Clifton M. (Clifton Melvin) Nichols

Life of Abraham Lincoln

Being a Biography of His Life From His Birth to His Assassination

Clifton M. (Clifton Melvin) Nichols

Life of Abraham Lincoln
Being a Biography of His Life From His Birth to His Assassination

ISBN/EAN: 9783337014438

Printed in Europe, USA, Canada, Australia, Japan

Cover: Foto ©Raphael Reischuk / pixelio.de

More available books at **www.hansebooks.com**

A. Lincoln
(1857.)

OF

ABRAHAM LINCOLN

Being a Biography of His Life from His Birth to His
Assassination; also a Record of His Ancestors,
and a Collection of Anecdotes
Attributed to Lincoln.

———

"His is the gentlest memory of our nation."

———

BY

CLIFTON M. NICHOLS.

———

ILLUSTRATED.

———

1896.
MAST, CROWELL & KIRKPATRICK.
NEW YORK CITY.   SPRINGFIELD, OHIO.   CHICAGO, ILL.

MAST, CROWELL & KIRKPATRICK,

SPRINGFIELD, OHIO.

LIFE OF ABRAHAM LINCOLN.

CHAPTER I.

PIONEER DAYS OF LINCOLN'S ANCESTORS IN KENTUCKY.

NEAR the point where the states of Virginia, Tennessee and Kentucky meet there is a wonderful gateway in the mountains, which was discovered in 1748, by Thomas Walker, and named Cumberland Gap, in honor of the Duke of Cumberland, prime minister to King George of England. He reported that it opened into a beautiful region inhabited by Indians and wild animals. From this gap north to where the waterways which form the Ohio river break through the mountains the rugged and towering Alleghenies present an almost impassable wall between Virginia and the country west. This barrier helped to protect the inhabitants against the warrior bands of western Indians, and for a time confined the march of the settler to the Shenandoah valley.

Daniel Boone had heard of the discovery of an opening in the mountains not far from his home, and thirsted for exploration of the unknown solitudes beyond, through which only Indians roamed. He was one of the elder sons of Squire Boone, who had come from Pennsylvania and settled in Wilkes county, North Carolina, on the Yadkin river. From his youth Daniel had shown a special fondness for hunting. Before he was ten years old he could shoot a deer while it was upon the run, and while yet a lad made long trips from home alone and was never lost. He was a born woodsman. He had the cunning and eye of an Indian, and could determine the points of the compass by the stars, like a mariner. In 1769, this intrepid hunter, in company with three companions, passed through Cumberland Gap into the wild territory west of the mountains, on a hunting and exploring expedition. As they advanced, the country and attractions improved. They traveled through vast reaches of somber forest, penetrating far into the interior. Boone and one of his companions were captured by the Indians, but made their escape. When they returned to their camp, the other two men had disappeared, and were never heard of again. Boone remained so long away from home that his younger brother, accompanied by a friend, came in search of him. Instead of returning, he sent his brother back for powder and bullets.

After being absent nearly a year, Boone* returned home, with a glowing account of the vastness and fertility of the new territory. He reported a country that abounded in possibilities for the settler. It was not rocky and mountainous. Streams were numerous and wild game was abundant. He organized and led forward a band of fifty hunters and trappers into the wilderness, and others soon followed. They built a rude fort, calling it Boonesborough. They were typical hunters and adventurers, with rifles on their shoulders and knives in their belts—the picket-line going on before the march of civilization.

At last the Revolutionary war was over. Peace relieved the restraint on the onward march of the pioneer, and the hunters' stories of a boundless country,

DANIEL BOONE ESCAPES FROM THE INDIANS.

renowned for soil and climate, across the mountains started an emigration fever. The rush of settlers from the Shenandoah valley counties of Virginia assumed striking proportions. Large groups of families from a single neighborhood banded themselves together for protection against the Indians while on the

*The Lincoln and Boone families were intimately associated for several generations. In the will of Mordecai Lincoln, recorded in the registry office at Philadelphia, dated 1735, George Boone, his "loving friend and neighbor," was made a trustee to assist in caring for the property. Squire Boone, the father of Daniel, was one of the appraisers. One of the numerous Abraham Lincolns was married to Anna Boone, a first cousin of Daniel Boone, July 10, 1760. It is thought that Abraham Lincoln, the president's grandfather, first became acquainted with Mary Shipley, whom he afterward married, while visiting the Boones on the Yadkin river, in North Carolina. It is known that intercourse between the families was kept up after they moved from Berks county, Pennsylvania.

journey. Their destination and route had been determined by Daniel Boone, for he and his father were known throughout the valley. He recommended the central and northern part of Kentucky for a location, which they reached by following his trail through the Cumberland Gap. They went in the usual backwoods manner, on horseback, the clothing and household goods being carried on pack-horses. Herds and flocks were driven along. Occasionally a party had tents; usually they slept in the open air. They carried a small stock of. provisions, including about thirty pounds of meal for each person. There was no meat, unless game was shot. The journey required from two to three weeks.

The trail was bad, especially where it climbed between the gloomy walls of Cumberland Gap. Even when undisturbed by prowling bands of red marauders, the trip was accompanied by much fatigue and exposure.

After traveling for many miles through dense forests, they came to the locality for which they had started. Here the emigrant train began to scatter. The heads of families would select a piece of ground and begin a pioneer's life, with an ax in one hand and a firebrand in the other—the evidence that the advance-guard of civilization had arrived. A spot for a home was selected, generally near a spring or a stream, and father and sons set to work felling trees to build a cabin. All settlers'

BOONE'S OLD TRAIL THROUGH THE MOUNTAINS.

cabins were alike—an oblong room, built of rough logs, with a door in one side and a fireplace in one end; the roof consisted of rafters made from poles covered with clapboards; the cracks between the logs were stopped up with clay; usually there were no windows or floors. When more room was needed, the space between the rafters was made into a loft, reached by climbing up pegs in the wall. The furniture of the pioneer's cabin was such as he could make from split boards with a few crude tools. They cooked by the open fire. Bread was baked by heating flat stones; or perhaps they were the possessors of a Dutch oven, an iron vessel about the size of a skillet, only twice as deep, with short legs and a lid. To bake, they placed it on the hearth and heaped live coals over it. Buffalo robes were their main bedding, and most of their clothing was made from the skins of animals. After the cabin was built, all hands set to work clearing ground for a crop. Trees were chopped down, the logs rolled in heaps, the brush piled on top, and burned.

The early settler's life was rough and monotonous; his surroundings were dreary; his cabin was destitute of the most common comforts; the blackened stumps and dead trees stood thick in his small field; neighbors were far apart; wild animals prowled around at night; and the settlers lived in mortal dread of the Indians, who were now thoroughly aroused against the white man for taking possession of their hunting-grounds, and were ever skulking around for a chance to take a scalp.

Such was the common lot of the early settlers in Kentucky, among whom were Abraham and Mary Shipley Lincoln, grandparents of President Lincoln.

A SHENANDOAH VALLEY SCENE, IN VIRGINIA.

A WINTER SCENE IN PIONEER DAYS IN KENTUCKY.

CHAPTER II.

IN 1782, Abraham Lincoln, grandfather of President Lincoln,* with his wife and five children, three sons and two daughters, left Rockingham county, Virginia, in the Shenandoah valley, with a party of emigrants, for Kentucky. They all rode horseback, and followed Daniel Boone's trail through Cumberland Gap.✔ They suffered all the hardships and mishaps usual to such a trip. They slept on the ground, were delayed by floods and harassed by Indians. Finally they reached Bear Grass Fort, in Mercer county, about fifty miles from what is now the city of Louisville. A farm of five hundred acres on Licking creek was selected. Here in the dense forest he cleared a few acres of ground, built a little log cabin, and became a pioneer settler on the western frontier. For generations past the Lincolns had been among those who kept on the crest of the wave of western settlement. They were typical pioneers, and marched along with those who pushed the frontier westward in the teeth of the forces of the wilderness. They conquered and transformed it. It was fighting work, only to be undertaken by these strong, brave, fearless men, who were familiar with woodcraft and knew how to find food and shelter in the forests—men who could outwit the Indian and endure the extremes of fatigue and exposure. They were uneducated; they lacked refinement; they were harsh, sturdy, courageous, tenacious, self-reliant, industrious men, faithful to their friends and dangerous to their enemies.

One day in the year 1784, while Abraham Lincoln was working in the clearing near his cabin with his three boys—Mordecai, ten years old; Josiah, eight,

---

*President Lincoln knew very little about his ancestry. In a letter written in 1848, he said: "My grandfather went from Rockingham county, Virginia, to Kentucky about 1782, and two years afterward was killed by the Indians. We have a vague tradition that my grandfather went from Pennsylvania to Virginia; that he was a Quaker; further than that I have never heard anything." Eager genealogists claim that they have since established his line back to the landing of the Lincolns from England, in 1638. In the records there is a similarity of Christian names; as Mordecai, Abraham, Thomas, Isaac, John and Jacob, but these same names are repeatedly found in the history of other families. We are told that President Lincoln's great-great-great-grandfather was one Mordecai Lincoln, who lived in Berks county, Pennsylvania, and died about 1735; that his great-great-grandfather was one John Lincoln, who emigrated to Rockingham county, Virginia; that his great-grandfather, Abraham Lincoln, had four brothers—John, Thomas, Isaac and Jacob. Abraham and his brother Thomas emigrated to Kentucky; Isaac to Tennessee; John and Jacob remained in Virginia. The latter was a lieutenant in the war of the Revolution, and took part in the siege of Yorktown. There is little doubt that it was on account of his intimate friendship with the famous Daniel Boone that President Lincoln's grandfather emigrated to Kentucky.

11

and Thomas, six—a bullet fired by an Indian pierced his heart. Mordecai, startled
by the shot, saw his father fall, and running to the cabin, seized the loaded rifle,
rushed to one of the loopholes cut through the logs of the cabin, and awaited
the approach of the savage. Josiah fled for the fort to give an alarm; the
Indian came up to take little Thomas Lincoln and carry him away. Suddenly
the crack of a rifle was heard, and the savage fell dead, shot by Mordecai.
Such was the tragedy in the life of Mary Shipley Lincoln, the grandmother of
the sixteenth president of the United States.

Soon after the death of her husband the widow moved to Washington county,
near the town of Springfield, where she lived until her death. No schools
had yet been established, and her children grew to manhood and womanhood

MORDECAI AVENGES THE MURDER OF HIS FATHER.

without the opportunity of securing an education. Both of the girls married,
and spent their lives in that section of the country. Under the law of entail in
Kentucky the eldest son inherited the estate of his father, and so Mordecai came
into possession of his father's property. Mordecai and Josiah Lincoln remained
in Washington county, and became the heads of good-sized families. They
were intelligent, well-to-do men, and owned slaves. Mordecai took part in the
Indian wars; he hated Indians bitterly ever after the murder of his father, and
to the day of his death never lost an opportunity of shooting them down.

A most remarkable and almost inexplicable fact is that to Thomas Lincoln
was "reserved the honor of an illustrious paternity." Thomas was about five feet
ten inches in height, weighed about two hundred pounds, had dark brown eyes,

dark skin and black hair. He was always poor and indolent. He was a man of great strength, but slow of movement. When he really tried he could accomplish a great deal at whatever he turned his hand, but he usually lacked the energy and perseverance necessary to make a success of his undertaking. He was a man of good intentions in all things and honest in all his dealings. He was a peaceful, law-abiding citizen, except when aroused to anger, and then he became a dangerous antagonist. He was of a nomadic disposition. One year he wandered off to his uncle's, on the confines of Tennessee. At another time he turned up in Breckinridge county. Finally, in 1806, at the age of twenty-eight, he drifted to Hardin county, and worked at the carpenter's trade in the shop of Joseph Hanks. While there

A CUPBOARD MADE BY THOMAS LINCOLN.

he married his employer's niece, Nancy Hanks. He then endeavored to set up for himself, but failed. He essayed farming at various times in Kentucky, Indiana and Illinois, but ill luck followed him. When he worked at the carpenter's trade at all, he preferred to make common benches, cupboards and bureaus. He was never a steady hand, but confined himself to doing odd jobs. He could neither read nor write until his wife taught him the letters of the alphabet, so he could spell his way slowly through the Bible, and knew how to write his name, which was the end of his attainments in this line. He was good-natured and fond of telling jokes, about the only trait he transmitted to his illustrious son. In politics he was a Democrat—a Jackson Democrat. In religion he was nothing at times and a member of various denominations by turns. It is believed, however, that he died in the faith of a Campbellite.

Very little is known of Nancy Hanks, the mother of President Lincoln. It seems that she was born in Virginia, in 1783; that her mother's given name was Lucy, and after she married Henry Sparrow the child did not remain long under her stepfather's roof, but went to live with her Aunt Betsey, who had married Thomas Sparrow. They had no children of their own. Besides Nancy, they took to raise her cousin, Dennis Hanks. Little Nancy became so identified with Thomas and Betsy Sparrow that a great many supposed that she was their child, and she was called Nancy Sparrow by her playmates. They were the only parents she ever knew, and she must have called them by names appropriate to that relationship. They took her with them to Mercer county, Kentucky. They reared her to womanhood, followed her to Indiana, died of the same disease at about the same time, and were buried close beside her.

Nancy Hanks was a beautiful girl, of pleasing manners and keen intellect. She was slender and symmetrical, above the ordinary height in stature, and had the appearance of one inclined to consumption. She was a brunette, with dark hair, soft hazel eyes, and had a high, intellectual-looking forehead. While in

ROCK SPRING.

One of the picturesque and romantic scenes of the Lincoln homestead on Nolin's creek, in Kentucky, is Rock Spring. In summer especially this is one of the most beautiful spots imaginable, and to its pleasing scenery is added the practical advantage of a never-failing supply of the finest quality of limestone water, for which central Kentucky is justly famous.

Virginia she attended school and received other advantages which placed her on a higher intellectual plane than most of those around her. She always wore a marked melancholy expression, which fixed itself upon the memory of every-one who ever saw or knew her, and though her life was seemingly beclouded by a spirit of sadness, she was in disposition amiable and generally cheerful; these traits she transmitted to her son. Her ancestors were probably English, who emigrated to America in the early days. Under favorable environments she likely would have become an accomplished and talented woman.

Thomas Lincoln and Nancy Hanks, parents of Abraham Lincoln, were married on June 12, 1806, near Beachland, Washington county, Kentucky, by the Rev. Jesse Head, a Methodist minister. Thomas was twenty-eight years of age and his wife twenty-three. They began married life in wretched poverty, in a dreary cabin about fourteen feet square, in Elizabethtown. Here, in the spring of 1807, their daughter, Sarah, was born. Thomas Lincoln soon wearied of Elizabethtown and carpenter-work. He thought he could do better as a farmer, and removed to a piece of land in La Rue county, three miles from Hodgensville, on the south fork of Nolin's creek. The land was poor and the landscape desolate. They took up their abode in a miserable cabin, which stood on a little knoll. Near by, a spring of excellent water gushed from beneath the rock, and was called "Rock Spring."

CHAPTER III.

ON February 12, 1809, a babe was born in a log cabin, located on Nolin's creek, in La Rue county, Kentucky, which was then a new and almost wild country. No doctors attended his birth. Only a few unskilled women were there to offer their willing services in caring for the mother. There was no fine linen ready in which to wrap the baby boy. His father was away from home. There was no food in the house, and had it not been for the kindness of neighbors he would have perished. But he was a child of destiny, and grew and waxed strong. They gave him his grandfather's name, Abraham—Abraham Lincoln! What a strange mingling of mirth and tears, of tragic and grotesque, of all that is gentle and just, humorous and honest, merciful, wise, laughable, lovable and divine, and all consecrated to the use of the man; while through all and over all an overwhelming sense of obligation, of chivalric loyalty to truth, and upon all the shadow of a tragic end.

The cabin in which Abraham Lincoln was born on that cold winter's night was a forlorn hovel with one door and no window. There were great chinks in the wall, through which the sun, rain and wind came driving in at pleasure. At night the stars were plainly visible, shining through cracks in the roof. The room was cold and bare, as it had scarcely anything in it that could be called furniture, and no floor except the beaten ground. In one end was a wide fireplace. It did not look as though a tender, new-born babe could live, much less grow and thrive, in such an uncomfortable place as this poor hut.

Here the mother gathered her infant son in her arms; here she went about her daily tasks, much of which was a routine of drudgery, getting something for her family to eat and wear. All of the cooking was done on the hearth, before the open fire. The food was simple, usually corn-bread and bacon or game. She had not sufficient strength, energy or health to make the most of life in a poor man's cabin. She craved better things—books, friends and the comforts of life. Frequently her husband would be gone for several days or weeks on hunting or boating trips, or at work at his trade, leaving her and the children alone. At night they could hear the snarl of the wolf, the cry of the panther and the hoot of the owl. From the door no human habitation could be seen, no familiar neighbors passed and repassed, for there were no roads. The children were a great comfort to her in this lonely place, their prattle was the sweetest of music to her. At dusk she took them on her lap and told them stories and sang them to sleep, when she tucked them away in their bed of leaves, covered with buffalo-robes. As they grew older, she taught them their A-B-C's and how to read and spell and write. Sarah and little Abe were always glad to see summer-time come, for then they could play out of doors, gather wild flowers, and carry little gourds of water for their mother from Rock Spring.

No school of any kind had ever been opened near Thomas Lincoln's home until Zachariah Riney, a wandering Roman Catholic priest, happened along, in the year 1813. He engaged an empty cabin, and sent word to the settlers that he would teach spelling and reading to all who would pay him. Although the Lincolns were very poor, it is a credit to the parents that Sarah and little Abe were found in the school. Logs split in two and turned flat side upward answered for benches, and the pupils included children and adults. The teacher

THE ALLEGED BIRTHPLACE OF LINCOLN.

The Lincoln family occupied the cabin on Nolin's creek for a period of four years after Abraham's birth, when they removed to the eastern end of the county. The farm on which Abraham was born passed into the hands of other and more energetic owners. The humble cabin was torn down, and the materials used in its construction were utilized otherwise, and ultimately destroyed in the manner common to the section and period. A more pretentious residence was erected on the site, but it, too, was built of logs. At a later period the farm again changed proprietors, and this second house was also torn down. The new owner built his residence at a different point. The logs used in the vacated dwelling were sold to a neighbor, and a portion of them remain at the present time in a dwelling occupied by Mr. John A. Davenport, and located about a mile from the old Lincoln homestead. For years after this the site of Abraham Lincoln's first home was cultivated in common with the surrounding land, and was marked only by a small mound, and a pear-tree, rugged, gnarled and sturdy, growing thereon. In 1895, the farm was purchased by New York speculators, who at once began its improvement with a view to its sale to the United States government for use as a national park. Many visitors suppose the cabin illustrated above to be the original Lincoln cabin, and certain recent Lincoln biographers give credence to the idea that it is. This, however, is a mistake. The present cabin is only a clever imitation of the original, built on the same plan, and with logs obtained from a very old, decaying house on an adjoining farm.

knew nothing outside of spelling and reading, and not much of these. The only book used was a speller, of which there were only a few copies. It was a great surprise to the teacher when he found that little Abe, only five years old, was far in advance of any of the children of his age, and even of many of the older pupils. Abe (that is what all his playmates called him) was tall of his age, and slender, had dark hair, gray eyes, and was of a quiet disposition. His sister, who was two years older, was large of her age, but not tall. She was a pretty child, with dark hair and gray eyes, and was very modest in the presence

A VIEW OF THE OLD THOMAS LINCOLN FARM IN KENTUCKY, WHERE ABRAHAM LINCOLN WAS BORN. (From a recent photograph.)

of strangers. With tattered speller, and lunch of corn-bread, she and Abe tramped through the woods to school the few weeks it kept open.

The church preceded the school-house in pioneer settlements. In Hodgensville, which consisted of a primitive mill and a few scattered cabins, the public-spirited had erected a log building. but had failed to provide glass for the windows. Occasionally a preacher came to the rude meeting-house, when the people flocked in from miles around. coming on foot or horseback. They did not all come for the purpose of hearing the religious services or to exhibit their clothing, but to see one another and exchange news, and hear what was going on in the world outside Hodgensville.   Mrs. Lincoln was a devout woman, attending church services whenever she could.   David Elkin, a traveling Baptist minister, was a special friend to the Lincolns, and took quite a fancy to Thomas Lincoln's boy.

Thomas Lincoln had made no headway in paying for his farm; in fact. no terms were easy enough for him.   He gave it up, and on September 12. 1813.

A SCENE ON THE ROLLING FORK.

bargained with a Mr. Slater for two hundred and thirty-eight acres.   The terms were that he was to pay one hundred and eighty pounds, all deferred payments. which were never met.   This land was situated about six miles from Hodgensville, on Knob creek, a very clear stream which empties into Rolling Fork two miles above the present site of New Haven.   The farm was somewhat hilly. well timbered. and had some rich little valleys, of which Thomas Lincoln succeeded in getting six acres under cultivation.   The cabin which he built here was even worse than the one they had left. if that were possible.   While here. Abraham entered his second school. which lasted about three months.   His teacher was Caleb Hazel.   He could teach reading and writing in an indifferent way. and a little arithmetic.   The school was located four miles from the Lincoln farm, and the Lincoln children had to tramp the entire distance. It was about this time that Dennis Hanks initiated Abraham into the mysteries of fishing. One day he and a companion named Gollaher were out on a little excursion, and while Abe was attempting to "coon" across a stream on a sycamore log, he lost his hold and fell into the water, and was saved only by the utmost exertions of Gollaher. Hunting ground-hogs was another favorite sport of the boys.

As time wore on, Thomas Lincoln became dissatisfied. and being a wanderer by natural inclination, he longed for a change. He was gaining neither riches nor credit, and attributed his luck to the country where he lived. He felt ill at ease and cramped in the presence of his more prosperous neighbors. He listened to the stories of the fertility and cheapness of the land in the new state of Indiana, across the Ohio river, and believed them. So he resolved to pull up stakes and locate once more in the wilderness. Among the many things which he had attempted was flatboating, and had been hired to make a few trips to New Orleans. When he concluded to make the removal to Indiana. he built a rude boat and loaded most of his scanty store of property and tools. and sold the rest for four hundred gallons of whisky. In those days whisky was a common article of commerce, and passed for so much coin in buying and selling. He started down Rolling Fork. then down Salt river. and reached the Ohio river without any mishaps, but here his boat capsized. He fished up whatever tools and property he could, and most of the whisky, and started on his way. finally landing at Thompson's Ferry, two and a half miles west of Troy, in Perry county. Indiana. Here he sold the boat, and put the property in the hands of a Mr. Posey. a settler living near. He then started out to find a location. and decided upon a spot sixteen miles distant, afterward returning to his family in Kentucky. walking the entire distance.

CHAPTER IV.

THOMAS LINCOLN and family moved from Kentucky to Indiana in the fall of 1816. Before they left, Mrs. Lincoln and the two children visited the grave of her third child, a boy, who died in infancy. The trip to Indiana was a hard journey, as there were no roads or bridges. They made the trip on horseback, borrowing two horses for the occasion. Besides their scanty bed and clothing, they carried with them a few cooking-utensils, including a Dutch oven and lid, a skillet and lid, and some tinware. They camped out on the way, and depended mostly upon game for subsistence.

After reaching Mr. Posey's house, Thomas Lincoln hired a wagon, into which he loaded his tools, the whisky, his few goods, his wife and children, and plunged into the forest. There were no roads or foot-paths, and many times a passageway had to be cut before they could proceed farther. At length they arrived at the spot which he had selected between Prairie and Pigeon creeks, and which has since become famous as the Lincoln farm. Lincoln was a "squatter," and did not enter his claim until October 15, 1817.

This part of the country was covered with thick forests of deciduous trees— poplar, oak, walnut, elm, beech and sugar. The land was fertile, the grazing excellent, and there was an immense amount of mast on the ground for hogs. Lincoln selected a beautiful site on an elevation for his home. The selection was wise, except that no running water was near, and they had to use that which collected in holes when it rained, until a well was dug. Here Thomas Lincoln built a temporary shelter called "a half-face camp," which is a shed built of poles and open on one side. It was as cold as outdoors, and not fit for a stable. They lived here all winter and until the next fall before he had the cabin completed. This cabin had neither floor nor window, and the doorway had to be closed by hanging skins of animals over it. It seems that Lincoln was too lazy to use his skill as a carpenter to improve his home, for the furniture was cruder than the house. The bed consisted of two poles, with one end of each stuck in between the logs in one corner of the cabin, while the corner of the bed where the poles crossed rested in a crotch of a forked stick sunk into the earthen floor. On these were thrown some rough boards, and on the boards a lot of leaves covered with skins and any old clothing they had. The table was a similar affair, and three-legged stools answered for chairs. They had a few pewter and tin dishes, and if they had knives or forks, it is unknown. Abraham slept on a bed of leaves in the loft, reached by climbing on pegs in the wall. In the fall of 1817 Thomas and Betsy Sparrow followed their adopted daughter to Indiana, and took up their abode in the old "half-face camp," which was about one hundred and fifty feet from the cabin. They brought with them their adopted son, Dennis Hanks, a cousin of Mrs. Lincoln's. For two years they continued to live along in' the old way. Lincoln did not like farming, and did not succeed in getting very much of his land under cultivation. He raised a small crop of corn and vegetables, and this, with the game, which was abundant, supplied the table.

LINCOLN'S INDIANA HOME.

Milk-sickness broke out in the Pigeon creek region in the summer of 1818. It was a terrible disease, common to new countries. It is supposed that it was contracted by cattle and sheep feeding on a poisonous weed, which grew in wild pasture-lands. It swept off the cattle which gave the milk, and the people who drank it. Among those who were attacked by it were Thomas and Betsy Sparrow and Mrs. Thomas Lincoln. The Sparrows were then removed from the "half-faced" camp to the Lincoln cabin, which was very little better. Many of the neighbors had already died of the disease, and Thomas Lincoln had made all of their coffins out of green lumber cut with a whip-saw. Toward fall the Sparrows and Mrs. Lincoln grew worse. The nearest doctor was at Yellow

Banks, Kentucky, thirty miles away, but they could not send for him, as they had no money with which to pay him. In the first part of October the Sparrows died. A day or so after, on October 5, 1815, Nancy Hanks Lincoln rested from her troubles, at the age of thirty-five years. Her husband sawed the lumber and made her rough coffin with his own hands.

Arnold describes the funeral thus:

"The country burying-ground where she was laid, half a mile southeast from their log cabin home, had been selected perhaps by herself, and was situated on the top of a forest-covered hill. There, beneath the dark shade of the woods, and under a majestic sycamore, they dug the grave of the mother of Abraham

THE LINCOLN FARM IN INDIANA. (From a recent photograph.)

Lincoln. The funeral ceremonies were very plain and simple, but solemn withal, for nowhere does death seem so deeply impressive as in such a solitude. At the time no clergyman could be found in or near the settlement to perform the usual religious rites. David Elkin, a traveling preacher whom the family had known in Kentucky, came, but not until some months afterward, traveling many miles on horseback through the wild forest to reach their residence; and then the family, with a few friends and neighbors, gathered in the open air under the great sycamore beneath which they had laid the mother's remains. A funeral sermon was preached, hymns were sung, and such rude but sincere and impressive services were held as are usual among the pioneers of the frontier."

Mrs. Lincoln's grave never had a stone, not even a head-board, to mark it, and the exact spot is unknown. Two or three children belonging to a neighbor, Levy Hall and wife, and the Sparrows, were buried near the grave. For years the graves remained uncared for. They were crumbled in and sunken and covered with bushes and wild vines. In 1879, Mr. P. E. Studebaker, of South Bend, Indiana, erected a stone over the graves, and a few of the leading citizens of Rockport, Indiana, built an iron railing around it. The

THE GRAVE OF NANCY HANKS LINCOLN.

inscription on the stone runs: "Nancy Hanks Lincoln, Mother of President Lincoln, Died Oct. 5, A. D. 1818, Aged 35 years. Erected by a friend of her martyred son, 1879."

The next year was a sorry and dreary one for the children in their cold and cheerless cabin. Sarah, now twelve years old, was housekeeper, and cooked what little they had to eat. Abe and Dennis were good-natured boys, and did what they could to pass away the long evenings and stormy days. In good weather the boys were busy getting up wood, doing the chores and hunting. Taking game with trap and rifle was a necessary occupation, as they needed the meat for food; and about their only source of income during the winter was from the sale of furs.

Thirteen months after the death of his first wife, Thomas Lincoln returned to Elizabethtown in search of another. He immediately called on Sarah Bush Johnston, whom he had courted before he married Nancy Hanks. Sarah married Daniel Johnston soon after Lincoln married Nancy. Johnston died in 1814, leaving three children—John, Sarah and Matilda—dependent on his wife. Sarah Bush was called a proud body when a girl, as she was very neat and tidy in her personal appearance, and was particular in the selection of her company. She "wanted to be somebody and have something." She was a woman of great energy, good sense, industrious and saving, and knew how to manage children. Mrs. Johnston agreed to marry Thomas Lincoln as soon as she could pay her debts. They were paid that day, and the couple were married the next morning, leaving for Indiana soon after. Mrs. Johnston was well supplied with furniture, clothing and household goods, and it required her brother's big wagon and a four-horse team to transport them to Indiana. Among the goods was a bureau that cost forty dollars. Thomas Lincoln thought it extravagance, and wanted her to turn it into

SARAH BUSH LINCOLN.

cash, which she flatly refused to do. When Mrs. Johnston, now Mrs. Lincoln, arrived at her new home, she was astonished beyond measure at the contrast between the glowing representations which her husband had made to her before leaving Kentucky and the real poverty and meanness of the place. She had evidently been given to understand that the bridegroom had abandoned his Kentucky ways, and was now a prosperous Indiana farmer. However, she made the best of a bad bargain, and immediately set to work making the place more comfortable and respectable. She had her husband put down a floor, hang windows and doors, and use his skill with tools to make improvements in the cabin. It was a strange experience for Sarah and Abe to sleep in warm beds, and to eat with knives and forks and have something warm and clean to wear. It was only a short time after the new mother came to the home until everything had changed. She had taken a fancy to Abe as a child in Kentucky, and now she cared for him with affection, and from that time on he appeared to live a new life. Sarah and Abe and the Johnston children soon became fast friends, and lived in the utmost harmony. Dennis Hanks also became a member of the household, and was Abe's companion from the time he was eight until twenty-two years of age. It is through him that students know much of this period of Abraham Lincoln's life.

When Thomas Lincoln first came to Indiana there were only a few settlers, in all seven or eight in the Pigeon creek country, who had come before him, and one of these was a Mr. Carter, whose acquaintance he had made in Kentucky, and who had induced Lincoln to locate there. The nearest town was Troy, on the Ohio river, about a mile from the mouth of Anderson creek. Harrison's victory over the Indians had won peace for Indiana, and heavy immigration set in. When Indiana was admitted as a state, in 1816, she had a population of 65,000. The Lincoln farm was in Perry county, with the county-seat at Troy, but afterward that part of the county was set off and became a part of Spencer county, with the county-seat at Rockport, twenty miles south.

JUDGE JOHN PITCHER, WHO LOANED LINCOLN LAW-BOOKS WHILE A BOY IN INDIANA.

In 1821, a state road was made, connecting Evansville and Corydon, which was then the state capital. In 1823, another road was built, connecting Rockport and Bloomington. These roads crossed just about a mile and a half from Thomas Lincoln's farm. The land near the cross-roads had been secured from the government by James Gentry, and the cross-roads made it a valuable trade center. In 1823, Gideon Romine started a store, and succeeded in getting a post-office in 1824. He soon sold his store to Gentry, after whom the place was named. Dennis Hanks helped to hew the logs for the first store-room in Gentryville.

CHAPTER V.

ABRAHAM LINCOLN began his school life in Indiana in 1819, soon after his stepmother came to the home. He was naturally quick in the acquisition of any sort of knowledge, and it is likely that by this time he could read and write a little. Mrs. Lincoln perceived that he was an unusually bright boy, and encouraged him all she could in his studies, and it was due to her efforts that he was able to attend school at all. It was necessary for him to work most of the time on the farm or in the shop, or hire out as a common laborer, in order to help support the family. If all the days which Abraham Lincoln attended school were added together, they would not make a single year's time, and he never studied grammar or geography or any of the higher branches in school. "Readin', writin' and cipherin'" was the limit. His first teacher in Indiana was Hazel Dorsey, who opened a school in a log school-house a mile and a half from the Lincoln cabin. The building had holes for windows, which were covered over with greased paper to admit light. The roof was just high enough for a man to stand erect. It did not take long to demonstrate that Abe was superior to any scholar in his class. His next teacher was Andrew Crawford, who taught in the winter of 1822-3, in the same little school-house. Abe was an excellent speller, and it is said that he liked to show off his knowledge, especially if he could help out his less fortunate schoolmates. One day the teacher gave out the word "defied." A large class was on the floor, but it seemed that no one would be able to spell it. The teacher declared he would keep the whole class in all day and night if "defied" was not spelled correctly. When the word came around to Katy Roby, she was standing where she could see Lincoln. She started, "d-e-f," and while trying to decide whether to spell the word with an "i" or a "y," she noticed that Abe had his finger on his eye and a smile on his face, and instantly took the hint. She spelled the word correctly, and the school was dismissed.

Among other things which Crawford tried to teach was *manners*. One of the pupils would retire, and then come in as a stranger, and another pupil would have to introduce him to all the members of the school in what was considered "good manners." As Abe wore a linsey-woolsey shirt, buckskin breeches which were too short and very tight, and low shoes, and was tall and awkward, he no

doubt created considerable merriment when his turn came. He was growing at
a fearful rate; he was fifteen years of age, and two years later attained his full
height of six feet four inches. Even at this early date he had learned to write
compositions, and even some doggerel rhyme, which he recited, to the great
amusement of his playmates. One of his first compositions was against cruelty
to animals. He was very much annoyed and pained at the conduct of the boys,
who were in the habit of catching terrapins and putting coals of fire on their
backs, which thoroughly disgusted Abraham. "He would chide us," said Nat
Grigsby, "tell us it was wrong, and would write against it."

The third and last school which he attended was taught by Mr. Swaney, and
was four and a half miles away. The distance was so great that he did not

LINCOLN AND HIS SISTER STUDYING BY FIRELIGHT.

attend long. By this time he knew more than any of his teachers, but he continued his studies wherever he happened to be, at home at nights, or in the fields
during the day. He was not particularly energetic when it came to hard manual
labor. When alone about his work his mind was on his lessons, and he would
frequently stop and be lost in deep thought. If he had company, he was constantly laughing and talking, cracking jokes and telling stories. One time Abe
said that his father taught him to work, but not to love it. He preferred to lie
under a shade-tree, or up in the loft of the cabin, and read or cipher or scribble.
At night he would sit before the fire and write on the shovel with charcoal. In
the daytime he would write on boards, and then shave the marks off and begin
again.

His stepmother said: "Abe read diligently; he read every book he could lay his hands on, and when he came across a passage that struck him, he would write it down on boards, if he had no paper, and keep it there until he did get paper; then he would rewrite, look at it, repeat it. He had a copy-book, a kind of scrap-book, in which he put down all things, and thus preserved them."

When Abe was fourteen years of age, John Hanks came from Kentucky and lived with the Lincolns. He describes Abe's habits thus: "When Lincoln and I returned to the house from work, he would go to the cupboard, snatch a piece of corn-bread, take down a book, sit down on a chair, cock his legs up as

SWIMMING-HOLE IN PIGEON CREEK, WHERE LINCOLN USED TO BATHE.

high as his head, and read. He and I worked barefooted, grubbed it, plowed, mowed, cradled together; plowed corn, gathered it, and shucked corn. Abe read constantly when he had an opportunity."

Among the books upon which Abe "laid his hands" were "Æsop's Fables," "Robinson Crusoe," Bunyan's "Pilgrim's Progress," "History of the United States," and Weems' "Life of Washington." All these he read many times, and transferred extracts from them to the boards and the scrap-book. He copied and worked out for himself nearly the whole of an arithmetic, some of the sheets of which are still in a fair state of preservation.

About this time he discovered that a Mr. Turnham, deputy constable in the neighborhood, had a copy of the Revised Statutes of Indiana, and he would go to his house and read and re-read the book. He borrowed Weems' "Life of Washington" from a neighbor, Joseph Crawford (not the school-teacher). It is said that Lincoln fairly devoured this book, and when not reading it, placed it between the logs of the wall. One night, while asleep, a rain came up and soaked the book thoroughly with mud and water. Abe told Mr. Crawford how it happened, and, as he had no money, offered to pay for it by work. Crawford agreed that if he would pull fodder three days he could have the book.

About the house Abe was kind and generous. Both his father and Dennis Hanks were good story-tellers, and, no doubt, with Mrs. Lincoln and the three girls, they had many pleasant times together in their back-woods fashion. Abe had a very retentive memory. When he was in the field he would mount a stump and begin to lecture, sometimes in humorous and sometimes in serious style. On Monday mornings he would frequently repeat almost the entire sermon which he had heard the day before, and frequently his father would break up his "meetings" and hustle him off in no gentle manner.

"OLD BLUE-NOSE" CRAWFORD.

He was put to work in the carpenter-shop, but did not learn the trade. His father hired him out to the neighbors, and Abe was always willing to make the transfer. His wit, humor and honesty were well known, which made him welcome wherever he went. He was especially popular with the women. It is said he was always ready to make a fire, carry water or nurse the baby.

In 1825, he worked for James Taylor, who lived at the mouth of Anderson's creek. He was here nine months, and his principal business was managing a ferry-boat plying the Ohio river and Anderson creek. He was compelled to act as a sort of "man-of-all-work" about the house and barn. He slept up-stairs with

Taylor's son, who said that Abe read until nearly midnight, and got up before daylight. Green was a hard master, and once struck the poor boy with an ear of hard corn and cut a gash over his eye. Abe's strength caused him to be in demand at hog-killing time, at which he earned thirty-one cents a day; and that was considered good pay.

He had never forgiven Joseph Crawford for making him pull fodder so long to pay for the "Life of Washington," and never lost an opportunity to crack a joke at his expense. Abe called him "Blue-nose Crawford," a name which stuck to him throughout his life. He worked for Crawford off and on. The first job

CRAWFORD'S HOUSE.

was to daub up the cracks between the logs of his house. While here, he always kept up his reading, and found several books at the Crawfords' which he studied thoroughly. Abe's sister was a hired girl in this same house. Even at this early date Lincoln was a good wrestler, and he was never better pleased than when he could inveigle Mr. Crawford into a tussle, and generally took the opportunity to throw Crawford to the ground several times. He was stronger and taller than any man in the neighborhood. He could strike with a maul a heavier blow, and could sink an ax deeper into wood than any man in that part of the country, and at splitting rails he had no superior.

2

There was an abundance of game in the Pigeon creek region, but Abe was not a hunter. He was a fair shot with a rifle, and killed some game, but he preferred to stay behind and read and talk, provided he had something to read. He did take part in the games and gatherings, and was found at the log-rollings and corn-huskings. If there was any literature to be written, especially for such occasions, Abe was called upon to do it.

By this time Gentryville was quite a "center of business." It had a blacksmith-shop, a store and a post-office. It was a great loitering-place for the young men, and Abe was immensely popular. His sallies of mirth and humor never failed to attract a crowd around him. He worked about the store some, but never reached the dignity of selling goods across the counter. They would sit up late at nights and read the papers and talk politics and tell stories. The

PIGEON CREEK GRAVEYARD, WHERE ABRAHAM LINCOLN'S SISTER IS BURIED.

blacksmith-shop was another favorite loafing-place of Lincoln's, as Baldwin was himself a famous story-teller. One cold night while going home in company with some young men, they found a man who had fallen by the wayside, dead drunk. The boys refused to help him, so Lincoln took him up in his arms and carried him to a cabin, built a fire, and saved the man's life.

Charles and Reuben Grigsby were married about this time, and returned home with their brides, when the infare feast and dance were held. Abe was not invited, and was very mad in consequence, his indignation finding vent in a highly descriptive piece of composition, entitled "The Chronicles of Reuben." They were sharp, witty and stinging. He dropped them on the road where the Grigsbys would find them. The Grigsbys were infuriated and wild with rage, and threatened to pound his face to a jelly and crack a couple of his ribs, but evidently Abe's tremendously long and muscular arms prevented them from trying it. What treasures of humor he must have wasted on that audience of "bumpkins!" In those days they had exhibitions or speaking-meetings in the school-house or church, and discussed such subjects as "The Bee and the Ant," "Water and Fire," "Which had the Most Right to Complain, the Negro or the Indian?" "Which was the Strongest, Wind or Water?" Abe's father was a Democrat, and at that time he agreed with him. He would frequently make political and other speeches to the boys and explain tangled questions. Booneville was the county-seat of Warrick county, situated about fifteen miles from Gentryville.

PIGEON CREEK CHURCH.

Thither Abe walked to be present at the sittings of the court, and listened attentively to the trials and the speeches of the lawyers. One of the trials was that of a murderer. He was defended by Mr. John Breckinridge, and at the conclusion of his speech Abe was so enthusiastic that he ventured to compliment him. Breckinridge looked at the shabby boy, thanked him, and passed on his way. Many years afterward, in 1862, Breckinridge called on the president, and he was told, "It was the best speech that I, up to that time, had ever heard. If I could, as I then thought, make as good a speech as that, my soul would be satisfied." At numerous times in Lincoln's youth, when his prospects of ever becoming president were apparently the slimmest of any boy living, he had hopes, and would assert that some day he would be a great man. Mrs. Crawford reproved him one day for bothering the girls in her kitchen, and asked him what he supposed would ever become of him, and he answered that he was going to be president of the United States. Abe usually did the milling for the family, and at first had to go a long distance, but later on a horse-mill was started near Gentryville. · Abe hitched his "old mare" to the mill and started her, with impatience. She did not move very lively, and he "touched her up" and started to say, "Get up, you old hussy!" The words "get up" fell from his lips, and then he became unconscious, caused by a kick from the mare. After several hours he

ABRAHAM LINCOLN WITNESSED SLAVERY FOR THE FIRST TIME.

came to, and the first thing he said was, ",You old hussy!" In after years he explained it thus: "Probably the muscles of my tongue had been set to speak the words when the animal's heels knocked me down, and my mind, like a gun, stopped half-cocked, and only went off when consciousness returned."

About a mile and half from the Lincoln cabin there lived a Mr. William Wood, who took two papers, one political and one temperance. Abe borrowed them, and read them faithfully over and over again, and became inspired with an ardent desire to write something on the subjects himself. He accordingly composed an article on temperance, which Mr. Wood thought was excellent, and was forwarded by a Baptist preacher to an editor in Ohio, by whom it was published, to the infinite gratification of Mr. Wood and his protege. Abe then tried his hand on national politics, which article was also published. In it he said: "The American government is the best form of government for an intelligent people. It ought to be kept sound, and preserved forever, that general education should be fostered and carried all over the country; that the Constitution should be saved, the Union perpetuated and the laws revered, respected and enforced." A lawyer named Pritchard chanced to pass that way, and, being favored with a perusal of Abe's "piece," declared that it was excellent, and had it printed in some obscure paper, causing the author an extraordinary access of pride.

In 1828, at the age of nineteen, Abe began to grow restless. He wanted to leave home, and consulted Mr. Wood about it, who advised him to remain with

LINCOLN RECEIVES TWO SILVER HALF DOLLARS.

his father until he should become of age. In the same spring, Abe went to work for a Mr. Gentry, and his son Allen and Lincoln took a flatboat-load of bacon and other produce to New Orleans. Abe was paid eight dollars per month, and ate and slept on board, and Gentry paid his passage back on the deck of a steamboat. While the boat was loading at Gentry's Landing, near Rockport, on the Ohio, Miss Roby, the girl whom he had helped to spell "defied," watched them. She afterward became Allen Gentry's wife. She says: "One evening Abe and I were sitting on the boat, and I said to him that the sun was going down. 'That is not so; it don't really go down, it seems so. The earth turns from west to east, and the revolution of the earth carries us under, as it were. We do the sinking, as you call it.' I replied, 'Abe, what a fool you are!' I know now that I was the fool, not Lincoln." At Madame Bushane's plantation, six miles below

Baton Rouge, while the boat was tied up to the shore in the dead hours of the night, and Abe and Allen were fast asleep in the bed, they were startled by footsteps on board. They knew instantly that it was a gang of negroes come to rob and perhaps murder them. Allen, thinking to frighten the negroes, called out: "Bring the guns, Lincoln, and shoot them!" Abe came without the guns, but he fell among the negroes with a huge bludgeon and belabored them most cruelly, following them onto the bank. They rushed back to their boat and hastily put out into the stream. It is said that he received a scar in this tussle which he carried with him to his grave. It was on this trip that he saw the workings of slavery for the first time. The sight of New Orleans was like a wonderful panorama to his eyes, for never before had he seen wealth, beauty, fashion and culture. He returned home with new and larger ideas and stronger opinions of right and injustice.

One day, while standing on the bank of the river, two passengers came up and asked to be taken to the steamer coming up the river. Abe agreed to take them out, and did so, and when he had them and their luggage on the boat, they threw him a silver half dollar each. One day, while the Cabinet was assembled in the White House, Mr. Lincoln related the incident to Seward, his secretary of state, and said: "I could scarcely believe my eyes. You may think it was a very little thing, but it was the most important instant of my life. I could scarcely believe that I, a poor boy, had earned a dollar in less than a day. The world seemed wider and fairer to me, and I was a more hopeful and confident being from that time."

CHAPTER VI.

THE "milk-sickness" was still prevalent in Indiana, and for this and other reasons a letter received from John Hanks, formerly of Elizabethtown, Kentucky, then of Decatur, Illinois, speaking of the vast reaches of prairie in his state, the richness of the soil, the winding rivers and creeks, and the beautiful groves of oak, maple and elm, met with a ready reception in the elder Lincoln's mind. Hanks promised that if Thomas Lincoln would come to Illinois he would select a quarter-section of land for him and have the logs cut for a cabin. Immigration had already set in, largely, to Illinois from Kentucky. One of the stepdaughters had married Levi Hall and the other Dennis Hanks, and all were willing to go. Abe's sister had married Aaron Grigsby, and in two years died. There were no dear friends to be left behind. Abe was now of age, but ready to cast his lot in with the rest. It was a long and tedious journey, but by early spring, in the year 1830, they could reach the end. They passed through snow, sleet, rain, mud and chilling winds; the rivers were filled with ice or overflowing their banks; they usually slept at night in their wagons. The father received the hearty co-operation of his stalwart son, who drove the team of four yoke of oxen, swung the ax to split rails to build a temporary shelter, and when the wagon sank in the mire, he put his shoulder to the wheel.

A little dog accompanied them, and the tenderness of Abe's heart is shown by the fact that one day when the dog was unwittingly left behind, howling, on the farther side of a stream, Abraham Lincoln had not the heart to leave it. Barefooted, he jumped into the water, crossed the stream, took the dog in his arms, and waded back with him, very much to the satisfaction of Abraham, and certainly very much to the delight of the dog.

At the spot near Decatur where Thomas Lincoln settled were found the logs which John Hanks had promised, ready for the new house, and Abraham Lincoln, "wearing a jean jacket, shrunken buckskin trousers, a coonskin cap, and driving an ox-team," became a citizen of Illinois. He was physically and mentally equipped for pioneer work. His first desire was to obtain a new and decent suit of clothes, but as he had no money, he was glad to arrange with Nancy Miller to make him a pair of trousers, he to split four hundred fence-rails for each yard of cloth—fourteen hundred rails in all. It was three miles from his father's cabin to her wood-lot, where he made the forest ring with the sound of his ax. Abraham had helped his father plow fifteen acres of land, and split enough rails to fence it, and he then helped to plow fifty acres for another settler.

Abraham now being over twenty-one, there was no one to restrain him from leaving home. He had been faithful to his parents, and there were no ties that bound him to his old associates, unless it was his good stepmother. He was free, and could go and do what he pleased, and attempt those things which were nearest his heart; but where he would find them, or how he would secure them, was a problem unsolved.

Illinois, now an empire with a commercial capital of over four million people, had in 1830 a little over fifty thousand inhabitants. Judge Arnold tells

GRAVEYARD WHERE SARAH GRIGSBY IS BURIED.
(Her grave is marked by the stone under flag.)

us that the Indian word from which the name of the state was derived was "Illini," signifying the "Land of full-grown men."

Thomas Lincoln moved at least three times in search of a location, and finally settled on Goosenest Prairie, in Coles county, near Farmington, where he died, in 1851, at the ripe old age of seventy-three. He had mortgaged his little farm of forty acres for two hundred dollars, but Abraham had paid the debt and taken a deed of the land, which contained the clause, "With a reservation of a life estate therein to them or the survivor of them." As soon as Abraham got up a little in the world, he began to send his stepmother money, and continued to do so until his own death. Sarah Bush Lincoln died April 10, 1869.

It was in April, 1830, that Lincoln left home for good. He did not go far, but sought work in the neighborhood among the settlers. Rail-splitting seemed to be the favorite kind of work. In March, 1831, he was fortunate in meeting a

LINCOLN CROSSING THE STREAM WITH THE DOG.

LINCOLN'S FIRST ILLINOIS HOME.

43

singular character known as Denton Offutt, of Springfield. Offutt was enterprising and aggressive, full of spirits in more senses than one, and kept things
moving along the line of the Sangamon. This man, who was at that time buying produce for the New Orleans market, employed Lincoln, John Hanks and
John Johnston to make a trip to New Orleans. They went down the Sangamon
to Jamestown, and walked to Springfield. It was but two years since Lincoln had
made the trip for Mr. Gentry, of Gentryville, Indiana, with Gentry's son Allen, and
therefore he knew something of the river, and of the great city near its mouth.

Offutt agreed to pay the three young men fifty cents a day each, and sixty
dollars for the trip, besides boarding them. He agreed to have the boat ready for

THE THOMAS LINCOLN CABIN, IN COLES COUNTY, ILLINOIS.

them at Judy's Ferry, five miles from Springfield, but after they had rowed down
the Sangamon to Springfield, they found Offutt exercising his social qualities
with the guests of the Buckhorn tavern, and increasing at a lively rate the
profits of the bar. But there was no boat. A boat was the first requisite for
the trip, and Offutt finally employed the boys to build one. Abraham was to
have charge of its construction, and he was well qualified for the task. Trees
on the government reservation, for which they had to pay nothing. were cut
down, and the ax, the saw, the chisel and the auger were used in the work.
Abraham, the "boss," did the cooking.

Two giants of the forest were hewed into timbers for the sides of the boat, to
which the planks for the bottom, which had been sawed out at Kirkpatrick's

sawmill, near by, were stoutly pinned, and the seams were calked and then pitched. It was a strong boat. Lincoln had had experience in building boats with his father, and knew just what to do and how to do it. The launching was a great affair. Offutt came out from Springfield with a large party and an ample supply of whisky, to give the boat and its builders a send-off. It was a sort of bipartizan mass-meeting, but there was one prevailing spirit, that born of rye and corn. Speeches were made in the best of feeling, some in favor of Andrew Jackson and some in favor of Henry Clay. Abraham Lincoln, the cook, told a number of funny stories, and it is recorded that they were not of too refined a character to suit the taste of his audience. A sleight-of-hand performer was present, and among other tricks performed, he fried some eggs in Lincoln's hat. Judge Herndon says, as explanatory to the delay in passing up the hat for the experiment, Lincoln drolly observed: "It was out of respect for the eggs, not care for my hat."

THE GRAVE OF THOMAS LINCOLN.

The boat was loaded with pork and beef in barrels, pork on foot, and corn. April 19, 1831, the boat and its load left Sangamon, and floated down the river toward New Salem, a town destined to be for awhile the scene of Lincoln's activities. A Mr. Rutledge, Mr. Coffin states, "had built a dam at a bend in the river and erected a mill on the western bank. The boat, instead of gliding over the dam, hung fast upon it. It was necessarily a ponderous affair in itself, and was heavily loaded. Lincoln was the man to discover a way out of the difficulty. Some of the barrels of pork and beef at the bow, "the forward end," as Mr. Coffin writes, were taken on shore. The boat, as a result of insufficient calking, was partly filled with water. Lincoln bored a hole, with a large auger, in the bottom of the end projecting over the dam, and the water ran out. Then the hole was plugged, the barrels near the stern rolled up in front, and the boat was floated successfully over the dam, reloaded, and went on its way. The people of New Salem were gathered on the banks, and recognized, with deep interest, the skill of the captain of the boat. A board sail which Lincoln had put up, for lack of canvas, excited much amusement at New Salem, Beardstown, Alton, St. Louis and other points on the route.

Offutt had purchased an additional number of pigs at Blue Bank, to put on board. Squire Godbey, of whom he bought them, and the three men undertook to drive them on board, but they refused to be driven. Lincoln had their eyelids sewed together, but that did not make the undertaking a bit more practicable. Finally, they were taken up, one by one, and carried on the boat. Lincoln then cut the threads from the eyes of the pigs, and the party proceeded on the journey.

DOWN THE SANGAMON.

CHAPTER VII.

IN this season of the year the trip down the majestic Mississippi, as she passes each day into a warmer atmosphere, is especially interesting, and Lincoln was daily learning more of life, and of the breadth and grandeur of the country over the destinies of which, thirty years afterward, he was to preside. Memphis, Vicksburg and Natchez were passed, after short stops at each, and Lincoln was again at a city which, in his eyes and in those of his companions, was a great metropolis. He saw the old sights and some new ones, and what he saw not only added to his knowledge of men and things, but stimulated his moral and humane impulses.

He had seen slaves in Kentucky when he was a small boy, and occasionally one in Illinois, nominally—by virtue of the Ordinance of 1787—a free state. But now, in his strolls about various portions of the city, he saw slaves from Kentucky and Tennessee, marching along on their way to sugar-cane and cotton plantations, and he finally came to a slave auction. Here men and women were sold from the block. His interest and his latent generous sympathies were touched by this sad, extraordinary sight. Human beings were treated like cattle, only worse. Comely maidens, sensitive, apprehensive, trembling, stood upon the block and were brutally handled by men who intended purchasing, and by others who merely wished to gratify their brutal tastes and propensities. The women and girls were pinched, coarsely questioned, made the objects of sport, their mouths opened and examined; and they were driven about to show whether they were sound in foot and limb, and then sold to men of whom they could know nothing and from whom they could only expect the worst. Husbands, wives and children wept as they were separated, in most instances never to meet in this world again.

What a spectacle was this in the American republic, the land of freedom, in which the Declaration of Independence had been adopted a little over half a century before! It is not strange that Abraham Lincoln's heart was profoundly stirred and. that the hot iron of this terrible wrong went into his soul. Just what Lincoln said on this occasion is not definitely known, as different versions are given, and some biographers deny that he said anything. But as to what he meant it is not difficult to guess. One of his biographers (Coffin) states that he said, with "quivering lips and soul on fire," to John Hanks: "John, if I ever get a chance to hit that institution, I'll hit it hard, by the Eternal God!" If he didn't say it, he ought to have done so. It is undoubtedly true that he felt it; and Judge Herndon says that Lincoln told him that he said it. The apparent profanity can be easily excused when the provocation is borne in mind. This was no doubt a crucial period in Lincoln's life. It gave him something to think about for long years, and when he came on the field of action, not long afterward, when the institution of slavery became a political problem, he felt that he had personal knowledge and had had a vivid experience as to its true nature.

LINCOLN AS A FLATBOATMAN.

The produce was disposed of at satisfactory prices. Offutt had gone down to New Orleans to attend to the selling, and he, Lincoln, Hanks and Johnston boarded a steamboat and started up the river. Judge Arnold quotes Lincoln's companions on the trip homeward as attempting to describe his indignation and grief. They said, "His heart bled; . . .   he was mad, thoughtful, abstracted, sad and depressed." Lincoln had been among people who were believers in premonitions and supernatural appearances all his life, and he once declared to his friends that he was "from boyhood superstitious." He said to the judge that "the near approach of the important events of his life were indicated by a presentiment or a strange dream, or in some other mysterious way it was impressed upon him that something important was to occur."

There is an old tradition that on this visit to New Orleans he and his companion, John Hanks, visited an old fortune-teller—a voodoo negress. Tradition says that "during the interview she became very much excited, and after various predictions-exclaimed: 'You will be president, and all the negroes will be free.' That the old voodoo negress should have foretold that the visitor would be president is not at all incredible. She doubtless told this to many aspiring lads, but the prophecy of the freedom of the slaves lacks confirmation."

The boat stopped at St. Louis; Offutt remaining to purchase goods for the "store" he was to establish at New Salem, and his companions continuing their journey on foot across the country to Farmington, where Thomas Lincoln was

SLAVE QUARTERS IN LOUISIANA.

indulging in his marked propensity by putting up a new house. This time it was a two-roomed structure. It was also made of hewed logs, and Abraham remained here a month, giving his father efficient help.

On an appointed day Abraham was to meet Offutt at New Salem, but while he was tarrying at Farmington his large dimensions attracted attention, and a certain Daniel Needham, the "champion wrestler of Coles county," began to resent the invasion of his territory by this big-limbed interloper. Needham had placed all of his muscular neighbors on their backs at one time or another, and was not slow to talk or to fight. Lincoln received from him a special challenge, and readily accepted it, and time and place were agreed upon. At Wabash Point the battle came off, and Needham, after a brief struggle, was placed on the ground, flat on his back.   Greatly chagrined, the defeated athlete demanded another trial, which was readily granted, with a like result.

On the day appointed, Lincoln became a citizen of New Salem. He was to be a clerk in Offutt's new store. He was now in a new atmosphere and in new surroundings, and was to attempt to carry on a new business. Lincoln had

CLEARING NEW GROUND IN PIONEER DAYS.

paddled down the river in a canoe and landed at Rutledge's mill. Offutt was there to welcome him and escort him to New Salem, then a prosperous village, located on a bluff a hundred feet high, and surrounded by an expanse of fertile fields and pastures. The Sangamon river skirted the base of the bluff, and presented a fine view from the summit. North of the town was the old mill over the dam of which Lincoln had taken his flatboat. Of the surrounding country Judge

Herndon writes: "The country in almost every direction is diversified by alternate stretches of hills and level lands, with streams between each, struggling to reach the river. The hills are bearded with timber—oak, hickory, walnut, ash and elm. Below them are stretches of rich alluvial bottom land, and the eye ranges over a vast expanse of foliage, the monotony of which is relieved by the alternating swells and depressions of the landscape. Between peak and peak, through its bed of limestone, sand and clay, sometimes kissing the feet of one bluff and then hugging the other, rolls the Sangamon river." Fine scenery often influences for good an impressionable and appreciative young person.

NEW SALEM STREET.

The site of New Salem, laid out in 1828, is now a desert. In 1836, it is said to have had twenty houses and one hundred inhabitants. . "How it vanished," one writer observes, "like a mist in the morning, to what distant place its inhabitants dispersed, and what became of the abodes they left behind, shall be questions for the local historian." One of these inhabitants, only twenty-eight years afterward, became an honored occupant of the White House.

Lincoln was nominally Offutt's clerk, but he had a few days of leisure before the goods arrived from St. Louis, which time he employed in making the acquain-

tance of as many of the people as possible. In the interval the annual election
came around. A Mr. Graham was clerk, but his assistant was absent, and it was
necessary to find a man to fill his place. Lincoln, a "tall young man," had
already concentrated on himself the attention of the people of the town, and Mr.
Graham easily discovered him. Asking him if he could write, he modestly
replied, "I can make a few rabbit-tracks." His rabbit-tracks proving to be leg-
ible and even graceful, he was employed. The voters soon discovered that the
new assistant clerk was honest and fair, and performed his duties satisfactorily,
and when, the work done, he began to "entertain them with stories," they discovered that their town had made a valuable personal and social acquisition.

LINCOLN STUDIES UNDER DIFFICULTIES.

During this interval an incident occurred that gave Lincoln something to do.
One of the citizens, a Dr. Nelson, decided to remove to Texas with his family
and goods, and employed Lincoln to take him to Beardstown, where he could
take a steamboat for St. Louis. The family and their household furniture and
other articles were put on a flatboat and floated down the Sangamon to the
Illinois river. The water was low, but the journey was safely accomplished.

Now began Lincoln's life as a "storekeeper." On the eighth of July, Offutt
received permission from the county authorities to "retail merchandise at New
Salem." The value of the goods was put at one thousand dollars—a large sum,
in those days, in a small town. A man worth ten thousand dollars cut as large

a figure as a man of the present day who assumes to be worth half a million. The building was a little log house. Dry-goods and groceries composed the stock, and doubtless there were other articles not included in these terms. Anything the people were thought likely to buy was kept, and sold when called for. Lincoln commenced business as a merchant, but he was not a business man, neither by nature nor training, and never became one.

At this period he found something much more attractive to him than the selling of goods, or of receiving money for them. It was Samuel Kirkham's

OLD MILL AT NEW SALEM.

English grammar, printed in Cincinnati, by N. and G. Guilford, in 1828. Gray-headed men of the present day do not recall this work with very pleasant recollections, but Lincoln found it exceedingly interesting—so much so that he may have neglected the little business which came straggling into the store. But he gave the book a thorough study, and he could soon repeat the rules and suggestions, word for word, and knew how to apply them. He learned how to construct sentences clearly and in understandable English. To this may be credited the fact that nobody who ever listened to Abraham Lincoln in later days failed to understand what he said or what he meant. To an acquaintance (Mentor Graham) he was indebted for the knowledge of the book, and he walked several miles to the house of a man named Vaner to obtain it.

Lincoln had periods in which there was nothing for him to do, and was therefore in circumstances that made laziness almost inevitable. Had people come to him for goods, they would have found him willing to sell them. He sold all that he could, doubtless. The store soon became the social center of the village. If the people did not care (or were unable) to buy goods, they liked to go where they could talk with their neighbors and listen to stories. These Lincoln gave them in abundance, and of a rare sort. Afterward Lincoln obtained a text-book on mathematics, and made good use of it. He never took a book in hand that he did not master.

ANDREW JACKSON, PRESIDENT 1829-37.

As much, however, as Lincoln lacked business training and the tact one requires to sell goods, his integrity was unquestioned. He watched the interest of his customers as much as that of his employer; he neglected neither. He early acquired the title of "Honest Abe," and many anecdotes are told of his square dealings. If he made a mistake in reckoning or in weighing, he was quick to rectify it. One day he found that a woman had paid him six and a quarter cents more than was due, and when the store was closed for the night, he hastened to correct the mistake, although she lived two miles away.

There were some rough people in the neighborhood. One of them used profane and vile language in the presence of some women, and Lincoln showed his gentlemanly instincts and true gallantry by resenting the affront. Herndon, in his "Life of Abraham Lincoln," gives the following account of the affair:

"'Do not use such language,' said Lincoln.

"'Who are you? I will swear when and where I please. I can lick you,' said the fellow.

"'When the ladies are gone I will let you have a chance to do so.'

"The ladies departed, and the man dared Lincoln to touch him. Suddenly he found himself lying flat upon his back, with blows falling upon him like the strokes of a hammer."

About eight miles from New Salem was a little place called Clary's Grove. The young men of that neighborhood had become, by their pugnacity and prowess, a "power in the land." They were muscular and aggressive. They were greatly addicted to larks, and were not at all particular as to the depredations they committed. Judge Herndon, who had a cousin living at New Salem, and who "knew personally" many of the "boys," describes them as follows:

"They were friendly and good-natured; they could trench a pond, dig a bog, build a house; they could pray or fight, make a village or create a state. They

LAST RUTLEDGE MILL, ON THE FOUNDATION OF THE MILL OF WHICH LINCOLN HAD CHARGE.

would do almost anything for sport or fun, love or necessity. Though rude and rough, though life's forces ran over the edge of the bowl, foaming and sparkling in pure deviltry for deviltry's sake, yet place before them a poor man who needed their aid, a lame or sick man, a defenseless woman, a widow or an orphaned child, they melted into sympathy and charity at once. They gave all they had, and willingly toiled or played cards for more. Though there never was under the sun a more generous parcel of rowdies, a stranger's introduction to them was likely to be the most unpleasant part of his acquaintance with them."

Denton Offutt was very proud of Lincoln, and was not at all reserved in his language when boasting of Abe's merits. He declared—was it with a prophet's prescience?—that he was "the smartest man in the United States," and proclaimed far and wide that Lincoln could "lift more, throw farther, run faster, jump higher and wrestle better than any man in Sangamon county!" There were a number of Armstrongs at Clary's Grove, and they were the chief among the "terrors" of the locality. They are said to have ridden through the neighborhood at night, whooping and swearing and frightening women and children. Hearing of Offutt's boasting, the boys were aroused, and determined to humble this new rival in the esteem of their fellow-citizens. They had no doubt that they could easily dispose of him, and one of the gang declared that Jack Armstrong would put Offutt's clerk on his back in a twinkling; but Lincoln's employer said that Lincoln would use Armstrong to wipe his feet on. Bill Clary then offered to bet that Jack was the better fellow, and Offutt took it, Lincoln consenting to a friendly wrestle. The match was arranged, and when the day arrived, there was much local excitement, and a large audience. The contest began —it was a severe struggle. None of Armstrong's usual devices seemed to work, and "Armstrong soon discovered that he had met his match. Neither could for some time throw the other, and Armstrong, convinced of this, tried a foul." This aroused Lincoln's anger, and a bystander says: "Lincoln no sooner realized the game of his antagonist than, furious with indignation, he caught him by the throat, and holding him out at arm's length, shook him like a child." Armstrong's friends rallied to his aid, but Lincoln held his own, and a little more, and an era of good feeling was soon organized. Even Jack Armstrong himself declared that Lincoln was "the best fellow who ever broke into the camp." That day the championship was transferred to Abraham Lincoln. He was the "best man" of the neighborhood, but in addition to being the champion, he was also a peacemaker. The Armstrongs became stout and lifelong friends of Lincoln, who had by his show of pluck and strength become immensely popular.

Much as Lincoln had learned from Kirkham, he had something to learn as to the sort of literature a practical knowledge of grammar could produce. Mr. George D. Prentice's Louisville *Journal* came regularly to the local postmaster, who was, almost as a matter of course, one of Lincoln's many friends, and to whom he was indebted for the reading of this fine, strong public journal, as famous then as Mr. Henry Watterson's *Courier-Journal* is now for clear English and a masterly treatment of current problems. Not only did Lincoln learn from this newspaper the news of the day, but he was greatly instructed by its bright, strong and able editorials.

Lincoln took much interest in local affairs. He was, as a matter of course, familiar with the important political and economical issues of the day involved in what were called internal improvements, the making of roads, canals, etc., by the general government as a means of developing the resources of the country. Lincoln favored this policy, much discussed at the time, and as a man of public spirit, he at once began to try to make a local application of the principle.

The Sangamon river, he thought, might be navigated. Much interest was manifested, and it was not long before Lincoln became the representative and champion of the idea. Indeed, he made several little speeches in favor of it. The Sangamon had been navigated up to this time only by canoes, flatboats and rafts Therefore, when Captain Vincent Bogue, of Springfield, in the spring of 1832, went to Cincinnati to buy a steamboat, with which he proposed to navigate the Sangamon and to connect Springfield and New Salem with tide-water, the people

PIONEERS MAKING CLAPBOARDS.

went wild. The steamer "Talisman" was purchased at Cincinnati and was started on its way down the Ohio; then steamed up the Mississippi and the Illinois to the vicinity of Alton, and thence up the Sangamon to the point in that stream nearest Springfield.

New Salem was a small town, but at once it was accepted as a fact that it had a great future. Certainly it had "great expectations.". Captain Bogue had inflated views as to the success of his enterprise, and at once made great promises. The round trip to Cincinnati and St. Louis was to be made once a week, and the merchants of Springfield advertised new goods "direct from the East, per steamer Talisman." Mails were also to be received once a week by steamer. All the land in the neighborhood of Springfield, New Salem and other towns on the river was platted and cut up into town lots. Many of the people seemed (to themselves) to be already rich. At Captain Bogue's suggestion, a number of men—Lincoln among them—went down from New Salem, with long-handled axes, to a point near Beardstown, to meet the boat as she entered the mouth of the Sangamon, and to cut away the branches on either side, so that she could pass on up the stream. Judge Herndon writes that he "and other boys on horseback followed the boat, riding along the river's bank as far as Bogue's mill, where she tied up; there we went aboard, and, lost in boyish wonder, feasted our eyes on the splendor of her interior decoration." Great excitement was created all along the route. Few of the people had ever seen a steamboat.

All Springfield was aroused, and materialized in full force at the landing. The people had been organizing themselves for the red-letter day in the history of the town. A grand reception awaited the captain and his crew, and the captain (not Captain Bogue) was prepared to make the most of an opportunity that never came to him again. A reception and a dance at the court-house were given to him and his men, and a gaudily attired woman whom he announced as "his wife." But the captain and his "wife" were both soon under the influence of ardent spirits, and Springfield's cultivated and refined ladies very naturally took offense and withdrew. Society was shocked to learn, the next day, that the woman was no wife, but an adventuress who had been picked up on the way to Springfield.

The Talisman remained a week at the landing, and the water in the river lowering, it was thought best to steam on down the several rivers to St. Louis. Much difficulty was encountered at various points, but Abraham Lincoln and Judge Herndon's brother were on deck and piloted her down to Beardstown. She then steamed down the Mississippi to St. Louis, where she caught fire at the warf and was burned to the water's edge. That was the last of the navigation of the Sangamon by steamboats, except in theory. Canoes, skiffs and flatboats have had no rivals there since that time.

CHAPTER VIII.

WE now come to an historical event of some importance—the breaking out, and the prosecution to its conclusion, of what is called the Black Hawk war. If it did nobody else any good, it was of benefit to Abraham Lincoln, as it opened to him an opportunity to do something for his country, but especially for himself. Denton Offutt, his old employer, had failed and removed elsewhere. Subsequent events showed that he became a resident of Baltimore, and presented to the public a scheme for taming wild horses by whispering in their ears. Captain Bogue's Talisman bubble bursted, leaving Lincoln disappointed and adrift.

In April, 1832, the people were startled by the appearance of a circular, which was scattered everywhere. It was an address to and a call upon the militia of the northwestern portion of the state, from Governor Reynolds, to rendezvous within a week at Beardstown, to repel an invasion by the Sac and other Indians, led by the famous Black Hawk. This great chief had formerly occupied the northwestern portion of the state, but on June 30, 1831, had solemnly promised Governor Reynolds and General Gaines, of the United States army, that none of his tribe should ever cross the Mississippi "to their usual place of residence, nor to any part of their old hunting-grounds east of the Mississippi, without permission of the president of the United States or the governor of the state of Illinois." The land formerly owned by the Indians was in 1804 sold to the United States government, but "with the provision that the Indians should hunt and raise corn there until it was surveyed and sold to settlers."

Black Hawk resisted the encroachments of the squatters, who had proved, like many another pioneer community of whites, to be the aggressors. But the whites, although the line agreed upon was fifty miles to the eastward, persisted in evading both the letter and spirit of the agreement, and Black Hawk, aggrieved, exasperated and broken-hearted, announced a theory that has been exploited by latter-day theorists. "My reason teaches me," Black Hawk wrote, "that *land cannot be sold.* The Great Spirit gave it to his children to live upon and cultivate, as far as it is necessary for their subsistence; and so long as they occupy and cultivate it, they have the right to the soil; but if they voluntarily leave, then any other people have a right to settle upon it. *Nothing can be sold but such things as can be carried away."*

Black Hawk had been known throughout the territory as an able and aggressive warrior, and as one who had sympathized and co-operated with the enemies of the country, especially the British. Here, however, he was justified in feeling that he had been wronged. He had not been allowed to plant his corn on the lands set aside to him for that purpose, and it is not strange that he was persuaded by another famous Indian (White Cloud, the prophet) to invade the Rock river country in 1831, and try to drive back the squatters. But he was driven back, and his wrongs were not righted. At this time he signed a formal treaty never to return east of the Mississippi.

Now Black Hawk, in his old age—at sixty-seven—became, in turn, the aggressor. He regretted that he had "touched the goose-quill" to the treaty.

BLACK HAWK.

Bad counsels of White Cloud "and his disciple Neapope," a promise of "guns, ammunition and provisions" from the British, his own treachery and obstinacy, and the hope of success, inspired him to trample upon treaties and to make another trial. On April 6, 1832, he crossed the Mississippi with about five hundred braves and his squaws and children, and advanced to Prophetstown, thirty-five miles up Rock river. It was ten days afterward that Governor Reynolds' proclamation and call for the services of the militia to assemble within a week at Beardstown, on the Illinois river, was issued. Lincoln, with nothing to do, and anxious to do something, dropped a personal canvass which he was then making in the interest of his own candidacy for a seat in the Illinois Legislature, and was one of the first to volunteer. A company was promptly raised, and by the twenty-second of April the men were at Beardstown.

Lincoln's personal campaign had here a little variation, but was really continued. He had worked for awhile, some time before, in a sawmill for a man named William Kirkpatrick, who had broken faith with him in a business transaction. Kirkpatrick pressed to the front and announced himself as a candidate for the captaincy. Lincoln, who had what politicians now call a "knife in his boot-leg," also announced himself as a candidate. His accounts with Kirkpatrick were squared by the result of the canvass. He took one position and Kirkpatrick another, the adherents of each gathering around their favorite—three fourths of the men around Lincoln, much to his surprise, as he afterward declared.

The men of the country proved to be a lot of very independent citizens, each with ideas and a will of his own. Each man also had a "uniform" of his own, but all knew how to handle and operate a gun. Coonskin caps and buckskin breeches were the prevailing style. But the captain and his men were without any sort of military knowledge, and both were forced to acquire such knowledge by attempts at drilling. Which was the more awkward, the "squad" or the commander, it would have been difficult to decide. In one of Lincoln's earliest military problems was involved the process of getting his company "endwise" through a gate. Finally he shouted, "This company is dismissed for two minutes, when it will fall in again on the other side of the gate!"

Lincoln was one of the first of his company to be arraigned for unmilitary conduct. Contrary to the rules he fired, a gun "within the limits," and had his sword taken from him. The next infringement of rules was by the men, who stole a quantity of liquor, drank it, and became unfit for duty, straggling out of the ranks the next day, and not getting together again until late at night. For allowing this lawlessness the captain was condemned to wear a wooden sword for two days. These were merely interesting but trivial incidents of the campaign. Lincoln was at the very first popular with his men, although one of them told him to "go to the devil," and he was daily showing qualities that increased their respect and admiration.

GOVERNOR JOHN REYNOLDS.

One day a poor old Indian came into the camp with a paper of safe conduct from General Lewis Cass in his possession. The members of the company were greatly exasperated by late Indian barbarities, among them the horrible murder of a number of women and children, and were about to kill him; they affected to believe that the safe-conduct paper was a forgery, and approached the old savage with muskets cocked to shoot him, when Lincoln rushed forward, struck up the weapons with his hands, and standing in front of the victim, declared to the Indian that he should not be killed. It was with great difficulty that the men could be kept from their purpose, but the courage and firmness of Lincoln thwarted them.

Lincoln's fame as a wrestler was somewhat diminished in this campaign. A man named Thompson (as Judge Herndon relates), a soldier from Union county, managed to throw him twice in succession. Lincoln's men declared that Thompson had been unfair, that he had been guilty of "foul tactics," and that Lincoln's defeat was due to a "dog fall." Lincoln, however, showed his true character by declaring that Thompson had acted fairly. William L. Wilson stated to Judge Herndon that in this campaign he wrestled with Lincoln, "two best in three," and "ditched" him. Lincoln was not satisfied, and the two tried a foot-race for a five-dollar bill, Wilson coming out ahead.

Naturally, under the circumstances, food was scarce, and the men learned the military art of "subsisting on the country," in which there was very little to subsist. One day a dove was caught and an unlimited amount of very weak soup was made. Chickens as tough as the hardy pioneers were found about the deserted cabins of the squatters, and roasted and devoured. They supplemented fresh pork nicely, and the voracious appetites of the men, whetted by their exposure and hardships, made their fare delicious.

ELIJAH ILES.

On the twenty-seventh of April, sixteen hundred men were organized into regiments and moved to the seat of the war. The weather was severe, and mud abounded in the roads. But the men were, hardy and muscular, and made light of the unfavorable conditions. Passing Yellow Banks, on the Mississippi, they reached Dixon, on Rock river, on the twelfth of May, and here, as Miss Tarbell states, "occurred the first bloodshed of the war." From Miss Tarbell's book we have a graphic account of Major Stillman's campaign and treachery: "A body of about three hundred and forty rangers, not of the regular army, under Major Stillman, asked to go ahead as scouts, to look for a body of Indians, under Black Hawk, rumored to be about twelve miles away. The permission was given, and on the night of May 14, 1832, Stillman and his men went into camp. Black Hawk heard of their presence. By this time the poor old chief had discovered that the promises of aid from the Indian tribes and the British were false, and, dismayed, had resolved to recross the Mississippi."

If he had been unmolested at this time, the famous Black Hawk war would have ceased without the shedding of a drop of blood. Miss Tarbell's narrative proceeds as follows: "When he heard that the whites were near, he sent three braves with a white flag to ask for a parley, and permission to descend the river.

Behind them he sent five men to watch proceedings. Stillman's rangers were in camp when the bearers of the flag of truce appeared. The men were many of them half drunk, and when they saw the Indian truce-bearers, they rushed out in a wild mob and ran them into camp. Then catching sight of the five spies, they started after them, killing two. The three who reached Black Hawk reported that the truce-bearers had been killed, as well as their two companions. Furious at this violation of faith, Black Hawk 'raised a yell,' and declared to the forty braves—all he had with him—that they must have revenge."

That Black Hawk's attack was vigorous and deadly does not need to be said. Stillman and his men were in search of the Indians, and they found them, to their sorrow. To Black Hawk's surprise, the rangers turned in dismay and put their legs to the best possible use, distancing the Indians, and never stopped running until they reached Dixon, twelve miles away, at midnight.

Among the men whom Captain Lincoln met in this campaign were Lieutenant-colonel Zachary Taylor, Lieutenant Jefferson Davis, and Lieutenant Robert Anderson, of the United States army. Judge Arnold, in his "Life of Abraham Lincoln," relates that Lincoln and Anderson did not meet again until some time in 1861. After Anderson had evacuated Fort Sumter, on visiting Washington, he called at the White House to pay his respects to the president. Lincoln expressed his thanks to Anderson for his conduct at Fort Sumter, and then said:

"Major, do you remember of ever meeting me before?"

"No, Mr. President, I have no recollection of ever having had that pleasure."

MAJOR ROBERT ANDERSON.

"My memory is better than yours," said Lincoln; "you mustered me into the service of the United States in 1832, at Dixon's Ferry, in the Black Hawk war."

When a member of Congress, Mr. Lincoln, in one of his speeches in reply to extravagant claims of heroism set up for General Lewis Cass, then a candidate for the presidency against General Zachary Taylor, said:

"By the way, Mr. Speaker, did you know of my military heroism? Yes, sir, in the days of the Black Hawk war I fought, bled and came away. Speaking of General Cass' career reminds me of my own. I was not at Stillman's defeat, but I was about as near to it as Cass was to Hull's surrender, and, like him, I saw the place very soon afterward. It is quite certain that I did not break my sword, for I had none to break, but I bent my musket pretty badly on one occasion."

An incident of much interest occurred during this campaign which showed the stamina of Colonel Zachary Taylor, afterward president of the United States. The volunteers were exasperated at the way in which the war was carried on, and wishing to go home, held a mass-meeting, and passed fiery resolutions, in which they declared that they would not pass over the state line in pursuit of the enemy. Taylor listened to them quietly, and then addressed them, good-naturedly but shrewdly, as follows:

" I feel that all gentlemen here are my equals; in reality, I am persuaded that many of them will, in a few years, be my superiors, and perhaps, in the capacity of members of Congress, arbiters of the fortunes and reputation of humble servants of the republic, like myself. I expect then to obey them as interpreters of the will of the people; and the best proof that I will obey them is now to observe the orders of those whom the people have already put in the place of

BLACK HAWK WAR RELICS.

authority to which many gentlemen around me justly aspire. In plain English, gentlemen and fellow-citizens, the word has been passed on to me from Washington to follow Black Hawk and to take you with me as soldiers. I mean to do both. There are the flatboats drawn up on the shore, and here are Uncle Sam's men drawn up behind you on the prairie."

The time of service of Lincoln's men had expired, and as their campaign had been one of much hardship and suffering, they were anxious to return to their homes. They were finally disbanded, and returned to New Salem and other places whence they came. Lincoln, however, and a companion named Harrison decided to remain, and both re-enlisted as privates, in Captain Elijah Iles' "Independent Spy Battalion." The men were mounted, had no camp duties to perform, and had regular rations; therefore, Lincoln was much better provided for as a private than he had been as captain of his old company.

The Black Hawk war was now rapidly approaching its close. But Black Hawk was desperate, and was devastating the country and murdering the settlers. The people were panic-stricken, and most of the settlements were abandoned. An old Illinois woman says, "We often left our bread dough unbaked to rush to the Indian fort near by." As all able-bodied men had volunteered, crops were necessarily neglected. One of America's great poets and journalists William Cullen Bryant, who visited his poet brother, Mr. John H. Bryant, in the year 1832, wrote home as follows:

"Every few miles on our way we fell in with bodies of Illinois militia proceeding to the American camp, or saw where they had encamped for the night. They generally stationed themselves near a stream or a spring in the edge of a wood, and turned out their horses to graze on the prairie. Their way was barked or girdled, and the roads through the uninhabited country were as much beaten and as dusty as the highways on New York island. Some of the settlers complained that they made war upon the pigs and chickens. They were a hard-looking set of men, unkempt and unshaved, wearing shirts of dark calico, and sometimes calico capotes."

WILLIAM G. GREEN.

William G. Green was a clerk in Offutt's store with Lincoln. He also saw Lincoln bore the hole in the bottom of the boat and take it over Rutledge's mill-dam. Mr. Green died in 1894, a wealthy man.

The army soon afterward marched up Rock river in pursuit of Black Hawk and his braves. The "rangers" were employed as scouts and spies. They proceeded with a brigade to the northwest. The nearest Lincoln ever came to a fight was when he was in the vicinity of the skirmish at Kellogg's Grove. The rangers arrived at the spot after the engagement and helped bury the five men who were killed. Lincoln told Noah Brooks, one of his biographers, that he "remembered just how those men looked as we rode up the little hill where their camp was. The red light of the morning sun was streaming upon them as they lay, heads toward us, on the ground. And every man had a round, red spot on the top of his head about as big as a dollar, where the redskins had taken his

3

scalp. It was frightful, but it was grotesque; and the red sunlight seemed to paint everything all over." Lincoln paused, as if recalling the vivid picture, and added, somewhat irrelevantly, "I remember that one man had on buckskin breeches."

The troops soon passed northward into what was then known as a part of the territory of Michigan, but is now the state of Wisconsin, and the month of July was devoted to following the Indians through forests and swamps. Black Hawk was disappointed, disheartened and nearly exhausted, and when finally encountered at Bad Ax, was an easy prey. At the last battle of the war, at Bad Ax, he was captured and the larger number of his braves massacred. The war was at last over. Lincoln and the other volunteers were mustered out by Lieutenant Robert Anderson (afterward famous as Major Robert Anderson, the hero of Fort Sumter), and wended their way homeward.

As further showing the generous qualities of Lincoln, and in the line of explaining one of the sources of his popularity, we quote from D. W. Bartlett's "Life and Speeches of Abraham Lincoln," published in 1860, a statement of his efficient service to his neighbors in the "Great Snow" of 1830-31:

"The deep snow which occurred in 1830-31 was one of the chief troubles endured by the early settlers of central and southern Illinois. Its consequences lasted through several years. The people were illy prepared to meet it, as the weather had been mild and pleasant—unprecedentedly so up to Christmas—when a snow-storm set in which lasted two days, something never before known even among the traditions of the Indians, and never approached in the weather of any winter since. The pioneers who came into the state (then a territory) in 1800 . . . say the average depth of snow was never, previous to 1830, more than knee-deep to an ordinary man, while it was breast-high all that winter. . . . It became crusted over, so as, in some cases, to bear teams. Cattle and horses perished, the winter wheat was killed, the meager stock of provisions ran out, and during the three months' continuance of the snow, ice and continuous cold weather the most wealthy settlers came near starving, while some of the poorer ones actually did. It was in the midst of such scenes that Abraham Lincoln attained his majority, and commenced his career of bold and manly independence. . . . Communication between house and house was often entirely obstructed for teams, so that the young and strong men had to do all the traveling on foot; carrying from one neighbor what of his store he could spare to another, and bringing back in return something of his store sorely needed. Men living five, ten, twenty and thirty miles apart were called 'neighbors' then. Young Lincoln was always ready to perform these acts of humanity, and was foremost in the counsels of the settlers when their troubles seemed gathering like a thick cloud about them."

CHAPTER IX.

LINCOLN'S military service had increased his already great popularity at New Salem, and he was ready to resume his campaign as a politician and a candidate for legislative honors. A. Y. Ellis describes his personal appearance at this time as follows: "He wore a mixed jean coat, claw-hammer style, short in the sleeves and bob-tailed; in fact, it was so short in the tail that he could not sit on it; flax and tow linen pantaloons and a straw hat. I think he wore a vest, but do not remember how it looked; he wore pot-metal boots."

He had announced himself as a candidate previous to enlisting, and it was only ten days before the election was to take place. He made his first speech at Pappsville. Judge Herndon describes the occasion as follows: "His maiden effort on the stump was on the occasion of a public sale at Pappsville, a village eleven miles west of Springfield. After the sale was over and speech-making [by the several candidates, for no nominating conventions were held in those days, and the race was open to all] had begun, a fight, 'a general fight,' as one of the bystanders relates, ensued, and Lincoln, noticing one of his friends about to succumb to the energetic attack of an infuriated ruffian, interposed to prevent it. He did so most effectually. Hastily descending from the rude platform, he edged his way through the crowd, and seizing the bully by the neck and the seat of his trousers, threw him, by means of his strength and long arms, as one witness stoutly insists, 'twelve feet away.' Returning to the stand, and throwing aside his hat, he inaugurated his campaign with the following brief but pertinent declaration:

"Fellow-citizens, I presume you all know who I am. I am humble Abraham Lincoln. I have been solicited by many friends to become a candidate for the Legislature. My politics are short and sweet, like the old woman's dance. I am in favor of the national bank; I am in favor of the internal improvement system and a high protective tariff. These are my sentiments; if elected, I shall be thankful; if not, it will be all the same."

The election occurred at the appointed time. There were twelve candidates in the field, and although Lincoln received the nearly unanimous vote of New Salem and Clary's Grove—Democrats as well as Whigs—he failed to receive enough to elect him.

He had at this time some further experience in commercial life. He and a
fellow named Berry bought out a grocery, and after a number of changes and
repeated losses, gave up the business. Lincoln told stories at one end of the store
and Berry drank whisky at the other end. Neither of the partners had much, if
any, business capacity. Reuben Radford decided to become a competitor with
Lincoln & Berry at this time, but he had not considered the cost of rivalry
with the favorite of the Clary's Grove boys. One night Radford left his store in
charge of a younger brother, and this, it seems, was the night of one of the
Clary's Grove boys' periodical larks. According to instructions, the young man
gave the members of the party two drinks each and refused a third, whereupon
the boys went to the barrel and helped themselves until all were drunk, and then
commenced shouting and dancing and proceeded to demolish the concern. What
remained of his stock was sold to Lincoln & Berry. Trade was dull that winter.

The farmers had very little
produce to sell, and consequently could not purchase
many goods. Berry the while
was drinking whisky and Lincoln was talking and musing
over politics. Finally the
store was sold to Trent Brothers. They had no money,
but gave their notes. Lincoln
& Berry had given their notes,
so all the transactions were
pretty much on notes. Berry
became a drunken sot. Lincoln was again adrift in the
world. His funds were ex-
hausted, and he was heavily

LINCOLN & BERRY'S STORE.
(Rear view, from a recent photograph.)

in debt, which indebtedness was not finally liquidated until Lincoln sent
portions of his salary home from Washington, when he was in Congress, to
Judge Herndon, to make the final payments.

On May 7, 1833, Lincoln was appointed postmaster at New Salem. The office
was afterward discontinued, and there was a balance of sixteen or eighteen
dollars due the government. This was overlooked by the Post-office Department,
and was not called for until some years afterward, Lincoln having removed to
Springfield. During the interval he had been in debt continuously, and, as usual,
poor. One day an agent of the department called on Dr. Henry, with whom
Lincoln at that time kept his law-office. Knowing Lincoln's poverty, Dr. Henry
offered to lend him the amount, but Lincoln asked the agent to be seated while
he went over to his trunk at the boarding-house. He soon returned with an old
blue sock, with a quantity of old silver and copper coin tied up in it, and
counted the coin, and handed over to the agent the exact amount to a cent in the

very identical bits which had been received by him from the people of New Salem.

The surveyor John Calhoun, although a Democrat, appointed Lincoln his assistant in the portion of the county in which he lived; he accepted, bought a compass and chain, "studied Flint and Gibson a little [Bartlett], and went at it." Calhoun was an educated and courteous gentleman, with some knowledge of human nature, and recognized the sterling qualities of his assistant. Calhoun was an accurate engineer, and was employed to plot and lay out new towns and villages. Lincoln, therefore, learned much, and the man who has been called the savior of his country became, as his predecessor, the father of his country, George Washington, had been, a good surveyor. He began to earn small amounts of money, was very frugal, but was still in financial straits, with his indebtedness hanging over him. He was, however, gradually reducing the debt. The people of the country should know what hardships and discouragements he endured. "In 1834," says Judge Arnold, "an impatient creditor seized his horse, saddle, bridle and surveying instruments, and sold them under execution." A

LINCOLN'S SURVEYING INSTRUMENTS.

friend in need—let us honor his name—Bowling Greene, was the bidder, and restored to Lincoln his property, waiting Lincoln's convenience for payment. Lincoln appreciated the kindness so much that at Mr. Greene's grave, in the year 1842, he tried in vain to deliver a funeral oration over his remains. Judge Arnold says: "When he rose to speak his voice was choked with emotion."

It was Lincoln's ambition to become a lawyer as well as a politician and a statesman. He had been reading Blackstone for some time, and was afterward given the range of the library of John T. Stuart, one of his old comrades in the Black Hawk war. Stuart lived in Springfield, and Lincoln would walk from New Salem, fourteen miles distant, to Springfield to exchange one book for another, and would often master thirty or forty pages of the new book on his way home. At New Salem he would sit under a tree, in warm weather, and "barefooted," while reading his books. Occasionally he would pursue his reading of Blackstone or Chitty on the top of a wood-pile. Every interval of leisure would be promptly and fully utilized, if it were no more than five minutes in duration. There was not much time at this period for exercising his story-telling propensities.

Lincoln soon after bought an old form-book, and acquired enough knowledge and proficiency to enable him to "draw up deeds, contracts and mortgages, and began to figure as a pettifogger before the justice of the peace," seldom making any charge for his services. He read other than law-books, studying natural philosophy and other scientific branches. He had also read historical books, having mastered Rollin and Gibbon. Novels of a fair sort also attracted his attention. It is a noticeable fact that at this period he read newspapers thoroughly. The Sangamon *Journal*, the Louisville *Journal*, the St. Louis *Republican*, and the old Cincinnati *Gazette*, then as now, with its "Commercial" attachment, a very strong paper, and at that time edited by the famous and popular "Charley" Hammond, were perused regularly, until he knew all that was in them.

Story-telling, however, was not entirely neglected. His reading embraced a wide range of funny sketches, all of which he learned by rote, thus adding to his

BOWLING GREENE'S HOUSE.

This cabin was located half a mile north of New Salem, where it still stands, used for an old stable. Lincoln began studying law while a boarder in this cabin. He was stretched out on the floor reading when he first met "Dick" Yates, then a college student home on a vacation, and who afterward became the great war governor.

personal store. He improved as a reciter and retailer of the stories he had read and heard, and as the reciter of tales of his own invention, and he had ready and eager auditors. Judge Herndon relates that as a mimic Lincoln was unequaled. An old neighbor said: "His laugh was striking. Such awkward gestures belonged to no other man. They attracted universal attention from the old and sedate down to the school-boy. Then in a few moments he was as calm and thoughtful as a judge on the bench, and as ready to give advice on the most important matters; fun and gravity grew on him alike."

Lincoln at this time fell very deeply in love with a beautiful young girl—Ann Rutledge, a daughter of James Rutledge, one of the founders of New Salem, and having the blood of a Revolutionary soldier in his veins. She is described as "being a blonde, with golden hair, lips as red as a cherry, a cheek like a wild rose, with blue eyes, and as sweet and gentle in manners and temper as attractive in person." This young lady was all the more interesting for having suffered already in a love affair, a long account of which is given by Lincoln's old partner, Judge Herndon. She and a worthy young man—John McNeil, who had not long before come to New Salem from an eastern state—became very deeply attached to each other. McNeil's partner in a store, Samuel Hill, also became attached to the young beauty, but his suit was not favorably regarded, and he good-naturedly retired from the contest, having been rejected. McNeil prospered, and finally decided to return to New York state and bring his parents to New Salem. He then told Ann, to whom he had become engaged, that his real name was McNamar, and that he had changed it so that his relatives would not discover him until he had made enough money to support them. This caused a change in the sentiment at New Salem, and Ann's friends tried to convince her that McNeil had committed a crime in his earlier days and had deserted her. The women of the community did much to destroy her faith in her lover.

At last Ann was convinced, at least in part, and at this point "the ungainly Lincoln" became her suitor, and was evidently smitten through and through. The Rutledges and all the people of New Salem were his friends and wished him success. The regard was finally found to be mutual, and Lincoln found courage to propose, but Ann asked him to wait until she had written to her old lover, asking him to release her. The answer was one of those letters that never came. Ann at last consented to become Lincoln's wife. To one of her brothers she said that when Lincoln's studies were completed she was to marry him. But her perplexity was not altogether removed, and finally her health was undermined and she was stricken down with fever. Her strength slowly passed away, and it was soon certain that she must die. She sent for her lover to come to her bedside. The two were alone in their supreme

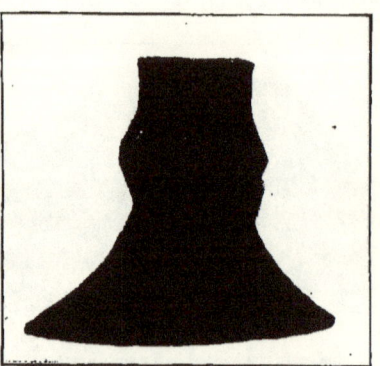

LINCOLN'S AX, USED WHILE AT NEW SALEM.

mutual sorrow. The poor girl soon died, in August, 1835. She used to sing very sweetly to her lover, and the last song she sang to him commenced:

> Vain man, thy fond pursuits forbear;
> Repent, thy end is nigh;
> Death at the farthest can't be far,
> Oh, think before thou die!

Lincoln was terribly distressed—almost heart-broken and crazed. The death of his mother had given him his greatest grief as a boy; the death of his affianced gave him the greatest grief of his young manhood. It was his old friend Bowling Greene who came to his rescue and "ministered to a mind diseased."

It is due to McNeil (or McNamar) to say that, after Ann's death, he returned with parents, brother and sister, thus showing his good faith.

It may be mentioned here that a year afterward Lincoln began to pay attention to Miss Mary S. Owens, a Kentucky girl, who was making, in 1836, a second

visit to New Salem. She had made some impression on him when she first came
to the town, in 1833. L. M. Greene describes her as follows: "She was tall and
portly, had large, blue eyes, and the finest trimmings I ever saw. She was jovial,
social, loved wit and humor, had a liberal education, and was considered wealthy.
None of the poets or romance-writers have ever given us a picture of a heroine
so beautiful as a good description of Miss Owens in 1836 would be." It seemed
that each was attracted to the other, but it became evident that neither was

GRAVE OF ANN RUTLEDGE.

really in love. One of his letters to Miss Owens is a very singular epistle. It
is certainly not very ardent. He, after the fashion of the lawyer, presents the
matter very cautiously, and pleads his own cause; then presents her side of the
case, advises her not "to do it," and agrees to abide by her decision. Miss
Owens, like other young women, liked an ardent lover, and although she
respected Lincoln, rejected him. She was afterward married, and became the
mother of five children. Two sons served in the Confederate army.

CHAPTER X

IN 1834, Lincoln, then twenty-five years of age, was again a candidate for the Legislature, and was elected, receiving a larger number of votes than any other man on either ticket. John T. Stuart, his Black Hawk war comrade, was also elected. Lincoln is spoken of by Judge Arnold as "the most popular man in Sangamon county." He was now a well-informed man. It could be safely said of him that he was self-educated. He knew much that the current literature of the day, the classics, school text-books and newspapers, contained. He was well up on all the political questions. Judge Arnold says: "He knew the Bible by heart. There was not a clergyman to be found so familiar with it as he. Scarcely a speech or paper prepared by him, from this time to his death. but contains apt allusions and striking illustrations from the sacred book. He could repeat all the poems of Burns, and was familiar with Shakspere. In arithmetic, surveying and the rudiments of other branches of mathematics he was perfectly at home. He had mastered Blackstone, Kent and the elementary law-books. He had considerable knowledge of physics and mechanics. He showed how much better it is to know thoroughly a few books than to know many superficially. Such had been his education. He was manly, just, gentle, truthful and honest. In conduct, kind and generous; so modest, so considerate of others, so unselfish, that everyone liked him and wished him success. True, he was homely, awkward and diffident, but he was, in fact, strictly a gentleman." A remarkable young man, this, at twenty-five. The writer of the foregoing was a careful man, who had the habit of weighing his words and of speaking with judicial fairness.

Lincoln was always a student, and at all times made the best possible use of his opportunities, which from this time were constantly increasing. He remained, as a matter of course, at Vandalia, the state capital, during his first term in the Legislature, and there met a cultivated class of men and women. He had here, also, a wider range of literature within his reach. During this first year of his experience as a legislator he listened attentively, thought much, but said little, and was a close student of public affairs.

It was in Lincoln's canvass for a second term, in 1836, that he began to be famous throughout a large portion of the state. He first spoke at Springfield

73

during this campaign. A meeting was advertised to be held in the court-house, at which candidates of opposing parties were to speak. This gave men of spirit and capacity a fine opportunity to show the stuff of which they were made. George Forquer was one of the most prominent citizens; he had been a Whig, but became a Democrat, possibly for the reason that by means of the change he secured the position of government land register, from President Andrew Jackson. He had the largest and finest house in the city, and there was a new and striking appendage to it, called a lightning-rod! The meeting was very large.

WILLIAM LLOYD GARRISON.

Seven Whig and seven Democratic candidates spoke, and Lincoln closed the discussion. A Kentuckian (Joshua F. Speed), who had heard Henry Clay and other distinguished Kentucky orators, stood near Lincoln, and states that he "never heard a more effective speaker; . . . the crowd seemed to be swayed by him as he pleased." What occurred during the closing portion of this meeting must be given in full, from Judge Arnold's book:

"Forquer, although not a candidate, then asked to be heard for the Democrats, in reply to Lincoln. He was a good speaker, and well known throughout the county. His special task that day was to attack and ridicule the young countryman from Salem. Turning to Lincoln, who stood within a few feet of him, he said: 'This young man must be taken down, and I am truly sorry that the task devolves upon me.' He then proceeded, in a very overbearing way, and with an assumption of great superiority, to attack Lincoln and his speech. He was fluent and ready with the rough sarcasm of the stump, and he went on to ridicule the person, dress and arguments of Lincoln with so much success that Lincoln's friends feared that he would be embarrassed and overthrown."

The Clary's Grove boys were present. and were restrained with difficulty from "getting up a fight" in behalf of their favorite, they and all his friends feeling that the attack was ungenerous and unmanly.

We quote the sequel, as follows:

"Lincoln, however, stood calm, but his flashing eye and pale cheek indicated his indignation. As soon as Forquer had closed, he took the stand, and first answered his opponent's arguments fully and triumphantly. So impressive were his words and manner that a hearer [Joshua F. Speed] believes that he can remember to this day and repeat some of the expressions. Among other things he said: 'The gentleman commenced his speech by saying that "this young man," alluding to me, "must be taken down." I am not so young in years as I am in the tricks and the trades of a politician, but,' said he, pointing to Forquer, 'live long or die young, I would rather die now than, like the gentleman, change my politics, and with the change receive an office worth three thousand dollars a year, and then,' continued he, 'feel obliged to erect a lightning-rod over my house, to protect a guilty conscience from an offended God!'"

Forquer was silenced and squelched.

Lincoln had several other encounters with distinguished Democrats, with similar results. "In this campaign," says Judge Arnold, "the reputation of Lincoln as a speaker was established, and ever afterward he was recognized as one of the great orators of the state."

JAMES SHIELDS.

Sangamon county had at this session two senators and seven members of the house, each one over six feet in height; they were called "the long nine." One of his Sangamon associates was Edward D. Baker, afterward a representative in Congress, then a member of the United States Senate, then a general in the field, dying at the engagement of Ball's Bluff. In the house was a young man from Vermont, Stephen Arnold Douglas, whom he first met at this period. There were also in the house James Shields, John A. Logan, John A. McClernand and others who afterward became famous. It should be stated here that in this canvass, as in that previous to it, Lincoln received the highest vote of any man on the ticket. He was a leader in the movement which resulted in removing the capital of the state from Vandalia to Springfield.

It was at this period that he made the important and prophetic declaration of principles, " I go for all sharing the privileges of the government who assist in bearing its burdens; consequently, I go for admitting all whites to the right of suffrage who pay taxes or bear arms, by no means excluding females." This was in 1836. Now, sixty years afterward, in many states women are allowed to vote. In 1836-7 Lincoln supported a measure for opening a great ship-canal from Lake Michigan, at Chicago, to the Illinois river. Now, sixty years later, such a canal is very near completion.

JOHN A. LOGAN.

At this time Lincoln began to wield his powerful personal and political influence against the aggressions of slavery. In 1820, as the result of an agreement between parties in Congress, Missouri was admitted to the Union without restriction as to slavery, but the act prohibited slavery thereafter, from the Atlantic to the Pacific, in the territory north of 36° 30′ north latitude. This agreement was called the Missouri Compromise, and it was part of a series of measures which created a sort of temporary fool's paradise called "an era of good feeling." It was evanescent; the controversy concerning slavery was not settled, but, on the other hand, increased in fury. Public sentiment at this time in Illinois was largely pro-slavery. The Legislature was nearly unanimous, as the result showed, in favor of slavery, and resolutions violently denouncing "abolitionists" and all persons who desired to abolish slavery and made efforts in that direction, or to restrict slavery, were whirled through the Legislature by an overwhelming vote. At this time there was a "black code," by which it was attempted to legalize severity and cruelty to negroes. Abraham Lincoln, thinking himself to be alone, stood up against the resolutions, but finally found one other member who had sufficient principle and nerve to stand with him. This seemed to be a turning-point in Abraham Lincoln's career. His conduct on this occasion was courageous and manly. Lincoln and Dan Stone, representatives from Sangamon county, made this protest, dated March 3, 1837, taken from the House Journal of the Illinois Legislature, 1836-37; pp. 817, 818:

"The following protest was presented to the House, which was read and ordered to be spread on the journals, to wit:

"Resolutions upon the subject of domestic slavery having passed both branches of the General Assembly at its present session, the undersigned have protested against the passage of the same.

"They believe that the institution of slavery is founded on both injustice and bad policy, but that the promulgation of abolition doctrine tends rather to increase than to abate its evils.

"They believe that the Congress of the United States has no power, under the Constitution, to interfere with the institution of slavery in the different states.

"They believe that the Congress of the United States has the power, under the Constitution, to abolish slavery in the District of Columbia, but that that power ought not to be exercised, unless at the request of the people of the District."

This utterance was conservative, and it represented the views of a great many

WILLIAM BUTLER.

men who were opposed to slavery, and especially to its extension, but, conservative and liberal as it was, it required great courage and stamina to present such a paper, under such circumstances, in a legislature whose members were moved by partizan bias and prejudice, and not by reason.

Lincoln was still a citizen of New Salem, and was also still a poor man. His salary as a member of the Legislature, beyond what was required to meet his board bills, was used to decrease his indebtedness. On his way home he had one of his periods of great depression. His associates in the Sangamon and Morgan county delegations were in high spirits over his and their success in getting the

capital removed to Springfield. But Lincoln, in his own words, was more concerned on the question as to how he should get capital for himself. William
Butler, a warm and strong friend, asked him what he "intended to do for a living," and he replied that he would like to leave New Salem, make his home in
Springfield and study law. Butler, who, with the other citizens, appreciated the
services he had rendered to Sangamon people, promptly told him that he could
make his (Butler's) house his home as long as he pleased. He afterward
accepted the hospitality, paying little attention to board bills.

STATE-HOUSE, SPRINGFIELD, ILLINOIS.

At Springfield he was honored by a reception and a banquet, at which the
following sentiment was given and unanimously and heartily approved: "He
[Lincoln] has fulfilled the expectation of his friends and disappointed the hopes
of his enemies." Of these, however, he had very few.

In 1837, Lincoln was twenty-eight years of age. He had come in contact
with the ablest men of the state, and was conscious of his growing power and
influence. It is true that he wished to be a lawyer, but lawyers abounded then
as now, and, so far as he knew, the custom that might come to him would be a

plant of slow growth. He had made the acquaintance and, very naturally, gained the friendship of Joshua Speed, who was a merchant, and kept what was called a "general store." Lincoln had brought his satchel, containing wearing-apparel and a few books, from New Salem, and threw it on the counter of Speed's store, in Springfield. Judge Herndon records the following colloquy that ensued:

Said Lincoln, "I want to get a room, and must have a bedstead and some bedding. How much will I have to pay?"

Mr. Speed took up his slate and jotted down the items—the cost of the bedstead, bedtick, sheets, blankets, wash-basin and towels. "Seventeen dollars," said the storekeeper.

LINCOLN'S LAW-OFFICE AT THE TIME OF HIS NOMINATION FOR PRESIDENT.

"I have no doubt it is cheap," replied Lincoln, "but I haven't the money to pay for the articles. If you could trust me until Christmas, and if I succeed in my experiment of being a lawyer, I will pay you then; if I fail, probably I shall never be able to pay you."

Mr. Speed had never seen him so dejected, but instantly solved the problem. "I can fix things better than that," said he. "I have a large room and a double bed up-stairs, and you are welcome to occupy the room and share the bed with me."

Taking his entire possessions, a satchel, or "saddle-bags," and two law-books, he took the bag and books up-stairs, and declared to Speed, with a radiant face, "I'm moved."

His old friend and compatriot, John T. Stuart, solved another problem for him by offering him a partnership, and the firm of Stuart & Lincoln was formed.

In 1838, Mr. Lincoln was for the third time elected to the Legislature, and received the Whig nomination for the speakership, being defeated by one vote

In 1840, he was returned to the Legislature for the fourth time. This was a period of great excitement throughout the country. An attempt had been made in 1828 to procure the passage of an amendment to the Constitution which would make Illinois a slave state. Free discussion of the slavery question was interfered with by mobs in many cities of the North, noticeably and very strangely in Boston. But public sentiment was influenced by merchants who sold goods in large quantities to southern customers. An attempt, happily futile, was made to hang William Lloyd Garrison, editor of *The Liberator*, at Boston, for his bold denunciations of slavery. But now the matter came nearer home.

Rev. Elijah P. Lovejoy, a plain-spoken, God-fearing man, of standing and ability, who was publishing a weekly religious paper at St. Louis, denounced the killing of a negro, who had, it is true, committed a horrible crime, but who had not had the benefit of a trial. Unfortunately, this sort of thing has not entirely passed away, North or South. Lovejoy showed how far he was in advance of his time, and how manly and true-hearted he was by denouncing, in strong terms, but in language that was true and fitting, the crime that had been committed, and a mob at once organized, entered his place, destroyed his types and threw his press into the river. Lovejoy then removed to Alton, in Illinois, a free state, at least by law and the provisions of the Constitution, and naturally hoped to be unmolested, but on receipt of press and types from Cincinnati, they were also destroyed by a mob. Lovejoy was of the stuff of which heroes were made. He therefore ordered another press and outfit of types. "It is our purpose," announced Lovejoy in behalf of his friends, to the mayor and other citizens, "to protect our property," and as he and his friends assembled with guns in hand, in the evening, the mayor nobly said to him, "You are acting in accordance with the law." The mob came, as expected, and fired into the building, and the firing was returned by Lovejoy's friends, and one of the men who made the assault was killed and another wounded. An attempt was then made to ascend to the top of the building and burn the roof. Lovejoy and others bravely stepped out on the street, and were about to fire at those on the ladder, when he was himself shot and mortally wounded. Then and there fell and died one of the greatest and bravest of America's martyrs to the freedom of speech and of the press.

At Cincinnati, Gamaliel Bailey, Jr.. the publisher of an anti-slavery paper— a courteous gentleman, a fair and good-tempered controversialist, but as firm as a rock in behalf of great principles—was mobbed in much the same way, but without the loss of his life. Afterward he removed to Washington, and commenced the publication of *The National Era*. in which. in 1850, appeared the several chapters of that immortal book, "Uncle Tom's Cabin," from the pen of Harriet Beecher Stowe—now living, in the year 1896.

The murder of Elijah P. Lovejoy did not frighten the opponents of slavery. Throughout the North fiery and righteous indignation moved in great waves, from city to city, and from commonwealth to commonwealth. The name of Lovejoy, a martyr to liberty, as well as to the freedom of the press, was honored and glorified. The mob that struck down Lovejoy had aimed an effective blow at the foundation of their own pet but ungodly "peculiar institution." From the very commencement of anti-slavery agitation no one event had so fired the hearts of the people, and to so great an extent made the institution of slavery universally odious, for the time, throughout the North, as this assassination of Lovejoy. Mass-meetings were held in hundreds of towns, and orators, with a theme that aroused them to the depths of their natures, spoke with unwonted eloquence and with electric effect.

It is not difficult to say, if we had no histories at all of the times, what Abraham Lincoln thought of the murder of the St. Louis negro and of this murderous and damnable assault on Lovejoy. He was a man who loved justice and loved liberty. This was in 1838, when Lincoln was twenty-nine years old. This was his first great opportunity. The young men of Springfield had already formed a lyceum for the discussion of public problems —and that relating to the

HARRIET BEECHER STOWE.

aggressions of human slavery, and the crimes committed in its name, was a problem that was actually blazing in all portions of the northern states. But Alton was near Springfield. Lincoln and his fellow-townsmen had often been there. The discussions of the lyceum were held in Mr. Speed's store, in the light and heat of one of the already old-fashioned large fireplaces, with the hickory back-log, and those who constituted the audience sat on boxes. nail-kegs, etc.

It seems to be a remarkable fact that two young men who were afterward among America's greatest orators and statesmen—certainly in the time in which they lived—should be members of and prominent debaters in this lyceum; and it seems a still more remarkable fact that one of these, Douglas, from Vermont, should take the side of the pro-slavery element, and that the native Kentuckian, Lincoln, should side with the enemies of slavery. There were no two brighter men of their age in the country at this time. Each acknowledged the other to be a foeman worthy of his steel. Differing politically, they were warm personal friends. Both had been in the Illinois Legislature together, and when the St. Louis and Alton murders came to be the topic of discussion, it proved to be one that brought out their best work. Speed's store soon was too small to accommodate the gatherings, and they were held in the First Presbyterian church.

FIRST PRESBYTERIAN CHURCH, SPRINGFIELD, ILLINOIS.

The discussions at Springfield, reported to some extent in the Sangamon *Journal*, had been heard of at Alton. The fame of Lincoln as a public speaker had reached that town long before, and now Lincoln was invited to Alton to deliver an address; and if Lincoln had not delivered in his subsequent career so many utterances that have become a part of the written history of his country, this utterance, made at Alton, would have been considered, at this day and henceforth, as wonderfully significant. The title of his address was, "The Perpetuation of Our Political Institutions." The very title was prophetic, as delivered over twenty years before the time when he stood up as the chief of those Americans who were the friends of the country's unity and integrity, on which principles were based its perpetuity. Let us read very carefully some portions of this address:

"In the great journal of things happening under the sun, the American people find our account running under date of the nineteenth century of the Christian era. We find ourselves in peaceful possession of the fairest portion of the earth as regards extent of territory, fertility of soil and salubrity of climate. We find ourselves under the government of a system of political institutions conducing more essentially to the ends of civil and religious liberty than any of which the history of former times tells us. We find ourselves the legal inheritors of these fundamental blessings. We toiled not in the acquirement or the establishment of them; they are a legacy bequeathed to us by a once hardy, brave and patriotic, but now lamented and departed, race of ancestors.

"Theirs was the task (and nobly they performed it) to possess themselves, and through themselves us, of this goodly land, and to rear upon its hills and in its valleys a political edifice of liberty and equal rights; 'tis

HENRY CLAY.

ours only to transmit these, the former unprofaned by the foot of the invader, the latter undecayed by the lapse of time. This our duty to ourselves and to our posterity, and love for our species in general, imperatively require us to perform.

"How, then, shall we perform it? At what point shall we expect the approach of danger? By what means shall we fortify against it? Shall we expect some transatlantic military giant to step across the ocean and crush us at a blow? Never! All the armies of Europe, Asia and Africa combined, with all the treasure of the earth (our own excepted) in their military chest, with a Bonaparte for a commander, could not, by force, take a drink from the Ohio, or make a track on the Blue Ridge in a trial of a thousand years.

"At what point, then, is the approach of danger to be expected? I answer, if it ever reaches us, it must spring up among us. It cannot come from abroad. If destruction be our lot, we must ourselves be its author and finisher. As a nation of freemen we must live through all time, or die by suicide. . . .

"There is even now something of ill omen among us. I mean the increasing disregard for law which pervades the country; the growing disposition to substitute the wild and furious passions in lieu of the sober judgment of courts, and the worse than savage mobs for the executive ministers of justice. This disposition is awfully fearful in any community, and that it now exists in ours, though grating to our feelings to admit, it would be a violation of truth and an insult to our intelligence to deny."

This is a most fitting prelude. Here spoke a man who, a great orator, was already showing qualities of great statesmanship, and now speaks the orator, statesman and prophet:

"There is no grievance that is a fit object of redress by mob law. Many great and good men, sufficiently qualified for any task they should undertake, may ever be found whose ambition would aspire to nothing but a seat in Congress, a gubernatorial or a presidential chair; but such belong not to the family of the lion or the brood of the eagle. What! Think you these places would satisfy an Alexander, a Cæsar or a Napoleon? Never!

"Towering genius disdains a beaten path. It seeks regions hitherto unexplored. It does not add story to story upon the monuments of fame erected to the memory of others. It denies that it is glory enough to serve under any chief. It scorns to tread in the footsteps of any predecessor, however illustrious. It thirsts and burns for distinction, and, if possible, will have it, whether at the expense of emancipating slaves or enslaving free men. Is it unreasonable, then, to expect that some man possessed with the loftiest genius, coupled with ambition sufficient to push it to its utmost stretch, will at some time spring up among us? And when such an one does, it will require the people to be united, attached to the government and laws, and generally intelligent, to successfully frustrate the design.

"Distinction will be his paramount object, and although he would as willingly, perhaps more so, acquire it by doing good as harm, yet that opportunity being passed, and nothing left to be done in the way of building up, he would sit down boldly to the task of pulling down. Here, then, is a probable case, highly dangerous, and such a one as could not have well existed heretofore."

Alluding to our Revolutionary ancestors, Mr. Lincoln says:

"In history we hope they will be read of, and recounted, so long as the Bible shall be read. But even granting that they will, their influence cannot be what it heretofore has been. Even then they cannot be so universally known. nor so vividly felt, as they were by the generation just gone to rest. At the close of that struggle nearly every adult male had been a participator in some of its scenes. The consequence was that of those scenes, in the form of a husband, a father, a son or a brother, a living history was to be found in every family—a history bearing the indubitable testimonies to its own authenticity, in the limbs mangled, in the scars of wounds received in the midst of the very scenes related; a history, too, that could be read and understood alike by all, the wise and the ignorant, the learned and the unlearned. But those histories are gone. They can be read no more forever. They were a fortress of strength; but what the invading foemen could never do, the silent artillery of time has done—the leveling of its walls. They are gone. They were a forest of giant oaks; but the resistless hurricane has swept over them, and left only here and there a lonely trunk, despoiled of its verdure, shorn of its foliage, unshading and unshaded, to murmur in a few more gentle breezes and to combat with its mutilated limbs a few more ruder storms, then to sink and be no more."

Herein is expressed reverence for law, a comprehension of the elements of a true and laudable ambition and the foresight of a truly great man.

CHAPTER XI.

M R. LINCOLN was at this time riding the circuit as an attorney. He was at all times a most interesting person. He and Speed boarded with William Butler, one of his stanchest friends, and afterward treasurer of the state of Illinois. It is related that on one occasion Lincoln, Speed and John J. Hardin, with a number of other lawyers, were on their return from court at Christiansburg, when Lincoln was suddenly missed.

"Where is Lincoln?" Mr. Speed asked.

"Oh," replied Mr. Hardin, "when I saw him last he had caught two young birds, which the wind had blown out of their nest, and he was hunting the nest to put them back."

In a short time Lincoln came up, having found the nest and replaced the young birds in it. The party laughed at him, but he said: "I could not have slept if I had not restored those little birds to their mother."

The United States courts were held in Springfield. John McLean, afterward famous as a justice of the Supreme Court, was the circuit judge, and Lincoln's associates at the bar included such men as John T. Stuart (his partner), Stephen T. Logan, Edward D. Baker, Ninian W. Edwards, and Josiah Limbon, of Springfield; Stephen Arnold Douglas, Lyman Trumbull, afterward United States senators; O. H. Browning, afterward senator and member of the Cabinet; William H. Bissell, afterward governor; David Davis, afterward governor, justice of the Supreme Court, senator and vice-president of the United States; Justin Butterfield, the ablest lawyer of Chicago, and other men afterward distinguished.

Court-houses of a pretentious charatcer were built of boards, but the greater number were built of logs. The furniture was very rude, as were the manners of the men who frequented them. The peculiarly American habit of elevating the heels higher than the head here prevailed. The lawyers were very free yet good-natured in their attitude to each other and their habits. They rode on horseback from one county-seat to another, with law-books, extra shirts, hair-brushes, etc., in their saddle-bags. Civilization had hardly achieved a shoe-brush at that period, in that region. Judge Arnold states that "sometimes two or three lawyers would unite and travel in a buggy, and the poorer and younger ones not seldom walked. But a horse was not an unusual fee, and in those days,

when horse-thieves, as clients, were but too common, it was not long before a
young man of ability found himself well mounted."

In 1840, Lincoln was again elected to the Legislature, and at this term he had
as his colleague John Calhoun. He was again a candidate for speaker.

Having been elected four times to as many biennial terms of the Legislature,
he declined again to be a candidate.

In the census of the United States for 1840 it was shown that there were
slaves in Illinois. Although it was nominally a free state, they had been
brought across the river from Kentucky. A case came to Mr. Lincoln which
greatly excited his sympathy. A Mr. Crowell sold his slave girl (Nancy) to a Mr.

Bailey, who gave his note, which was
not paid when due, and Mr. Crowell
brought suit. Lincoln, then thirty-
two years of age, gave his services
in behalf of the slave woman, who
was the real party to the suit. Probably this was his first case in the
Supreme Court. Stephen T. Logan,
afterward to become his law partner,
and subsequently a judge, was attorney on the other side.

"May it please the court," said
Lincoln, "the Ordinance of 1787,
which prohibited slavery in the
Northwest Territory, would give
Nancy her freedom. The constitution of the state prohibits the holding of slaves; she cannot, therefore,
be held as a slave; she cannot be sold
as a slave; a note given for the sale

STEPHEN A. DOUGLAS.

of a slave in a free state can have no
value; neither Crowell nor Bailey
can hold Nancy—she is entitled to freedom, and Crowell is not entitled to the
money which Bailey promised to pay him."

The court promptly decided in his favor, and that decision put an end to the
holding of slaves in Illinois.

In one of Lincoln's law-cases at this period a colt was used as a witness.
The dispute was between two men as to the ownership of the colt. Lincoln
suggested that the mares should be brought to the vicinity of the court-house
and that the colt should be allowed to choose between them. The colt
whinnied for his mother; there was an answering whinny from one of the mares,
and that answered the question. The court decided in favor of Lincoln.

In this year Mr. Lincoln supported William Henry Harrison, of North Bend,
near Cincinnati, Ohio, for the presidency. General Harrison was born, as was

Lincoln, in a log cabin, and having defeated the Indians in a well-fought battle at Tippecanoe, Indiana, he became popularly known as "Old Tippecanoe." The campaign was remarkable and unprecedented in its popular demonstration. Log cabins were erected everywhere, as they were half a century later, when Benjamin Harrison, the general's grandson, was a candidate for the same office, and was elected. Pine and ash liberty-poles were erected by the Whigs, the friends of Harrison, and hickory poles were put up by the Democrats, who had renominated Van Buren. Canoes were made out of logs and given prominent places in the processions. "Tom Corwin, the Wagon-boy," was a candidate for governor in Ohio, and Abraham Lincoln, who already ranked with Corwin as a wit and orator, easily lead the columns of the Whigs in Illinois. He was in demand everywhere for political addresses, and went whenever and wherever possible.

The charges against Van Buren, in this campaign, must be acknowledged as trivial. Too many gold spoons and too much rich furniture had been purchased for the White House. The campaign poet blossomed out in full, and Whig songs were sung with a will in every neighborhood. Campaign papers were printed at political centers and distributed in large numbers. In this year Horace Greeley, of New York, first became known by the remarkable little newspaper, called *The Log Cabin*, which he published, and which

FIRST COURT-HOUSE AT DECATUR, ILLINOIS.

gained at once a remarkably large circulation. Its editorials, written in clear, concise and plain but very forcible English, were the strongest journalistic utterances of that campaign. Lincoln discovered Greeley, and the two had much to do with each other in after years.

Van Buren was defeated by Harrison by a large vote. Two years afterward Van Buren, who was a very affable and congenial gentleman, met Lincoln. Mr. Van Buren and Ex-Secretary of the Navy Paulding, while on a western tour, stopped at Rochester, near Springfield, one night, and Judge Peck, a Democrat, Mr. Lincoln and others called on the ex-president to pay their respects. Lincoln got to telling his best stories in the best manner, and Judge Peck said that he never spent a more joyous night. Mr. Van Buren did his part in telling stories, giving incidents of the leading members of the New York bar, back to the days of Hamilton and Burr. Mr. Van Buren stated afterward that the only drawback to his enjoyment on this occasion was that his sides were sore for a week thereafter from laughing at Lincoln's stories. While Lincoln was at the White House, John, Martin Van Buren's gifted and witty son, called upon him, and the president related to him the occasion when he had met his father in Illinois.

In 1839, Lincoln made a courageous speech in the hall of the Illinois House of Representatives. His early friend John Calhoun, the former surveyor, was a fellow-member and a Democrat. A series of debates was decided upon. Douglas, Lambourn and others spoke for the Democrats, and Lincoln, Edward D. Baker and Browning spoke for the Whigs. Lambourn taunted the Whigs with the hopelessness of their struggle, to which Lincoln replied:

WILLIAM HENRY HARRISON.

"Address that argument to cowards and knaves. With the free and the brave it will effect nothing. It may be true; if it must, let it. Many free countries have lost their liberties, and ours may lose hers, but if it shall, let it be my proudest plume, not that I was the last to desert, but that I never deserted her."

Mr. Lincoln declared that he would never bow to the denunciation and persecution of his opponents, and then said: "Here before heaven, and in the face of the world, I swear eternal fidelity to the just cause of the land of my life, my liberty and my love. . . . The cause approved of our judgment and our hearts, in disaster, in chains, in death, we never faltered in defending."

On February 22, 1842, he delivered before the Washingtonian Temperance Society, at Springfield, an address upon temperance, in which he said: "When the victory shall be complete, when there shall be neither slave nor a drunkard on the earth, how proud the title of that land which may claim to be the birthplace and cradle of those revolutions that shall have ended in that victory."

Judge Arnold, in the following, describes an important period in Lincoln's life:

"Wishing to devote his time exclusively to his profession, he did not, as had already been stated, seek, in 1840, re-election to the Legislature. He had been associated as partner with one of the most prominent lawyers at the capital of the state, and he himself was leader of his party, and altogether the most popular man in central Illinois. In August, 1837, Stuart, his partner, was elected to Congress over Stephen A. Douglas, after one of the severest contests which ever occurred in the state. The district then extended from Springfield to Chicago, and embraced nearly all the northern part of Illinois. Stuart was re-elected in 1839. Their partnership terminated on April 14, 1841, and on the same day Lincoln entered into a new partnership with Judge Stephen T. Logan, one of the ablest and most successful lawyers of the state, and at that time universally recognized as at the head of the bar at the capital."

Lincoln was the candidate for Congress at the time of the presidential election in 1840. Colonel Coffin describes an incident in the campaign of that year, from Judge Herndon's account, as follows:

MARTIN VAN BUREN.

"Edward Dickinson Baker was born in London, England. He was two years younger than Abraham Lincoln, and came to America early in life. He made Springfield his home. He was a young lawyer, and, like Lincoln, an ardent Whig. His voice was musical. He could play the piano, sing songs and write poetry. He was an earnest advocate for the election of Harrison as president, and made a speech in the court-house to a great crowd. Many who gathered to hear him were Democrats. They were rough men; chewed tobacco, drank whisky, and became angry at what Baker was saying.

"The office of Stuart & Lincoln was over the court-room. A trap-door for ventilation, above the platform of the court-room, opened into their office. Lincoln, desiring to hear what Baker was saying, lifted the door, stretched himself upon the floor, and looked down upon the swaying crowd. Baker was talking about the stealings of the Democratic officials in the land-offices.

"'Wherever there is a land-office there you will find a Democratic newspaper defending its corruptions,' said Baker.

"'Pull him down! Put him out! It's a lie!' was the cry from a fellow in the crowd whose brother was editor of a Democratic paper. There was a rush for the platform. Great was the astonishment of the crowd at seeing a pair of long legs dangle from the scuttle, and then the body, shoulders and head of Abraham Lincoln, who let himself down to the platform. He lifted his hand, but the fellows did not heed his gesture. Then they saw him grasp a stoneware water-pitcher and heard him say, 'Hold on, gentlemen! This is a free country— a land for free speeches. Mr. Baker has a right to speak; let him be heard. I am here to protect him, and no man shall take him from this platform if I can prevent it.' Baker made his speech without further molestation."

CHAPTER XII.

AT about this time Lincoln again had time and inclination to resume love-making. Miss Mary Todd, of Kentucky, was this time the young lady who attracted his attention. She was the daughter of Hon. Robert S. Todd, and grandniece of John Todd, who, in company with General George Rogers Clark, in 1778, was present at the capture of Kaskaskia and Vincennes, Indiana, and who was appointed by Patrick Henry, governor of Virginia, "county lieutenant, or commandant, of the county of Illinois, in the state of Virginia." He was the founder of the state, and was killed at the battle of Blue Licks, Kentucky, in 1782. Miss Todd came to Springfield in 1839, to visit her sister, the wife of the Hon. Ninian W. Edwards. She was at this time twenty-one years of age. Her mother died when Mary was very young, and she had been taught in a boarding-school at Lexington. She is described by Judge Arnold as "intelligent and bright, full of life and animation, with ready wit and quick at repartee and satire. Her eyes were grayish blue, her hair abundant and dark brown in color. She was a brunette, with a rosy tinge in her cheeks, of medium height, and form rather full and round."

She was at once received in what really were the best families, and soon showed herself worthy to move in the highest social circles. She had at an early period become acquainted, very naturally, with a large number of educated young men, most of them lawyers or in some way prominently connected with public affairs. Both the young men and the young women of the town were greatly interested in politics, and not a few of them were ambitious. This was true of the Lexington belle who had so recently made her advent in Springfield. She had her eyes quite wide open, and gave these young men a close inspection. Mr. Lincoln was the most famous member of the group. He was at this time serving his last term in the Legislature; he was one of the best orators and stump-speakers in the state of Illinois. And socially, too, he was very prominent. An old resident says that "every lady wanted to get near Lincoln, to hear him talk." An old gentleman told Judge Arnold that when dining one day at the same table with Miss Todd and Lincoln, he said to her after dinner, half in jest and half in earnest: "Mary, I have heard that you have said you want to marry a man who will be president. If so, Abe Lincoln is your man."

Lincoln had been introduced to Miss Todd by Mr. Speed, a friend of both. The young lady especially interested him, as she was a personal friend of his great exemplar, Henry Clay. But he was attracted, also, by her personal beauty and her sprightliness. He had not forgotten Ann Rutledge, whom he had tenderly loved and to whose memory he was loyal, but, nevertheless, he and Miss Todd evidently grew more and more attached to each other daily. It is to her credit that in spite of his awkwardness she recognized his sterling qualities, and had glimpses, perhaps, of his future illustrious career. Miss Todd was

MRS. ABRAHAM LINCOLN.

an ardent lover, while Lincoln had the deliberation of a lawyer as well as the heart of a man. Lincoln and Miss Todd were at last engaged, and a day in January, 1841, was fixed for the wedding, to be celebrated at the house of Judge Edwards. Elaborate preparations were made, and the expectant bride was radiant and happy, but Mr. Lincoln, most unfortunately, was attacked by one of his periods of deep depression—of doubt, anxiety and fear. It seemed to him that he did not love the girl well enough to marry her, and he remained away. The disappointment, sorrow and mortification of Miss Todd could not adequately be expressed. Mr. Speed sought his friend, and found him, "pale, haggard and in the deepest melancholy."

To Hon. John T. Stuart Mr. Lincoln wrote these sentences: "I am the most miserable man living. If what I feel were equally distributed to the whole human family, there would not be a cheerful face on earth. Whether I shall ever be better I cannot tell; I awfully forebode I shall not. To remain as I am is impossible. I must die or be better."

Lincoln's true and loyal friend, Joshua F. Speed, who had closed his business in Springfield and was about to return to Louisville, persuaded the young man to accompany him. There he was graciously and affectionately greeted by the mother of Mr. Speed, one of those noble Christian women whose radiant lives witness the truth of the religion they represent. Mr. Speed tried in vain to arouse Lincoln to make an effort to overcome the weight of his sorrow. It remained for Mr. Speed's mother to lead him to the Great Comforter who offers help to all who come to him. Lincoln was deeply impressed and strongly influenced by this good woman. Lucy Gilman Speed was as warm-hearted as she was refined. She was a delight and comfort to all who knew her. Above all, she was a devoted, loving and very intelligent Christian woman, of a deep and broad spiritual nature, and was capable of leading this brilliant and intellectual man, who was often in doubt, into the clear, warm, bright, invigorating and vivifying atmosphere of Christian knowledge and experience. Mrs. Speed gave Mr. Lincoln an Oxford Bible, which he retained and read all his life.

From the Speed residence Lincoln, greatly and strongly comforted, took passage on a steamer, with "new hopes and ambitions," on his way to Springfield. On his way he had another opportunity to observe some of the barbarous customs due to the toleration of slavery.

AN EARLY PORTRAIT OF LINCOLN.

"A fine example was presented on board the boat for contemplating the effect of condition upon human happiness. A gentleman had purchased twelve negroes in different parts of Kentucky, and was taking them to a farm in the South. They were chained six and six together; a small iron clevis was around the left wrist of each, and this was fastened to the main chain by a shorter one at a convenient distance from the others, so that the negroes were strung together precisely like so many fish upon a trout-line. In this condition they were being separated forever from the scenes of their childhood, their friends, their fathers and mothers and brothers and sisters, and many of them from their wives and children, and going into perpetual slavery, where the lash of the master is proverbially more ruthless than anywhere else; and yet amid all these distressing circumstances, as we would think them, they were the most cheerful and apparently happy people on board. One, whose offense for which he was sold was an overfondness for his wife, played the fiddle almost continually, and others danced, sang, cracked jokes, and played various games with cards from day to day. How true it is that 'God tempers the wind to the shorn lamb,' or, in other words, that he renders the worst of human conditions tolerable, while he permits the best to be nothing better than tolerable."

On his return, Lincoln applied himself to the law, and continued his practice with great vigor. To all appearances the memory of his engagement to Mary Todd did not disturb him. The pain of separation was over, their paths leading in different directions, and the whole thing was a matter of the past. And so might it have ever remained but for the intervention of Mrs. Simeon Francis. She was a leader in society, and an admirer of Mary Todd's. Her husband, who was editor of the Sangamon *Journal*, was warmly attached to Lincoln. Lincoln

HOUSE WHERE LINCOLN WAS MARRIED, AND WHERE MRS. LINCOLN DIED.

was a frequent contributor, and practically controlled the editorial columns of the *Journal*. Mrs. Francis took it upon herself to bring about a reconciliation between Lincoln and Miss Todd. She arranged for a gathering at her house, inviting them, and both attended, neither suspecting the other's presence until the hostess brought them together, with the request, "Be friends again," thereby renewing the courtship. At first their meetings were secret at the home of their good friends, Mr. and Mrs. Francis. Miss Todd's sister was not aware of the reconciliation for several weeks afterward.

It was a time of great financial depression; the state was heavily in debt from great expenditure in internal improvements, and James Shields, the auditor of state, who was thought to have overstepped his duties in collecting taxes, was bitterly denounced. Shields was from Tyrone, Ireland. He was quite prominent and popular in social circles, and was proud and high-spirited. Miss Todd, who was a keen observer, thought Shields a good mark for shafts of ridicule, especially as he appeared to be somewhat vain. She therefore wrote a series of satirical papers for the Sangamon *Journal*, entitled "Aunt Rebecca, or the Lost Township." Judge Herndon describes the affair as follows:

"It was written from 'Lost Township,' a place not found on any map. The writer was a widow, and signed herself 'Rebecca.' The widow gave an account of a visit to her neighbor, whom she found very angry. 'What is the matter, Jeff?' she asked. 'I'm mad Aunt 'Becca! I've been tug-ging ever since harvest, get-ting out wheat and hauling it to the river to raise state bank paper enough to pay my tax this year and a little school debt I owe; and now, just as I've got it, here I open this infernal *Extra Register* [Democratic news-paper], expecting to find it full of Glorious Democratic Victories and High Com'd Cocks, when, lo and behold! I find a set of fellows, calling themselves officers of the state, have forbidden the tax collectors and school com-missioners to receive any more state paper at all; so here it is, dead on my hands.'

HORACE GREELEY.
(Founder of the New York *Tribune.*)

"The widow went on to tell how her neighbor used some bad words. 'Don't swear so,' she said, in expos-tulation, to Jeff; 'you know I belong to the meetin', and swearing hurts my feelings.'

"'Beg pardon, Aunt 'Becca, but I do say that it is enough to make one swear, to have to pay taxes in silver for nothing only that Ford may get his $2,000, Shields his $2,400, and Carpenter his $1,600 a year, and all without danger of loss from state paper.'"

Shields, like most vain men, was very sensitive to ridicule, and sought the editor of the paper, demanding the name of the author, which demand was refused. The editor, knowing something of the relations between Lincoln and

Miss Todd, advised him of the circumstances, whereupon Lincoln assumed the authorship, and was challenged by Shields to meet him on the "field of honor." Meanwhile Miss Todd increased Mr. Shields' ire by writing another letter to the paper, in which she said: "I hear the way of these fire-eaters is to give the challenged party the choice of weapons, which being the case, I'll tell you in confidence that I never fight with anything but broom-sticks, or hot water, or a shovelful of coals, the former of which, being somewhat like a shillalah, may not be objectionable to him." Lincoln accepted the challenge, and selected broad-

CALEB B. SMITH.

swords as the weapons. Mutual friends attempted to bring about a peaceful termination of what seemed likely to be a tragedy. Judge Herndon gives the closing of this affair, as follows:

"The laws of Illinois prohibited duelling, and he [Lincoln] demanded that the meeting should be outside the state. Shields undoubtedly knew that Lincoln was opposed to fighting a duel—that his moral sense would revolt at the thought, and that he would not be likely to break the law by fighting in the state. Possibly he thought Lincoln would make an humble apology. Shields was brave but foolish, and would not listen to overtures for explanation. It was arranged that the meeting should be in Missouri, opposite Alton. They proceeded to the place selected, but friends interfered, and there was no duel. There is little doubt that the man who had swung a beetle and driven iron wedges into gnarled hickory logs could have cleft the skull of his antagonist, but he had no such intention. He repeatedly said to the friends of Shields that in writing the first article he had no thought of anything personal. The auditor's vanity had been sorely wounded by the second letter, in regard to which Lincoln could not make any explanation except that he had had no hand in writing it. The affair set all Springfield to laughing at Shields, but it detracted from the happiness of Lincoln. By accepting the challenge he had violated his sense of right and outraged his better nature. He would gladly have blotted it from memory. It was ever a regret."

On November 4, 1842, the wedding, so unhappily postponed, was held, under most happy auspices. The officiating clergyman, the Rev. Mr. Dresser, used the Episcopal church service for marriage. Lincoln placed the ring upon the bride's finger, and said, "With this ring I now thee wed, and with all my worldly goods I thee endow." Judge Thomas C. Browne, who was present, and had a pre-eminently legal mind, exclaimed: "Good gracious, Lincoln! the statute fixes all that."

Mr. and Mrs. Lincoln took rooms in the Globe tavern, at Springfield, about two hundred yards southwest of the old state-house. They were pleasantly situated, paying four dollars a week for board and rooms.

CHAPTER XIII.

THE partnership between Judge Logan and Mr. Lincoln was dissolved September 20, 1843, and on the same day Mr. Lincoln associated himself with a promising young lawyer named William H. Herndon, one of the ablest and most interesting of his biographers. Mr. Herndon was an out-and-out abolitionist, in full sympathy with William Lloyd Garrison, Wendell Phillips and other old abolitionist agitators, and anti-slavery newspapers and pamphlets were plentiful in Lincoln's office.

Mr. Lincoln at that time thought the immediate abolishing of slavery was not practical—the institution being recognized by the Constitution and existing in one half the states composing the Union. The abolitionists denounced the Constitution and the Union. Mr. Lincoln could not go so far as that; he had long been a champion of the Constitution and of the Union.

In 1844, Mr. Lincoln bought of Rev. Nathan Dresser a roomy "frame" house, quite cozy and comfortable, in which he lived until he went to Washington to occupy the White House.

In 1839, Mr. Lincoln's old comrade and partner, Hon. John T. Stewart, had been elected to Congress, defeating Stephen A. Douglas. In 1842, Lincoln, Edward D. Baker and John J. Hardin, all personal friends, were congressional candidates. Baker carried the delegation from Sangamon county, and Lincoln, one of the delegates, was instructed to vote for him, which he did gracefully, saying to his friends, "I shall be fixed a good deal like the fellow who is made groomsman to the man who cut him out and is marrying his girl." Hardin, however, was nominated and elected. In 1843, Baker was nominated and elected, and in 1846 Lincoln was elected. Lincoln's opponent was the famous old Methodist pioneer preacher, Peter Cartwright, but Lincoln received a vote much exceeding his party strength. In this campaign Mr. Lincoln's friends raised two hundred dollars toward paying his campaign expenses, and he returned one hundred and ninety-nine dollars and twenty-five cents, stating that his only expense was seventy-five cents.

In 1847, he was in the house at Washington; there he met the great men of that day. Among them were Robert C. Winthrop, John Quincy Adams and Caleb B. Smith, of Indiana; Andrew Johnson, of Tennessee; Alexander H.

Stephens, Howell Cobb, Robert Toombs, of Georgia, and Barnwell Rhett, of South Carolina. In the other house, the Senate, were Stephen A. Douglas, recently elected from Illinois; Daniel Webster, of Massachusetts; John P. Hale, of New Hampshire; John A. Dix, of New York; Lewis Cass, of Michigan; Thomas H. Benton, of Missouri; John C. Calhoun, of South Carolina, and Jefferson Davis, of Mississippi.

At Washington he saw gangs of slaves marching away from the prison to be sold in southern markets, and when a member from New York introduced a resolution prohibiting the slave trade in the District of Columbia, Mr. Lincoln favored it. He asserted further that he would make free all children born after January 1, 1850, and if owners of slaves were willing to part from them, he would have the government purchase their freedom; but at once bitter opposition appeared on the part of the southern members.

Mr. Lincoln was the only Whig representing Illinois, the six other members being Democrats.

In 1844, Mr. Lincoln had made many speeches in behalf of Henry Clay, the Whig candidate for the presidency. One of these he made at Pigeon creek, Indiana, his old home. His neighbors of former days gathered around him and

WENDELL PHILLIPS.

listened in surprise and delight to the eloquence of the man whom they had known as a boy. The election of James K. Polk over his favorite, Henry Clay, was a great blow to Lincoln personally. He afterward embraced an opportunity to see and hear his idol, and get some comfort and consolation from his personal presence. Clay was to deliver an address on the "Gradual Emancipation of the Slaves," at Lexington. This town was Mr. Lincoln's old home, and he decided to go and hear the address, and, if possible, meet Mr. Clay. He went into the hall and listened, but with a feeling of great disappointment. Mr. Clay was there, but not the great orator. There was no fire in the eye, no music in the speech. The address was a tame affair, as was the personal greeting when Mr. Lincoln made himself known. Mr. Clay was courteous, but cold. He may never have heard of the man in his presence who was to secure, without solicitation, the pri: which he for many years had unsuccessfully sought. Lincoln was disenchanted; his ideal was shattered. One reason why Clay had never reached the goal of his ambition had become apparent. Two men who were radically different had met at Lexington on this occasion. Both had commenced life as poor boys, and in the state of Kentucky; both had fought their way to high honors; both were great orators. Clay had a great name at home and abroad; Lincoln's fame was mainly confined to his own and neighboring

LINCOLN'S HOME IN SPRINGFIELD, ILLINOIS, FROM 1844 TO 1861.

states. But Clay was cool and dignified, while Lincoln was cordial and hearty. Clay's hand was bloodless and frosty, with no vigorous grip in it; Lincoln's was warm, and its clasp was expressive of kindliness and sympathy.

Mr. Lincoln did more than occupy his seat and respond at roll-call, notwithstanding he was a new member, from a region that was then called "the West." The Mexican war was in progress. The object of this war, expressed in plain English, was to increase, through the enlargement of the limits of the state of Texas, a greater breadth of territory to be utilized by slave-owners. Mr. Lincoln was at heart opposed to slavery; he desired that, as soon as possible, the District of Columbia should be made free. He was opposed to the addition of territory to the United States simply for the purpose of dividing it into new slave states, and thereby giving the institution greater power for harm in the councils of the nation than they already possessed. He did not build wiser than he knew, in his time, but, much wiser than the mass of the people who were his contemporaries knew.

The question of slavery as connected with the war with Mexico was quite intricate. He was a patriot, and at the same time was a representative of the cause of human freedom. He voted for men and money to carry on the war.

PETER CARTWRIGHT.

He honored the brave men who responded to the call of their country. His old friend Hardin, who had represented his own district in Congress, fell at Buena Vista. Yet Mr. Lincoln, who had been faithful as a patriot, could not be persuaded or forced to admit or vote to the effect that the war had been righteously begun by President Polk. "But," said Mr. Lincoln afterward, in his joint debate with Stephen A. Douglas, replying to the charge of Douglas that he had taken the part of the common enemy, "whenever they asked for any money, or land warrants, or anything to pay the soldiers there, during all that time I gave the same vote that Judge Douglas did. You can think as you please as to whether that was consistent. Such is the truth, and the judge has the right to make all he can out of it. But when he, by a general charge, conveys the idea that I withheld supplies from the soldiers who were fighting in the Mexican war, or did anything else to hinder the soldiers, he is, to say the least, grossly and altogether mistaken."

During this session of Congress Mr. Lincoln introduced what his opponents called the "Spot" resolutions, their purpose being to ridicule him. Nevertheless they were very much annoyed and worried by them. They gave President Polk a great deal of worry and trouble. He had tried to convey, in his message, the impression that the Mexicans were the aggressors, and that the war was undertaken to repel invasion and to avenge the shedding of the "blood of our fellow-citizens on our own soil." No president, before nor since, was ever so peculiarly or trenchantly arraigned as on this occasion. The resolutions are given in full below:

"*Resolved by the House of Representatives*, That the President of the United States be respectfully requested to inform this House—

"1st. Whether the spot on which the blood of our citizens was shed, as in his messages declared, was or was not within the territory of Spain, at least after the treaty of 1819, until the Mexican revolution.

"2d. Whether that spot is or is not within the territory which was wrested from Spain by the revolutionary government of Mexico.

"3d. Whether that spot is or is not within a settlement of people, which settlement has existed ever since long before the Texas revolution, and until its inhabitants fled before the approach of the United States army.

"4th. Whether that settlement is or is not isolated from any and all other settlements by the Gulf and the Rio Grande on the south and west, and by wide uninhabited regions on the north and east.

"5th. Whether the people of that settlement, or a majority of them, or any of them, have ever submitted

JAMES K. POLK.

themselves to the government or laws of Texas or of the United States, by consent or by compulsion, either by accepting office, or voting at elections, or paying tax, or serving on juries, or having process served upon them, or in any other way.

"6th. Whether the people of that settlement did or did not flee from the approach of the United States army, leaving unprotected their homes and their growing crops, *before* the blood was shed, as in the messages stated; and whether the first blood so shed was or was not shed within the inclosure of one of the people who had thus fled from it.

"7th. Whether our *citizens*, whose blood was shed, as in his messages declared, were or were not, at that time, armed officers and soldiers, sent into that settlement by the military order of the President, through the Secretary of War.

"8th. Whether the military force of the United States was or was not so sent into that settlement after General Taylor had more than once intimated to the War Department that, in his opinion, no such movement was necessary to the defense or protection of Texas."

Action on these resolutions was never taken, but they did their work. On January 12, 1848, Mr. Lincoln commented on them in a speech, in which, as Henry J. Raymond says, "he discussed, in his homely and forcible manner, the absurdities and contradictions of Mr. Polk's message, and exposed its weakness."

Let us hope that Henry Clay, a man of integrity, as eminent for patriotism as for his matchless oratory, lived long enough to discover the sort and style of man Abraham Lincoln was.

Mr. Lincoln was still the friend of internal improvements, and made a speech in Congress advocating and defending the system they represented.

CHAPTER XIV.

IN 1848, Lewis Cass, of Michigan, was the Democratic candidate for the presidency in opposition to General Zachary Taylor, who was heartily supported by Mr. Lincoln. The friends of General Cass made much of and exploited his military services during the campaign. Mr. Lincoln knew something about their character, and had investigated Cass' accounts with the treasury. These accounts Lincoln alluded to in detail (July 28, 1848), and then said:

"I have introduced General Cass' accounts here chiefly to show the wonderful physical capacities of the man. They show that he not only did the labor of several men at *the same time,* but he often did it in *several places* many hundred miles apart *at the same time.* And as to eating, too, his capacities are shown to be quite as wonderful. From October, 1821, to May, 1822, he ate ten rations a day in Michigan, ten rations a day here in Washington, nearly $5 worth a 'day, besides partly on the road between the two places. And then there is an important discovery in his example—the act of being paid for what one eats, instead of having to pay for it. Hereafter, if any nice young man shall owe a bill which he cannot pay in any other way, he can just board it out. We have all heard of the animal standing in doubt between two stacks of hay and starving to death; the like of that would never happen to General Cass. Place the stacks a thousand miles apart, and he would stand stock-still midway between them and eat them *both at once;* and the green grass along the line would be apt to suffer some, too, at the same time. By all means, make him president, gentlemen. He will feed you bounteously, if—if—there is any left after he shall have helped himself."

In the campaign in behalf of Taylor and against Cass, Mr. Lincoln made a speech in which he said:

"But in my hurry I was very near closing on the subject of military coat-tails before I was done with it. There is one entire article of the sort I have not discussed yet; I mean the military tail you Democrats are now engaged in dovetailing onto the great Michigander. Yes, sir, all his biographers (and they are legion) have him in hand, tying him to a military tail, like so many mischievous boys tying a dog to a bladder of beans. True, the material they have is very limited, but they drive at it might and main. He *in*vaded Canada without resistance, and he *out*vaded it without pursuit. As he did both under orders, I suppose there was to him credit in neither of them; but they are made to constitute a large part of the tail. He was volunteer aid to General Harrison on the day of the battle of the Thames, and as you said in 1840 that Harrison was picking whortleberries, two miles off, while the battle was fought, I suppose it is a just conclusion with you to say Cass was aiding Harrison to pick whortleberries. This is about all, except the mooted question of the broken sword. Some authers say he broke it; some say he threw it away, and some others, who ought to know, say nothing about it. Perhaps it would be a fair historical compromise to say,

ALEXANDER H. STEPHENS.

if he did not break it, he did not do anything else with it."

President Taylor offered to make Lincoln governor of the territory of Oregon, but he declined the honor.

His opposition in Congress to the Mexican war made him temporarily unpopular in his district, and prevented his re-election. He took the ground that the Mexican war was unnecessarily and unconstitutionally commenced by the president.

Of a speech made by Alexander H. Stephens, in Congress, Mr. Lincoln wrote to William Herndon, as follows: "I just take up my pen to say that Mr. Stephens, of Georgia, a little, slim, pale-faced, consumptive man, with a voice like Logan, has just concluded the very best speech of an hour's length I ever heard. My old, withered, dry eyes are full of tears yet!" Lincoln's letters to Herndon, who was his law partner in Springfield, Illinois, while in Congress or out on the circuit, and even while president, are invaluable in judging Lincoln's character.

This same Alexander Stephens, vice-president of the southern confederacy, writing, seventeen years after Lincoln's death, and recalling their service together in Congress, from 1847 to 1849, says: "I knew Mr. Lincoln well and intimately, and we were both ardent supporters of General Taylor for president in 1848. Mr. Lincoln, Toombs, Preston, myself and others formed the first congressional Taylor club, known as 'The Young Indians,' and organized the Taylor movement, which resulted in his nomination. . . .

"Mr. Lincoln was careful as to his manners, awkward in his speech, but was possessed of a very strong, clear, vigorous mind. . . . . He always attracted and riveted the attention of the House when he spoke. His manner of speech as well as thought was original. He had no model. He was a man of strong convictions, and what Carlyle would have called an earnest man. He abounded in anecdote. He illustrated everything he was talking about by an anecdote, always exceedingly apt and pointed, and socially he always kept his company in a roar of laughter."

During the Taylor-Cass campaign Mr. Lincoln made his first visit to the East, speaking at New York and Boston, and attracting much attention. He made a notable address at Worcester, Massachusetts. On his way home he conceived a device for raising steamboats in low water, which he patented. •

At the second session of Congress, Mr. Lincoln introduced a bill looking to the emancipation of the slaves in the District of Columbia, but it was ultimately laid on the table, and remained there. The introduction and advocacy of the bill covers, however, a significant and honorable leaf in his public record.

In 1849, Mr. Lincoln resumed the practice of law in Springfield. The year 1849 will be forever memorable in the annals of the country. In the year before, James W Marshall was digging a mill-race for John A. Sutter, in California. Some "yellow stuff" was discovered by Marshall in a shovelful of dirt. That "yellow stuff" was to produce a commercial and financial revolution Marshall took a lot of this yellow stuff to the small collection of houses called San Francisco, and showed it to Isaac Humphrey, who had been a miner of precious metals in Georgia. Said Humphrey, "It is gold." ‌

There were no telegraph lines or railways across the continent at that time, although it had long been predicted that a railroad would be built. The news of the discovery of gold, however, traveled as rapidly as steamships could carry it. It went down to the Isthmus, was then taken overland from the Pacific to the Gulf of Mexico, and thence by water to New York. It was then spread in the newspapers to all portions of the country. Many of the "forty-niners" are still living, and some of them are hale and hearty. They rushed to the new El Dorado in great numbers, if traveling by steamboat and on foot or mule-back can be called rushing. The steamers were crowded with emigrants, and soon the gold region was swarming with them. Those of the common miners first in the field were making hundreds of dollars a day, which was something extraordinary and unprecedented. By February, 1850, more than 8,000 miners, from all portions of the United States, were in the field, and seventy ships were being made ready for California trips. Western men made the overland trip, across the plains, through the mountains, on foot or in wagons. Hundreds of thousands of dollars were in store in San Francisco. More than 400 vessels were floating in the bay, and the population of this city was put at 20,000. From these small beginnings grew and developed an empire on the Pacific coast.

Of the host of hardy, enterprising men who flocked to her from the East and from foreign lands, in 1849 and afterward, many returned, some of them rich and some very poor, while a large number remained, to dig farther for gold or to cultivate the soil.

But with the founding of this new empire there arose new and important political issues. Should this tract of California, a slice of Old Mexico, become free soil and a land of free men and not of slaves? It is true that the line of latitude of 36° 30′—the line of that Missouri Compromise—decided this and set apart the territory to freedom, but imaginary lines, even when fixed by law and by the consent of all parties, were no bar to pro-slavery presumption.

In 1846, when President Polk asked for $2,000,000 as a basis for the negotiation of peace, David Wilmot, representative in Congress from Pennsylvania, had moved what is known as the Wilmot Proviso, which declared that it should be a condition to the acquisition of any territory from Mexico "that neither slavery nor involuntary servitude should ever exist in any part thereof, except for crime, whereof the party should be duly convicted." At two different times this compromise was adopted in the House, but rejected in the Senate. An appropriation of $3,000,000 was finally passed without the proviso, but the proposed measure had made David Wilmot famous as a champion of free soil. The principles of the Wilmot Proviso formed the foundation of a new political movement.

CHAPTER XV.

FROM 1849 to 1854 Mr. Lincoln was engaged in the work of his profession as a lawyer. Zachary Taylor was inaugurated president March 4, 1849, having been elected not only by a plurality, but by a majority, of the vote of the Electoral College, although some southerners had voted against him because he had not come out squarely in favor of the extension of slavery. On the third of June, General B. Riley, military governor of California, issued a call for a convention of the people of California, to form a state constitution. This convention was held, and adopted a constitution, by the terms of which slavery was expressly prohibited. President Taylor presented the constitution to Congress, and the representatives of the new state, all Democrats, stood knocking at the door for admission to the Union for many weary months. Had Congress been faithful to the Missouri Compromise, California would have been admitted at once.

A matter of such great political importance could not fail to be of intense interest to Mr. Lincoln, and to ultimately draw him from his law-books and practice into the political arena.

On June 3, 1849, Senator Henry Clay submitted the basis of a new compromise, which seemed to him to be necessary to the solution of the present difficulty, and his proposition had the support of the greatest statesmen of the day. Mr. Clay's "Compromise of 1850" had this for its first resolution:

"That California, with suitable boundaries, ought, upon her application, to be admitted as one of the states of this Union, without the imposition by Congress of any restriction in respect to the exclusion or introduction of slavery within those boundaries."

The resolution declared that it was inexpedient to abolish slavery in the District of Columbia; but that it *was* expedient to prohibit the slave trade within the District, and that "more effectual provision ought to be made by law, according to the requirement of the Constitution, *for the restitution and delivery of persons bound to service or labor, in any state, who may escape into any other state or territory in the Union.*" After much discussion, Senator Stephen A. Douglas, of Illinois, reported a bill, March 25, 1850, for the admission of California into the Union, and also one to establish territorial governments for Utah and New Mexico. On the eighth of May following, Senator Henry Clay, from a special

111

committee, presented and recommended a series of "bases" for a "general compromise." This report was similar to the resolutions already alluded to as having been introduced by Mr. Clay; but it provided, also, for the establishment
of territorial governments for New Mexico and Utah, *without the Wilmot Proviso*," and prohibited the slave trade, but did not abolish slavery, in the District
of Columbia. Finally, in August, the Senate passed a bill providing for the
admission of California as a state without slavery, and on the admission of New
Mexico and Utah as territories without restriction, and these, and other bills

suggested by Mr. Clay in his
compromise, passed both
Houses and became laws.

On January 23, 1854,
Senator Douglas surprised
both his friends and opponents by presenting a bill for
the admission of two tracts
lying between parallels 36°
30' on the south, and 43° 30'
on the north as territories,
one to be called Kansas and
the other Nebraska, the bill
providing that "*all questions
pertaining to slavery in the
territories, and in the new
states to be formed* therefrom,
*be left to the people residing
therein.*"

Mr. Douglas afterward
moved an amendment, stat-
ing that it was the true intent
and meaning of the act "not
to legislate slavery into any
territory or state, nor to
exclude it therefrom, but to
leave the people thereof per-

EDWARD D. BAKER.

fectly free to form and regulate their domestic institutions in their own way, subject
to the Constitution of the United States." This represented the political doctrine
of "squatter sovereignty" that was so frequently and earnestly exploited by Mr.
Douglas, and so vehemently attacked by Mr. Lincoln, in debates which followed.
Indeed, this action by Douglas struck Lincoln with amazement. His bill, in
becoming a law, repealed the very Missouri Compromise which Douglas had
declared "to be sacred," and a law which "no human hand should destroy."

A law for the recovery of fugitive slaves from free territory, passed in 1850,
had been the means of causing universal excitement and commotion throughout

the North. The law was but a twin to the compromise measure adopted the same year. The efforts of slaveholders to capture their slaves created great indignation everywhere that an attempt was made to enforce it.

Unnecessary brutality was frequently shown by the slave-catchers, and the sympathies of the people in the North were aroused in behalf of the fugitives. In many instances popular feeling and excitement were at the highest pitch. The slave-catchers continued their work during the period reaching from 1850 to the breaking out of the rebellion. In some instances, the pursuers and capturers of slaves were themselves arrested for kidnapping, and were glad to relinquish their claims to secure their own freedom.

HOWELL COBB.

Franklin Pierce, of New Hampshire, was president, in 1854, when Douglas' Kansas-Nebraska Bill was passed, and he was in full sympathy with the distinguished senator.

This bill passed the Senate March 3. 1854. It is a singular fact that Sam Houston, the man who had been the leader in achieving the independence of Texas, and who represented that state in the Senate, voted against the bill, and in the closing portion of his speech used the language given below. Pointing to the eagle, he said:

"Yon proud symbol above your head remains enshrouded in black, as if deploring the misfortune that has fallen upon us, and as a fearful omen of the future calamities which await our nation in the event that this bill becomes a law."

Here spoke another prophet!

In the House of Representatives, the venerable statesman, Thomas H. Benton, of Missouri. at this time a member of the House, most vigorously opposed the passage of the bill. Mr. Benton, although living in a slave state, was indignant at the "violation of the compact," foreseeing very clearly, as did Senator Houston, the danger that would follow. But the bill passed the House May 8,

1854, and it was a foregone conclusion that Pierce would sign it and make it a law. The friends of slavery, and especially of slavery extension, were in transports of delight. Cannon were fired from Capitol Hill, and demonstrations of rejoicing were made in various portions of the South. The friends of freedom everywhere felt that a great wrong and outrage had been committed. Douglas was denounced in all portions of the North as a betrayer of a sacred trust, and the charge was freely made that the presidential bee buzzing in his ears had drawn his attention from the peculiar political enormity of his conduct. He had been the leader in the repeal of the Missouri Compromise, as he had previously been one of the loudest in its praise; consequently, his apparent sacrifice of principle was supposed to have for its object the promotion of his own political aspirations.

There was at once organized by the slaveholders a scheme to colonize and occupy the southern portion of this territory, called Kansas, for the purpose of making it a slave state. But the friends of freedom, fully awake to the importance of the crisis, determined that it should be free.

Armed bodies of slaveholders crossed the line of Missouri, and proceeded to make settlements; but what were called "free-state" men were also on the march. There were two lines of emigrants, from the two sections of the country. The free-state emigrants took farming tools, Bibles. hymn-books, and Sharp's rifles, for which they afterward found good use. John Brown, who soon became known as Ossawatomie Brown, and afterward attempted to create a revolution which should free the slaves, at Harper's Ferry, and was hanged, at Charleston, Virginia, December 2, 1859, was one of the leaders. Charles Robinson, afterward governor, and Messrs. Pomeroy and Lane, afterward generals, were prominent in the movement. The whole country was in a state of excitement. The new emigrants had the sympathy of millions behind them. They were sustained by the money as well as the moral support of the great commonwealths north of Mason and Dixon's line. A national society was formed in Massachusetts to aid the free-state men, and Abraham Lincoln was a member of the executive committee. Throughout the greater portion of this period Mr. Lincoln had been engaged assiduously in the practise of his profession, but he was now called from his retirement to take a most prominent part in the great events which were to bring about a revolutionary change in the political and moral conditions of the country.

CHAPTER XVI.

IN the meantime, Mr. Lincoln had been developing his legal talents and spreading his fame as one of the ablest lawyers in the West. In a reaper patent case, tried in Cincinnati in 1857, between Cyrus McCormick and Mr. Manny, McCormick employed the famous Reverdy Johnson, of Baltimore, and Manny had secured the services of George Harding, of Philadelphia, and Abraham Lincoln. Afterward Manny employed Edwin M. Stanton, of Steubenville, Ohio. Lincoln had prepared himself with great care, as usual, and was ready for his task. Judge John McLean presided. Manny's three attorneys met to consult as to the management of the case. Judge Herndon describes this episode as follows:

"Only two of them could be heard by the court. Mr. Harding, by mutual consent, was to present the mechanical features of the invention. Who should present the legal points, Lincoln or Stanton? By custom it was Lincoln's right. He was prepared; Stanton was not. 'You will speak, of course,' said Stanton. 'No, you,' the courteous reply. 'I will,' the answer, and Mr. Stanton abruptly and discourteously left the room. He had taken a great dislike to Lincoln, who overheard him in an adjoining room say to a friend, 'Where did such a lank creature come from? His linen duster is blotched on his back with perspiration and dust, so that you might use it for a map of the continent.'"

This was the first meeting of two great men, afterward to be very closely united in the service of their country. Lincoln felt the indignity, but history shows very plainly that he never bore any malice toward the great war secretary of 1861.

One of the most notable of Lincoln's law-cases was that in which he defended William D. Armstrong, charged with murder. The case was one which was watched during its progress with intense interest, and it had a most dramatic ending. The defendant was the son of Jack and Hannah Armstrong. The father was dead, but Hannah, who had been very motherly and helpful to Lincoln during his life at New Salem, was still living, and asked Lincoln to defend him. Young Armstrong had been a wild lad, and was often in bad company. One night, in company with a lot of other wild fellows, he went to a camp-meeting. Rowdies tried to disturb and break up the meeting, and a row ensued in which a man was killed. It was charged that Armstrong was the murderer, and he was placed in prison. Li ..n responded as follows to Hannah Armstrong's request for legal advice and aid:

SPRINGFIELD, ILLINOIS, September 18—.

DEAR MRS. ARMSTRONG:—I have just heard of your deep affliction, and the arrest of your son for murder. I can hardly believe that he can be guilty of the crime alleged against him. It does not seem possible. I am anxious that he should have a fair trial, at any rate; and gratitude for your long-continued ..dness to me in adverse circumstances prompts me to offer my humble services gratuitously in his behalf. It will afford me an opportunity to requite, in a small degree, the favors I received at your hand, and that of your lamented husband, when your roof afforded me grateful shelter, without money and without price.

Yours truly,
ABRAHAM LINCOLN.

ROBERT TOOMBS.

The case came on for trial in 1858, only two years before Lincoln was nominated for the presidency, and it was exploited very widely in the campaign. A man by the name of . Morris was arrested with him. convicted, and sent to the penitentiary.

Judge Arnold says: "The evidence against Bill was very strong. Indeed, the case for the defense looked hopeless. Several witnesses swore positively to his guilt. The strongest evidence was that of a man who swore that at eleven o'clock at night he saw Armstrong strike the deceased on the head; that the moon was shining brightly and was nearly full, and that its position in the sky was just about that of the sun at ten o'clock in the morning, and that by it he saw Armstrong give the mortal blow. This was fatal, unless the effect could be broken by contradiction or impeachment. Lincoln quietly looked up an almanac, and found that, at the time this, the principal witness, declared the moon to have been shining with full light, there was *no moon at all*. There were some contradictory statements made by other witnesses, but on the whole the case seemed almost hopeless. Mr. Lincoln made the closing argument. 'At first,' says Mr. Walker, one of the counsel associated with him, ' he spoke slowly and

arefully, reviewed the testimony, and pointed out its contradictions, discrep-
ncies and impossibilities. When he had thus prepared the way, he called for
he almanac, and showed that, at the hour at which the principal witness swore
e had seen, by the light of the full moon, the mortal blow given, there was no
noon at all.'

"This was the climax of the argument, and, of course, utterly disposed of the
rincipal witness. But it was Lincoln's eloquence which saved Bill Armstrong.
Iis closing appeal must have been irresistible. His associate says: 'The last
fteen minutes of his speech was as eloquent as I ever heard. . . . The
ury sat as if entranced, and when he was through, found relief in a gush of
ears.' One of the prosecuting attorneys says: 'He took the jury by storm.
. . There were tears in Lincoln's eyes while he spoke, but they were
enuine. . . . I have said an hundred times that it was Lincoln's speech
hat saved that criminal from the gallows.' . . . The jury in this case knew
nd loved Lincoln, and they could not resist him. He told the anxious mother,
Your son will be cleared before sundown.' When Lincoln closed, and while the
tate's attorney was attempting to reply, she left the court-room and 'went down
o Thompson's pasture,' where, all alone, she remained awaiting the result. Her
nxiety may be imagined, but before the sun went down that day, Lincoln's mes-
enger brought to her the joyful tidings, 'Bill is free. Your son is cleared.'
'or all of this Lincoln would accept nothing but thanks."

Another biographer, M. Louise Putnam, says:

"The jury retired, and at the expiration of half an hour returned with the
erdict, 'Not guilty.'

"The poor widow dropped into the arms of her son, who, tenderly supporting
er, told her to behold him free and innocent. Then crying out, 'Where is Mr.
incoln?' he rushed across the court-room and grasped his deliverer's hand with-
ut uttering a word; his emotion was so great he could not speak. Mr. Lincoln
ointed to the West, and said, 'It is not yet sundown, and *you are free.*'"

CHAPTER XVII.

NATHANIEL P. BANKS, of Massachusetts, a friend of free soil, was chosen speaker of the national House of Representatives in 1855, over Aiken, of South Carolina. The revolution of public sentiment was still in progress in the North. The course of the Democrats in Congress had alienated many distinguished men of the party, among them Martin Van Buren and his witty and eloquent son, John. The seceders in New York state were known as barn-burners, and they first materialized in a convention held at Buffalo—which convention, however, was really national in its scope. The friends of freedom began to call themselves Republicans, and the Republican party was born February 22, 1856. It was a notable and most enthusiastic gathering. On May 29th, in the same year, a convention composed of the representatives of the people of Illinois, who were opposed to the extension of slavery, was held at Bloomington, and here, Judge Arnold declares, "the Republican party was organized." The convention was composed of both Democrats and Whigs—partizans who had never acted together before. The members of the committee on resolutions were unable to agree, and the representative man of Illinois, Abraham Lincoln, was sent for Judge Arnold says:

"He [Lincoln] suggested that all could unite on the principles of the Declaration of Independence and hostility to the extension of slavery. 'Let us,' said he, 'in building our new party, make our corner-stone the Declaration of Independence—let us build on this rock, and the gates of hell shall not prevail against us." The problem was mastered, and the convention adopted the following:

"*Resolved*, That we hold, in accordance with the opinions and practices of all the great statesmen of all parties for the first sixty years of the administration of the government, that, under the Constitution, Congress possesses full power to prohibit slavery in the territories; and that while we will maintain all constitutional rights of the South, we also hold that justice, humanity, the principles of freedom, as expressed in our Declaration of Independence and our national Constitution, and the purity and perpetuity of our government require that that power should be exerted to prevent the extension of slavery into territories heretofore free.

"Thus was organized the party which, against the potent influence of Douglas, revolutionized the state of Illinois, and elected Lincoln to the presidency. Lincoln's speech to this convention has rarely been equaled. 'Never,' says one of the delegates, 'was an audience more completely electrified by human eloquence. Again and again during the delivery the audience sprang to their feet, and by long-continued cheers, expressed how deeply the speaker had roused them. It fused the mass of incongruous elements into harmony and union.

"Delegates were appointed to the national convention, which was to meet in Philadelphia, to nominate candidates for president and vice-president."

R. BARNWELL RHETT.

In June, 1856, the first nominating convention of the Republican party was held at Philadelphia. John C. Fremont was named for the presidency, and William L. Dayton for the vice-presidency. Abraham Lincoln's Bloomington "plank" was accepted as the chief portion of the platform adopted, and it became apparent that, as Lincoln was already the leader of the new party in the Northwest, he was to become the leader of the free-soil sentiment throughout the nation.

The Democrats met at Cincinnati on the second of June, and on the sixteenth ballot nominated James Buchanan, of Pennsylvania, for the presidency, and John C. Breckinridge, of Kentucky, for the vice-presidency. The convention refused to nominate the aspiring Douglas, but it "indorsed the compromise measures of 1850 and Douglas' Kansas-Nebraska Bill."

The Whigs of the South and certain conservative Whigs of the North, who were popularly called the "Silver Grays," nominated Millard Fillmore for the presidency.

There was now a clear understanding of the great political issue of the day, and a hard-fought campaign followed. At one time it seemed likely that Fremont and Dayton would be elected. Abraham Lincoln was constantly speaking, and with great effect, but finally Buchanan managed to carry the doubtful states of Pennsylvania and Indiana, and the contest was virtually ended.

Buchanan was elected, receiving in the electoral college 172 votes, Fremont receiving 114, and Fillmore those to which Maryland was entitled.

Meanwhile the struggle in Kansas continued. The pro-slavery men had formed at Lecompton a constitution which was designed to make of Kansas a slave state. The free-soil advocates adopted a free-state constitution at Topeka. This was submitted to the people and adopted. Thus was the issue clearly defined; the friends of the two constitutions came into collision, and in Kansas the civil war was virtually begun.

In 1856, Congress appointed an investigating committee, of which John Sherman, of Ohio, was a member. This committee did thorough and exhaustive work, and finally reported that "every election held under the auspices of the United States officials had been controlled, not by actual settlers, but by non-residents from Missouri, and that every officer in the territory owed his election to these non-residents."

Meanwhile the free-state officers had been arrested, and the free-state legislation dispersed by "the regular army of the United States, *acting under orders of the president*. It was thus that Kansas was to be brought into the Union as a slave state." [Herndon.]

Buchanan, very naturally, sent a message to Congress, December 9, 1857, asking that body to admit Kansas, with its fraudulent slave-state constitution. The personal friends of Stephen A. Douglas were surprised and glad to see him at once announce his condemnation of the proposal. One of his ablest and most commendable speeches was made on this occasion. " Why," said he, "force this constitution down the throats of the people in opposition to their wishes, and in violation of our pledges? . . . The people want a fair vote, and will never be satisfied without it. . . . If it is to be forced upon the people, under a submission that is a mockery and an insult, I will resist it to the last."

Buchanan remonstrated with Mr. Douglas, and proceeded to warn him of personal consequences. Recalling the fact that the senator had always been an admirer of General Jackson, Buchanan, the time-server, said:

"You are an ambitious man, Mr. Douglas, and there is a brilliant future for you, if you retain the confidence of the Democratic party; if you oppose it, let me remind you of the fate of those who in former times rebelled against it. Remember the fate of Senators Rives and Talmadge, who opposed General Jackson, when he removed the government deposits from the United States bank. Beware of their fate, Mr. Douglas."

"Mr. President," said Douglas, "General Jackson is dead. Good-morning, sir!"

The celebrated decision in the Dred Scott case was most important, and had great influence on public sentiment. The decision was made by the Supreme Court early in Mr. Buchanan's administration.

Dred Scott had been one of the slaves of Dr. Emerson, of Missouri, a United States army surgeon. Emerson moved first to Rock Island, Illinois, and then to

Fort Snelling, Minnesota, at which latter place, in 1836, Scott was married to a negro woman whom Emerson had bought. After the birth of two children all the family were taken back to St. Louis and sold. Dred brought suit for his freedom, and after the Circuit and Supreme Courts of Missouri had heard the case, it was, in May, 1854, appealed to the United States Supreme Court. The decision read by Chief-justice Taney held that "negroes, whether free or slaves, *were not citizens of the United States,* and could not become such by any process known to the Constitution;" that under the laws of the United States "a negro

could neither sue nor be sued, and therefore the court had no jurisdiction over Dred Scott's cause;" that "a slave was to be regarded in the light of a personal chattel, and might be removed from place to place by his owner as any other piece of property;" that "the Constitution gave to every slave-holder the right of removing to or through any state or territory with his slaves, and of returning at his will with them to a state where slavery was recognized by law; and that therefore the Missouri Compromise of 1820 and the compromise measures of 1850 were unconstitutional and void."

Judge Taney did not announce this decision because he wished to of his own accord, but he was pursued and hounded on by the champions of slavery until it seemed to him that he was forced to it. Retiring to his home after the act, he fell on the neck of his black body-servant, and declared that he was a ruined man.

JOHN BROWN.

Six of the associate justices—Wayne, Nelson, Grier, Daniel, Campbell and Catron—concurred, but Judges McLean and Curtis dissented. The president had hoped that this would allay the excitement, but it had a contrary effect. The South affected satisfaction, but the free-soil party became exasperated, and the passage of personal liberty bills resulted in several of the antislavery states. By means of the enactment of these measures the efforts of the slave-catchers were often thwarted—conspicuously so in the noted Oberlin-Wellington case, in Ohio, where a slave was taken from a sheriff and spirited away. It is true that Professor Peck, J. M. Fitch, Simeon Bushnell and others were kept in jail in Cleveland for months, and tried for their "crime," but they were finally released by the prosecutor, under state law.

John Brown's raid at Harper's Ferry, Virginia, October 16, 1859, was the next excitement for the slave states. The details of the daring attempt, its failure and the trial, condemnation and execution of John Brown and six of his

JAMES BUCHANAN.

companions, are incidents too well and widely known to justify recapitulation here. This affair, and the rapid growth of the Free-Soil party in Kansas, while widening the breach between North and South, threw into the nineteenth presidential election campaign of 1860 the apple of discord destined to precipitate the clash of arms.

A United States senator was to be chosen in Illinois, in 1854, to take the place of Senator Shields. Lincoln took a prominent part in the campaign. Douglas was the champion of " popular," or " squatter," sovereignty. Lincoln met Douglas on two occasions before the people. The first time was at a meeting of the state fair, at Springfield, on October 4th. Lincoln had great vantageground, Douglas having proved recreant to his former principles, so solemnly announced by him. He said: "My distinguished friend says it is an insult to the emigrants of Kansas and Nebraska to suppose that they are not able to govern themselves. We must not slur over an argument of this kind because it happens to tickle the ear. It must be met and answered. I admit that the emigrant of Kansas and Nebraska is competent to govern himself, *but I deny his right to govern any other person without that person's consent."* The two opponents met again in Peoria. When the Legislature convened, Lincoln gave way to Lyman Trumbull, who was elected senator.

CHIEF-JUSTICE TANEY.

Early in June, 1857, Douglas made his famous speech in Springfield, in which he declared that he meant to sustain all the acts of what was called the Lecompton convention, even though a pro-slavery constitution should be formed. He further expressed his approval of the Dred Scott decision in this same speech.

Lincoln replied to him at Springfield two weeks later. He defended the course of action which the Republicans of Kansas had adopted in behalf of free territory. This was but a sort of prelude to the famous senatorial contest between Douglas and Lincoln the next year. The measure known as the English Bill was made a law April 30, 1858.

Douglas' term was on the eve of expiring, and he returned to Illinois, after the adjournment of Congress. He had come in open contact with the administration through his course on the Lecompton Bill, and had really made himself quite popular with the Republicans of Illinois, some of whom were inclined to think it would not be wise to oppose his re-election. But they knew that he was in no sense a Republican, and that he had declared he "did not care whether slavery was voted down or not." Abraham Lincoln was nominated as a candidate for Douglas' place in the Senate, June 17, 1858. Mr. Douglas had already been indorsed and "virtually renominated" by the Democratic state convention.

Lincoln delivered his first speech in Chicago, July 9th, and Douglas said of it that it was "well prepared and carefully written." We quote from the first paragraph of a speech made by Lincoln, at Springfield, as follows:

"If we could first know where we are, and whither we are tending, we could better judge what to do and how to do it. We are now far into the fifth year since a policy was initiated with the avowed object and confident promise of putting an end to slavery agitation. Under the operation of that policy that

INTERIOR OF SENATE CHAMBER.

agitation has not only not ceased, but has constantly augmented. In my opinion, it will not cease until a crisis shall have been reached and passed. '*A house divided against itself cannot stand.' I believe this government cannot endure permanently half slave and half free.*"

After several speeches had been made by each gentleman, Lincoln addressed a letter to Douglas challenging him to a series of debates during the campaign. The challenge was accepted, and arrangements were made by which Douglas was to have four opening and closing speeches to Mr. Lincoln's three, Mr. Lincoln not objecting to the disparity.

CHAPTER XVIII.

A T Ottawa, Illinois, August 21, 1858, was commenced one of the most remarkable political debates ever known. There were actual intellectual giants in
those days: Stephen A. Douglas, a Vermonter, who had arisen rapidly into a
large degree of fame since he had become a citizen of Illinois, was one of those
giants, and Abraham Lincoln was another. Not only were the two men great,
but they discussed great vital principles. The Ordinance of 1787, the Missouri
Compromise, the Compromise of 1850, the Kansas-Nebraska Bill (finally passing
as the English Bill, and so framed as to deceive and defraud the people of Kansas,
who decided, nevertheless, to make theirs a free state), were frequently touched
in the discussion.

Seven joint debates were held—at Ottawa, Freeport, Jonesboro, Charleston,
Galesburg, Quincy and Alton. Mr. Douglas rode about from place to place in a
special saloon-car, furnished by the general superintendent of the road, George
B. McClellan, afterward a prominent Union general, and Democratic candidate
for the presidency. Mr. Lincoln and his famous saddle-bags went from place to
place in an ordinary car. There was firing of cannon, music by bands, great
processions, and immense audiences at each of these meetings.

Henry J. Raymond, the famous editor of the New York *Times,* epitomizes
in his book on Lincoln the matter of the first debate, as follows:·

"In the first of these joint debates, which took place at Ottawa, Mr. Douglas
again rung the changes upon the introductory passage of Mr. Lincoln's Springfield speech, 'A house divided against itself,' etc. Mr. Lincoln reiterated his
assertion, and defended it in effect, as he did in his speech at Springfield. Then
he took up the charge he had previously made, of the existence of a conspiracy
to extend slavery over the northern states, and pressed it home, citing as proof
a speech which Mr. Douglas himself had made on the Lecompton Bill, in which
he had substantially made the same charge against Buchanan and others. He
then showed again that all that was necessary for the accomplishment of the
scheme was a decision of the Supreme Court to the effect that no state could
exclude slavery, as the court had already decided that no territory could exclude
it, and the acquiescence of the people in such a decision; and he told his hearers
that Douglas was doing all in his power to bring about such acquiescence in

advance, by declaring that the true position was, not to care whether slavery 'was voted down or up,' and by announcing himself in favor of the Dred Scott decision, not because it was right, but because a decision of the court is to him a 'Thus saith the Lord,' and thus committing himself to the next decision just as firmly as to this."

The next meeting was to be held at Freeport, and as Mr. Douglas in the Ottawa debate had asked Mr. Lincoln several questions, which he had promptly answered, Lincoln prepared four questions to be asked of Douglas at Freeport.

· CHARLES SUMNER.

One of America's greatest orators and uncompromising antislavery advocates. He was born 1811, and died 1874.

The third question was:

"If the Supreme Court of the United States shall decide that states cannot exclude slavery from their limits, are you in favor of acquiescing in, adopting, and following such decision as a code of political action?"

"Douglas," said Lincoln's friends, "will reply by affirming this decision as an abstract principle, but denying its political application."

"If he does that he can never be president," said Lincoln.

"That is not your lookout; you are after the senatorship."

"No, gentlemen; I am killing larger game. *The battle of 1860 is worth a hundred of this.*"

Douglas evaded the question. The senator had stated that he did not care whether slavery was voted into or out of the territories; that the negro was not *his* equal: the Declaration of Independence was not intended to include the negro. Mr. Lincoln replied to these propositions, at Freeport, as follows:

"The men who signed the Declaration of Independence said that all men are created equal, and are endowed by their Creator with certain inalienable rights—life, liberty, and the pursuit of happiness. This was their majestic interpretation of the economy of the universe. This was their lofty and wise and noble understanding of the justice of the Creator to his creatures—yes, gentlemen, to all his creatures, to the whole great family of man. In their enlightened belief, nothing stamped .with the divine image and likeness was sent into the world to be trodden on and degraded and imbruted by its fellows. They grasped not only the whole race of man then living, but they reached forward and seized upon the farthest posterity. They erected a beacon to guide their children, and their children's children, and the countless myriads who should inhabit the earth in other ages. Wise statesmen as they were, they knew the tendency of posterity to breed tyrants, and so they established these great self-evident truths, that when in the distant future some man, some faction, some interest, should set up the doctrine that none but rich men, none but white men, or none but Anglo-Saxon white men, were entitled to life, liberty, and the pursuit of happiness, their posterity might look up again to the Declaration of Independence, and take courage to renew the battle which their fathers began; so that truth and justice and mercy and all the humane and Christian virtues might not be extinguished from the land; so that no man would hereafter dare to limit and circumscribe the great principles on which the temple of liberty was being built.

"Now, my countrymen, if you have been taught doctrines conflicting with the great landmarks of the Declaration of Independence; if you have listened to suggestions which would take away from its grandeur, and mutilate the fair symmetry of its proportions; if you have been inclined to believe that all men are not created equal in those inalienable rights enumerated by our chart of liberty, let me entreat you to come back. Return to the fountain whose waters spring close by the blood of the Revolution. Think nothing of me; take no thought for the political fate of any man whomsoever, but come back to the truths that are in the Declaration of Independence. You may do anything with me you choose if you will but heed these sacred principles. You may not only defeat me for the Senate, but you may take me and put me to death. While pretending no indifference to earthly honors, I do claim to be actuated in this contest by something higher than an anxiety for office. I charge you to drop every paltry and insignificant thought for any man's success. It is nothing; I am nothing; Judge Douglas is nothing. But do not destroy that immortal emblem of humanity—the Declaration of American Independence."

Mr. Lincoln had a majority of four thousand in the popular vote of the state, but the legislative districts had been so unfairly constructed that Douglas received a majority of the ballots in the Legislature. The debates, however, attracted universal attention throughout the country and brought Mr. Lincoln to the front as an able and eloquent champion of free-soil principles.

In 1859, the Democrats of Ohio, having nominated their candidate for governor, Mr. Douglas, as the champion of "popular sovereignty" was invited to take part in the canvass, with great expectations as to the results on the part of the Democracy. Naturally, the Republicans at once asked Lincoln to come to the state, and he promptly responded, making two remarkable speeches (he could have made no other kind at that time), one at Columbus, the other at Cincinnati.

5

Mr. Douglas had had printed in *Harper's Magazine* an elaborate and carefully prepared article, explaining his views on the principles of which he was the chief representative. This was a golden opportunity for Mr. Lincoln, and at Columbus he made mince-meat of Mr. Douglas' elaborate essay. Mr. Lincoln tersely described what Judge Douglas' proposed popular sovereignty really was. He said: "It is, as a principle, no other than that if one man chooses to make a slave of another man, neither that other man nor anybody else has a right to object. Applied to the government as he means to apply it, it is this: If, in a new territory into which a few people are beginning to enter for the purpose of making their homes, they choose to exclude slavery from their limits or establish it there, however 'one or the other may affect the persons to be enslaved, or the infinitely greater number of persons who are afterward to inhabit that territory, or the other members of the families of communities of which they are but incipient members, or the general head of the family of states, as parent of all—however their action may affect one or the other of these, there is no power or right to interfere. That is Douglas' popular sovereignty applied. He has a good deal of trouble with popular sovereignty. His explanations explanatory of explanations explained are interminable." Mr. Lincoln proceeded to say, "Did you ever, five years ago, hear of anybody in the world saying that the negro had no share in the Declaration of National Independence: that it did not mean negroes at all; and when 'all men' were spoken of, negroes were not included?"

JOHN CHARLES FREMONT.

Familiarly known as the "Pathfinder." He was born 1813, and was the first Republican candidate for president.

Mr. Lincoln at Cincinnati addressed largely the Kentuckians. his old neighbors, and after advising them to nominate Mr. Douglas as their candidate for the presidency at the approaching Charleston convention, showed them how, by so doing, they would the more surely protect their cherished institution of slavery.

The Ohio Republican state committee was so well pleased with Mr. Lincoln's speeches that it requested permission to publish in a pamphlet or book the verbatim report of the debate between Mr. Douglas and himself in Illinois, of which they printed a very large edition and distributed it widely as a campaign document.

In December, 1859, by invitation, Lincoln visited Kansas, as the great champion of the freedom of their territory. He spoke at Atchison, Troy, Leavenworth and other towns near the border.

In February, 1860, he was invited to speak in New York, and at Cooper Institute, on the evening of February 27, 1860, he made one of the grandest of all his public utterances, exciting by his strong points and his eloquence an enthusiasm that was tremendous in its manifestations. It was accepted at once as the most

THE WIGWAM WHERE LINCOLN WAS NOMINATED FOR PRESIDENT.

important contribution to the solution of the immensely important current political problems of the day that had been uttered, and reported as it was, in the New York *Tribune* (Horace Greeley's paper) and other New York journals, it had a wide circulation throughout the United States, and did much to create public opinion in the exciting times which were to follow.

Subsequently, Mr. Lincoln spoke in Connecticut, Rhode Island and New Hampshire, creating great enthusiasm everywhere, and talk of his becoming a candidate for the presidency seemed to be spontaneous. A good many New-Yorkers and others desired the nomination of William Henry Seward for the presidency, and were so considerate (!) as to consent that Mr. Lincoln might have the second place on the ticket.

What were Mr. Lincoln's pecuniary circumstances at this time? To an Illinois acquaintance, whom he met at the Astor House, in New York, he said: "I have the cottage at Springfield, and about three thousand dollars in money. If they make me vice-president with Seward, as some say they will, I hope I shall be able to increase it to twenty thousand dollars, *and that is as much as any man ought to want.*"

At New York, in company with a friend, he went to visit the Five Points Mission, and addressed the children. After having spoken, the superintendent, Mr. Pease, asked his name. He courteously replied, "It is Abraham Lincoln, of Illinois."

CHAPTER XIX.

THE CHICAGO CONVENTION AND CAMPAIGN OF 1860.

L INCOLN, who had received a respectable number of votes for the presidential nomination in the convention at Philadelphia, which nominated Fremont and Dayton, was now prominently mentioned by the people East and West as an available candidate for the Republican nomination in 1860. A prominent and formidable opponent was Mr. Seward, the man who advanced the doctrine that there was a higher law, even, than the Constitution of the United States—the law of the Supreme Being. Mr. Seward was a man of great popularity, of decided ability as a public man and a statesman, besides having had long experience as a politician. He had been twice elected governor of the state of New York.

The Republicans of Illinois gathered in state convention at Decatur, on May 9 and 10, 1860, and determined to present Abraham Lincoln as their candidate for the presidency at the national Republican convention, called to meet at Chicago on the sixteenth. At this Decatur convention, Lincoln's cousin, John Hanks, brought in "two historical rails," as Judge Herndon writes, of a lot "which both had made in the Sangamon bottom, and which served the double purpose of electrifying the Illinois people and kindling the fire of enthusiasm that was destined to sweep over the nation." Judge Herndon quotes one ardent delegate as saying: "These rails were to represent the issue in the coming contest between labor free and labor slave; between democracy and aristocracy; little did I think of the mighty consequences of this little incident; little did I think that the tall and angular and bony rail-splitter who stood in girlish diffidence, bowing with awkward grace, would fill the chair once filled by Washington, and that his name would echo in chants of praise along the corridors of all coming times."

By this time the whole North had come to recognize in Mr. Lincoln those qualities of which statesmen are made, and his name was heard everywhere in discussions as to the most available man to lead the Republican party to victory. Mr. Seward, however, a man of wider experience, was the favorite candidate in certain portions of the East.

One of Mr. Lincoln's old friends, David Davis, afterward senator and a member of the Supreme Court, engaged rooms in the Tremont House, Chicago, to be used as the Lincoln headquarters during the convention. An immense wooden structure was erected on the lake front, opposite the site on which the Auditorium now

stands—that great hall in which President Benjamin Harrison, the grandson of
President William H. Harrison, was nominated in 1888. This structure was called
"The Wigwam," and it has gone into history by that name. Great crowds of
people from all portions of the East, North and West were gathered in Chicago
on this occasion.

The convention opened May 16th. There were 465 delegates, and a large
attendance of politicians from all parts of the country. Salmon P. Chase, Mr.
Cameron, of Pennsylvania, Mr. Bates, of Missouri, as well as Mr. Seward and Mr.

LINCOLN IN 1861.

Until after Lincoln's nomination for the presidency
he never wore a beard. The portrait above was taken in
Springfield about three months later, in January, 1861,
just before his departure for Washington. It was one of
the first and best showing him with a beard. It is an old-
fashioned wet plate, and is well preserved. When a portrait was to be painted for the Illinois state-house, all the
various pictures of the martyred president were spread
out before the committee of old friends and neighbors,
and this sitting was chosen for a model of the painting.

Lincoln, were named as candidates, but it was soon evident
that either Seward or Lincoln
would be the chosen one.

Judge Wilmot, author of
that famous free-soil measure,
the Wilmot Proviso, was made
temporary chairman, and
George Ashmun, of Mass-
achusetts, permanent chairman. On the seventeenth the
committee on resolutions reported a platform, which was
received with great enthusiasm
and unanimously adopted.
Mr. Seward, to whom we must
award additional praise, was a
man of great patriotism and
ability, and was thought to be
the man who would receive the
honor of the nomination. A
motion was made to nominate
on the seventeenth, but an
adjournment was taken until
morning.

During the night there
were new developments. The
Republicans of Illinois turned
out in large numbers and rent
the air with their shouts for
Lincoln. Mr. Seward's adherents marched the streets with
flags and bands of music, and

were enthusiastic for their candidate. The air was filled with music.

The balloting was reached the next day. The first ballot gave Mr. Seward 173½
to 102 for Lincoln, with quite a number of "scattering" votes. On the second

ballot the chairman of the Vermont delegation, which delegation had given a divided vote on the first ballot, announced that "Vermont gave her ten votes for the young giant of the West, Abraham Lincoln." On the second ballot Mr. Seward had 184½ votes, Mr. Lincoln 181; and on the third ballot Mr. Lincoln received 230 votes, being within one and one half of a majority. The vote was not announced, but so many everywhere had kept the count of the ballot that it was known throughout the convention at once. Mr. David K. Carter, of Ohio, rose and announced a change in the vote of the Ohio delegation of four votes in favor of Lincoln, and at once the convention burst out in a state of the wildest excitement. Instantly cannons blazed and roared, bands played, banners waved, and the excited Republicans of Illinois and Chicago shouted themselves hoarse; while the telegraph i n s t r u m e n t s clicked the glad news to all portions of the country.

When the convention settled down again, other states changed their votes in favor of Mr. Lincoln, and it was announced as the result of the third ballot that Abraham Lincoln, of Illinois, had received 354 votes out of 465, and that he was nominated by the Republican party for the office of president of the United States. The nomination was then, on the motion of William H. Evarts, of New York, made unanimous, and the convention took a recess until the

HANNIBAL HAMLIN, OF MAINE.
Vice-president with Lincoln the first term. He was born 1809, and died 1891.

afternoon, when it completed its work by nominating Hannibal Hamlin, of Maine, for the vice-presidency.

Mr. Lincoln was at his proper place—at home—at this time. Let us give Mr. Raymond's significant paragraph describing what occurred at Springfield:

"He [Mr. Lincoln] had been in the telegraph-office during the casting of the first and second ballots, but then left and went over to the office of the *State Journal*, where he was sitting conversing with friends while the third ballot was being taken. In a few moments came across the wires the announcement of the result. The superintendent of the telegraph company, who was present, wrote on a scrap of paper, 'Mr. Lincoln, you are nominated on the third ballot,' and a boy ran with the message to Mr. Lincoln. He looked at it in silence amid the shouts of those around him; then rising and putting it in his pocket, he said quietly, 'There's a little woman down at our house would like to hear this; I'll go down and tell her.'"

Mr. Raymond relates that, "Tall Judge Kelly, of Pennsylvania, who was one of the committee to advise Mr. Lincoln of his nomination, and who is himself a great many feet high, had meanwhile been eying Mr. Lincoln's lofty form with

AN OVATION FROM NEIGHBORS, AFTER THE NOMINATING CONVENTION.

a mixture of admiration and possibly jealousy; this had not escaped Mr. Lincoln, and as he shook hands with the judge he inquired, "What is your height?"

"'Six feet three. What is yours, Mr. Lincoln?'

"'Six feet four.'

"'Then,' said the judge, 'Pennsylvania bows to Illinois. My dear man, for years my heart has been aching for a president that I could look up to, and I've found him at last in the land where we thought there were none but "little" giants.'"

The presidential campaign that followed was the most remarkable that had been conducted in the country since the time that William Henry Harrison was the Whig candidate for the presidency in 1840, twenty years before. The enthusiasm throughout the North was spontaneous and overwhelming. Abraham Lincoln had come to be regarded as the man of all others to represent the principles and bear the standard of the new party. The popular demonstrations everywhere were enthusiastic and decidedly original. The whole North was organized into companies, battalions, regiments, brigades, etc., and the members of these organizations were known far and wide as "Wide-Awakes." They were uniformed with oil capes and glazed caps, and they turned out with full ranks of old and middle-aged men, youth and boys, at all public demonstrations. They paraded with bands of martial music, sang songs and shouted for the "rail-splitter of Illinois." No man of that period had gained so strong a hold on the hearts of the people. The magic words, "Old Abe" and "Honest Old Abe" were on thousands of banners.

EDWARD EVERETT.

The significant fact with regard to all these demonstrations, remembered with great interest by millions of men still living, is that they were representative of a great principle, involving the freedom of individuals, of commonwealths, and of the nation.

John G. Whittier, William Cullen Bryant, James Russell Lowell, Henry W. Longfellow, and other American poets, had written stirring lines against slavery, and Mrs. Stowe's immortal work, "Uncle Tom's Cabin," written years before, had produced a powerful influence against the "peculiar institution" of the South. Then there was the brave work of the martyr John Brown, of Ossawatomie, a native of Connecticut, afterward a resident of North Elba, New York, where a monument now stands to his memory. He had fired, at Harper's Ferry, a shot in behalf of the freedom of the slaves that was heard in every slave cabin in the world. He died on the scaffold six months before the Chicago convention was held.

At the Democratic convention, held at Charleston, South Carolina, in April, 1860, Stephen A. Douglas was in the lead as a presidential candidate. The convention took a recess until the eighteenth of June to reassemble at Baltimore, and Douglas was finally nominated for the presidency of the United States, and Herschell B. Johnson, of Georgia, was named for the vice-presidency. So Lincoln and Douglas were again in the field against each other.

On the twenty-eighth of June, also at Baltimore, southern Democrats who had seceded at Charleston convened, and nominated as their candidate John C. Breckinridge, of Kentucky, for the presidency and Joseph Lane for the vice-presidency. Previous to this, however, in May, the Constitutional Union National Convention was held, and the principal plank in its platform adopted declared that "it is both the part of patriotism and of duty to recognize no political principles other than the constitution of the country, the union of the states, and the enforcement of the laws." John Bell, of Tennessee, was the candidate for the presidency, and Edward Everett, of Massachusetts, was named for the vice-presidency.

With four national tickets in the field, representing as many conflicting principles and sectional interests, it is no wonder that the campaign of 1860 was one of the most exciting in the history of the country.

It is quite true that some of the Republican politicians were disappointed and chagrined. Statesmen who had had a national reputation before Lincoln had become a prominent figure in political affairs felt that their "claims" had been slighted. But the people were more than satisfied. Popular Lincoln demonstrations were almost continuous throughout the North. Fence-rails were a feature of the campaign. Great armies of Republicans, uniformed with oil-cloth caps and capes, and carrying torches at night, marched the streets of every city and village, and gathered in great mass-meetings in commercial and political centers.

The election was held on the sixth of November; the result showed a popular vote for Lincoln of 1,857,610; for Douglas, 1,365,976; for Breckinridge, 847,953; and for Bell, 590,631. In the electoral college Lincoln received 180 votes, Breckinridge 72, Bell 39, and Douglas 12.

CHAPTER XX.

FINALLY, February 11, 1861, Mr. Lincoln left Springfield for Washington. It may be that Mr. Douglas was traveling about the country at this time in George B. McClellan's magnificent saloon-car, but Mr. Lincoln was not riding about on horseback with saddle-bags from one part of the country to another, nor in a common railway coach. A special train had been provided, and a man of the name of Wood (recommended to Mr. Lincoln by Mr. Seward) had been placed in charge of the party, which was composed of the president-elect, his wife, his sons, Robert, William and Thomas, his brother-in-law, Dr. W. S. Wallace, David Davis, Norman B. Judd, Elmer Ellsworth (who was afterward killed at Alexandria, Virginia), and the president's two secretaries, John G. Nicolay and John Hay. Colonel Sumner, of the United States army, was also in the car, and Governor Yates, Judge O. H. Browning and others were of the party. Before leaving the station, Lincoln addressed his old neighbors and friends, as follows:

"Friends, no one who has never been placed in like position can understand my feelings at this hour, nor the oppressive sadness I feel at this parting. For more than a quarter of a century I have lived among you, and during all that time I have received nothing but kindness at your hands. Here I have lived from my youth, until now I am an old man; here the most sacred ties of earth were assumed; here all my children were born, and here one of them lies buried. To you, dear friends, I owe all that I am. All the checkered past seems to crowd now upon my mind. To-day I leave you; I go to assume a task more difficult than that of Washington, and unless the great God, who assisted him, shall be with and aid me, I must fail; but if the same Almighty arm shall guide and support me, I shall not fail, I shall succeed. Let us all pray that the God of our fathers will not forsake us now. To him I commend you all. Permit me to ask that with equal sincerity and faith you will invoke his guidance for me. With this, friends, one and all, I must now bid you an affectionate farewell."

The trip from Springfield to Washington was much like a "royal progress." It is doubtful, however, whether any king on a tour about his country among his people was ever greeted with such enthusiastic and loyal receptions. Multitudes of people gathered at all places where the train stopped, and brief addresses were made from time to time.

At Pittsburgh he advised deliberation, and begged the American people to keep their temper on both sides of the line. In front of Independence Hall, he assured his listeners that "under his administration there would be no bloodshed until it was forced upon the government, and then it would be compelled to act in self-defense."

A little incident illustrative of Mr. Lincoln's sympathy with children may not be out of place here. In the beautiful village of Westfield, Chautauqua county, New York, lived little Grace Bedell. During the campaign she saw a portrait of

THE DEPOT AT SPRINGFIELD, ILLINOIS, FEBRUARY 11, 1861.

Mr. Lincoln, for whom she felt the love and reverence that was common in Republican families, and his smooth, homely face rather disappointed her. She said to her mother: "I think, mother, that Mr. Lincoln would look better if he wore whiskers, and I mean to write and tell him so."

The mother gave her permission.

Grace's father was a Republican; her two brothers Democrats. Grace wrote at once to the "Hon. Abraham Lincoln, Esq., Springfield, Illinois," in which she told him how old she was, and where she lived; that she was a Republican; that she thought he would make a good president, but would look better if he would let his whiskers grow. If he would do so she would try to coax her brothers to vote for him. She thought the rail fence around the picture of his cabin was very pretty. "If you have not time to answer my letter, will you allow *your little girl to reply for you?*"

Mr. Lincoln was much pleased with the letter, and decided to answer it, which he did at once, as follows:

Miss GRACE BEDELL.   SPRINGFIELD, ILLINOIS, October 19, 1860.

My Dear Little Miss:—Your very agreeable letter of the fifteenth is received. I regret the necessity of saying I have no daughter. I have three sons; one seventeen, one nine and one seven years. of age. They, with their mother, constitute my whole family. As to the whiskers, having never worn any, do you not think people would call it a piece of silly affectation if I should begin it now? Your very sincere well-wisher,

A. LINCOLN.

When on the journey to Washington, Mr. Lincoln's train stopped at Westfield. He recollected his little correspondent, and spoke of her to ex-Lieutenant-governor George W. Patterson, who called out and asked if Grace Bedell was present. There was a large, surging mass. of people gathered about the train, but Grace was discovered at a distance; the crowd opened a pathway to the coach, and she came, timidly but gladly, to the president-elect, who told her

GRACE BEDELL BILLINGS.

that she might see that he had allowed his whiskers to grow at her request. Then, reaching out his long arms, he drew her up to him and kissed her. The act drew an enthusiastic demonstration of approval from the multitude. Grace is now, in 1896, a married lady, living in Kansas, and the wife of a banker. Her present name is Grace Bedell Billings.

Great precaution was used in Mr. Lincoln's passage from Harrisburg, Pennsylvania, to Washington, and many accounts, differing in their statements, have been printed. Threats had been made that Mr. Lincoln, on his way to Washington, should never pass through Baltimore. Mr. Herndon says, in his "Life of Lincoln," that "it was reported and believed that conspiracies had been formed to attack the train and blow it up with explosives, or in some equally effective way dispose of the president-elect. Mr. Seward and others were so deeply impressed by the reports that Allen Pinkerton, a noted detective of Chicago, was employed to investigate the reports and ferret out the conspiracy, if any existed. This shrewd detective opened an office as a stock-broker, and, with his assistants, the most noted of whom was a woman, was soon in possession of inside information. A change of plans and trains at Harrisburg was due to his management and advice.

Mr. Lincoln had advised General Scott of the threats of violence on the inauguration day. The veteran commander was lying propped up in his bed by pillows, and weak and trembling from physical debility, his feelings were very

LINCOLN'S NIGHT TRIP FROM HARRISBURG
TO WASHINGTON.

much wrought up by Mr. Lincoln's communication. Adjutant-general Thomas Mather called upon Mr. Scott in Lincoln's behalf, and was addressed by Scott as follows: "General Mather, present my compliments to Mr. Lincoln when you return to Springfield, and tell him I expect him to come on to Washington as soon as he is ready; say to him that I will look after those Maryland and Virginia rangers myself; I will plant cannon at both ends of Pennsylvania avenue, and if any of them show their heads or raise a finger, I'll blow them to hell."

Only the members of the party knew when Mr. Lincoln left Harrisburg, or when he arrived at Washington. The secessionists of Baltimore were utterly thwarted, and long after his train had passed on its way to Washington were doubtless brooding over their fiendish conspiracy.

Mr. Lincoln arrived at Washington a few days before the fourth of March, and took quarters at Willard's hotel, then and now a famous hostelry. On the morning of March 4, 1861, he rode to the Capitol in a barouche with President Buchanan. The oath of office was administered by the venerable Chief-justice Taney, and he was at last president of our great republic. Mr. Buchanan accompanied him to the White House, and here the retiring chief magistrate bade him farewell, bespeaking for him a peaceful, prosperous and successful administration. His inaugural address, delivered immediately after taking the oath, could have been, under the circumstances and on as supreme occasion as this, nothing less than remarkable. The closing paragraphs are as follows:

"In your hands, my dissatisfied fellow-countrymen, and not in mine, is the momentous issue of civil war. The government will not assail you. You can have no conflict without being yourselves the aggressors. You have no oath registered in heaven to destroy the government, while I shall have the most solemn one to 'preserve, protect and defend it.' I am loath to close. We are not enemies, but friends. We must not be enemies. Though passion may have strained, it must not break our bonds of affection. The mystic cord of memory, stretching from every battle-field and patriot grave to every living heart and hearthstone all over this broad land will yet swell the chorus of the Union, when again touched, as surely they will be, by the better angels of our nature."

Sublime and beautiful prophecy! How much was to occur before it was finally fulfilled!

LINCOLN ENTERS WASHINGTON, FEBRUARY 23, 1861.

Judge Isaac N. Arnold says that on New-Year's day, 1861, Senator Douglas made this statement at Washington: "The cotton states are making an effort to draw the border states into their scheme of secession, and I am but too fearful they will succeed. If they do, there will be the most fearful civil war ever known." Pausing a moment, he looked like one inspired, while he proceeded, "Virginia, over yonder across the Potomac," pointing toward Arlington, "will become a charnel-house, but in the end the Union will triumph. They will try to get possession of this Capitol to give them prestige abroad; but in that effort they will never succeed; the North will rise en masse to defend it, but Washington will become a city of hospitals; the churches will be used for the sick and wounded. This house, the Minnesota block, will be devoted to that purpose." Before the end of the war this prediction was literally fulfilled. Nearly all of the churches were used for the wounded, and the Minnesota block, and the very room in which this remark was made, became the Douglas hospital.

President Lincoln appointed his Cabinet as follows· William H. Seward, secretary of state; Simon Cameron, secretary of war; Salmon P. Chase, secretary of the treasury, Gideon Wells, secretary of the navy; Caleb P. Smith, secretary of the interior; Montgomery Blair, postmaster-general; Edward Yates, attorney-general.

What men were these! Mr. Seward and Mr. Chase, of Ohio, were among the ablest, most intellectual statesmen of their day. They were sterling patriots. They were both ambitious, and possibly somewhat jealous of Mr. Lincoln, whom they believed, in their inmost hearts, was inferior to them. Certainly both were polished gentlemen. Seward was affable; Chase was of a most commanding presence. Caleb B Smith, of Indiana, was also a man of power, as was Simon Cameron, of Pennsylvania. Montgomery Blair was a patriot from a slave state.

LINCOLN ENTERED THE WHITE HOUSE MARCH 4, 1861.

CHAPTER XXI.

A FEW words should here be written covering the condition of things during the later months of Mr. Buchanan's administration. He was evidently in great perplexity. His Cabinet was largely composed of disloyal men, who were doing their utmost to excite the southern people into revolt. Outside of the Cabinet there were many of the same ilk. Early in the Lincoln campaign, representative men in South Carolina and other southern states threatened to secede, and declared that the South would not live under a black Republican government. After it was known that Lincoln was elected, great effort was made in various southern states to induce South Carolina to raise the banner of revolt and secession; and not without success. Federal officers in that state sent their resignations to Washington. In Georgia, Governor Brown, on November 12th, asserted the right of secession, and declared it the duty of Georgia to stand by South Carolina. There were some southern men who at heart were still true to the Union. In that same month Alexander H. Stephens attempted bravely to stem the tide of the coming rebellion. Still, in a speech before the Georgia Legislature, November 14th, he said: "Should Georgia determine to go out of the Union, I shall bow to the will of the people."

James Buchanan was doubtless as deserving of pity as he was of blame. He was old and ill, suffering still from the National hotel poisoning. In his Cabinet were Howell Cobb, of Georgia, John B. Floyd, of Virginia, and other bitter secessionists, by whom he was dominated. Buchanan showed great weakness in his last message, and but prepared the way for the conspirators. In Congress and out there were attempts to conciliate the secessionists and avert the impending outbreaks, but, unhappily, without effect. Grand old Ben Waller in the Senate, John A. Logan and Owen Lovejoy, of Illinois, and other noble and brave men in the House, stood at the front, doing their best to stamp out treason and promote sentiments of loyalty to the Union and the flag.

When Mr. Lincoln took his seat as president, the work of the conspirators against the Union was well advanced. The secession members of Buchanan's Cabinet, especially Floyd, the secretary of war, had robbed the treasury of its funds to be used in equipping a rebel army and navy. Military posts in the South, with all their equipments, had been put in the hands of armed traitors.

Seven states, South Carolina at the head, had already passed ordinances of secession, and a confederate government had been organized at Montgomery, Alabama. North Carolina still hesitated, and in some other states there was a conflict of opinion. Some of the rebel leaders believed that the North would not fight; that it was divided, and that vast numbers of its people would oppose "coercion" and perhaps fight on the side of the rebellion. Benjamin F. Butler, of Massachusetts, had been a supporter of Breckinridge, and it was naturally supposed by southern conspirators that he would be with them. Of one of them Mr. Butler asked, "Are you prepared for war?"

"But there will be no war; the North will not fight," was the very prompt reply.

Said Mr. Butler, "The North will fight; the North will send the last man and expend the last dollar to maintain the government."

"But," said his southern friend, "the North cannot fight; we have too many allies."

"You have friends," said Butler, "in the North so long as you fight your battles in the Union, but the moment you fire on the flag, the northern people will be a unit against you, and you may be assured, if war comes, slavery ends."

By the close of May, 1861, eleven states were in rebellion.

LINCOLN WHILE PRESIDENT.

Robert Lincoln, son of the martyred president, was shown sixty sittings of his father. In reply to the question as to which was the best picture, he picked out the one above reproduced.

During the last days of Mr. Buchanan's administration, Major Robert Anderson was in command of Fort Sumter, at the mouth of Charleston harbor. Anderson was a Kentuckian, and the conspirators all about him in Charleston assumed that he would take sides with the South.. Anderson listened to their talk in the social circles of Charleston, but kept his own counsel, and when it was rendered certain in his mind as to their traitorous purpose, he quietly withdrew to the fort and ran up the stars and stripes. This surprised, excited and enraged the people of Charleston. The first thing to be done by the government was to provision the fort. The secessionists in the Cabinet opposed this, but finally two steamers loaded with supplies sailed from New York to Sumter. Jefferson Davis and his Cabinet were in consultation at Montgomery, and were waiting for the secession of Virginia. Roger A. Pryor, present from that state, said, " I will tell you what will put Virginia in the Southern Confederacy in less than an hour; *sprinkle blood in their faces!*"

General Beauregard, located at Charleston, was ordered to demand the immediate surrender of Fort Sumter. Major Anderson replied promptly, "I cannot surrender the fort; I shall await the first shot, and if you do not batter me to pieces, I shall be starved out in three days." In the early morning of April 12, 1861, the first shot was fired on Sumter, and the echoes of that first shot reverberated throughout the civilized world.

It fired the brain and heart of the entire North, which was instantly convulsed with excitement; there was a great awakening, the like of which had never been known in America, or probably in the world. The masses of the people of the North were tremendously wrought up and thoroughly aroused. The people of the South had been excited and aroused and preparing for war for years. The great body of the men of the North were "Wide-Awakes" indeed, and were ready now to carry guns instead of simple banners and transparencies, and they were anxiously awaiting a call for troops. The first shot at Sumter had made the people, with very few individual exceptions, of one heart, one opinion, one mind, and of one purpose. They were in a condition of exalted, and even exultant, patriotism, and filled with an enthusiasm of a sort that had never been known. The new patriotism born of this new crisis in the affairs of the country shone in the white faces and blazing eyes of men and women, and even children, throughout the North. The issue was plain. Should the Union be preserved? Should the flag still float? Should the republic stand?

CHAPTER XXII.

MAJOR ANDERSON'S provisions were gone, and he departed from Fort Sumter, April 14, 1861. The people of Charleston were wild with excitement. Governor Pickens thanked God that the day had come. It seemed quite evident to these men that the battle had already been at last half won. President Lincoln, on April 15th, three days after the fall of Fort Sumter, issued a proclamation calling for 75,000 men, and summoned Congress to meet in extra session on July 4, 1861. The people were ready for it. Never was a call for troops more promptly and even enthusiastically met; there was hardly a syllable of protest in any part of the northern states. Many uniformed regiments in various states reported at places of rendezvous in their entirety. Thousands of individuals commenced the raising of companies. Some men recruited entire regiments, and it was not long before the 75,000 men were ready for duty. The most extraordinary promptness and efficiency were shown in equipping the troops and gathering supplies. Never were the noblest and grandest qualities of the American people displayed to better advantage than in this great emergency. The patriotism of the young men of the North was universal, spontaneous and sublime, and the spirit of the women corresponded with that of the men.

Two days later Virginia seceded from the Union; Arkansas followed May 6th, and North Carolina lowered the stars and stripes on the twentieth. There were so many strong and true Union men in the mountains of East Tennessee that the disunionists could not withdraw that state until June 8th. In Missouri there was a conflict between unionists and disunionists, and Kentucky tried to be neutral. Maryland was divided in sentiment, but some of the bitterest and most insidious foes of the Union were gathered in and about Baltimore.

On April 19th, the president issued a proclamation providing for the blockading of the forts of the seceded states.

On the same day, the anniversary of the battle of Lexington, the first regiment of Massachusetts volunteers attempted to pass through Baltimore. On the eighteenth the first section of Pennsylvania troops had passed through quietly and unmolested. The Sixth Massachusetts and the Seventh Pennsylvania regiments arrived at eleven in the morning. Meanwhile the passions of the people had been still further excited by the announcement of the evacuation of Harper's Ferry by the Federal troops. The Massachusetts regiment occupied eleven cars, and these were, according to the then existing regulations, drawn through the streets of the city, singly, by horses to the Camden street depot. An ominous-looking mob had assembled, but at first a sullen silence was maintained. Ere the cars had gone a couple of blocks, however, the crowd became so dense that the horses could barely force their way through. Then began a chorus of hoots and yells, mingled with threats. The troops remained quiet, and this, instead of appeasing, appeared to anger the rioters. Brickbats and stones were hurled, and it became evident that these missiles were not *accidentally* at hand. Many of the men were wounded, but the first eight cars reached Camden street depot without serious damage. The ninth car was not so fortunate, for a defective brake caused a halt at Gay street, and the mob, now numbering from 8,000 to 10,000, made a furious onslaught. This car, with some damage, also reached the Camden street depot. Behind it, however, were two other cars confronted by a barricade hastily constructed of anchors and other materials dragged from the wharf. Finding further transportation impossible, the soldiers were ordered to leave the cars, and were formed into close columns under Captain A. S. Follansbee, of Company C, of Lowell. With fixed bayonets they advanced on the double-quick in the direction of the Washington station. The mob closed on them, muskets were snatched away, and amid throwing of missiles, revolver-shots, and bullets from the stolen muskets, the patience of the troops at last gave way. Two of their number had been killed, and several wounded had been taken within the solid square which was now

NORMAN B. JUDD.

Intimate friend and fellow-attorney. Mr. Judd was the chairman of the Illinois delegation to the convention that nominated Lincoln. He was chairman of the state central committee of Illinois during the canvass. He was born in 1815, and died in 1878.

formed. An order was given to turn and fire singly; there was no platoon firing, or the carnage in that dense mass would have been appalling. On Pratt street, near Gay street, one man was crushed by a stone or heavy piece of iron thrown from a window. After a protracted struggle the troops reached the depot, bearing with them their dead, now increased to three, and nine wounded comrades, one of them mortally injured. They were hustled into the train and sent off, but the mob followed for a considerable distance, and made frantic efforts to throw the cars from the track. In the streets nine of the Baltimorians had been killed and a great number wounded. The mayor of Baltimore had headed the column for a short time, but he could not allay the storm he had raised, and finding his person in danger, he disappeared.

The Philadelphia troops, not yet armed, were with difficulty extricated from the mob and taken back to Philadelphia.

HARPER'S FERRY, VIRGINIA.

On the twentieth, Norfolk was attacked, and the Federal troops spiked the guns and retired.

Virginia was rapidly filled with southern volunteers, and, as they were aggressive, even the city of Washington was threatened.

The Massachusetts Eighth and the famous New York Seventh were in Washington by April 25th, and the Capitol was safe forever thereafter.

Cairo, Illinois, was also occupied by Union troops. John M. Johnson, senator from Kentucky, sent a solemn protest to the president, who promptly replied: "If I had suspected that Cairo, in Illinois, was in Doctor Johnson's senatorial district, I would have thought twice before sending troops to Cairo." This ended that controversy.

By May 24th, about twenty thousand troops had arrived in Washington. The rebels had been flaunting their new flag at Alexandria, Virginia, but troops were sent across the Potomac to take possession of the place. Among them were Colonel Ellsworth's zouaves. Colonel Ellsworth, who had studied law in Lincoln's office at Springfield, and who was one of the party who accompanied him to Washington, saw a Confederate flag waving above the Marshall house, kept by a

Mr. Jackson. He went to the roof and tore it down, and upon reaching the foot of the stairs, was shot down by Jackson, who, in turn, was promptly killed by a New York zouave.

On the third of May, Mr. Lincoln saw the necessity of calling for more troops, and issued a proclamation asking for 83,000 men, to be enlisted *for three years or during the war!*

The Union army, which had been organized at Washington, crossed the Potomac on the long bridge May 24th, and entered Virginia. General McGruder had a band of Confederates at Bethel church; Union troops were sent to dislodge him, but were driven back, with loss. General George B. McClellan, the former Illinois railway superintendent, had undertaken the conquest of West Virginia, and gained a victory at Rich Mountain, July 11th. General Rosecrans defeated Floyd at Carnifex Ferry, August 10th, and Robert E. Lee was driven back from Cheat Mountain, September 14th, thus restoring West Virginia to Federal authority.

Men who pretended to be in favor of peace, but whose real purpose was to prevent warlike demonstrations on the part of the government, while seeming to have no desire that preparations of the same sort should be suspended at the South, made themselves very conspicuous with their advice to the government, and continued their demonstrations throughout the entire conflict.

Congress met in extra session July 4th, in response to the president's proclamation. The Republicans had control of both houses, and a large number of Democrats joined the Republicans in standing by the president in his efforts to preserve the Union.

The ablest and yet the fairest man among the Confederates was Alexander H. Stephens, the man whose speech Mr. Lincoln had so greatly admired so many years before. Jefferson Davis was far inferior to him in force and dignity. He was a small man, and physically very feeble, but in intellectual power he was a giant, and in spite of his environments, was really in favor of peace and union. But, as we have already stated, Mr. Stephens had declared that he would go with his state. He went out of the Union, and was now vice-president of the Confederacy, with Davis as chief executive.

The headquarters of the Confederacy were removed from Montgomery, Alabama, to Richmond, Virginia, July 20th. Prior to that time Robert E. Lee, of Virginia, had resigned his office of colonel in the United States army and had accepted a general's commission in the Confederate army.

Lieutenant-general Winfield Scott was now in command of the Union forces. The stanch old patriot had been approached by a deputation of southerners and offered the command of the military forces of Virginia, but he had promptly declined the offer. In his reply to the deputation he had said:

"I have served my country under the flag of the Union for more than fifty years, and as long as God permits me to live I will defend that flag with my sword, even if my own native state assails it." About the same time General Scott, April 21st, telegraphed to Senator Crittenden, of Kentucky: "I have not changed; have no thought of changing; always a Union man."

CHAPTER XXIII

BEAUREGARD and Joseph E. Johnston had concentrated the Confederate troops in Virginia, at no great distance from the Potomac, and on July 16th, the Union army made an advance toward the enemy. The first clash of arms took place between Centerville and Bull Run. The Unionists then pressed on, and on the morning of the twenty-first came upon the Confederates, well posted, at a point between Bull Run and Manassas Junction. The first great battle of the war was here fought, and with great valor on both sides. At midday it seemed that the Union general, McDowell, would gain the victory, but finally, in the crisis of the conflict, General Joseph E. Johnston arrived from the Shenandoah valley with nearly six thousand fresh troops, made an attack on the Union forces, and the tide was turned. McDowell's whole army was hurled back, and his men were soon in full retreat toward Washington. The Union loss in killed, wounded and prisoners was 2,952; that of the Confederates, 2,050. Happily, the victors were too badly crippled to pursue. This engagement was known at the North as the battle of Bull Run; the southerners called it the battle of Manassas.

The defeat of the Federal army covered the entire North with gloom. The friends of the Union had expected a great victory. But the lesson was wholesome. The people became more determined than ever, and their quality was shown in immense contributions for the support of the Union cause. Meanwhile the southern people were in transports over a dearly bought and decidedly doubtful victory—a victory that in the end caused them much more harm than would have resulted from a defeat.

During the summer several naval expeditions were sent out.

The Confederates made strong efforts to capture Missouri. Camp Jackson was formed by them near St. Louis, but it was broken up by Captain Nathaniel Lyon. The rebel General Price defeated Colonel Mulligan at Lexington. General John C. Fremont was in command in Missouri, but he was superseded by General David Hunter, and he in turn by General Halleck. Lexington was subsequently retaken by the Federals, and Price retired into Arkansas.

In November, 1861, General Winfield Scott sent his resignation to the president, which was received with great regret. General George B. McClellan succeeded Scott. McClellan was spoken of by some as a "political" general, and it was charged that while he desired to put down the rebellion, he seemed quite anxious that the institution of human slavery should not be interfered with. On the other hand, General John C. Fremont, who had been honored by being the first Republican candidate for the presidency (and who was a son-in-law of Thomas H. Benton), contended that the abolition of slavery was one great purpose of the war. But Abraham Lincoln soon gave not only William H. Seward, his secretary of state, but these generals, who were exceeding their authority on one side or the other, to understand that he was president. No man can imagine the immense responsibility that was resting upon the mind and heart of this supremely great man, elevated to this high position through the providence of God to save the country, and to make it a

UNITED STATES CAPITOL, WASHINGTON, D. C.

free land. There was no stronger man in America, and therefore none upon whom he could lean. He was at this time the greatest representative of the rights of man in all the world. No such political or national emergency had ever arisen before; every disaster caused him the deepest sorrow; every Union success on the battle-field gave him comfort. No man was ever more widely advised, nor did ever the advice given by men differ more radically. He was asked to do all sorts of things, and not to do all sorts of things. Bodies of preachers advised him to bring about peace. These men had prayed over the matter, and had had direct advice from the Almighty that their course was approved. Others were praying for the immediate emancipation of the slaves, and they also claimed to have advices from the same source that confirmed their opinions.

It is not to be supposed that Abraham Lincoln was to be kept in ignorance of the purposes and will of the Almighty. Perhaps he heard voices, such as Joan of Arc had heard in another century, and on another continent. At any rate, he was not only the greatest man of his time, but the wisest and the strongest. His settled purpose reached out to a time and to an event of which his immediate friends were not advised, and the problem of the age, fortunately for him and for the present generation, was being providentially worked out.

DOUGLAS MONUMENT, CHICAGO.

In November, 1861, the rebels Mason and Slidell, of Virginia, who had been appointed as commissioners from the Confederate states to England and France, took passage on the British mail-steamer Trent, which was hailed on the eighth by the United States frigate San Jacinto, Captain Wilkes, and brought to by a shot across her bows. Mason and Slidell were taken prisoners, brought to the United States, and lodged in Fort Warren. Although this act of Captain Wilkes excited much admiration and exultation, it was almost instantly seen by the president and his advisory that the act was illegal and must be disavowed, and the men were promptly released, with an apology. In this matter the practical wisdom and prudence of William H. Seward, then secretary of state, was conspicuously shown. He was one of the greatest men who ever held this high position.

Toward the close of the year there was a decided change for the better in the situation, as viewed from the Federal standpoint. Not only were the Confederate forces dislodged from West Virginia, but they were driven out of Kentucky and Missouri, reviving the hope throughout the North that the war would not be of long duration, and that it would end in the triumph of the Union cause.

CHAPTER XXIV.

AT the opening of 1862 the Union army was 450,000 strong. Edwin M. Stanton succeeded Simon Cameron as secretary of war, having been called into the Cabinet by the same "long, lank" individual whom he had affected so to despise many years before at the trial of the famous "reaper case." General McClellan was organizing the Army of the Potomac in the vicinity of Washington, while General Don Carlos Buell commanded a strong force at Louisville, Kentucky.

Colonel James A. Garfield (the future president of the United States, who was to die as did Mr. Lincoln, by the bullet of an assassin) defeated a force of Confederates on January 9th, on the Big Sandy river, in Kentucky. Ten days later, at Mill Spring, General George H. Thomas, afterward one of the greatest of Union generals, defeated Crittenden and Zollicoffer in the same neighborhood, and Zollicoffer was killed.

Fort Henry, on the Tennessee river, in Kentucky, and Fort Donelson, in Tennessee, on the Cumberland, had been erected and operated by the Confederates. Commodore Foote was sent up the Tennessee with a flotilla, and compelled the evacuation of Fort Henry, the rebels retiring, with some loss, to Donelson. The gunboats were then ordered to Donelson. Ulysses S. Grant, of Illinois, who had been with Foote at Fort Henry, now advanced to Fort Donelson and began to besiege it. Grant had 30,000 men, and after two days' fighting, forced General Buckner to an "unconditional and immediate surrender." Buckner's army of ten thousand men were made prisoners of war, and valuable stores of ammunition, guns and supplies were taken.

There was universal rejoicing throughout the North over this great victory. As a consequence of the capture of Donelson, Governor Harris, of Tennessee, gathered up his archives and evacuated Nashville.

Grant ascended the Tennessee to Pittsburg Landing, where the memorable battle of Shiloh was fought. He was there attacked on the morning of March 6th, by Albert Sidney Johnston and Beauregard, with a large force. There was hard fighting during the day, with the advantage apparently in favor of the rebels, but at night Buell arrived with a large number of troops from Nashville, and Grant assumed the offensive. Johnston had already fallen, and on the second day of the battle Beauregard was driven, with the remainder of his army, from the field, on the route toward Corinth, Mississippi. The slaughter on both sides during the two days' fighting was terrible, each army losing 10,000 men.

In March, 1862, a bill was passed providing for the abolition of slavery in the District of Columbia, and President Lincoln sent a message to Congress announcing his approval of the bill. Mr. Lincoln then proposed to Congress a resolution providing that the United States, in order to co-operate with any state which may adopt gradually the abolition of slavery, give to such state pecuniary aid, to be used by such state at its discretion. No state offered to accept this proposition.

At about this time General Butler, in command at Fortress Monroe, advised Lincoln that he had determined to regard all slaves coming into his camps as contraband of war, and to employ their labor under fair compensation; and the secretary of war replied to him, in behalf of the president, approving his course, and saying, "You are not to interfere between master and slave on the one hand, nor surrender slaves who may come within your lines." This was a significant milestone of progress to the great end that was thereafter to be reached.

In May, Senator Douglas died at Chicago. By his patriotic course he had turned the great multitude of his followers in the North to the support of Lincoln.

LEONARD SWETT.

Mr. Swett became acquainted with Lincoln in 1848, and was very intimate with him until the time of his assassination. They traveled the circuit together, and Mr. Swett and David Davis were the two Illinois friends who were consulted in forming the first Cabinet. Lincoln spoke of Swett as the "intimate friend who never sought office."

Lincoln's eldest son, Robert Todd, was at this time in Harvard University, but Willie and Tom were in the White House with their father and mother. Both of the boys were seized with illness, and Willie died. This naturally added to the burden which was already weighing so heavily upon the president.

On the sixth of March, General Curtis defeated 20,000 Confederates and Indians at Pea Ridge, Arkansas.

About this time important events were occurring at Fortress Monroe, in Virginia, on the Atlantic coast. Captain John Ericsson, an inventor, and a man of wealth, great liberality and patriotism, had invented and completed a "peculiar war-vessel, with a single round tower of iron exposed above the water line." [Ridpath.]

The Confederates had raised the frigate Merrimac, which had been sunk by the Union forces at the Norfolk navy-yard, and had plated it with "impenetrable mail of iron." Reaching the immediate vicinity of Fortress Monroe on March 8th, this formidable vessel attacked and sunk the United States vessels Cumberland and Congress. But here its conquering career suddenly came to an end, for, during the night, Captain Ericsson's strange vessel, which was called the Monitor, arrived from New York, and on the morning of the ninth these two monsters of the deep turned their guns upon each other. After five hours of fighting, the rebel ironclad gave up the contest, and slipped away, badly damaged, to Norfolk.

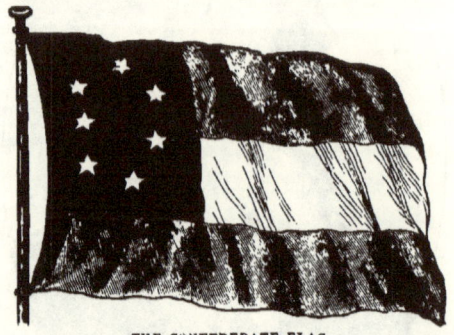

THE CONFEDERATE FLAG.

Earlier than this, General Burnside and Commodore Goldsborough had captured Roanoke island. Burnside also captured Newberne, North Carolina, March 14th, and Beaufort, South Carolina, April 25th. General Quincy A. Gilmore took Fort Pulaski, at the mouth of the river Savannah, April 11th. Early in the same month a powerful squadron, commanded by General Benjamin F. Butler and Admiral Farragut, entered the Mississippi and proceeded as far as Fort Jackson and St. Phillip, thirty miles above the mouth of the river. Here they commenced a furious bombardment of the forts, which were situated on opposite sides of the river. Finally, April 24th, they ran the batteries, broke the blockade, and on the memorable day of April 25, 1862, reached New Orleans, and took possession of the city, thus closing the mouth of the great Mississippi against the Confederates. This was one of the great achievements of the war.

At this period there was a great pressure on the president in behalf of the emancipation of slaves. It is now well known that his purpose to free them at the proper time was as strong as the purpose of any man in his country. He had his own plan, and the result shows that it was the only one that was practicable.

Two men at this time were contributing in no small degree toward relieving the minds of the president and the people of their burden of anxiety and worry,

by writing humorous articles for the press on the situation. These men were
Charles Farrar Browne, known as "Artemus Ward," and David R. Locke, known
as "Rev. Petroleum Vesuvius Nasby." Lincoln laughed heartily at Artemus
Ward's badly spelled but exceedingly droll utterances, and it is undoubtedly true
that they had a tendency to relieve the strain of his mind and nervous system.
Petroleum V. Nasby assumed to be a Kentucky Democrat, opposed to the war to
uphold the government; his letters were the literary features of the hour. He so
truthfully represented the utterances of the anti-war Democrats, especially those

PRESIDENT LINCOLN AND GENERAL McCLELLAN.

This picture was made by the government photographer when the president was calling
on General McClellan, at his tent at Antietam, October 3, 1862. Before them, on the table, are
maps and plans, and these great characters are discussing the situation.

of the border states, that the pretended letters were believed to be genuine in
many quarters. Indeed, it was found necessary by some of these Democrats to
disavow the sentiments therein expressed; the so-called arguments placed these
Democrats who were opposing the war, and organizing to resist drafts, in such a
light as to make them utterly and supremely ridiculous in the eyes of patriots.

On July 14th, the president called for an army of four hundred thousand men,
and for four hundred millions of dollars in money. Both requests were promptly

ranted.   At this time the cry was, "On to Richmond!" and great expectations
·ere entertained of General McClellan, who had exceptional qualifications by
ature and training for.organizing, equipping and drilling an army, but seemed
lmost utterly lacking in power of making aggressive military movements.

The rebels, under General Kirby Smith, took the aggressive August 30th,
lvancing toward the Ohio river.   General Bragg co-operated with him,
lvancing from Chattanooga to Mumfordsville, where, on September 17th, he
)ok 4,500 Federal prisoners.   Bragg then started for Louisville, but was inter-
pted by General Buell.
mith's objective point was
incinnati, but General Lew
Vallace was there; tens of
ousands of Ohio and In-
iana "squirrel-hunters," as
hey were called, rallied at ·
is call, and Smith, after
oming in sight of the Queen
ity, took a sober second
hought and retired.

Rosecrans and Grant de-
ated Price at Iuka, Septem-
er 19th.   Price was again
pulsed October 3d, when,
ith Van Dorn, he advanced
n Corinth.

In December occurred the
reat battle of Murfreesbor-
ugh, in which Bragg was
efeated on the banks of
tone river, by Rosecrans.
n the first day's conflict a
ortion of the Union forces
ras shattered.   The brunt
f the battle now fell on·
homas, and he was crowded
ack.   Rosecrans, however,
cadjusted his lines, and as

JUDGE N. M. BROADWELL.

One of Lincoln's personal friends and colleagues at
the Springfield bar.

he result of "the unparalleled heroism of William B. Hazen, who, with 1,800
nen," stayed the onward course of the rebels, the Federal lines were com-
)letely restored.   New-Year's morning, 1863, found Rosecrans strongly posted,
ind ready for renewal of the conflict.   On the second the battle was renewed,
ind finally Bragg and his host were driven back, with great slaughter.

In Virginia, Banks met one of the greatest and most effective of Confederate
generals, "Stonewall" Jackson, and was driven back.   The Union forces were

defeated at Fort Royal. Fremont drove back Jackson at Cross Keys, and Jackson then defeated General Shields at Port Republic, and passed on to assist in defending Richmond, the rebel capital.

At last, March 10, 1862, McClellan, with 200,000 men, the Army of the Potomac, began the long march to the Confederate capital; the cry of "On to Richmond!" had at last had its effect. At Manassas Junction the Confederates fell back. McClellan, at this point, changed his plan and embarked 120,000 of his men to Fortress Monroe. This force advanced to Yorktown, which was taken. An advance was then made to Williamsburg, where the rebels were defeated, with a severe loss, as they were again at West Point, and the Union forces passed on to the Chickahominy, crossed it, and were within ten miles of Richmond.

Meanwhile, May 10th, General Wool advanced on Norfolk and captured it; on the eleventh the rebels sunk their own ironclad, the Virginia, which the Monitor had disabled, at Fortress Monroe. May 31st, McClellan advanced to within seven miles of Richmond, at Fair Oaks, or Seven Pines, where he met the Confederates, and after two days' fighting, drove them back, with considerable loss. Robert E. Lee, the greatest and most popular of the rebel military leaders, now took the chief command, and became aggressive. After seven days of continuous and very severe fighting, Lee was beaten at Malvern Hill, twelve miles from Richmond, and McClellan might then have advanced and captured the Confederate capital. Instead, however, he retired to Harrison's Landing, a few miles down the river.

Lee, now confident that Richmond was safe from capture by McClellan, moved northward, about the middle of August, with the purpose of invading Maryland. Meanwhile Stonewall Jackson was flying about, attacking and harassing the Union forces. An undecisive second battle, August 28th and 29th, was fought at Manassas Junction, the old Bull Run battle-ground. There were several collisions and much hard fighting, and Lee finally crossed the Potomac into Maryland at Point of Rocks, and on September 6th took possession of Frederick. McClellan's whole force had followed Lee, and on the night of the fourteenth were at Antietam creek. Hooker was with McClellan. On September 17th was fought the great battle of Antietam, in which the Confederates were disastrously defeated. Lee, in the month's operation, had lost 30,000 men. McClellan followed the retreating Confederates back into Virginia.

A series of changes in the command of the Army of the Potomac began October 7th. The president, finally yielding to his own convictions, spurred on by outside pressure, relieved General McClellan, appointing General Burnside as his successor. Burnside was defeated in his first battle after assuming command of the army, the battle of Fredericksburg, and the year 1862 ended in gloom.

CHAPTER XXV.

ON September 22, 1862, after much thought and discussion, Mr. Lincoln issued his famous Emancipation Proclamation, declaring that unless the states fighting against the government laid down their arms previous to January, 1863, he should issue an edict giving freedom to the slaves. The issuing of his memorable document was another surprise to the people of the country. Lincoln had promised himself that if God would give him a Union victory he would issue this proclamation, and whether in response to this promise or not, the Union victory at Antietam, Maryland, in which the rebels were defeated and driven back across the Potomac, furnished a pretext.

In November, 1862, Horatio Seymour, an anti-war Democrat, but a man of splendid ability and great personal influence, was elected governor of New York. This and similar occurrences gave great encouragement to northern Democrats who were opposed to the war. Clement L. Vallandigham, of Ohio, had shown himself, in the national House of Representatives and elsewhere, one of the bitterest and most outspoken of all the men of this class. At a political meeting held at Mount Vernon, Ohio, he declared that it was the design of "those in power to establish a despotism," and that they had "no intention of restoring the Union." He denounced the conscription which had been ordered, and declared that men who submitted to be drafted into the army were "unworthy to be called free men." He spoke of the president as "King Lincoln." Such utterances at this time, when the government was exerting itself to the utmost to recruit the armies, were dangerous, and Vallandigham was arrested, tried by court-martial at Cincinnati, and sentenced to be placed in confinement during the war. General Burnside, in command at Cincinnati, approved the sentence, and ordered that he be sent to Fort Warren, in Boston Harbor; but the president ordered that he be sent "beyond our lines into those of his friends." He was therefore escorted to the Confederate lines in Tennessee, thence going to Richmond. There he did not meet with a very cordial reception, and finally ran the blockade to Nassau and went thence to Canada.

On January 1, 1863, occurred the greatest event of the war—the issuing of the promised and long-expected Emancipation Proclamation. This great paper, written by Abraham Lincoln's own hand, and coming from his great heart, must stand in history as the direct fruit of, and must rank in history with, the immortal Declaration of Independence. The Confederates had been duly warned, in a proclamation issued in September, that if they remained in rebellion the slaves would be set free.

PROCLAMATION.

Whereas, On the 22d day of September, in the year of our Lord one thousand eight hundred and sixty-two, a proclamation was issued by the President of the United States, containing, among other things, the following, to-wit:

"That on the first day of January, in the year of our Lord one thousand eight hundred and sixty-three, all persons held as slaves within any state or designated part of a state, the people whereof shall then be in rebellion against the United States, shall be then, thenceforward and forever free; and the Executive Government of the United States, including the military and naval authority thereof, will recognize and maintain the freedom of such persons, and will do no act or acts to repress such persons, or any of them, in any efforts they may make for their actual freedom.

WILLIAM HENRY SEWARD.

"That the Executive will, on the first day of January aforesaid, by proclamation, designate the states and parts of states, if any, in which the people thereof, respectively, shall then be in rebellion against the United States; and the fact that any state, or the people thereof, shall on that day be in good faith represented in the Congress of the United States, by members chosen thereto at elections wherein a majority of the qualified voters of such state shall have participated, shall, in the absence of strong countervailing testimony, be deemed conclusive evidence that such state, and the people thereof, are not then in rebellion against the United States."

Now, therefore, I, Abraham Lincoln, President of the United States, by virtue of the power in me vested as Commander-in-Chief of the Army and Navy of the United States in time of actual armed rebellion against the authority and government of the United States, and as a fit and necessary war measure for suppressing said rebellion, do, on this first day of January, in the year of our Lord one thousand eight hundred and sixty-three, and in accordance with my purpose so to do, publicly proclaimed for the full period of one hundred days from the day first above mentioned, order and designate, as the states and parts of states wherein the people thereof, respectively, are this day in rebellion against the United States, the following, to-wit:

Arkansas, Texas, Louisiana (except the parishes of St. Bernard, Plaquemines, Jefferson, St. John, St. Charles, St. James, Ascension, Assumption, Terre Bonne, LaFourche,

Ste. Marie, St. Martin, and Orleans, including the city of New Orleans), Mississippi, Alabama, Florida, Georgia, South Carolina, North Carolina and Virginia (except the forty-eight counties designated as West Virginia, and also the counties of Berkeley, Accomac, Northampton, Elizabeth City, York, Princess Anne and Norfolk, including the cities of Norfolk and Portsmouth), and which excepted parts are, for the present, left precisely as if this proclamation were not issued.

And by virtue of the power, and for the purpose aforesaid, I do order and declare that all persons held as slaves within said designated states and parts of states are and henceforward shall be free, and that the Executive Government of the United States, including the military and naval authorities thereof, will recognize and maintain the freedom of said persons.

And I hereby enjoin upon the people so declared to be free to abstain from all violence, unless in necessary self-defense; and I recommend to them, that, in all cases, when allowed, they labor faithfully for reasonable wages.

GENERAL GRANT'S OLD HOME, GALENA, ILLINOIS.

And I further declare and make known that such persons, of suitable condition, will be received into the armed service of the United States, to garrison forts, positions, stations and other places, and to man vessels of all sorts in said service.

And upon this act, sincerely believed to be an act of justice, warranted by the Constitution, upon military necessity, I invoke the considerate judgment of mankind and the gracious favor of Almighty God.

In testimony whereof I have hereunto set my name and caused the seal of the United States to be affixed.

Done at the City of Washington, this first day of January, in the year of our [L. S.] Lord one thousand eight hundred and sixty-three, and of the Independence of the United States the eighty-seventh.

By the President: ABRAHAM LINCOLN.
WILLIAM H. SEWARD, Secretary of State.

This proclamation was received with satisfaction and great joy by the loyal people of the United States, and President Lincoln was at once crowned as the greatest of emancipators.

There were important military movements in various portions of the South. Efficiency and bravery were shown everywhere by Union officers and private soldiers. Lincoln had loyal and most helpful allies in Congress and in the field. A large number of Union generals had already gained great victories and

PRESIDENT LINCOLN AND GENERAL McCLELLAN.

This is a very interesting picture, as it gives an idea how Lincoln looked in a crowd of men. The picture is from a Brady negative, taken at the headquarters of the Army of the Potomac, at Antietam, on October 4, 1862.

acquired most honorable places in history. Among these were Ulysses S. Grant, William T. Sherman, George H. Thomas, Phil. Sheridan, and others. The president had made repeated calls for troops and money, and Congress had responded promptly, so that he had now about half a million men in the field. But there were some discordant notes, and the condition of the country was such that Congress passed a law, March 3, 1803, authorizing the president to suspend the writ of habeas corpus throughout the United States when, in his opinion, public safety might require it.

General Butler had, by occupying New Orleans, closed the mouth of the Mississippi to the rebels, but in order to open the river throughout its length to the Union gunboats and vessels, it was necessary to capture Vicksburg, the great objective point of the campaign in the West. Vicksburg was to be taken in the West, and the army of Lee was to be destroyed in the East.

Grant arrived in the vicinity of Vicksburg February 2, 1803, and assumed command. The siege was most remarkable; slowly the work proceeded of closing all the approaches to the city. The operations of the land and naval forces were very elaborate; canals were cut, fortifications erected. Admiral Porter co-operated with General Grant.

The capture of Port Gibson, on the Mississippi, below Vicksburg, by Union troops gave encouragement to Grant; and Johnston's army moved with the purpose of relieving Vicksburg and to take Pemberton, who was in command of the rebel forces in that city, out of the cage in which he found himself; but Johnston was defeated, and several victories won, in quick succession, by the Union troops,

SIMON CAMERON, OF PENNSYLVANIA.

Secretary of war under Lincoln, from March 4, 1860, to January 11, 1862.

and Pemberton and his men were finally driven into their works and the city completely invested.

Grant now decided to take the city by assault, and on May 22d, the attack was made with great vigor, but without success. There was great suffering on the part of the besieged troops, and citizens were reduced to great extremities, and, finally, on July 3d, Pemberton sent a letter to Grant proposing an armistice and commissioners to arrange terms of capitulation. The result of this was that the city and garrison of Vicksburg was surrendered on July 4, 1863.

In the siege of Vicksburg and preceding battles, the general loss to the rebels was 37,000 taken prisoners, including fifteen general officers, 10,000 killed and wounded, and a large quantity of ammunition. Thus the Mississippi was free to the Union forces, and to trade throughout its entire length.

The Confederates, in June, 1863, formed another purpose to beard the loyal lion in his very den. On the twenty-eighth, Lee invaded Pennsylvania with a very large force, occupied Chambersburg promptly, and advanced on Gettysburg.

On the twenty-seventh, General Meade had succeeded General Hooker in command of the Army of the Potomac. General Reynolds, of the Union forces, came unexpectedly upon the enemy at Gettysburg, and was at first driven back. On the morning of July 1, 1863, the battle of Gettysburg began, and during the forenoon of July 4th, after one of the most terrible series of battles recorded in history, it was evident that Lee was preparing to retreat. The Confederates had made a tremendous effort to capture Cemetery Hill, the key to the Union position. Pickett's charge on this occasion is known as one of the severest and most heroic demonstrations ever made by the Confederates, but after repeated attempts, and after pressing up to the very muzzles of the artillery, the rebels· were met with such storms of grape and canister that the survivors threw down their arms and surrendered, rather than run the gauntlet of retreat. Three thousand prisoners were taken.

On July 4, 1863, General Meade, in a dispatch dated at 8:30 P. M., to the secretary of war, said, "The enemy opened at 1:00 P. M., from about one hundred and fifty guns. They concentrated upon my left center, continuing without intermission for about three hours, at the expiration of which time they assaulted my left center twice, being upon both occasions handsomely repulsed, with severe loss to them, leaving in our hands nearly three thousand prisoners."

The effect of these two great victories, the capture of Vicksburg and the repulse of the rebel forces at Gettysburg, was tremendous. The president and all loyal people were greatly encouraged and strengthened. It was evident to men of observation and foresight that the tide of events had turned, and that the crushing down and out of the Confederacy was only a matter of time.

CHAPTER XXVI

THE rejoicing and gratitude of the friends of the Union found expression in a proclamation issued by their beloved president July 15, 1863: "It has pleased Almighty God to hearken to the supplications and prayers of an afflicted people, and to vouchsafe to the army and the navy of the United States victories on the land and on the sea so signal and so effective as to furnish reasonable ground for augmented confidence that the union of these states will be maintained, their constitution preserved, and their peace and prosperity permanently restored. But these victories have been accorded not without sacrifice of life, limb, health and liberty incurred by brave, loyal and patriotic citizens. Domestic affliction in every part of the country follows in the train of these fearful bereavements. It is meet and right to recognize and confess the presence of the Almighty Father, and the power of his hand, equally in these triumphs and these sorrows."

The president then invited the people to assemble August 4th for thanksgiving, praise and prayer, and to render homage to the Divine Majesty, for the wonderful things he had done in the nation's behalf; and he called upon the people to invoke his Holy Spirit to subdue the anger which had been produced and so long sustained a needless and cruel rebellion; to change the hearts of the insurgents; to guide the councils of the government with wisdom, and to visit with tender care and consolation those who through the vicissitudes of battles and sieges had been brought to suffer in mind, body or estate, and finally to lead the whole nation through the paths of repentance and submission to the Divine will, to unity and fraternal peace. That the people responded to this invitation heartily does not need to be said.

On November 19th, the battle-field at Gettysburg, which had been set apart as a national cemetery, was consecrated to its pious purpose by impressive ceremonies. The president and his Cabinet, governors and officials of several states, and large masses of people assembled on this occasion. Edward Everett, late secretary of state, and senator from Massachusetts, one of the greatest public speakers of the day, with an international reputation, was the orator of the occasion. President Lincoln, however, while in the cars on his way from the White House, was notified that he would be expected to make "some remarks also." He made a few notes while in the car, and when the time came for him

PICKETT'S CHARGE AT GETTYSBURG.

to speak, he delivered the now famous Gettysburg address, the finest, strongest and one of the briefest orations ever made on this continent. From a literary point of view, this speech has come to be regarded as an American classic. Mr. Everett was a good and great man; his memory will be affectionately cherished; but his splendid sentences have already been forgotten, while Lincoln's few impressive words have already an imperishable place in the history and literature of the world. Here is the address:

"Fourscore and seven years ago our fathers brought forth on this continent a new nation, conceived in liberty, and dedicated to the proposition that all men are created equal.

GENERAL ULYSSES S. GRANT.

"Now we are engaged in a great civil war, testing whether that nation, or any nation so conceived and so dedicated, can long endure. We are met on a great battlefield of that war. We have come to dedicate a portion of that field as the final resting-place for those who here gave their lives that that nation might live. It is altogether fitting and proper that we should do this.

"But, in a larger sense, we cannot dedicate—we cannot consecrate—we cannot hallow—this ground. The brave men, living and dead, who struggled here have consecrated it, far above our poor power to add or detract. The world will little note, nor long remember, what we *say* here, but it can never forget what they *did* here. It is for us, the living, rather to be dedicated here to the unfinished work which they who fought here have thus far so nobly advanced. It is for us, rather, to be here dedicated to the great task remaining before us, that from these honored dead we take increased devotion to that cause for which they gave the last full measure of devotion, that we here highly resolve that these dead shall not have died in vain; that this nation, under God, shall have a new birth of freedom; and that government of the people, by the people, for the people, shall not perish from the earth."

On September 19th and 20th, the famous battle of Chickamauga was fought, in which General Thomas, commanding the center of Rosecran's army, firmly withstood and beat back the rebels under Bragg. General Garfield especially distinguished himself in this battle.

General Grant arrived at Louisville October 19th, and assumed the command of the military division of the Mississippi. Rosecrans was then relieved, and

LINCOLN AND TAD.

An interesting story is related of this picture. While in the White House, Mr. Lincoln made many sittings at the request of Mr. Brady, the historical photographer of Washington. Upon one occasion the president was accompanied by his favorite son, "Tad." Mr. Brady made an exposure, and went into the dark-room to change the plate. During the delay, Mr. Lincoln picked up an album of Brady's celebrated pictures and was showing them to Tad. When Mr. Brady came back, his artistic eye was impressed by the pose, and he induced them to remain just as they were while he took the picture. The above was told by Hon. Robert Lincoln, of Chicago, in January, 1896.

Thomas became commander of the Army of the Cumberland. Thomas retired to Chattanooga, after the battle of Chickamauga, where Grant joined him October 22d, and they determined to storm and carry the heights of Lookout mountain and Missionary ridge. On November 24th, Sherman's men gained possession of the north end of the last-named height. Thomas attacked the center and drove the enemy back to the hills. Hooker pushed around Lookout mountain, and drove the enemy up its western slope, capturing their rifle-pits.

The men recognized at once their great opportunity, and pressed the rebels with impetuous ardor until they reached the very summit, above the clouds and smoke, and spectators in the valley could get occasional glimpses of their battle-flags, waving in triumph. The next day Bragg was in full retreat. On the twenty-fifth the scene of Lookout mountain was repeated on the summit of Missionary ridge. Bragg withdrew then to Ringgold, Georgia.

Meanwhile the Confederate siege of Knoxville, in East Tennessee, was in progress, with Burnside in command of the Union forces. General Sherman finally marched to his relief; Longstreet raised the siege and marched into Virginia.

On September 6th, the forts in Charleston harbor were taken by the Union forces, and the city was now at their mercy. The situation had greatly changed since the

ANDREW JOHNSON.

Vice-president with Lincoln in the campaign of 1864, and successor in office. He was born in 1808, and died 1875.

rebels had fired their first shot at Sumter, in 1861. During the spring and summer of 1863 there was much fighting, as usual, in Virginia. Lee and Jackson made a furious attack on General Hooker, May 2d, at Chancellorsville, and Jackson was mortally wounded by a shot from his own ranks.

On March 3, 1863, it was found necessary by Congress to pass a conscription law, and two months afterward the president ordered a general draft for 300,000 men. All able-bodied men over twenty and under forty-five were liable to conscription. The anti-war people were very bitter, and did what they could do safely in the line of resisting the officers who had the management of the conscription. In some instances their indignation broke out in mob violence. An armed mob of large proportions burned a New York asylum for colored orphans, July 13th, attacked the police, and killed about a hundred people. An unsuccessful attempt was made to wreck the New York *Tribune* building. Governor Seymour made a mild speech, promising that the draft should be suspended, and advising the rioters to disperse. His promise was unauthorized and void of force, and Union troops came into the city, and soon put down the insurrection with a strong hand. But resistance to the draft broke out so violently elsewhere that August 19th, President Lincoln, in a proclamation, suspended the privilege of the writ of habeas corpus throughout the Union. Only about 50,000 men were drafted, but volunteering was greatly stimulated, and in October the president issued another call for 300,000 men. On June 20th, in this year, West Virginia became a state and was admitted to the Union.

CHAPTER XXVII.

THE Emancipation Proclamation was issued by Mr. Lincoln in the sincere belief that "it was an act of justice warranted by the Constitution, and upon military necessity." In its publication, he had invoked "the considerate judgment of mankind and the gracious favor of Almighty God." Slavery had been abolished at the Capitol, prohibited in the territories, and all negro soldiers in the Union army had been declared free. The fugitive-slave laws had been repealed, as had all laws which recognized or sanctioned slavery. The states not embraced in the proclamation had emancipated their slaves, so that slavery now existed only in the rebel states.

After all that had been done by Congress, by war and by the president, one thing alone remained to complete and make permanently effective these great anti-slavery measures. This was to introduce into the Constitution itself a provision to abolish slavery in the United States, and to prohibit its existence in any part thereof forever.

Senator Lyman Trumbull, February 10, 1864, reported from the judiciary committee the proposed amendment, in these words:

"Article XIII., Section 1.—Neither slavery nor involuntary servitude, except as a punishment for crime, whereof the party shall have been duly convicted, shall exist within the United States, or any place subject to their jurisdiction.

"Section 2.—Congress shall have power to enforce this article by appropriate legislation."

The resolution passed the Senate April 8th. The debate on the subject in the House began on January 6, 1865, and James A. Garfield, of Ohio, afterward president, took a prominent part in the discussion. On January 13th, the measure was passed by a vote of one hundred and nineteen ayes and fifty-six nays. When the speaker made the formal announcement, "The constitutional majority of two thirds having voted in the affirmative, the joint resolution is passed," it was received with great demonstrations of applause. It was an important fact that quite a number of Democrats voted for the measure.

The amendment to the Constitution was put to a vote of the states and was adopted.

There had been much opposition to the renomination of Lincoln for the presidency by prominent Republicans, some of them being aspirants for the honor. The Republican convention met at Baltimore, June 8, 1864. Rev. Robert J. Breckinridge, uncle of the rebel leader, John C. Breckinridge, was elected as temporary chairman, and, in a bold and fervid speech, commenced the business of the convention. He delared slavery to be "contrary to the spirit of Christian religion, and incompatible with the natural rights of man." Ex-Governor William Dennison, of Ohio, the first of the famous war governors, was

THE FEDERALS BOMBARDING FORT SUMTER.

made president. Singularly enough, in view of the opposition that had been manifested previous to the convention, Lincoln was unanimously renominated for the presidency, and Andrew Johnson, of Tennessee, was nominated for the vice-presidency.

The Democratic convention met at Chicago, August 29th, and nominated George B. McClellan for president, and George H. Pendleton, of Ohio, for vice-president. Vallandigham, having returned to Ohio from the rebel lines, attended this convention as a delegate, and was chairman of the committee on resolution. The second resolution declared that "after four years of trying to restore the Union by war, immediate efforts should. be made for the cessation of hostilities." The war for the maintenance of the Union was formally declared to be "a failure." To the credit of the candidate, General McClellan, he was not fully in accord with the platform upon which he had been placed.

The campaign was fought on this issue. The questions to be settled were: Should the war be prosecuted by the government to a successful conclusion, or should there be a cessation of hostilities and a compromise effected? The campaign was one of great interest and excitement. The friends of Mr. Lincoln had almost every advantage. The rebels were losing ground at nearly every point. The repeated assertions of the Democracy that the Union could not be restored by force of arms in the existing state of things had become ridiculous, and Lincoln was re-elected almost by acclamation, receiving every electoral vote except those of New Jersey, Delaware and Kentucky.

As soon as the result was known, General Grant telegraphed from City Point his congratulations, and added that "the election having passed off quietly . . . is a victory worth more to the country than a battle won." At a late hour on the evening of the election, Mr. Lincoln, in response to a serenade, said: " I am thankful to God for this approval of the people. But while deeply grateful for this mark of their confidence in me,

GEORGE B. McCLELLAN.

if I know my own heart, my gratitude is free from any taint of personal triumph. It is not in my nature to triumph over any one, but I give thanks to Almighty God for this evidence of the people's resolution to stand by free government and the rights of humanity." But it was a tremendous personal triumph for which any man might be properly grateful; it was a vindication by the people of the sterling worth and unfaltering courage of the president.

Lincoln was reinaugurated March 4, 1865, and in a clear but sometimes saddened voice, he pronounced his second but last inaugural, a most impressive address, the closing paragraph of which is as follows:

"With malice toward none, with charity for all, with firmness in the right as God gives us to see the right, let us finish the work we are in, to bind up the nation's wounds, to care for him who shall have borne the battle, and for his widow and his orphans, to do all which may achieve and cherish a just and lasting peace among ourselves and with all nations."

Mr. Lincoln, as the champion of the Union cause, had among his most zealous friends the loyal women of the North. Many books might be written about what these women did for the good of the soldiers in the field and in hospitals and for the Union cause. They contributed largely to the public opinion of the North. They organized themselves into aid societies, and gathered and prepared supplies for the hospitals and such articles of food as were adapted to the needs of sick and wounded soldiers. In many cities of the North there were headquarters where food supplies were prepared by women, and old men unfit for military duty, and forwarded to Union camps. The aggregate amount of good accomplished by these women can never be known. No doubt thousands of lives were saved through their humane and Christian efforts.

BENJAMIN F. BUTLER.

The sanitary commission of 1865 was one of the most wonderful and effective organizations of the time.

The loyal press of the country was also of immense and incalculable help to the president. There were sharp newspaper criticisms of the administration, but they were from men who were patriots and loyal to the Constitution and the Union. "On to Richmond," and "A more vigorous prosecution of the war," were phrases that were iterated and reiterated day after day. The editors at the desk co-operated with the commanders and the common soldiers in the field. In many communities there were disloyal utterances, and in Indiana especially the Knights of the Golden Circle proved to be conspirators against the Union and the flag. Under these circumstances the Union men at home—especially those in charge of newspapers—had a most difficult task, and accomplished a most noble work in fighting disunionists at home and in firing and encouraging loyal hearts.

The first military movements of 1864 began, as in 1863, in the West. William Tecumseh Sherman loomed up as a conspicuous military figure, and during the year proved to be one of the greatest generals of the time. In February, General Sherman left Vicksburg and advanced into Alabama; but meeting with a repulse, he returned to Vicksburg. General Banks commanded a successful expedition in the Red river country. The rebel General Forest captured Fort Pillow, on the Mississippi, and massacred a large number of negro soldiers. On May 7th, Sherman had one hundred thousand men in his command at Chattanooga, and began a series of movements which ended in his great march to the sea, and in the cutting of the very heart of the Confederacy in two. He burned Atlanta, November 14th, Columbia, South Carolina, was surrendered to him February 17th following, and soon thereafter Charleston itself was abandoned by the Confederates.

Kilpatrick, in a fight with Hampton, showed a conspicuous bravery and persistence, which gave him a brilliant victory. In August, Commodore Farragut sealed up the harbor of Mobile. Johnston was in the field, and there was vigorous fighting, with varied results, but the trend of events was in the line of Union success.

CHAPTER XXVIII

PRESIDENT LINCOLN placed Ulysses S. Grant in command of all the armies of the United States, March 2, 1864. The rank of lieutenant-general was revived by act of Congress, and conferred upon him. Seven hundred thousand Union soldiers were ready to move at his command. This greatest of generals had a plan for putting down the rebellion, and he proceeded to carry it out by striking and defeating the Confederates at all points; by pounding away at them day after day, and week after week, and month after month, until they were forced to surrender. General Sherman's movements, to which we have alluded, were at his suggestion, and under his direction. Grant was in Virginia, at a point on the James river, laying his plans to capture Richmond. After varying fortunes, Butler arrived at Bermuda Hundred, where Grant joined him. On June 17th and 18th, an ineffectual attempt was made to take Petersburg. Sigel, Hunter and Averill were operating in the Shenandoah valley. Early crossed the Potomac, but was driven back by General Lew Wallace. Afterward, however, Early again crossed the Potomac, invading Pennsylvania, burning Chambersburg, and returning to the valley laden with spoil.

An event of great military importance was the placing of General Philip H. Sheridan in command of the consolidated Union army on the Upper Potomac. Sheridan was the great cavalry officer of the Union army, fearless, daring, aggressive, and commanding victory by his great genius as well as by his tremendous courage and dash. He had 40,000 men at his disposal, and he used them with great effect. On October 19, 1864, Early surprised the Union camp near Winchester, and pursued the Union forces as far as Middletown. Sheridan, at Winchester, heard the sound of battle, and rode at breakneck speed a distance of twenty miles, met the flying Federal troops, rallied them with a word, turned upon the rebels, and gained one of the most glorious victories of the war. At the request of the great tragedian James E. Murdoch, who had interested and inspired the Union troops in many a camp by his patriotic recitations, Thomas Buchanan Read, poet and artist, commemorated this event in a' stirring poem, entitled "Sheridan's Ride." There were many men, unknown at the breaking out of the war, who gained honor and fame in the Virginia campaigns. To name them all would take up many a page of this book. Among them was

Joseph Warren Keifer, of Springfield, Ohio, afterward speaker of the national House of Representatives. He never lost a battle or made a military mistake. Then there were General Garfield, General J. D. Cox, and really a host of others, whose names are luminous and are dear to the hearts of all patriots.

During the summer of 1864, efforts to bring about peace were renewed. Horace Greeley, editor of the New York *Tribune*, and the most influential

PRESIDENT LINCOLN, ALLEN PINKERTON AND GENERAL McCLERNAND.

The central figure of this picture is the president; the one on the right, in uniform, is General McClernand, and the gentleman at the left is Allen Pinkerton, the distinguished detective. This photograph was taken at Antietam, on October 3, 1863, when President Lincoln visited the army in the field. It is from a negative taken by Brady and Gardner, for the government.

journalist of his time, wrote the president as follows: "I venture to remind you that our bleeding, bankrupt, almost dying country longs for peace, shudders at the prospect of fresh conscriptions, of further wholesale devastations, and of new rivers of human blood," etc.

Mr. Greeley asked the president to consent to negotiations looking toward the ending of the war. In response, the president announced his willingness to negotiate with commissions authorized by Jefferson Davis to negotiate. July 20, 1864, Greeley crossed into Canada to confer with refugee rebels at Niagara. He bore with him this paper from the president: "To whom it may concern:

Any proposition which embraces the restoration of peace, the integrity of the whole Union, and the abandonment of slavery, and which comes by and with an authority that can control the armies now at war with the United States, will be received and considered by the executive government of the United States, and will be met by liberal terms and other substantial and collateral points, and the bearer or bearers thereof shall have safe conduct both ways."

To this Jefferson Davis replied, "*We are not fighting for slavery: we are fighting for independence.*"

Mr. Lincoln and Mr. Seward met Alexander H. Stephens February 3, 1865, on the River Queen, at Fortress Monroe. Stephens was enveloped in overcoats and shawls, and had the appearance of a fair-sized man. He began

EDWIN M. STANTON.

to take off one wrapping after another, until the small, shriveled old man stood before them. Lincoln quietly said to Seward, "This is the largest shucking for so small a nubbin that I ever saw." R. M. T. Hunter was with Mr. Stephens.

Lincoln had a friendly conference, but presented his ultimatum—that the one and only condition of peace was that Confederates "must cease their resistance."

In the fall of 1864 and the winter of 1865, Grant was pressing in upon and around the center of the Confederacy, Petersburg and Richmond, and pounding away with ponderous blows. A mine was exploded under one of the Petersburg forts, July 30th, but with little influence in favor of the Federals.

SURRENDER OF GENERAL LEE TO GENERAL GRANT.

CHAPTER XXIX.

GRANT gained a substantial victory at Five Forks, April 1, 1865, capturing 6,000 men. This was one of a series of conflicts. On the second he made a general assault upon and captured Petersburg, and on the night of that day Lee and his army, and the members of the Confederate government, evacuated Petersburg. The rebel soldiers set the warehouses of their old capital on fire, and large portions of the city were consumed.

Grant took possession of Richmond April 3d. Lincoln immediately went to the front, going up in a man-of-war to the landing called Rocketts, about a mile below the city, accompanied by his young son, "Tad," and Admiral Porter, and went to the city in a boat. The sailors who accompanied him, armed with carbines, composed his only military guard. He walked up the streets toward General Weitzel's headquarters, in the house occupied but two days before by Jefferson Davis, who took French leave before the surrender. The news of his arrival spread as he walked, and from all sides the colored people came running together, with cries of intense exultation, to greet their deliverer. A writer in the *Atlantic Monthly* describes the scene as follows:

"They gathered around the president, ran ahead, hovered upon the flanks of the little company, and hung like a dark cloud upon the rear. Men, women and children joined the constantly increasing throng. They came from all the by-streets, running in breathless haste, shouting and hallooing, and dancing with delight. The men threw up their hats, the women waved their bonnets and handkerchiefs, clapped their hands. and sang, "Glory to God! glory, glory!" rendering all the praise to God, who had heard their wailings in the past, their moanings for wives, husbands, children and friends sold out of their sight, had given them freedom, and after long years of waiting, had permitted them thus unexpectedly to behold the face of their great benefactor.

"I thank you, dear Jesus, that I behold President Linkum!" was the exclamation of a woman who stood upon the threshold of her humble home, and with streaming eyes and clasped hands gave thanks aloud to the savior of men.

"Another, more demonstrative in her joy, was jumping and striking her hands with all her might, crying, "Bless de Lord! Bless de Lord! Bless de Lord!" as if there could be no end to her thanksgiving.

"The air rang with a tumultuous chorus of voices. The street became almost impassable on account of the increasing multitude, till soldiers were summoned to clear the way.

"The walk was long, and the president halted a moment to rest. 'May the good Lord bless you, President Linkum!' said an old negro, removing his hat and bowing, with tears of joy rolling down his cheeks. The president removed his own hat, and bowed in silence; but it was a bow which upset the forms, laws, customs and ceremonies of centuries. It was a death-shock to chivalry and a

HOUSE IN WHICH GENERAL LEE SURRENDERED TO GENERAL GRANT.

mortal wound to caste. Recognize a nigger! Faugh! A woman in an adjoining house beheld it, and turned from the scene in unspeakable disgust."

Lee was followed at once by our troops, and after a series of great battles—each forming an important chapter in the history of the war—was surrounded. He finally surrendered at Appomatox Court House, on April 9, 1865. Grant and Lee met in the parlor of William McLean's house, where, in a memorable inter-. view, the terms of surrender were agreed upon.

The spontaneous and universal rejoicings of the people of the country at this complete overthrow of the rebellion were such as had never been witnessed before on any continent. Men laughed, cried, shouted, and shook hands with each other; there were parades by day, and at night America was illuminated by discharges of fireworks, and thousands of flaming torch-light processions. The war was over. Peace stretched her white wings over our beloved land.

William T. Sherman's great march "from Atlanta to the sea" ended at Raleigh, April 13th, and here, thirteen days after his arrival, he received the surrender of General Joseph E. Johnston. Both Lee and Johnston were treated with consideration and magnanimity.

Jefferson Davis was captured at Irwinsville, Georgia, May 10th, by General Wilson's cavalry. He was conveyed to Fortress Monroe. He was taken to Richmond, tried on a charge of treason, released on bail, and finally dismissed.

Friday, April 14th, the anniversary of the surrender of Fort Sumter in 1861, was selected by the president as the day when General Robert Anderson should raise the American flag upon the same fort. Lincoln's humanity and magnanimity were never more conspicuously shown than at this period. There was no vengeance in his heart to be exploded upon the men who had arrayed themselves in armies against the government. The hate of the conspirators, however, had not passed away; there were rumors of plots in various parts of the country and Canada, and many warnings were sent to the president, who had forebodings of disaster.

Mr. Lincoln sent a message by Mr. Colfax, April 14th, to the miners in the Rocky mountains, and in the regions bounded by the Pacific ocean, in which he assayed to stimulate their operations, and said: "Now that the rebellion is overthrown, and we know pretty nearly the amount of our national debt, the more gold and silver we mine, we make the payment of that debt so much easier." "Now," said he, speaking with more emphasis, "I am going to encourage that in every possible way. We shall have hundreds of thousands of disbanded soldiers, and many have feared that their return home in such great numbers might paralyze industry by furnishing, suddenly, a greater supply of labor than there will be demand for. I am going to try to attract them to the hidden wealth of our mountain ranges, where there is room enough for all. Immigration, which even the war has not stopped, will land upon our shores hundreds of thousands more per year from overcrowded Europe. I intend to point them to the gold and silver that wait for them in the West. Tell the miners for me that I shall promote their interests to the utmost of my ability; because their prosperity is the prosperity of the nation; and," said he, his eye kindling with enthusiasm, "we shall prove, in a very few years, that we are indeed the treasury of the world." Here spoke the political economist, the philanthropist, the statesman and the prophet.

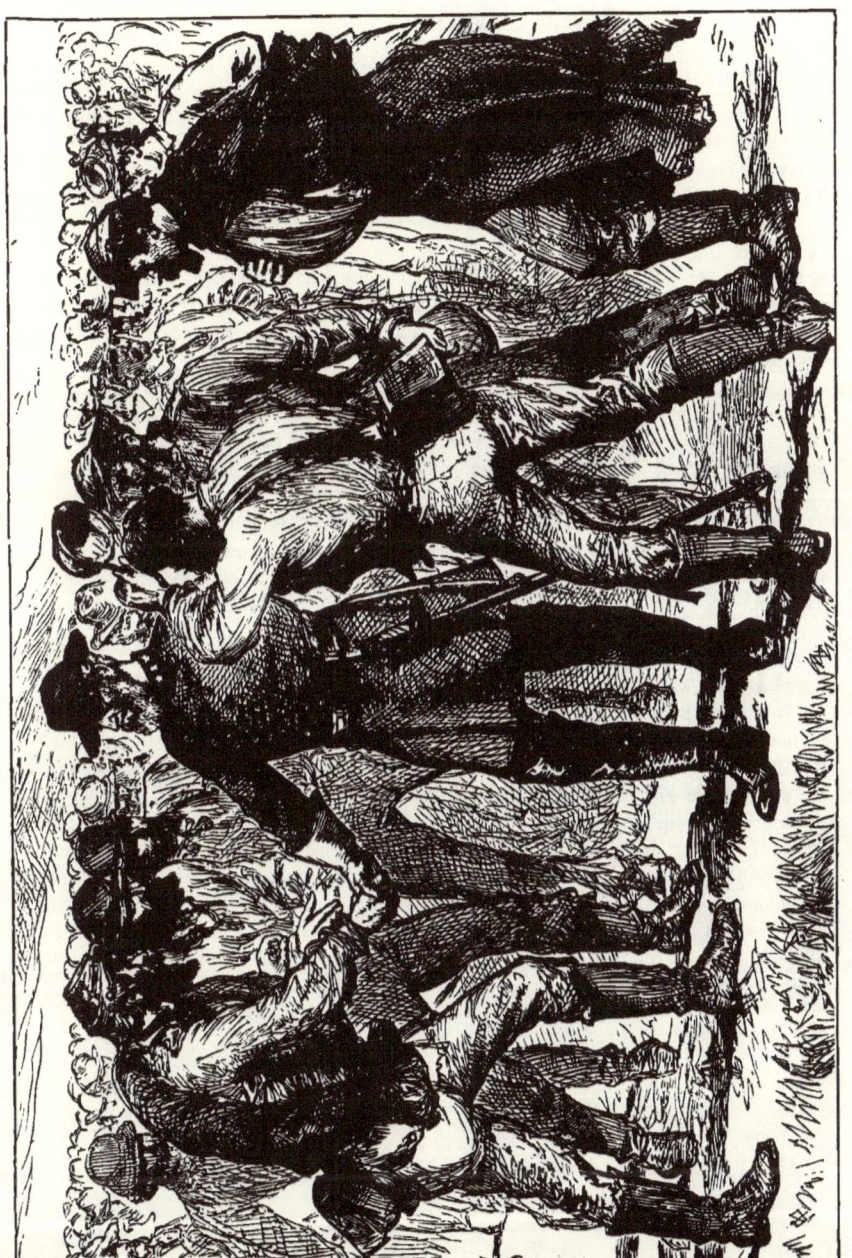

GENERAL LEE BIDDING FAREWELL TO HIS SOLDIERS.

CHAPTER XXX.

AT this time the friends of the Union cause were in transports of delight. Earnest, devout thanksgivings were on every tongue, flaring forth from every heart. Banners were in every breeze. Bonfires blazed on every street. Never were a people at such a height of exultation and rejoicing.

On the afternoon of April 14th, the president, with Mrs. Lincoln, drove about the city of Washington, and were received everywhere with affectionate greetings. At a meeting of the Cabinet that day, he had said, "I have no desire to kill or hang the Confederates." To his wife he said, "When these four years are over, Mary, we will go back to Illinois, and I will again be a country lawyer. God has been very good to us."

On the night of that same day he attended Ford's theater, and occupied a box. He was accompanied by Mrs. Lincoln, Major H. R. Rathbone and Miss Clara W. Harris. The play for that evening was the "American Cousin." The party was greeted with great applause from the people, who came to witness a comedy, but who saw the most terrible of tragedies.

The orchestra played "Hail to the Chief." The president was pleased, and acknowledged the courtesy. The curtain rose upon the second scene in the last act. Laura Keene, personating "Mrs. Montchessington," was saying to "Asa Trenchard:"

"You don't understand good society. That alone can excuse the impertinence of which you are guilty."

"I guess I know enough to turn you inside out," was the reply of Trenchard.

Just here there was the report of a pistol, and the laughter of the audience turned to demonstrations of alarm. At fifteen minutes after ten, John Wilkes Booth, an actor by profession, passed along the passage behind the spectators in the dress-circle, showed a card to the president's messenger, and stood for two or three minutes, looking down upon the stage and the orchestra below. He then entered the vestibule of the president's box, closed the door behind him, and fastened it by bracing a short plank against it from the wall, so that it could not be opened from the outside. He then drew a small silver-mounted Derringer pistol, which he carried in his right hand, holding a long, double-edged dagger in his left. All in the box were intent upon the proceedings upon the stage; but

189

President Lincoln was leaning forward, holding aside the curtain of the box with his left hand, and looking, with his head slightly turned toward the audience. Booth stepped within the inner door into the box, directly behind the president, and holding the pistol just over the back of the chair in which he sat, shot him through the back of the head. Mr. Lincoln bent slightly forward, with his eyes closed, but in every other respect his attitude remained unchanged.

Major Rathbone, turning his eyes from the stage, saw a man standing between him and the president. He instantly sprang toward him and seized him; but Booth wrested himself from his grasp, and dropping the pistol, struck at him with the dagger, inflicting a severe wound upon his left arm near the shoulder. Booth then rushed to the front of the box and shouted, "*Sic semper tyrannis!*" put his

hand upon the railing in front of the box, and leaped over it upon the stage below. As he went over, his spur caught in the flag which draped the front, and he fell; but recovering himself immediately, he rose, brandished the dagger, and facing the audience, shouted, "*The South is avenged!*"

The assassin escaped into Virginia, and found a temporary refuge among the rebel sympathizers of lower Maryland. He was afterward caught and shot to death by one of the soldiers that were sent in pursuit of him. An attempt was made to assassinate Mr. Seward, secretary of state, at the same time, but without success.

The private box in Ford's theater, Washington, where President Lincoln was assassinated by John Wilkes Booth, April 14, 1865.

The president was borne to a small house across the street, Mrs. Lincoln, dazed and wild with grief, following him. At a little past seven o'clock in the morning Abraham Lincoln died, with inexpressible peace upon his face. "Now he belongs to the ages," said Secretary Stanton.

From the most extravagant demonstrations of rejoicing and triumph, the people of the entire North, with many in the border states, and many in the territory of the late Confederacy, were plunged into grief, and almost into despair. Never was there such a transition from the most transporting joy to the profoundest sorrow as was experienced by the American people the next day, on the memorable fifteenth of April, 1865, when the news of the assassination of their beloved president was sent by telegraph and cable to all parts of the civilized world. The whole people were stricken with a sorrow that was too great for tears. People gathered in the streets of great cities and small villages, and were wringing their own hands, in their great brief, instead of joyously shaking hands with each other, as they had so recently done over great and final victories.

But one such scene had ever been known in history. That was when, nearly three hundred years before, in the sixteenth century, the fiendish assassin Balthazar Gerard, the proto-type of John Wilkes Booth, shot to death William the Silent, the father and re-deemer of the noble, liberty-loving people of Holland. On that occasion, says John Lothrop Motley, "the little children of Holland shed tears" over the strik-ing down of the liberator of the Dutch people. The Hol-landers were lovers of liberty; they had passed through a cruel and prolonged crisis, and suffered beyond the pow-er of pen to describe, but at last the power of the despot was broken, and Holland and the Dutch people enjoyed freedom of person and of religious belief. The grief of the American people over the smiting down of the great liberator of the nine-teenth century was like that of the Hollanders, only on an immensely larger scale.

HOUSE IN WHICH PRESIDENT LINCOLN DIED.

The feeling of the people of the United States at this time, broken-hearted as they were at the loss of their president, was, possibly, more intense than the feelings of the Hollanders. Abraham Lincoln, and the people who so loved him, had not striven and suffered in behalf of their own freedom, but of the freedom of an enslaved and despised race. If ever there was a cause that was approved in heaven; if ever a cause that received the active interposition of Divine Providence, it was the cause of national unity and human freedom, which was now triumphant.

What pen can paint the portrait of Abraham Lincoln? A great poet said:

> Some angel guide my pencil while I draw
> The picture of a good man.

No angel could give us a portrait of Abraham Lincoln. None but a saint in heaven of the highest rank; one who had suffered here on earth in the cause of his Master, and had trodden the thorny path and highway of tears, could appreciate the true character, and the self-sacrificing and exalted career of the martyred president.

THE CAPTURE OF BOOTH.

Mr. Lincoln was, as we said in the beginning of this book, of all others a man of the people. His tender but strong heart was always full of sympathy for each and all. All classes, from the richest to the poorest of the poor,

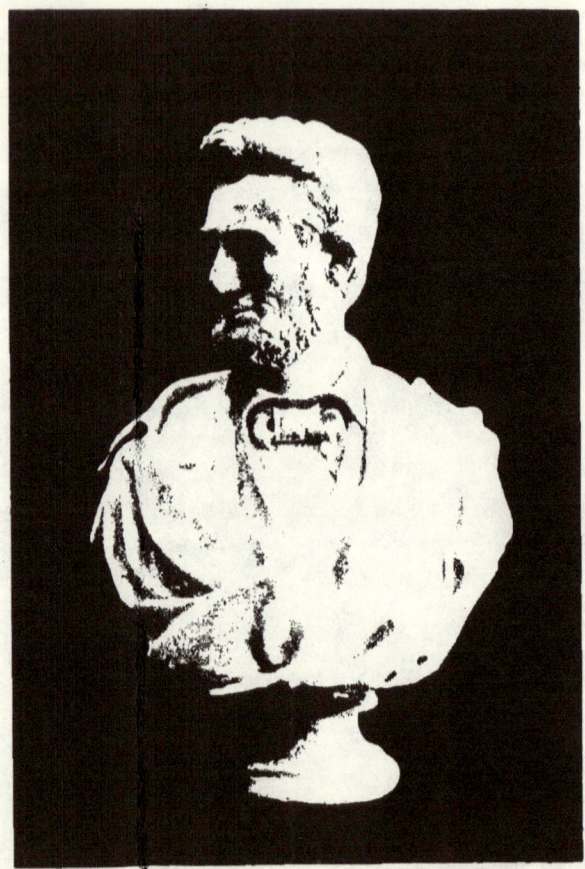

BUST OF THE MARTYRED PRESIDENT.

received his courteous attention, and in occasions of sorrow, his most sympathetic feeling and efficient help. It is not strange that in very many instances his pity overcame his prudence, but in no instance was it to anybody's real injury.

7

Not only were the skies thick with the smoke of battle, but schemes to thwart his great purpose, and plots to destroy his best efforts, had constantly to be contended against. Men of patriotism and purity of purpose; men who estimated him and loved him, and whose services were of great value, mercilessly criticized

LINCOLN MONUMENT, AT SPRINGFIELD, ILLINOIS.
"Here sleeps the apostle of human liberty."

his course; loyal but impatient patriots hounded him on to public acts against his better judgment, but his patience was God-like; he had a purpose clearly formed; he seemed to see long in advance the very strokes that would break the rebellion and restore peace to the country.

There was one Counselor who never failed him, and to whom he often went for comfort and wisdom. He promised the Almighty that if he would give him a victory he would publicly issue his proclamation, and give freedom to the slaves. To this we may well believe the response was given, and immediately the pledge was fulfilled.

No man was ever more viciously abused by apparent friends, or by secret or open foes. The "father of his country" was assailed with venomous attacks repeatedly during his beneficent career. The best men the world has ever known have been those who have suffered the meanest and most venomous attacks.

Mr. Lincoln replied to few or none of these. He was so faithful and constant in the discharge of his supremely important duties that he felt it would be a waste of time to attempt to undertake his own vindication. He well knew that history would do him justice. Now, at last, an appreciation of his greatness and his goodness and of the inestimable service he had rendered his country and its people was universally felt to the bottom of the common people. The passage of his mortal remains from Washington through various cities to Springfield, Illinois, has gone into the history of the country. Again the fountains of the great depths of sorrow were opened. Everywhere along the route the funeral train was met by crowds of people with demonstrations of deepest mourning. Now monuments stand in various cities of the Union to the memory of Abraham Lincoln, the emancipator, and many streets and avenues are named in his honor. One noble monument stands at Chicago, where Mr. Lincoln was first nominated for the presidency, and another stands at his old home, in Springfield, Illinois.

CHAPTER XXXI.

IT is thirty years since the close of the war. We are at last a united people. The term "rebel" has passed away, and is only used in honest, records of the past, and without malice. Our American nation has for its individual constituents a united, patriotic and loyal people. No men when they meet greet each other's faces or shake each other's hands with more heartiness and deeper feelings of good will than the gray-headed soldiers of the Union and of the Confederate armies. Men of both armies meet under the "stars and stripes" at the graves of the dead on Memorial day. There are no more graceful or hearty' tributes to the high·character and the great work of Abraham Lincoln than appear in the utterances on the platform of a former Confederate general, John B. Gordon, of Georgia, and the former editor of the *Chattanooga Rebel*, Henry Watterson. There is now no North, no South. Near the battle-fields of the late civil war iron furnaces and cotton factories have been erected by men from New England, Ohio and other northern states, and the hum of new industries fills the ambient air of a new and redeemed South.

Mason and Dixon's line has been efficiently and forever abolished. There are Democratic governors in northern states; there are Republican governors in southern states; and whenever people of the different sections of the country meet, there are demonstrations of unity, patriotism, brotherly affection and peace.

Abraham Lincoln was the greatest man of his time. He had his faults and defects, but who cares to dwell on them? What were the elements of his greatness? He could see farther into the pregnant future than any man of his day. He had the largest heart and the broadest sympathies of any man known at the time when he lived. His patience and forbearance were Christ-like. He had a wonderfully keen intellect, instant in its workings, and seemingly incapable of mistakes. He was a great statesman. In the emancipation of the slaves was involved the problem of ages. He was urged by strong and great men to issue the Emancipation Proclamation long. before he did. He was urged by equally strong and great men to delay its issue. He therefore stood alone, and was forced to act for himself, and results show that he acted not a day too soon nor a day too late. He had a keen and comprehensive military mind. He had been a student of the military records of the past. He gave his greatest generals pre-eminently practical and effective suggestions. He was the greatest orator of his age, if great oratory means the utterance of great thoughts and announcement of great principles, in a manner that most moves and changes men, and that secures for them a permanent place in the annals of a nation, and of the world. The greatness of the theme paralyzes the pen. All patriots and all friends of their race, in all countries and climes, uncover their heads as they recall the memory of ABRAHAM LINCOLN!

THOUGHTS AND SAYINGS

OF

ABRAHAM LINCOLN.

THOUGHTS AND SAYINGS

OF

ABRAHAM LINCOLN.

THE VALUE OF EDUCATION.

(Address at New Salem, Illinois, March 9, 1835, when a candidate for the Legislature.)

Upon the subject of education, not presuming to dictate any plan or system respecting it, I can only say that I view it as the most important subject which we, as a people, can be engaged in.

That every man may receive at least a moderate education, and thereby be enabled to read the histories of his own and other countries, by which he may duly appreciate the value of our free institutions, appears to be an object of vital importance; even on this account alone, to say nothing of the advantages and satisfaction to be derived from all being able to read the Scriptures and other works, both of a religious and moral nature, for themselves.

For my part, I desire to see the time when education, by its means, morality, sobriety, enterprise and integrity, shall become much more general than at present, and should be gratified to have it in my power to contribute something to the advancement of any measure which might have a tendency to accelerate the happy period.

Every man is said to have his peculiar ambition. Whether it be true or not, I can say, for one, that I have no other so great as that of being truly esteemed of my fellow-men. How far I shall succeed in gratifying this ambition is yet to be developed. I am young, and unknown to many of you. I was born, and have ever remained, in the most humble walks of life. I have no wealthy popular relations or friends to recommend me. My case is thrown exclusively upon the independent voters of the county; and, if elected, they will have conferred a favor upon me for which I shall be unremitting in my labors to compensate.

But if the good people in their wisdom shall see fit to keep me in the background, I have been too familiar with disappointment to be very much chagrined.

SPEECH ON THE DRED SCOTT DECISION.

(Delivered at Springfield, Illinois, June 26, 1857.)

The chief-justice does not directly assert, but plainly assumes as a fact, that the public estimate of the black man is more favorable now than it was in the days of the Revolution.

In those days, by common consent, the spread of the black man's bondage to the new countries was prohibited; but now Congress decides that it will not continue the prohibition, and the Supreme Court decides that it could not if it would.

In those days, our Declaration of Independence was held sacred by all, and thought to include all; but now, to aid in making the bondage of the negro universal and eternal, it is assailed and sneered at, and constructed and hawked at, and torn, till, if its framers could rise from their graves, they could not at all recognize it.

All the powers of earth seem rapidly combining against him; Mammon is after him, ambition follows, philosophy follows, and the theology of the day is fast joining the cry.

THE TEMPERANCE CAUSE.

(Address before the Washingtonian Temperance Society, Springfield, Illinois, February 22, 1842.)

The cause itself seems suddenly transformed from a cold abstract theory to a living, breathing, active and powerful chieftain going forth "conquering and to conquer." The citadels of his great adversary are daily being stormed and dismantled; his temples and altars, where the rites of his idolatrous worship have long been performed, and where human sacrifices have long been wont to be made, are daily desecrated and deserted.

The trump of the conqueror's fame is sounding from hill to hill, from sea to sea, and from land to land, and calling millions to his standard at a blast.

When one who has long been known as a victim of intemperance bursts the fetters that have bound him, and appears before his neighbors "clothed in his right mind," a redeemed specimen of long-lost humanity, and stands up with tears of joy trembling in his eyes, to tell of the miseries once endured, now to be endured no more forever; of his once naked and starving children, now clad and fed comfortably; of a wife, long weighed down with woe, weeping, and a broken heart, now restored to health, happiness and a renewed affection; and how easily it is all done, once it is resolved to be done—how simple his language! There is a logic and eloquence in it that few with human feelings can resist.

It is an old and true maxim that "a drop of honey catches more flies than a gallon of gall." So with men. If you would win a man to your cause, first convince him that you are, his sincere friend. Therein is a drop of honey that catches his heart; which, say what he will, is the great highroad to his reason, and when once gained, you will find but little trouble in convincing his judgment of the justice of your cause, if, indeed, that cause really be a just one. On the contrary, assume to dictate to his judgment, or to command his action, or to mark him as one to be shunned and despised, and he will retreat within himself, close all the avenues to his head and his heart, and though your cause be naked truth itself, transformed to the heaviest lance, harder than steel, and sharper than steel can be made, and though you throw it with more than hurculean force and precision, you shall be no more able to pierce him than to penetrate the hard shell of a tortoise with a rye straw.

Of our political revolution of '76 we are all justly proud. It has given us a degree of political freedom far exceeding that of any other nation of the earth. But with all these glorious results, past, present and to come, it had its evils, too. It breathed forth famine, swam in blood, and rode in fire; and long, long after, the orphans' cry and the widows' wail continued to break the sad silence that ensued. These are the price, the inevitable price, paid for the blessings it brought.

Turn now to the temperance resolution. In it we shall find a stronger bondage broken, a viler slavery manumitted, a greater tyrant deposed—in it more of want supplied, more disease healed, more sorrow assuaged. By it, no orphans starving, no widows weeping. By it, none wounded in feeling, none injured in interest; even the dram-maker and dram-seller will have glided into other occupations so gradually as never to have felt the change, and will stand ready to join all others in the universal song of gladness.

And what a noble ally this, to the cause of political freedom; with such an aid, its march cannot fail to be on and on, till every son of earth shall drink in rich fruition the sorrow-quenching draughts of perfect liberty!

Happy day when, all appetite controlled, all passions subdued, all matter subjugated, mind—all-conquering mind—shall live and move, the monarch of the world! Glorious consummation! Hail, fall of fury! Reign of reason, all hail!

And when the victory shall be complete—when there shall be neither a slave nor a drunkard on earth—how proud the title of that land which may truly claim to be the birthplace and cradle of both those resolutions that shall have ended in that victory! How nobly distinguished that people who shall have planted, and nurtured to maturity, both the political and moral freedom of their species!

This is the one hundred and tenth anniversary of the birthday of Washington—we are met to celebrate this day.

Washington is the mightiest name on earth—long since the mightiest in the cause of civil liberty, still mightiest in moral reformation.

On that name a eulogy is expected. It cannot be. To add brightness to the sun or glory to the name of Washington is alike impossible. Let none attempt it.

In solemn awe pronounce the name, and, in its naked, deathless splendor, leave it shining on.

HOPELESS PEACEFUL EMANCIPATION OF THE SLAVE.

(Letter to Hon. George Robertson, Lexington, Kentucky, August 15, 1855.)

So far as peaceful voluntary emancipation is concerned, the condition of the negro slave in America, scarcely less terrible to the contemplation of a free mind, is now as fixed and hopeless of change for the better as that of the lost souls of the finally impenitent.

The autocrat of all the Russias will resign his crown, and proclaim his subjects free republicans, sooner than will our American masters voluntarily give up their slaves.

Our political problem now is, Can we as a nation continue together permanently, forever, half slave and half free? The problem is too mighty for me. May God in his mercy superintend the solution!

"I SWEAR ETERNAL FIDELITY TO THE JUST CAUSE."

(Speech at Springfield, Illinois, during the Harrison presidential campaign, 1840.)

Many free countries have lost their liberty, and ours may lose hers; but if she shall, be it my proudest plume, not that I was last to desert, but that I never deserted her.

I know that the great volcano at Washington, aroused and directed by the evil spirit that reigns there, is belching forth the lava of political corruption in a current broad and deep, which is sweeping with frightful velocity over the whole length and breadth of the land, bidding fair to leave unscathed no green spot or living thing.

I cannot deny that all may be swept away. Broken by it, I, too, may be; bow to it I never will. The possibility that we may fail in the struggle ought not to deter us from the support of a cause which we believe to be just. It shall not deter me.

If ever I feel the soul within me elevate and expand to those dimensions not wholly unworthy of its Almighty Architect, it is when I contemplate the cause of my country, deserted by all the world beside, and I standing up boldly alone, and hurling defiance at her victorious oppressors.

Here, without contemplating consequences, before heaven, and in the face of the world, *I swear eternal fidelity to the just cause*, as I deem it, of the land of my life, my liberty, and my love; and who that thinks with me will not fearlessly adopt the oath that I take?

Let none falter who thinks he is right, and we may succeed.

But if, after all, we shall fail, be it so; we have the proud consolation of saying to our consciences, and to the departed shade of our country's freedom, that the cause approved of our judgment, and, adorned of our hearts in disaster, in chains, in death, we never faltered in defending.

REVIEW OF THE UNION ARMIES AT WASHINGTON.

REDEMPTION OF THE AFRICAN RACE.

(Eulogy on the life and character of Henry Clay, Springfield, Illinois, July 16, 1852.)

This suggestion of the possible ultimate redemption of the African race and African continent was made twenty-five years ago. Every succeeding year has added strength to the hope of its realization. May it indeed be realized! Pharaoh's country was cursed with plagues, and his hosts drowned in the Red sea for striving to retain a captive people who had already served them more than four hundred years. May like disaster never befall us!

If, as the friends of colonization hope, the present and coming generations of our countrymen shall, by any means, succeed in freeing our land from the dangerous presence of slavery, and at the same time restoring a captive people to their long-lost fatherland, with bright prospects for the future, and this, too, so gradually that neither races nor individuals shall have suffered by the change, it will, indeed, be a glorious consummation.

And if to such a consummation the efforts of Mr. Clay shall have contributed, it will be what he most ardently wished; and none of his labors will have been more valuable to his country and his kind.

THE INJUSTICE OF SLAVERY.

(Speech at Peoria, Illinois, October 16, 1854.)

This declared indifference, but, as I must think, covert zeal, for the spread of slavery I cannot but hate. I hate it because of the monstrous injustice of slavery itself ; I hate it because it deprives our republic of an example of its just influence in the world; enables the enemies of free institutions with plausibility to taunt us as hypocrites; causes the real friends of freedom to doubt our sincerity; and especially because it forces so many really good men among ourselves into an open war with the very fundamental principles of civil liberty, criticizing the Declaration of Independence and insisting that there is no right principle of action but self-interest.

The doctrine of self-government is right—absolutely and eternally right—but it has no just application, as here attempted. Or, perhaps, I should rather say that whether it has such just application depends upon whether a negro is not, or is, a man. If he is not a man, in that case he who is a man may, as a matter of self-government, do just what he pleases with him. But if the negro is a man, is it not to that extent a total destruction of self-government to say that he, too, shall not govern himself ?

When the white man governs himself, that is self-government; but when he governs himself, and also governs another man, that is more than self-government—that is despotism.

What I do say is that no man is good enough to govern another man without that other's consent.

The master not only governs the slave without his consent, but he governs him by a set of rules altogether different from those which he prescribes for himself. Allow all the governed an equal voice in the government; that, and that only, is self-government.

Slavery is founded in the selfishness of man's nature—opposition to it, in his love of justice. These principles are an eternal antagonism; and when brought into collision so fiercely as slavery extension brings them, shocks and throes and convulsions must ceaselessly follow.

Repeal the Missouri Compromise—repeal all compromise—and repeal the Declaration of Independence—repeal all past history—still you cannot repeal human nature.

I particularly object to the new position which the avowed principles of the Nebraska law gives to slavery in the body politic. I object to it because it assumes that there can be moral right in the enslaving of one man by another. I object to it as a dangerous dalliance for a free people—a sad evidence that, feeling prosperity, we forget right—that liberty as a principle we have ceased to revere.

Little by little, but steadily as man's march to the grave, we have been giving up the old for the new faith. Near eighty years ago we began by declaring that all men are created equal; but now from that beginning we have run down to the other declaration that for some men to enslave others is a "sacred right of self-government." These principles cannot stand together. They are as opposite as God and Mammon.

Our republican robe is soiled and trailed in the dust. Let us purify it. Let us turn and wash it white, in the spirit, if not in the blood, of the Revolution. Let us turn slavery from its claims of "moral right" back upon its existing legal rights, and its arguments of "necessity." Let us return it to the position our fathers gave it, and there let it rest in peace.

Let us readopt the Declaration of Independence, and the practices and policy which harmonize with it. Let North and South—let all Americans—let all lovers of liberty everywhere, join in the great and good work.

If we do this, we shall not only have saved the Union, but shall have so saved it as to make and to keep it forever worthy of saving. We shall have so saved it that the succeeding millions of free, happy people, the world over, shall rise up and call us blessed to the latest generations.

"THOSE WHO DENY FREEDOM TO OTHERS."

(Letter to the Republicans of Boston, April, 1859.)

This is a world of compensation, and he who would *be* no slave, must consent to *have* no slave. Those who deny freedom to others deserve it not for themselves, and under a just God cannot long retain it.

"ALL MEN ARE CREATED EQUAL."

(Speech at the Republican banquet, Chicago, Illinois, December 10, 1856, after the presidential campaign.)

Our government rests in public opinion. Whoever can change public opinion can change the government practically just so much. Public opinion, on any subject, always has a "central idea," from which all its minor thoughts radiate. That "central idea" in our political public opinion at the beginning was, and until recently has continued to be, "the equality of man." And although it has always submitted patiently to whatever of inequality there seemed to be as a matter of actual necessity, its constant working has been a steady progress toward the practical equality of all men.

Let everyone who really believes, and is resolved, that free society is not and shall not be a failure, and who can conscientiously declare that in the past contest he has done only what he thought best—let every such one have charity to believe that every other one can say as much.

Thus, let bygones be bygones; let party differences as nothing be, and with steady eye on the real issue, let us reinaugurate the good old "central ideas" of the republic. We can do it. The human heart is with us; God is with us. We shall again be able not to declare that "all states as states are equal," nor yet that "all citizens as citizens are equal," but to renew the broader, better declaration, including both these and much more, that "all men are created equal."

"THE ONE RETROGRADE INSTITUTION IN AMERICA."

(Reply to Stephen A. Douglas, on the Kansas-Nebraska Bill, Springfield, Illinois, October 4, 1854.)

Be not deceived. The spirit of the Revolution and the spirit of Nebraska are antipodes; and the former is being rapidly displaced by the latter. Shall we make no effort to arrest this? Already the liberal party throughout the world expresses the apprehension "that the one retrograde institution in America is undermining the principles of progress, and fatally violating the noblest political system the world ever saw." This is not the taunt of enemies, but the warning of friends. Is it quite safe to disregard it, to disparage it? Is there no danger to liberty itself in discarding the earliest practice and first precept of our ancient faith?

In our greedy haste to make profit of the negro, let us beware lest we cancel and rend in pieces even the white man's character of freedom.

My distinguished friend Douglas says it is an insult to the emigrant to Kansas and Nebraska to suppose they are not able to govern themselves. We must not slur over an argument of this kind because it happens to tickle the ear. It must be met and answered.

I admit the emigrant to Kansas and Nebraska is competent to govern himself, but *I deny his right to govern any other person without that person's consent.*

"A HOUSE DIVIDED AGAINST ITSELF CANNOT STAND."

(The following speech, afterward severely criticized by many of the author's own friends, was delivered by Mr. Lincoln at Springfield, Illinois, June 17, 1858, at the close of the Republican state convention which nominated him for the United States Senate.)

If we could first know where we are, and whither we are tending, we could better judge what to do and how to do it. We are now far into the fifth year since a policy was initiated with the avowed object and confident promise of putting an end to slavery agitation. Under the operation of that policy that agitation has not only not ceased, but has constantly augmented.

In my opinion, it will not cease until a crisis shall have been reached and passed.

"A house divided against itself cannot stand." I believe this government cannot endure permanently half slave and half free. I do not expect the Union to be dissolved; I do not expect the house to fall; but I do expect it will cease to be divided. It will become all one thing or all the other.

Either the opponents of slavery will arrest the further spread of it, and place it where the public mind shall rest in the belief that it is in the course of ultimate extinction, or its advocates will push it forward, till it shall become alike lawful in all the states—old as well as new, North as well as South.

Our cause, then, must be intrusted to and conducted by its own undoubted friends—those whose hands are free, whose hearts are in the work—who *do care* for the result.

The result is not doubtful. We shall not fail—if we stand firm, we *shall not fail*. Wise counsels may accelerate, or mistakes delay it, but sooner or later the victory is sure to come.

"THIS NATION CANNOT LIVE ON INJUSTICE."

(Remarks defending his speech, June 17, 1858, "A House Divided Against Itself," etc.)

Friends, I have thought about this matter a great deal, have weighed the question well from all corners, and am thoroughly convinced the time has come when it should be uttered; and if it must be that I must go down because of this speech, then let me go down *linked to truth*—die in the advocacy of what is *right* and *just*.

This nation cannot live on injustice. "A house divided against itself cannot stand," I say again and again.

"WISEST THING I EVER DID."

(Reply to friends at Bloomington, Illinois, in regard to the "House Divided" speech.)

You may think that speech was a mistake; but I have never believed it was, and you will see the day when you will consider it the wisest thing I ever did.

THE WHITE HOUSE, APRIL 14, 1865.

LINCOLN'S OLD HOME, SPRINGFIELD, ILLINOIS, MAY 16, 1865.

THE LINCOLN AND DOUGLAS JOINT DEBATE.

(First joint debate, Ottawa, Illinois, August 21, 1858.)

I have no purpose, directly or indirectly, to interfere with the institution of slavery in the state where it exists. I believe I have no lawful right to do so, and I have no inclination to do so. I agree with Judge Douglas: he [the negro] is not my equal in many respects—certainly not in color; perhaps not in moral or intellectual endowment. But in the right to eat the bread—without the leave of anybody else—which his own hand earns, *he is my equal, and the equal of Judge Douglas, and the equal of every living man.*

I think, and shall try to show, that it is wrong, wrong in its direct effect, letting slavery into Kansas and Nebraska—and wrong in its prospective principle; allowing it to spread to every other part of the wide world, where men can be found inclined to take it.

I have no prejudice against the southern people. They are just what we would be in their situation. If slavery did not now exist among them, they would not introduce it. If it did now exist among us, we should not instantly give it up. This I believe of the masses North and South. Doubtless there are individuals on both sides who would not hold slaves under any circumstances, and others who would gladly introduce slavery anew, if it were out of existence.

When southern people tell us they are no more responsible for the origin of slavery than we, I acknowledge the fact. When it is said that the institution exists, and that it is very difficult to get rid of it in any satisfactory way, I can understand and appreciate the saying. I surely will not blame them for not doing what I should not know how to do myself. If all earthly power were given me, I should not know what to do as to the existing institution.

With public sentiment, nothing can fail; without it, nothing can succeed. Consequently, he who molds public sentiment goes deeper than he who enacts statutes or pronounces decisions. He makes statutes and decisions possible or impossible to be executed.

(Second joint debate, Freeport, Illinois, August 27, 1858.)

Answers to the seven questions propounded by Mr. Douglas:

I do not now, nor ever did, stand in favor of the unconditional repeal of the Fugitive Slave Law.

I do not now, nor ever did, stand pledged against the admission of any more slave states into the Union.

I do not stand pledged against the admission of a new state into the Union, with such a constitution as the people of that state may see fit to make.

I do not stand to-day pledged to the abolition of slavery in the District of Columbia.

I do not stand pledged to the prohibition of the slave trade between the different states.

I am impliedly, if not expressly, pledged to a belief in the *right* and *duty* of Congress to prohibit slavery in all the United States territories.

I am not generally opposed to honest acquisition of territory; and, in any given case, I would or would not oppose such acquisition, accordingly as I might think such acquisition would or would not aggravate the slavery question among ourselves.

(Third joint debate, Jonesboro, Illinois, September 15, 1858.)

I say, in the way our fathers originally left the slavery question, the institution was in the course of ultimate extinction, and the public mind rested in the belief that it *was* in the course of ultimate extinction. I say, when this government was first established, it was the policy of its founders to prohibit the spread of slavery into the new territories of the United States, where it had not existed.

All I have asked or desired anywhere is that it should be placed back again upon the basis that the fathers of our government originally placed it. I have no doubt that it *would* become extinct for all time to come, if we but readopt the policy of the fathers by restricting it to the limits it has already covered —restricting it from the new territories.

(Fourth joint debate, Charleston, Illinois, September 18, 1858.)

I have always wanted to deal with everyone I meet candidly and honestly. If I have made any assertion not warranted by facts, and it is pointed out to me, I will withdraw it cheerfully..

The Kansas-Nebraska Bill was introduced four years and a half ago, and if the agitation is ever to come to an end, we may say we are four years and a half nearer the end. So, too, we can say we are four years and a half nearer the end of the world; and we can just as clearly see the end of the world as we can see the end of this agitation.

If Kansas should sink to-day, and leave a great vacant space in the earth's surface, this vexed question would still be among us. I say, then, there is no way of putting an end to the slavery agitation amongst us but to put it back upon the basis where our fathers placed it, no way but to keep it out of our new territories—to restrict it forever to the old states where it now exists. Then the public mind *will* rest in the belief that it is in the course of ultimate extinction.

(Fifth joint debate, Galesburg, Illinois, October 7, 1858.)

And now it only remains for me to say that I think it is a very grave question for the people of this Union to consider whether, in view of the fact that this slavery question has been the only one that has ever endangered our republican institutions—the only one that has ever threatened or menaced a dissolution of the Union, that has ever disturbed us in such a way as to make us fear for the perpetuity of our liberty—in view of these facts, I think it is an exceedingly interesting and important question for this people to consider—whether we shall engage in the policy of acquiring additional territory, discarding altogether from our consideration while obtaining new territory the question how it may affect us in regard to this, the only endangering element to our liberties and national greatness.

(Sixth joint debate, Quincy, Illinois, October 13, 1858.)

We have in this nation this element of domestic slavery. It is the opinion of all the great men who have expressed an opinion upon it that it is a dangerous element. We keep up a controversy in regard to it. That controversy necessarily springs from differences of opinion, and if we can learn exactly—can reduce to the lowest elements—what that difference of opinion is, we perhaps shall be better prepared for discussing the different systems of policy that we would propose in regard to that disturbing element.

I suggest that the difference of opinion, reduced to its lowest terms, is no other than the difference between the men who think slavery a wrong and those who do not think it wrong. We think it is a wrong, not confining itself merely to the persons or to the states where it exists, but that it is a wrong in its tendency, to say the least, that extends itself to the existence of the whole nation.

Because we think it wrong, we propose a course of policy that shall deal with it as a wrong. We deal with it as with any other wrong, in so far as we can prevent its growing any larger, and so deal with it that, in the run of time, there may be some promise of an end to it.

(Seventh and last joint debate, Alton, Illinois, October 15, 1858.)

It may be argued that there are certain conditions that make necessities and impose them upon us, and to the extent that if a necessity is imposed upon a man he must submit to it. I think that was the condition in which we found ourselves when we established this government.

We had slaves among us; we could not get our Constitution unless we permitted them to remain in slavery; we could not secure the good we did secure if we grasped for more; and having by necessity submitted to that much, it does not destroy the principle that is the charter of our liberties. Let the charter remain as a standard.

I think the authors of that notable instrument intended to include *all* men, but they did not mean to declare all men equal *in all respects*.

They defined with tolerable distinctness in what they did consider all men created equal; equal in certain inalienable rights, among which are life, liberty, and the pursuit of happiness. This they said, and this they meant. They did not mean to assert the obvious untruth that all men were then actually enjoying that quality, or yet that they were about to confer it immediately upon them. In fact, they had no power to confer such a boon. They meant simply to declare the *right*, so that the enforcement of it might follow as fast as circumstances should permit.

They meant to set up a standard-maxim for free society, which should be familiar to all, constantly looked to, constantly labored for, and even though never perfectly attained, constantly approximated, and thereby constantly spreading and deepening its influence and augmenting the happiness and value of life to all people, of all colors, everywhere.

There, again, are the sentiments I have expressed in regard to the Declaration of Independence upon a former occasion—sentiments which have been put in print and read wherever anybody cared to know what so humble an individual as myself chose to say in regard to it.

MESSAGE TO HIS DYING FATHER.

(Letter to his brother-in-law, John Johnston, January 12, 1851.)

I sincerely hope father may yet recover his health; but, at all events, tell him to remember to call upon and confide in our great and good and merciful Maker, who will not turn away from him in any extremity. He notes the fall of a sparrow, and numbers the hairs of our heads; and he will not forget the dying man who puts his trust in him.

Say to him, if we could meet now it is doubtful whether it would not be more painful than pleasant; but that, if it be his lot to go now, he will soon have a joyous meeting with the loved ones gone before, and where the rest of us, through the help of God, hope ere long to join them.

DISADVANTAGES THE REPUBLICANS LABOR UNDER.

(Speech at Springfield, Illinois, July 17, 1858.)

Senator Douglas is of world-wide renown. All the anxious politicians of his party, or who have been of his party for years past, have been looking upon him as a certainty, at no distant day, to be the president of the United States. They have seen, in his round, jolly, fruitful face, post-offices, land-offices, marshalships and cabinet appointments, chargeships and foreign missions, bursting and sprouting out in wonderful exuberance, ready to be laid hold of by their greedy hands.

On the contrary, nobody has ever expected me to be president. In my poor, lean, lank face nobody has ever seen that any cabbages were sprouting out. These are disadvantages, all taken together, that the Republicans labor under. *We* have to fight this battle upon principle, and upon principle alone.

I am, in a certain sense, made the standard-bearer in behalf of the Republicans. I was made so merely because there had to be some one so placed, I being nowise preferable to any other one of the twenty-five—perhaps a hundred—we have in the Republican ranks.

Then, I say, I wish it to be distinctly understood and borne in mind that we have to fight this battle without many—perhaps without any—of the external aids which are brought to bear against us. So I hope those with whom I am surrounded have principle enough to nerve themselves for the task, and leave nothing undone that can be fairly done to bring about the right result.

LINCOLN'S OFFICE CHAIR, TABLE AND SADDLE-BAGS, WHILE A LAWYER.

VIEW OF THE REAR PARLOR OF THE OLD LINCOLN HOMESTEAD. (From a recent photograph.)

215

NATURAL RIGHTS OF THE NEGRO.

(Speech delivered at Columbus, Ohio, September, 1859.)

I have no purpose to introduce political and social equality between the white and the black races. There is a physical difference between the two which in my judgment will probably forbid their ever living together upon the footing of perfect equality, and inasmuch as it becomes a necessity that there must be a difference, I, as well as Judge Douglas, am in favor of the race to which I belong having the superior position.

I have never said anything to the contrary, but I hold that notwithstanding all this, there is no reason in the world why the negro is not entitled to all the natural rights enumerated in the Declaration of Independence, the right to life, liberty, and the pursuit of happiness.

In the right to eat the bread—without leave of anybody else—which his own hands earn, *he is my equal, and the equal of Judge Douglas, and the equal of every living man.*

KINDLY FEELING FOR HIS OPPONENTS.

(Speech at Cincinnati, Ohio, September, 1859, addressed particularly to Kentuckians.)

I will tell you, so far as I am authorized to speak for the opposition, what we mean to do with you. We mean to treat you, as near as we possibly can, as Washington, Jefferson and Madison treated you. We mean to leave you alone, and in no way to interfere with your institution; to abide by all and every compromise of the Constitution, and, in a word, coming back to the original proposition, to treat you so far as degenerated men (if we have degenerated) may, according to the examples of those noble fathers—Washington, Jefferson and Madison.

We mean to remember that you are as good as we; that there is no difference between us other than the difference of circumstances. We mean to recognize and bear in mind always that you have as good hearts in your bosoms as other people, or as we claim to have, and treat you accordingly. We mean to marry your girls when we have a chance—the white ones, I mean—and I have the honor to inform you that I once did have a chance in that way.

The good old maxims of the Bible are applicable to human affairs, and in this, as in other things, we may say here that he who is not for us is against us; he who gathereth not with us scattereth.

I should be glad to have some of the many good and able and noble men of the South to place themselves where we can confer upon them the high honor of an election upon one or the other end of our ticket. It would do my soul good to do that thing.

It would enable us to teach them that inasmuch as we elect one of their number to carry out our principles, we are free from the charge that we mean more than we say.

EXTRACTS FROM FIRST INAUGURAL ADDRESS, MARCH 4, 1861.

Apprehension seems to exist among the people of the southern states that by the occasion of a Republican administration their property and their peace and personal security are to be endangered. There has never been any reasonable cause for such apprehension. Indeed, the most ample evidence to the contrary has all the while existed, and been open to their inspection. It is found in nearly all the published speeches of him who now addresses you.

I do but quote from one of those speeches, when I declared that " I have no purpose, directly or indirectly, to interfere with the institution of slavery in the states where it exists."

I believe I have no lawful right to do so, and I have no inclination to do so.

It is seventy-two years since the first inauguration of a president under our national Constitution. During that period, fifteen different and very distinguished citizens have in succession administered the executive branch of the government. They have conducted it through many perils, and generally with great success. Yet, with this scope for precedent, I now enter upon the same task, for the brief constitutional term of four years, under great and peculiar difficulties.

I hold that in the contemplation of universal law and the Constitution, the union of these states is perpetual.

Why should there not be a patient confidence in the ultimate justice of the people? Is there any better or equal hope in the world? In our present differences, is either party without faith of being in the right? If the Almighty Ruler of nations, with his eternal truth and justice, be on your side of the North, or on your side of the South, that truth and that justice will surely prevail by the judgment of this great tribunal—the American people.

VIEWS REGARDING A PROTECTIVE TARIFF.

(Letter to Dr. Edward Wallace, October 11, 1859.)

I believe if we could have a moderate, carefully adjusted protective tariff, so far acquiesced in as not to be a perpetual subject of political strife, squabbles, changes and uncertainties, it would be better for us.

THE HUMBLEST OF ALL THE PRESIDENTS.

(Speech to the Legislature, Albany, New York, February 18, 1861.)

It is true that while I hold myself, without mock modesty, the humblest of all the individuals who have ever been elected president of the United States, I yet have a more difficult task to perform than any one of them has ever encountered.

FORMAL ANNOUNCEMENT OF HIS NOMINATION FOR THE PRESIDENCY.

(Reply to the president of the convention, at the homestead, Springfield, Illinois, May 19, 1860.)

I tender to you, and through you to the Republican national convention, and all the people represented in it, my profoundest thanks for the high honor done me, which you now formally announce.

Deeply, and even painfully, sensible of the great responsibility which is inseparable from this high honor—a responsibility which I could almost wish had fallen upon some one of the far more eminent men and experienced statesmen whose distinguished names were before the convention, I shall, by your leave, consider more fully the resolutions of the convention, denominated the platform, and, without any unnecessary or unreasonable delay, respond to you, Mr. Chairman, in writing, not doubting that the platform will be found satisfactory, and the nomination gratefully accepted.

———

ABRAHAM LINCOLN'S AUTOBIOGRAPHY.

The following autobiography was written by Mr. Lincoln's own hand, at the request of J. W. Fell, of Springfield, Illinois, December 20, 1859. In the note which accompanied it the writer says:

"Herewith is a little sketch, as you requested. There is not much of it, for the reason, I suppose, that there is not much of me.

"I was born February 12, 1809, in Hardin county, Kentucky. My parents were both born in Virginia, of undistinguished families, second families, perhaps I should say. My mother, who died in my tenth year, was of a family of the name of Hanks, some of whom now reside in Adams county, and others in Mason county, Illinois. My paternal grandfather, Abraham Lincoln, emigrated from Rockingham county, Virginia, to Kentucky, about 1781 or 1782, where, a year or two later, he was killed by Indians, not in battle, but by stealth, when he was laboring to open a farm in the forest. His ancestors, who were Quakers, went to Virginia from Berks county, Pennsylvania. An effort to identify them with the New England family of the same name ended in nothing more definite than a similarity of Christian names in both families—such as Enoch, Levi, Mordecai, Solomon, Abraham and the like.

"My father, at the death of his father, was but six years of age, and grew up literally without any education. He removed from Kentucky to what is now Spencer county, Indiana, in my eighth year. We reached our new home about the time the state came into the Union. It was a wild region, with many bears and other wild animals still in the woods. There I grew up. There were some schools, so called, but no qualification was ever required of a teacher beyond 'readin', writin', and cipherin'' to the rule of three. If a straggler, supposed to understand Latin, happened to sojourn in the neighborhood, he was looked upon as a wizard. There was absolutely nothing to excite ambition for education. Of course, when I came of age I did not know much. Still, somehow, I could read, write, and cipher to the rule of three, but that was all. I have not been to school since. The little advance I now have upon this store of education I have picked up from time to time under the pressure of necessity.

"I was raised to farm work, at which I continued till I was twenty-two. At twenty-one I came to Illinois, and passed the first year in Macon county. Then I got to New Salem, at that time in Sangamon, now in Menard county, where I remained a year as a sort of clerk in a store. Then came the Black Hawk war, and I was elected a captain of volunteers—a success which gave me more pleasure than any I have had since. I went into the campaign, was elected, ran for the Legislature the same year (1832), and was beaten—the only time I have ever been beaten by the people. The next and three succeeding biennial elections I was elected to the Legislature. I was not a candidate afterward. During the legislative period I had studied law, and removed to Springfield to practise it. In 1846, I was elected to the lower house of Congress. Was not a candidate for re-election. From 1849 to 1854, both inclusive, practised law more assiduously than ever before. Always a Whig in politics, and generally on the Whig electoral ticket, making active canvasses. I was losing interest in politics, when the repeal of the Missouri Compromise aroused me again. What I have done since then is pretty well known.

"If any personal description of me is thought desirable, it may be said I am in height six feet four inches, nearly; lean in flesh, weighing, on an average, one hundred and eighty pounds; dark complexion, with coarse black hair and gray eyes—no other marks or brands recollected."

WOULD NOT BUY THE NOMINATION FOR THE PRESIDENCY.

To a party who wished to be empowered to negotiate reward for promises of influence in the Chicago convention, 1860, Mr. Lincoln replied:

"No, gentlemen; I have not asked the nomination, and I will not now buy it with pledges. If I am nominated and elected, I shall not go into the presidency as the tool of this man or that man, or as the property of any factor or clique."

THE PLEDGE WITH COLD WATER.

(Remarks to the committee that notified him, at his home, May, 1860, of his nomination.)

Gentlemen, we must pledge our mutual health in this most healthy beverage which God has given man. It is the only beverage I have ever used or allowed in my family, and I cannot conscientiously depart from it on the present occasion. It is pure Adam's ale from the well.

The above is a picture of the tools and the men who broke into the Lincoln monument, on the night of November 7, 1876. They succeeded in getting the lead casket containing Lincoln's body out of the sarcophagus, and while waiting for a wagon to come and haul the body away, they were frightened away by the officers, who had notice that an attempt would be made to steal the body that night.

LINCOLN'S HORSE.

This horse was ridden and driven by Mr. Lincoln for seven years. Just before he left for Washington, 1861, he sold him for $75. The horse was traded around, and was finally purchased by a drayman. When the news of the assassination of the president came, the man on the right went immediately and purchased the horse from the drayman for $75. He put him on exhibition, and the first day took in $80, and before the horse died, the man is said to have made over $25,000 showing him about the country.

DEFENDS THE SECRETARY OF WAR.

(Remarks at a war meeting, Washington, August 6, 1862.)

General McClellan has sometimes asked for things that the secretary of war did not give him. General McClellan is not to blame for asking what he wanted and needed, and the secretary of war is not to blame for not giving when he had none to give. And I say here, as far as I know, the secretary of war has withheld no one thing at any time in my power to give him. I have no accusation against him. I believe he is a brave and able man, and I stand here, as justice requires me to do, to take upon myself what has been charged on the secretary of war, as withholding from him.

"ALL HONOR TO JEFFERSON."

(Letter, April 6, 1861.)

All honor to Jefferson; to a man who, in the concrete pressure of a struggle for national independence by a single people, had the coolness, forecast and capacity to introduce into a merely revolutionary document an abstract truth, applicable to all men and all times, and so to embalm it there that to-day and in all coming days it shall be a rebuke and a stumbling-block to the harbingers of reappearing tyranny and oppression!

HIS "EARLY HISTORY."

(Reply to a gentleman who asked for a sketch of his life.)

My early history is perfectly characterized by a single line of Gray's "Elegy,"

The short and simple annals of the poor.

"WE SHALL TRY TO DO OUR DUTY."

(Speech at Leavenworth, Kansas, spring of 1860.)

If we shall constitutionally elect a president, it will be our duty to see that you also submit. Old John Brown has been executed for treason against a state. We cannot object, even though he agreed with us in thinking slavery wrong. That cannot excuse violence, bloodshed and treason. It could avail him nothing that he might think himself right. So, if we constitutionally elect a president, and, therefore, you undertake to destroy the Union, it will be our duty to deal with you as old John Brown has been dealt with. We shall try to do our duty. We hope and believe that in no section will a majority so act as to render such extreme measure necessary.

"ALL AMERICAN CITIZENS ARE BROTHERS."

(Rejoicing over the November election, Springfield, Illinois, November 20, 1860, at a political meeting.)

I I rejoice with you in the success which has so far attended the Republican cause, yet in all our rejoicing let us neither express nor cherish any hard feelings toward any citizen who by his vote differed with us. Let us at all times remember that all American citizens are brothers of a common country, and should dwell together in the bonds of fraternal feeling.

———

LABOR THE SUPERIOR OF CAPITAL.

(Message to Congress, December 3, 1861.)

Labor is prior to and independent of capital. Capital is only the fruit of labor, and could never have existed if labor had not first existed. Labor is the superior of capital, and deserves much the higher consideration. Capital has its rights, which are as worthy of protection as any rights, nor is it denied that there is, and probably always will be, a relation between labor and capital, pro-ducing mutual benefits.

———

"LET US HAVE FAITH THAT RIGHT MAKES MIGHT."

(Speech at Cooper Institute, February 27, 1860.)

I defy any one to show that any living man in the whole world ever did, prior to the beginning of the present century (and I might almost say prior to the beginning of the last half of the present century), declare that, in his under-standing, any proper division of local from Federal authority, or any part of the Constitution, forbade the Federal government to control as to slavery in the Federal territories.

To those who now so declare, I give, not only "our fathers who framed the government under which we live," but with them all other living men within the century in which it was framed, among whom to search, and they shall not be able to find the evidence of a single man agreeing with them.

I do not mean to say we are bound to follow implicitly in whatever our fathers did. To do so would be to discard all the lights of current experience, to reject all progress, all improvement. What I do say is that if we could sup-plant the opinions and policy of our fathers in any case, we should do so upon evidence so conclusive, and argument so clear, that even their authority, fairly considered and weighed, cannot stand; and most surely not in a case whereof we ourselves declare they understood the question better than we.

Let all who believe that "our fathers who framed the government under which we live" understood this question just as well, and even better than we do now, speak as they spoke, and act as they acted upon it.

It is exceedingly desirable that all parts of this great confederacy shall be at peace and in harmony one with another. Let us Republicans do our part to have it so. Even though much provoked, let us do nothing through passion and ill-temper.

Even though the southern people will not so much as listen to us, let us calmly consider their demands, and yield to them, if in our deliberate view of our duty we possibly can. Judging by all they say and do, and by the subject and nature of their controversy with us, let us determine, if we can, what will satisfy them.

Wrong as we think slavery is, we can yet afford to let it alone where it is, because that much is due to the necessity arising from its actual presence in the nation. But can we, while our votes will prevent it, allow it to spread into the national territories, and to overrun us here in these free states?

If our sense of duty forbids this, then let us stand by our duty, fearlessly and effectively. Let us be diverted by none of those sophistical contrivances wherewith we are so industriously plied and belabored—contrivances such as groping for some middle ground between the right and the wrong, vain as the search for a man who should be neither a living man nor a dead man; such as a policy of "don't care" on a question about which all true men do care; such as Union appeals beseeching true Union men to yield to disunionists, reversing the divine rule, and calling, not the sinners, but the righteous to repentance; such as invocations to Washington imploring men to unsay what Washington said, and to undo what Washington did.

Let us have faith that right makes might, and in that faith let us, to the end, dare to do our duty as we understand it.

ACKNOWLEDGMENT TO GENERAL GRANT.

(Letter to General Grant, July 13, 1863.)

I do not remember that you and I ever met personally. I write this now as a grateful acknowledgment for the almost inestimable service you have done the country.

I write to say a word further. When you first reached the vicinity of Vicksburg, I thought you should do what you finally did—march the troops across the neck, run the batteries with the transports, and thus go below; and I never had any faith, except a general hope, that you knew better than I, that the Yazoo Pass expedition, and the like, could succeed. When you got below and took Port Gibson, Grand Gulf and vicinity, I thought you should go down the river and join General Banks; and when you turned northward, east of Big Black, I feared it was a mistake.

I now wish to make the personal acknowledgment that you were right and I was wrong.

"AS LIKELY TO CAPTURE THE 'MAN IN THE MOON.'"

(Dispatch to General Thomas, at Harrisburg, Pennsylvania, July 8, 1863.)

Forces now beyond Carlisle to be joined by regiments still at Harrisburg, and the united force again to join Pierce somewhere, and the whole to move down the Cumberland valley, will, in my unprofessional opinion, be quite as likely to capture the "man in the moon" as any part of Lee's army.

"BEWARE OF RASHNESS."

(To General Hooker, in giving him command of the Army of the Potomac.).

And now, beware of rashness, beware of rashness, but, with energy and sleepless vigilance, go forward and give us victories.

READING THE EMANCIPATION PROCLAMATION TO HIS CABINET.

(Remarks at the meeting, September 22, 1862.)

Gentlemen, I have, as you are aware, thought a great deal about the relation of this war to slavery, and you all remember that several weeks ago I read to you an order that I had prepared upon the subject, which, on account of objections made by some of you, was not issued. Ever since then my mind has been much occupied with this subject, and I have thought all along that the time for acting on it might probably come.

I have got you together to hear what I have written down. I do not wish your advice about the main matter, for that I have determined for myself. This I say without intending anything but respect for any one of you. But I already know the views of each on this question. They have been heretofore expressed, and I have considered them as thoroughly and carefully as I can. What I have written is that which my reflections have determined me to say. If there is anything in the expressions I use, or in any minor matter, which any one of you think had best be changed, I shall be glad to receive your suggestions.

One other observation I will make. I know very well that many others might, in this matter as in others, do better than I can; and if I was satisfied that the public confidence was more fully possessed by any one of them than by me, and knew of any constitutional way in which he could be put in my place, he should have it. I would gladly yield to him. But though I believe I have not so much of the confidence of the people as I had some time since, I do not know that, all things considered, any other person has more; and, however this may be, there is no way in which I can have any other man put where I am. I am here; I must do the best I can, and bear the responsibility of taking the course which I feel I ought to take.

INTERIOR OF MEMORIAL HALL. (Lincoln Monument, Springfield, Ill.)

Some of the most interesting objects are arranged in the foreground. On the left is seen a bust of the martyred president, and a cast of the hand that wrote the Emancipation Proclamation. On the right is a stone taken from a fragment of a wall built about twenty-four hundred years ago, during the reign of Servius Tullius, its sixth king, around the city of Rome, Italy. The inscription on it reads: "To Abraham Lincoln, president for the second time of the American republic, citizens of Rome present this stone, from the wall of Servius Tullius, by which the memory of each of those brave asserters of liberty may be associated, Anno, 1865." The old chair in front of the column contains a seat of hickory bark, put in by Mr. Lincoln in 1834. The surveying instruments were owned and used by him from 1832 until 1837. The powder-horn was worn by his grandfather, Abraham Lincoln, as a Revolutionary soldier from Virginia. He was killed by an Indian while wearing it, in Kentucky, in 1782. The framed pieces hanging about the marble walls are chiefly made up from about one thousand such sent to Mrs. Lincoln after the death of her husband, and contain expressions of sympathy and condolence.

OBSERVANCE OF THE SABBATH DAY IN THE ARMY AND NAVY.

(General Orders, November 15, 1862.)

The importance for man and beast of the prescribed weekly rest, the sacred rights of Christian soldiers and sailors, a becoming deference to the best sentiments of a Christian people, and a due regard for the divine will, demand that Sunday labor in the army and navy be reduced to the measure of strict necessity.

The discipline and character of the national forces should not suffer, nor the cause they defend be imperiled, by the profanation of the day or name of the Most High. "At this time of public distress"—adopting the words of Washington in 1776—"men may find enough to do in the service of God and their country without abandoning themselves to vice and immorality."

The first general order issued by the father of his country after the Declaration of Independence indicates the spirit in which our institutions were founded and should ever be defended:

" *The general hopes and trusts that every officer and man will endeavor to live and act as becomes a Christian soldier defending the dearest rights and liberties of his country.*"

"PRESERVE THE UNION AND LIBERTY."

(In response to an address of welcome by Governor O. P. Morton, Indianapolis, February 11, 1861.)

In all trying positions in which I shall be placed, and, doubtless, I shall be placed in many such, my reliance will be placed upon you and the people of the United States; and I wish you to remember, now and forever, that it is your business, and not mine, that if the union of these states and the liberties of this people shall be lost, it is but little to any one man of fifty-two years of age, but a great deal to the thirty millions of people who inhabit these United States, and to their posterity in all coming time.

It is your business to rise up and preserve the Union and liberty for yourselves, and not for me.

ANNOUNCES HIMSELF AS A CANDIDATE.

(Letter to the Sangamon *Journal*, Springfield, Illinois, June 13, 1836.)

I go for all sharing the privileges of the government who assist in bearing its burdens, consequently I go for admitting all whites to the right of suffrage who pay taxes or bear arms (by no means excluding females).

While acting as their representative I shall be governed by their will on all subjects upon which I have the means of knowing what their will is; and upon all others I shall do what my own judgment teaches me will best advance their interests, whether elected or not.

STORY-TELLING WAS A RELIEF.

(To a congressman who objected to the president telling a story when he had important business to present.)

You cannot be more anxious than I am constantly; and I say to you now, that if it were not for this occasional vent, I should die.

WOULD LEAVE IT TO THE WORLD UNERASED.

When Dr. Long said to his friend, " Well, Lincoln, that foolish speech will kill you—will defeat you for all offices for all time to come," referring to the "House Divided" speech, Mr. Lincoln replied:

"If I had to draw a pen across and erase my whole life from existence, and I had one poor gift or choice left, as to what I should save from the wreck, I should choose that speech, and leave it to the world unerased."

LETTER, OCTOBER 8, 1862.

I sincerely wish war was an easier and pleasanter business than it is, but it does not admit of holidays.

"MY PARAMOUNT OBJECT IS TO SAVE THE UNION."

(Reply to an editorial of complaint in the New York *Tribune*, by Horace Greeley, August 19, 1862.)

My paramount object is to save the Union, and not either to save or to destroy slavery. If I could save the Union without freeing any slave, I would do it. If I could save it by freeing all the slaves, I would do it; and if I could do it by freeing some and leaving others alone, I would also do that. What I do about slavery and the colored race, I do because I believe it helps to save this Union; and what I forbear, I forbear because I do not believe it would help to save the Union. I shall do less whenever I shall believe what I am doing hurts the cause, and I shall do more whenever I believe doing more will help the cause.

HIS VOW BEFORE GOD.

(Remarks to Secretary Salmon P. Chase.)

I made a solemn vow before God that if General Lee was driven back from Pennsylvania I would crown the result by the declaration of freedom to the slaves.

GOD BLESS THE WOMEN OF AMERICA.

(Speech at a ladies' fair for the benefit of the soldiers, Washington, March 16, 1864.)

I appear to say but a word. This extraordinary war in which we are engaged falls heavily upon all classes of people, but the most heavily upon the soldiers. For it has been said, "All that a man hath will he give for his life," and, while all contribute of their substance, the soldier puts his life at stake, and often yields it up in his country's cause. *The highest merit, then, is due the soldiers.*

In this extraordinary war extraordinary developments have manifested themselves such as have not been seen in former wars; and among these manifestations nothing has been more remarkable than these fairs for the relief of suffering soldiers and their families, and the chief agents in these fairs are the women of America!

I am not accustomed to the use of language of eulogy; I have never studied the art of paying compliments to women; but I must say that if all that has been said by orators and poets since the creation of the world in praise of women were applied to the women of America, it would not do them justice for their conduct during the war.

I will close by saying, God bless the women of America!

"NOT ONE WORD OF IT WILL I EVER RECALL."

(Remarks to some friends concerning the Emancipation Proclamation, New-Year's evening, 1863.)

The signature looks a little tremulous, for my hand was tired, but my resolution was firm.

I told them in September, if they did not return to their allegiance, and cease murdering our soldiers, I would strike at this pillar of their strength. And now the promise shall be kept, and not one word of it will I ever recall.

LAST VISIT TO HIS LAW-OFFICE.

(Conversation with his law partner, William H. Herndon, before leaving for Washington, 1861.)

I love the people here, Billy, and owe them all that I am. If God spares my life to the end, I shall come back among you and spend the remnant of my days.

WOULD WILLINGLY EXCHANGE PLACES WITH THE SOLDIER.

(To Hon. Schuyler Colfax, upon receiving bad news from the army.)

How willingly would I exchange places to-day with the soldier who sleeps on the ground in the Army of the Potomac!

IN DISPENSING PATRONAGE THE DISABLED SOLDIER TO HAVE THE PREFERENCE.

(Letter to the postmaster-general, July 27, 1863.)

Yesterday little indorsements of mine went to you in two cases of post-masterships, sought for widows whose husbands have fallen in the battles of this war. These cases, occurring on the same day, brought me to reflect more attentively than what I had before done as to what is fairly due from us here in the dispensing of patronage toward the men who, by fighting our battles, bear the chief burden of saving our country.

My conclusion is that, other claims and qualifications being equal, they have the right, and this is especially applicable to the disabled soldier and the deceased soldier's family.

PARDON FOR A DESERTER.

(Remarks to Hon. Schuyler Colfax, who asked for a respite.)

Some of our generals complain that I impair discipline and subordination in the army by my pardons and respites, but it makes me rested, after a day's hard work, if I can find some good excuse for saving a man's life; and I go to bed happy as I think how joyous the signing of my name makes him and his family.

"ALREADY TOO MANY WEEPING WIDOWS."

(Reply to a general who insisted on the president signing the warrants for the execution of twenty-four deserters.)

There are already too many weeping widows in the United States. For God's sake, don't ask me to add to the number, for I won't do it.

DISPATCH TO GENERAL BURNSIDE AT CINCINNATI, JULY 27, 1863.

General Grant is a copious worker and fighter, but a meager writer or telegrapher.

A PRESENTIMENT.

(Remarks to Mrs. Harriet Beecher Stowe.)

Whichever way it ends, I have the impression that I shall not last long after it is over.

REPLY TO A PLEA FOR THE LIFE OF A SOLDIER.

Well, I think the boy can do us more good above the ground than under it.

LINCOLN MONUMENT, SPRINGFIELD, ILLINOIS.
(See description on opposite page.)

LINCOLN MONUMENT, SPRINGFIELD, ILLINOIS.

(See another view on page 194.)

This view is from a point a little east of north from the monument, and across a ravine running west through Oak Ridge cemetery. The vault at the foot of the bluff is the receiving-tomb for the cemetery. Mr. Lincoln's remains were deposited in that vault May 4, 1865. A flight of iron steps, commencing about fifty yards east of the vault, ascends in a curved line to the monument, an elevation of more than fifty feet. The door seen in the picture of the monument is the entrance to the catacomb. That is where the thieves entered on the night of November 7, 1876, when they tried to steal the remains of President Lincoln.

Excavation for this monument commenced September 9, 1869. It is built of granite, from quarries at Biddeford, Maine. The rough ashlers were shipped to Quincy, Massachusetts, where they were dressed to perfect ashlers and numbered, thence shipped by railroad to Springfield. It is 72½ feet from east to west, 119½ feet from north to south, and 100 feet high. The total cost is about $230,000, to May 1, 1888. All the statuary is orange-colored bronze. The whole monument was designed by Larkin G. Mead; the statuary was modeled in plaster by him in Florence, Italy, and cast by the Ames Manufacturing Company, of Chicopee, Massachusetts. The statue of Lincoln and Coat of Arms were first placed on the monument; the statue was unveiled and the monument dedicated October 15, 1874. The Infantry and Naval Groups were put on in September, 1877, the Artillery Group, April 13, 1882, and the Cavalry Group, March 13, 1883.

The principal front of the monument is on the south side, the statue of Lincoln being on that side of the obelisk, over Memorial Hall. Presuming that the reader will, in imagination, ascend with me one of the four flights of steps leading to the terrace, and, beginning at the southeast corner, we will study for a short time the Cavalry Group, move along to the northeast corner and study the Naval Group, at the northwest corner the Artillery Group, and at the southwest corner the Infantry Group. On the east side are three tablets, upon which are the letters U. S. A. To the right of that, and beginning with Virginia, we find the abbreviations of the original thirteen states in the order they were settled as colonies, ending with Georgia. Next comes Vermont, the first state admitted after the Union was perfected, the states following in the order they were admitted, ending with Nebraska on the east, thus forming the cordon of thirty-seven states, composing the United States of America when the monument was erected. There have been eight new states admitted since the monument was built, thus beginning a new century of states, with Colorado under Virginia, continuing around with North and South Dakota, Montana, Washington, Idaho, Wyoming and Utah.

We will now take a position on the terrace immediately over the door leading to Memorial Hall. We are in the presence of the grandest and most imposing object-lessons of patriotism ever expressed by inert matter. The statue of President Lincoln, as commander-in-chief of the army and navy, takes its position over all. The Infantry is assigned to the post of honor, the advance on the right. The Cavalry, second in honor and efficiency, takes the advance on the left. The Artillery is placed in the rear on the right. The Navy, in the rear on the left, acts independently or co-operates with all, as the good of the service and the wisdom of the commander-in-chief dictates. Let us give the combination a brief study, beginning with the Coat of Arms, which we see is modified by the olive branch of peace, President Lincoln having tendered the same to the southern people, with whom he plead in the most pathetic terms, in his first inaugural address, not to begin the war. The response, all the world knows, was the bombardment of Fort Sumter, thus trampling the olive branch under foot, leaving no alternative to the nation but cruel, bloody war, which raged until the government, represented by the American eagle in the Coat of Arms, severed the chains of slavery. In a larger sense, the artist says that the president, standing above the Coat of Arms, treats it as a pedestal, emblematic of the Constitution of the United States, and with the Infantry, Cavalry, Artillery and Navy marshaled around him, wields all for holding the states together in a perpetual bond of union, without which he could never hope to effect the great enemy of human freedom. The grand climax is indicated by President Lincoln, with his left hand holding out as a golden scepter the Emancipation Proclamation, while in his right he holds the pen with which he has just written it. The right hand is resting on another badge of authority, the American flag, thrown over the fasces. At the foot of the fasces lies a wreath of laurel, with which to crown the president as the victor over slavery and rebellion.

REMARKS TO NEGROES IN THE STREETS OF RICHMOND.

The president walked through the streets of Richmond—without a guard except a few seamen—in company with his son "Tad," and Admiral Porter, on April 4, 1865, the day following the evacuation of the city. Colored people gathered about him on every side, eager to see and thank their liberator. Mr. Lincoln addressed the following remarks to one of these gatherings:

"My poor friends, you are free—free as air. You can cast off the name of slave and trample upon it; it will come to you no more. Liberty is your birth-right. God gave it to you as he gave it to others, and it is a sin that you have been deprived of it for so many years.

"But you must try to deserve this priceless boon. Let the world see that you merit it, and are able to maintain it by your good works. Don't let your joy carry you into excesses; learn the laws, and obey them. Obey God's command-ments, and thank him for giving you liberty, for to him you owe all things. There, now, let me pass on; I have but little time to spare. I want to see the Capitol, and must return at once to Washington to secure to you that liberty which you seem to prize so highly."

"WITH MALICE TOWARD NONE, WITH CHARITY FOR ALL."

(Second inaugural address, March 4, 1865.)

Fellow-countrymen, at this second appearing to take the oath of the pres-idential office, there is less occasion for an extended address than there was at the first. Then a statement, somewhat in detail, of a course to be pursued seemed fitting and proper. Now, at the expiration of four years, during which public declarations have been constantly called forth on every point and phase of the great contest which still absorbs the attention and engrosses the energies of the nation, little that is new could be presented.

The progress of our arms, upon which all else chiefly depends, is as well known to the public as to myself, and it is, I trust, reasonably satisfactory and encouraging to all. With high hope for the future, no prediction in regard to it is ventured.

On the occasion corresponding to this, four years ago, all thoughts were anxiously directed to an impending civil war. All dreaded it; all sought to avert it. While the inaugural address was being delivered from this place, devoted altogether to saving the Union without war, insurgents' agents were in the city seeking to destroy it without war—seeking to dissolve the Union and divide its effects by negotiation.

Both parties deprecated war; but one of them would make war rather than let the nation survive, and the other would accept war rather than let it perish. And the war came.

The prayer of both could not be answered—those of neither have not been answered fully. The Almighty has his own purposes. "Woe unto the world because of offenses! for it must needs be that offenses come; but woe to that man by whom the offense cometh."

If we shall suppose that American slavery is one of those offenses which, in the providence of God, must needs come, but which having continued through his appointed time, he now wills to remove, and that he gives to North and South this terrible war as the woe due to those by whom the offense came, shall we discern therein any departure from those divine attributes which the believers in a living God always ascribe to him?

Fondly do we hope, fervently do we pray, that this mighty scourge of war may soon pass away.

Yet, if God wills that it continue until all the wealth piled by the bondsman's two hundred and fifty years of unrequited toil shall be sunk, and until every drop of blood drawn by the lash shall be paid by another drawn with the sword, as was said three thousand years ago, so still it must be said, "The judgments of the Lord are true and righteous altogether."

With malice toward none, with charity for all, with firmness in the right, as God gives us to see the right, let us strive on to finish the work we are in; to bind up the nation's wounds; to care for him who shall have borne the battle, and for his widow and for his orphan; to do all which may achieve and cherish a just and lasting peace among ourselves, and with all nations.

NEGROES KNEEL AT THE PRESIDENT'S FEET.

While the president was walking through the streets of Richmond, Virginia, April 4, 1865, some negroes knelt at his feet and thanked him for their freedom. The president replied, in his characteristic way, as follows:

"Don't kneel to me—that is not right. You must kneel to God only, and thank him for the liberty you will hereafter enjoy; I am but God's humble instrument; but you may rest assured that as long as I live no one shall put a shackle on your limbs, and you shall have all the rights which God has given to every other free citizen of this republic."

SECOND NOMINATION FOR THE PRESIDENCY.

(Response to an address by George W. Dennison, president of the national Republican convention at Baltimore, notifying Mr. Lincoln of his nomination. The committee met at the White House on June 9, 1864.)

I will neither conceal my gratification nor restrain the expression of my gratitude, that the Union people throughout this country, in the continued effort to save and advance the nation, have deemed me not unworthy to remain in my present position.

THE NAVY GROUP. (Lincoln Monument, Springfield, Ill.)

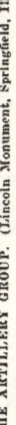

THE ARTILLERY GROUP. (Lincoln Monument, Springfield, Ill.)

The Artillery Group, in clay, was shipped by the artist, Mr. Larkin G. Mead, at Florence, Italy, and arrived in Chicopee, Massachusetts, October, 1880. It was cast in orange-colored bronze by the Ames Manufacturing Company, shipped in February, and placed on the northwest pedestal of the monument, April 13, 1882. It weighs 4,433 pounds, and cost $13,700. This piece is the reproduction of a single detachment of artillery in action. The enemy has gained the strongest point in artillery fighting, having dismounted the gun by knocking the carriage into splinters, and at the same time killing and wounding some of the men. The officer in command escapes unhurt, and with drawn saber mounts his dismounted piece, and is looking defiance at the approaching enemy, either infantry or cavalry, on a charge. The wounded and prostrate soldier, with a look of intense pain, bravely keeps his face toward the enemy. The youthful soldier, with uplifted hands, probably in his first battle, fails to give any attention to the approaching enemy, being too much horrified in consequence of the havoc beneath and around him. It is reasonable to presume that the flying pieces of the gun-carriage have killed and wounded half a dozen of his comrades, giving him sufficient cause to feel as his appearance would indicate.

ANSWER TO AN APPLICATION FOR PARDON.

The following reply was made by Mr. Lincoln to an application for the pardon of a soldier who had shown himself very brave in war, and had been severely wounded, but afterward deserted:

"Did you say he was once badly wounded? Then, as the Scriptures say that in the shedding of blood is the remission of sins, I guess we'll have to let him off this time."

HAPPIEST DAY OF THE FOUR YEARS.

The following remarks were made by the president to Admiral David D. Porter, while on board the flagship Malvern, on the James river, in front of Richmond, the day the city surrendered:

"Thank God that I have lived to see this! It seems to me that I have been dreaming a horrid dream for four years, and now the nightmare is gone. I want to see Richmond."

MR. LINCOLN SEEKS RELAXATION.

Seeking relaxation from the engrossing cares which confronted him night and day, Mr. Lincoln remarked to Schuyler Colfax, as he went to the theater one evening after receiving intelligence of what he regarded as reverses to the army of General Grant in the wilderness:

"People may think strange of it, but I *must* have some relief from this terrible anxiety, or it will kill me."

REGARDING HIS SECOND INAUGURAL ADDRESS.

(Letter to Thurlow Weed, March 15, 1865.)

Everyone likes a compliment. Thank you for yours on my little notification speech and on the recent inaugural address. I expect the latter to wear as well as, perhaps better than, anything I have produced; but I believe it is not immediately popular.

Men are not flattered by being shown that there has been a difference of purpose between the Almighty and them.

To deny it, however, in this case is to deny that there is a God governing the world.

It is a truth which I thought needed to be told, and, as whatever of humiliation there is in it falls most heavily on myself, I thought others might afford for me to tell it.

"HOLD ON WITH A BULLDOG GRIP."

(Dispatch to General Grant, August 17, 1864.)

have seen your dispatch expressing your unwillingness to break your hold where you are. Neither am I willing. Hold on with a bulldog grip.

NOT SCARED ABOUT HIMSELF.

Reply to Schuyler Colfax, when told how uneasy all had been at his going to Richmond:

" Why, if any one else had been president and had gone to Richmond, I would have been alarmed; but I was not scared about myself a bit."

LAST WRITTEN WORDS OF ABRAHAM LINCOLN.

Given to Mr. Ashmun as the President and Mrs. Lincoln were leaving the White House, a few minutes before eight o'clock, on the evening of April 14, 1865:

"Allow Mr. Ashmun and friend to come to see me at 9 o'clock A. M., to-morrow, April 15, 1865."

REMARKS TO HIS WIFE ON THE FATAL DAY.

Remarks made by the president to his wife while they were out driving in an open carriage on the afternoon of April 14, 1865, when Mrs. Lincoln said: "You almost startle me by your cheerfulness.")

And well I may feel so, Mary, for I consider this day the war has come to a close. We must both be more cheerful in the future; between the war and the loss of our darling Willie we have been very miserable.

LAST PUBLIC ADDRESS OF ABRAHAM LINCOLN.

(Remarks on April 11, 1865, to a gathering at the White House on the fall of Richmond.)

We meet this evening not in sorrow, but in gladness of heart.

The evacuation of Petersburg and Richmond, and the surrender of the principal insurgent army, give hope of a righteous and speedy peace, whose joyous expression cannot be restrained.

In the midst of this, however, He from whom all blessings flow must not be forgotten. Nor must those whose harder part gives us the cause of rejoicing be overlooked; their honors must not be parceled out with others.

I myself was near the front, and had the high pleasure of transmitting the good news to you; but no part of the honor, for plan or execution, is mine. To General Grant, his skilful officers and brave men, all belongs.

SERMON ON THE DEATH OF LINCOLN.

BY HENRY WARD BEECHER, APRIL 23, 1865.

EVEN he who now sleeps has, by this event, been clothed with new influence. Dead, he speaks to men who now willingly hear what before they refused to listen to. Now his simple and mighty words will be gathered like those of Washington, and your children and your children's children shall be taught to ponder the simplicity and deep wisdom of utterances which, in their time, passed, in the party heat, as idle words. Men will receive a new impulse of patriotism for his sake, and will guard with zeal the whole country which he loved so well; I swear you, on the altar of his memory, to be more faithful to the country for which he has perished. Men will, as they follow his hearse, swear a new hatred to that slavery against which he warred, and which in vanquishing him has made him a martyr and a conqueror; I swear you, by the memory of this martyr, to hate slavery with an unappeasable hatred. Men will admire and imitate his unmoved firmness, his inflexible conscience for the right; and yet his gentleness, as tender as a woman's, his moderation of spirit, which not all the heat of party could inflame, nor all the jars and disturbances of this country shake out of its place; I swear you to an emulation of his justice, his moderation and his mercy.

You I can comfort; but how can I speak to that twilight million to whom his name was as the name of an angel of God? There will be wailing in places which no ministers shall be able to reach. When, in hovel and in cot, in wood and in wilderness, in the field throughout the South, the dusky children, who looked upon him as that Moses whom God sent before them to lead them out of the land of bondage, learn that he has fallen, who shall comfort them? Oh, thou Shepherd of Israel, that didst comfort thy people of old, to thy care we commit the helpless, the long wronged, and grieved!

And now the martyr is moving in triumphal march, mightier than when alive. The nation rises up at every stage of his coming. Cities and states are his pall-bearers, and the cannon beats the hours with solemn progression. Dead—dead—dead—he yet speaketh! Is Washington dead? Is Hampden dead? Is David dead? Is any man dead that ever was fit to live? Disenthralled of flesh, and risen to the unobstructed sphere where passion never comes, he begins his illimitable work. His life now is grafted upon the Infinite, and will be fruitful as no earthly life can be. Pass on, thou that hast overcome! Your sorrows, O people, are his peace! Your bells, and bands, and muffled drums sound triumph in his ear. Wail and weep here, God makes it echo joy and triumph there. Pass on, thou victor!

ABRAHAM LINCOLN.

FROM THE ODE RECITED AT THE HARVARD COMMEMORATION,
JULY 21, 1865.

L IFE may be given in many ways,
  And loyalty to Truth be sealed
As bravely in the closet as the field,
  So bountiful is Fate;
  But then to stand beside her,
  When craven churls deride her,
To front a lie in arms and not to yield,
    This shows, methinks, God's plan
    And measure of a stalwart man,
    Limbed like the old heroic breeds,
    Who stands self-poised on manhood's solid earth,
  Not forced to frame excuses for his birth,
Fed from within with all the strength he needs.

Such was he, our Martyr-Chief,
    Whom late the Nation he had led,
    With ashes on her head,
Wept with the passion of an angry grief:
Forgive me, if from present things I turn
To speak what in my heart will beat and burn,
And hang my wreath on his world-honored·urn.
    Nature, they say, doth dote,
    And cannot make a man
    Save on some worn-out plan,
    Repeating us by rote:
For him her Old World moulds aside she threw.
    And, choosing sweet clay from the breast
    Of the unexhausted West,
With stuff untainted shaped a hero new,
Wise, steadfast in the strength of God, and true.
    How beautiful to see
Once more a shepherd of mankind indeed,
Who loved his charge, but never loved to lead ;
One whose meek flock the people joyed to be,
  Not lured by any cheat of birth,
  But by his clear-grained human worth,

238

And brave old wisdom of sincerity!
  They knew that outward grace is dust;
  They could not choose but trust
In that sure-footed mind's unfaltering skill,
  And supple-tempered will
That bent like perfect steel to spring again and thrust.
  His was no lonely mountain-peak of mind,
  Thrusting to thin air o'er our cloudy bars,
  A sea-mark now, now lost in vapors blind:
  Broad prairie rather, genial, level-lined,
  Fruitful and friendly for all humankind,
Yet also nigh to heaven and loved of loftiest stars.
    Nothing of Europe here,
Or, then, of Europe fronting mornward still,
    Ere any names of Serf and Peer
    Could Nature's equal scheme deface
    And thwart her genial will;
    Here was a type of the true elder race,
And one of Plutarch's men talked with us face to face.
  I praise him not; it were too late;
And some innative weakness there must be
In him who condescends to victory
  Such as the Present gives, and cannot wait,
    Safe in himself as in a fate.
    So always firmly he:
    He knew to bide his time,
    And can his fame abide,
Still patient in his simple faith sublime,
    Till the wise years decide.
  Great captains, with their guns and drums,
    Disturb our judgment for the hour,
    But at last silence comes;
  These all are gone, and, standing like a tower,
  Our children shall behold his fame,
    The kindly-earnest, brave, foreseeing man,
Sagacious, patient, dreading praise, not blame,
  New birth of our new soil, the first American.
                    —*James Russell Lowell.*

BIOGRAPHICAL SKETCH.

JAMES RUSSELL LOWELL was born in Cambridge, Massachusetts, February 22, 1819. His father was the Rev. Charles Lowell, and was a direct descendant of English settlers. After graduating from Harvard (1838), he entered law. In 1841, "A Year's Life," his first volume of poems, was given to the public. In 1844, he was married to Maria White. The well-known "Bigelow Papers" made Mr. Lowell's name widely known; they appeared in the Boston *Courier* in 1846-8. In 1845, "The Vision of Sir Launfal" was issued. It is one of the grandest poems in the English language; the beautiful portrayal of a right gospel pervades it from beginning to end. He succeeded Longfellow as professor of belles-lettres at Harvard in 1855. He was a constant contributor to leading magazines, especially to the *Atlantic Monthly*. From 1863-72 he was one of the editors of *The North American Review*. He was appointed minister to Spain by President Hayes, in 1877, and, in 1880, was transferred to London. He loved England almost as his own America, and was greatly admired and beloved by the English people. Oxford honored him with D.C.L., and Cambridge by making him an LL.D. His death occurred August 1, 1891.

ORATION ON LINCOLN.

BY WILLIAM McKINLEY, EX-GOVERNOR OF OHIO.

IT requires the most gracious pages in the world's history to record what one American achieved. The story of this simple life is the story of a plain, honest, manly citizen, true patriot and profound statesman, who, believing with all the strength of his mighty soul in the institutions of his country, won, because of them, the highest place in its government, then fell a precious sacrifice to the Union he held so dear, which Providence had spared his life long enough to save.

We meet to do honor to this immortal hero, Abraham Lincoln, whose achievements have heightened human aspirations and broadened the field of opportunity to the races of men. . . .

What were the traits of character which made Abraham Lincoln prophet and master, without a rival, in the greatest crisis in our history? What gave him such mighty power? To me the answer is simple:

Lincoln had sublime faith in the people. He walked with and among them. He recognized the importance and power of an enlightened public sentiment and was guided by it. Even amid the vicissitudes of war he concealed little from public view and inspection. In all he did he invited, rather than evaded, examination and criticism. He submitted his plans and purposes, as far as practicable, to public consideration with perfect frankness and sincerity. There was such homely simplicity in his character that it could not be hedged in by pomp of place, nor the ceremonials of high official station. He was so accessible to the public that he seemed to take the whole people into his confidence.

Here, perhaps, was one secret of his power. The people never lost their confidence in him, however much they unconsciously added to his personal discomfort and trials. His patience was almost superhuman, and who will say that he was mistaken in his treatment of the thousands who thronged continually about him? More than once when reproached for permitting visitors to crowd upon him he asked, in pained surprise, "Why, what harm does this confidence in men do me? I get only good and inspiration from it."

Horace Greeley once said: "I doubt whether man, woman or child, white or black, bond or free, virtuous or vicious, ever accosted or reached forth a hand to Abraham Lincoln and detected in his countenance or manner any repugnance or

INFANTRY GROUP. (On Lincoln Monument, Springfield, Ill.)

CAVALRY GROUP. (On Lincoln Monument, Springfield, Ill.)

The Cavalry Group, in plaster, was shipped by Mr. Mead, the artist, with that of the Artillery, from Florence, Italy, and arrived at Chicopee, Massachusetts, in October, 1880. The casting in bronze and finishing was completed by the Ames Manufacturing Company, in the summer of 1882. It was placed on the southeast pedestal of the monument, March 13, 1883; weighs 5,500 pounds, and cost $13,700.

field and patriot grave to every living heart and hearthstone all over this broad land, will yet swell the chorus of the Union when again touched, as surely they will be, by the better angels of our nature."

But his words were unheeded. The mighty war came, with its dreadful train. Knowing no wrong, he dreaded no evil for himself. He had done all he could to save the country by peaceful means. He had entreated and expostulated, now he would do and dare. He had, in words of solemn import, warned the men of the South. He had appealed to their patriotism by the sacred memories of the battle-fields of the Revolution, on which the patriot blood of their ancestors had been so bravely shed, not to break up the Union. Yet all in vain. "Both parties deprecated war, but one would make war rather than let the nation survive, and the other would accept war rather than let it perish. And the war came."

Lincoln did all he could to avert it, but there was no hesitation on his part when the sword of rebellion flashed from its scabbard. He was from that moment until the close of his life unceasingly devoted and consecrated to the great purpose of saving the Union. All other matters he regarded as trivial, and every movement, of whatever character, whether important or unimportant of itself, was bent to that end.

The world now regards with wonder the infinite patience, gentleness and kindness with which he bore the terrible burden of that four years' struggle. Humane, forgiving and long-suffering himself, he was always especially tender and considerate of the poor, and in his treatment of them was full of those "kind little acts which are of the same blood as great and holy deeds." As Charles Sumner so well said, "With him as president the idea of republican institutions, where no place is too high for the humblest, was perpetually manifest, so that his simple presence was a proclamation of the equality of all men."

During the whole of the struggle he was a tower of strength to the Union. Whether in defeat or victory, he kept right on, dismayed at nothing, and never to be diverted from the pathway of duty. Always cool and determined, all learned to gain renewed courage, calmness and wisdom from him, and to lean upon his strong arm for support. · The proud designation, "Father of his country," was not more appropriately bestowed upon Washington than the affectionate title, "Father Abraham," was given to Lincoln by the soldiers and loyal people of the North.

The crowning glory of Lincoln's administration, and the greatest executive act in American history, was his immortal proclamation of emancipation. Perhaps more clearly than any one else Lincoln had realized years before he was called to the presidency that the country could not continue half slave and half free. He declared it before Seward proclaimed the "irrepressible conflict." The contest between freedom and slavery was inevitable; it was written in the stars. The nation must be either all slave or all free. Lincoln with almost supernatural prescience saw it. His prophetic vision is manifested through all his utterances; notably in the great debate between himself and Douglas. To him was given the duty and responsibility of making that great classic of liberty, the Declaration of Independence, no longer an empty promise, but a glorious fulfillment.

Many long and thorny steps were to be taken before this great act of justice could be performed. Patience and forbearance had to be exercised. It had to be demonstrated that the Union could be saved in no other way. Lincoln, much as he abhorred slavery, felt that his chief duty was to save the Union, under the Constitution and within the Constitution. He did not assume the duties of his great office with the purpose of abolishing slavery, nor changing the Constitution, but as a servant of the Constitution and the laws of the country then existing. In a speech delivered in Ohio in 1859, he said: "The people of the United States are the rightful masters of both Congress and the courts, not to overthrow the Constitution, but to overthrow the men who would overthrow the Constitution."

This was the principle which governed him, and which he applied in his official conduct when he reached the presidency. We now know that he had emancipation constantly in his mind's eye for nearly two years after his first inauguration. It is true he said at the start, "I believe I have no lawful right to interfere with slavery where it now exists, and have no intention of doing so;" and that the public had little reason to think he was meditating general emancipation until he issued his preliminary proclamation, September 22, 1862.

Just a month before, exactly, he had written to the editor of the New York *Tribune:*

"My paramount object is to save the Union, and not either to save or destroy slavery. If I could save the Union without freeing any slave, I would do it; if I could save it by freeing all the slaves, I would do it; and if I could do it by freeing some and leaving others alone, I would also do that."

The difference in his thought and purpose about "the divine institution" is very apparent in these two expressions. Both were made in absolute honor and sincerity. Public sentiment had undergone a great change, and Lincoln, valiant defender of the Constitution that he was, and faithful tribune of the people that he always was, changed with the people. The war had brought them and him to a nearer realization of our absolute dependence upon a higher power, and had quickened his conceptions of duty more acutely than the public could realize. The purposes of God, working through the ages, were, perhaps, more clearly revealed to him than any other.

Besides, it was as he himself once said, "It is a quality of revolutions not to go by old lines or old laws, but to break up both and make new ones." He was naturally "antislavery," and the determination he formed, when as a young man he witnessed an auction in the slave-shambles in New Orleans, never forsook him. It is recorded how his soul burned with indignation, and that he then exclaimed, "If I ever get a chance to hit that thing, I'll hit it hard!" He "hit it hard" when as a member of the Illinois Legislature he protested that "the institution of slavery is founded on both injustice and bad policy." He "hit it hard" when as a member of Congress he "voted for the Wilmot Proviso as good as forty times." He " hit it hard" when he stumped his state against the Kansas-Nebraska Bill, and on the direct issue carried Illinois in favor of the restriction of slavery by a majority of 4,414 votes. He " hit it hard " when he approved the law abolishing slavery in the District of Columbia, an antislavery measure that he had voted for in Congress. He " hit it hard " when he signed the acts abolishing slavery in all the territories and for the repeal of the fugitive-slave law. But it still remained for him to strike slavery its death-blow. He did that in his glorious proclamation of freedom. . . .

In all the long years of slavery agitation, unlike any of the other antislavery leaders, Lincoln always carried the people with him. In 1854, Illinois cast loose from her old Democratic moorings and followed his leadership in a most emphatic protest against the repeal of the Missouri Compromise. In 1858, the people of Illinois indorsed his opposition to the aggressions of slavery, in a state usually Democratic, even against so popular a leader as the "Little Giant." In 1860, the whole country indorsed his position on slavery, even when the people were continually harangued that his election meant the dissolution of the Union. During the war the people advanced with him step by step to its final overthrow. Indeed, in the election of 1864 the people not only indorsed emancipation, but went far toward recognizing the political equality of the negro. They heartily justified the president in having enlisted colored soldiers to fight side by side with the white man in the noble cause of union and liberty. Aye, they did more. They indorsed his position on another and vastly more important phase of the race problem. They approved his course as president in reorganizing the government of Louisiana, and a hostile press did not fail to call attention to the fact that this meant eventually negro suffrage in that state.

Perhaps, however, it was not known then that Lincoln had written the new free-state governor, March 13, 1864:

"Now you are about to have a convention, which, among other things, will probably define the elective franchise. I barely suggest for your private consideration whether some of the colored people may not be let in—as, for instance, the very intelligent, and especially those who have fought gallantly in our ranks. They would probably help, in some trying time to come, to keep the jewel of liberty within the family of freedom."

Lincoln had that happy, peculiar habit which few public men have attained, of looking away from the deceptive and misleading influences about him—and none are more deceptive than those of public life in our capitals—straight into the hearts of the people. He could not be deceived by the self-interested host of eager counselors who sought to enforce their own particular views upon him as the voice of the country. He chose to determine for himself what the people were thinking about and wanting him to do, and no man ever lived who was a more accurate judge of their opinions and wishes.

The battle of Gettysburg turned the scale of the war in favor of the Union, and it has always seemed to me most fortunate that Lincoln declared for emancipation before rather than after that decisive contest. A later proclamation

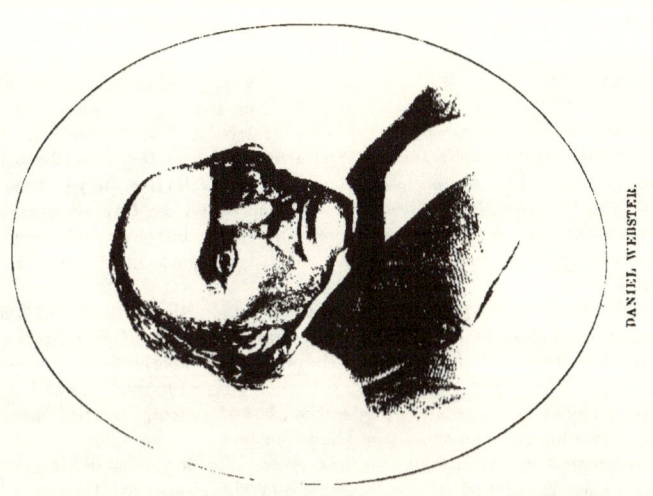

DANIEL WEBSTER.

MILLARD FILLMORE.

218

might have been construed as a tame and cowardly performance, not a challenge of truth to error for mortal combat. The ground on which that battle was fought is held sacred by every friend of freedom. But important as the battle itself was, the dedication of it as a national cemetery is celebrated for a grander thing. The words Lincoln spoke there will live "until time shall be no more"—through all eternity. Well may they be forever preserved on tablets of bronze upon the spot where he spoke, but how infinitely better it would be if they could find a permanent lodging-place in the soul of every American! . . .

It is not difficult to place a correct estimate upon the character of Lincoln. He was the greatest man of his time, especially approved of God for the work he gave him to do. History abundantly proves his superiority as a leader, and establishes his constant reliance upon a higher power for guidance and support. The tendency of this age is to exaggeration, but of Lincoln certainly none have spoken more highly than those who knew him best.

The greatest names in American history are Washington and Lincoln. One is forever associated with the independence of the states and formation of the Federal Union, the other with the universal freedom and the preservation of that Union. Washington enforced the Declaration of Independence as against England, Lincoln proclaimed its fulfillment, not only to a downtrodden race in America, but to all people, for all those who may seek the protection of our flag. These illustrious men achieved grander results for mankind within a single century—from 1775 to 1865—than any other men ever accomplished in all the years since first the flight of time began. Washington engaged in no ordinary revolution. With him it was not who should rule, but what should rule. He drew his sword, not for a change of rulers upon an established throne, but to establish a new government, which should acknowledge no throne but the tribune of the people. Lincoln accepted war to save the Union, the safeguard of our liberties, and re-established it on "indestructible foundations" as forever "one and indivisible." To quote his own grand words:

"Now, we are all contending that this nation, under God, shall have a new birth of freedom, and that the government of the people, by the people, for the people, shall not perish from the earth."

Each lived to accomplish his appointed task. Each received the unbounded gratitude of the people of his time, and each is held in great and ever-increasing reverence by posterity. The fame of each will never die. It will grow with the ages, because it is based upon imperishable service to humanity—not to the people of a single generation or country, but to the whole human family, wherever scattered, forever.

The present generation knows Washington only from history, and by that alone can judge him. Lincoln we know by history also; but thousands are still living who participated in the great events in which he was leader and master. Many of his contemporaries survive him; some are here yet in almost every locality. So Lincoln is not far removed from us. Indeed, he may be said to be still known to the millions; not surrounded by the mists of antiquity, nor by the halo of idolatry that is impenetrable.

He never was inaccessible to the people. Thousands carry with them yet the words which he spoke in their hearing; thousands remember the pressure of his hand; and I remember, as though it were but yesterday, and thousands of my comrades will recall, how, when he reviewed the Army of the Potomac immediately after the battle of Antietam, his indescribably sad, thoughtful, far-seeing expression pierced every man's soul. Nobody could keep the people away from him, and when they came to him he would suffer no one to drive them back. So it is that an unusually large number of American people came to know this great man, and that he is still so well remembered by them. It cannot be said that they are mistaken about him, or that they misinterpreted his character and greatness.

; Men are still connected with the government who served during his entire administration. There are at least two senators, and perhaps twice as many representatives, who participated in his first inauguration; men who stood side by side with him in the trying duties of his administration, and have been without interruption in one branch or another of the public service ever since. The Supreme Court of the United States still has among its members one whom Lincoln appointed, and so of other branches of the Federal judiciary. His faithful private secretaries are still alive, and have rendered posterity a great service in their history of Lincoln and his times. They have told the story of his life and public services with such entire frankness and fidelity as to exhibit to the world "the very inner courts of his soul." This host of witnesses, without exception, agree as to the true nobility and intellectual greatness of Lincoln. All proudly claim for Lincoln the highest abilities and the most distinguished and self-sacrificing patriotism.

Lincoln taught them, and has taught us, that no party or partizan can escape responsibility to the people; that no party advantage, or presumed party advantage, should ever swerve us from the plain path of duty, which is ever the path of honor and distinction. He emphasized his words by his daily life and deeds. He showed to the world by his lofty example, as well as by precept and maxim, that there are times when the voice of partizanship should be hushed and that of patriotism only be heeded.

He taught that a good service done for the country, even in aid of an unfriendly administration, brings to the men and the party who rise above the temptation of temporary partizan advantage a lasting gain in the respect and confidence of the people. He showed that such patriotic devotion is usually rewarded, not only with retention in power and the consciousness of duty well and bravely done, but with the gratification of beholding the blessings of relief and prosperity, not of a party or section, but of the whole country. This, he held, should be the first and great consideration of all public servants.

When Lincoln died, a grateful people, moved by a common impulse, immediately placed him side by side with the immortal Washington, and unanimously proclaimed them the two greatest and best Americans. That verdict has not changed, and will not change, nor can we conceive how the historians of this or any age will ever determine what is so clearly a matter of pure personal opinion as to which of these noble men is entitled to greatest honor and homage from the people of America.

A recent writer says: "The amazing growth Lincoln made in the esteem of his countrymen and the world, while he was doing his great work, has been paralleled by the increase of his fame in the years since he died." He might have added that, like every important event of his life, Lincoln's fame rests upon a severer test than that of any other American. Never, in all the ages of men, have the acts, words, motives—even thoughts—of any statesman been so scrutinized, analyzed, studied or speculated upon as his. Yet from all inquirers, without distinction as to party, church, section or country, from friend and from foe alike, comes the unanimous verdict that Abraham Lincoln must have no second place in American history, and that he never will be second to any in the reverent affections of the American people.

Says the gifted Henry Watterson, in a most beautiful, truthful and eloquent tribute to the great emancipator: "Born as lowly as the son of God, reared in penury and squalor, with no gleam of light nor fair surroundings, it was reserved for this strange being, late in life, without name or fame, or seeming preparation, to be snatched from obscurity, raised to supreme command at a supreme moment, and intrusted with the destiny of a nation. Where did Shakspere get his genius? Where did Mozart get his music? Whose hand smote the lyre of the Scottish plowman and staid the life of the German priest? God alone, and as surely as these were raised by God, inspired of God was Abraham Lincoln; and a thousand years hence no story, no tragedy, no epic poem will be filled with greater wonder than that which tells of his life and death. If Lincoln was not inspired of God, then there is no such thing on earth as special providence or the interposition of divine power in the affairs of men."

My fellow-citizens, a noble manhood, nobly consecrated to man, never dies. The martyr to liberty, the emancipator of a race, the savior of the only free government among men, may be buried from human sight, but his deeds will live in human gratitude forever.

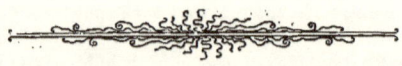

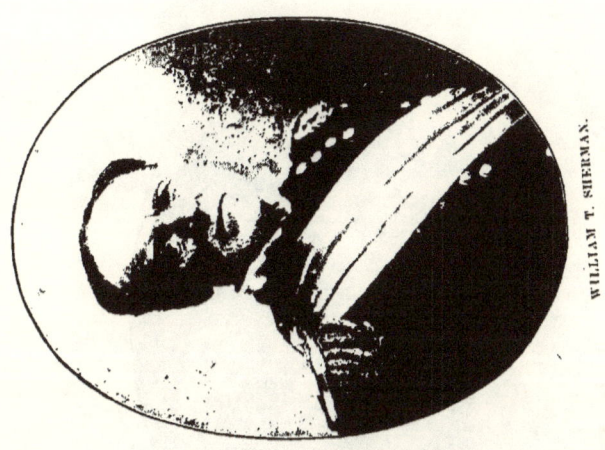

WILLIAM T. SHERMAN.

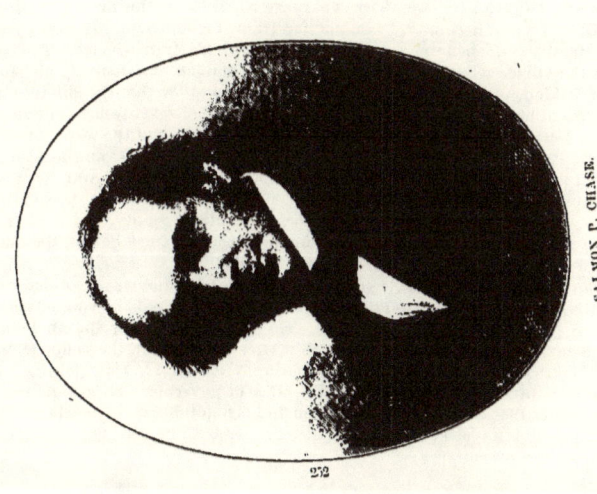

SALMON P. CHASE.

BIOGRAPHICAL SKETCH.

MAJOR McKINLEY was born February 26, 1844, in the manufacturing town of Niles, Trumbull county, Ohio, not far from Youngstown. It was a hamlet then, and the family residence was a modest and comfortable frame house. The boy William entered the village school when five years of age, and later on took up his studies in the town of Poland, to which his parents had moved, in order that the children might avail themselves of better educational facilities. At the age of seventeen he entered Allegheny College. His studies were soon interrupted by the outbreak of the war. The slight, pale-faced, gray-eyed and patriotic young student flung aside his books and decided to shoulder a musket for the preservation of the Union. At the close of the war he was mustered out as captain and brevet-major of the same regiment in which he had enlisted. He read law, and was elected prosecuting attorney of Stark county, and held that position for some years. While at Canton he won the heart of Miss Saxon, the daughter of a local newspaper publisher, and the two were married.

Major McKinley was first elected to Congress in 1876, and was re-elected two and four years after. In 1882, he received the certificate of election, but the vote was close, and his opponent, Jonathan Wallace, was seated. He again entered the lists in 1884, with success, and continued in Congress until 1890. After his defeat in the congressional election of 1890, Major McKinley turned his attention from national to state politics. He became the candidate of Ohio Republicans for the office of governor. So general was the favorable sentiment that there was no opposition to his nomination. The triumphant election which followed is a matter of common history. In 1893, he was again elected to serve as the state's chief executive.

"OH! WHY SHOULD THE SPIRIT OF MORTAL BE PROUD?"

LINCOLN'S FAVORITE POEM.

Oh! why should the spirit of mortal be proud?—
Like a swift-fleeing meteor, a fast-flying cloud,
A flash of the lightning, a break of the wave,
He passeth from life to his rest in the grave.

The leaves of the oak and the willow shall fade,
Be scattered around and together be laid;
And the young and the old, and the low and the high,
Shall moulder to dust and together shall lie.

The infant, a mother attended and loved;
The mother, that infant's affection who proved;
The husband, that mother and infant who blest,—
Each, all, are away to their dwellings of rest.

The maid on whose cheek, on whose brow, in whose eyes,
Shone beauty and pleasure—her triumphs are by,
And the memory of those who loved her and praised,
Are alike from the minds of the living erased.

The hand of the king, that the scepter hath borne,
The brow of the priest, that the miter hath worn,
The eye of the sage and the heart of the brave,
Are hidden and lost in the depths of the grave.

The peasant, whose lot was to sow and to reap,
The herdsman, who climbed with his goats up the steep,
The beggar, who wandered in search of his bread,
Have faded away like the grass that we tread.

The saint, who enjoyed the communion of heaven,
The sinner, who dared to remain unforgiven,
The wise and the foolish, the guilty and just,
Have quietly mingled their bones in the dust.

So the multitude goes—like the flower or the weed,
That withers away to let others succeed;
So the multitude comes—even those we behold,
To repeat every tale that has often been told;

254

For we are the same our fathers have been;
We see the same sights our fathers have seen;
We drink the same stream, we view the same sun,
And run the same course our fathers have run.

The thoughts we are thinking, our fathers would think;
From the death we are shrinking, our fathers would shrink;
To the life we are clinging, they also would cling—
But it speeds from us all, like the bird on the wing.

They loved—but the story we cannot unfold;
They scorned—but the heart of the haughty is cold;
They grieved—but no wail from their slumber will come;
They joyed—but the tongue of their gladness is dumb.

They died—ay, they died—we things that are now,
That walk on the turf that lies over their brow,
And make in their dwellings a transient abode,
Meet the things that they met on their pilgrimage road.

Yea! hope and despondency, pleasure and pain,
Are mingled together in sunshine and rain;
And the smile and the tear, the song and the dirge,
Still follow each other, like surge upon surge.

'Tis the wink of an eye—'tis the draught of a breath,
From the blossom of health to the paleness of death;
From the gilded saloon to the bier and the shroud:—
Oh! why should the spirit of mortal be proud?
                              —*Alexander Knox.*

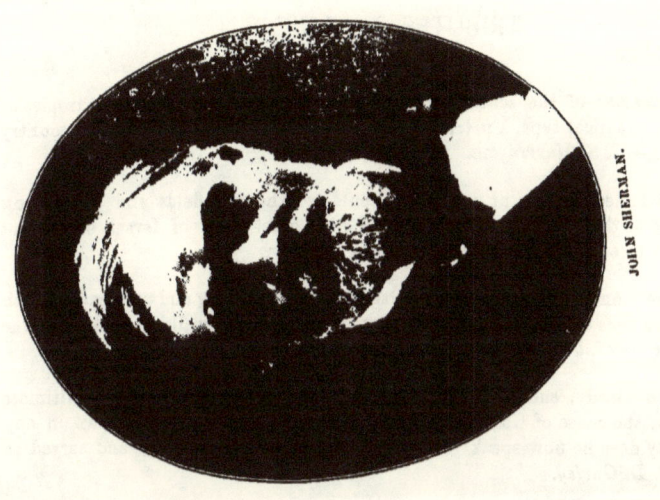

JOHN SHERMAN.

WILLIAM M. EVARTS.

TRIBUTES TO LINCOLN.

A statesman of the school of sound common sense, and a philanthropist of the most practical type, a patriot without a superior, his monument is a country preserved.—*C. S. Harrington.*

He ascended the mount where he could see the fair fields and the smiling vineyards of the promised land. But, like the great leader of Israel, he was not permitted to come to the possession.—*Seth Sweetser.*

At the moment when the stars of the Union, sparkling and resplendent with the golden fires of liberty, were waving over the subdued walls of Richmond, the sepulcher opens, and the strong, the powerful enters it.—*Sr. Rebello da Silva.*

By his steady, enduring confidence in God, and in the complete ultimate success of the cause of God, which is the cause of humanity, more than in any other way does he now speak to us, and to the nation he loved and served so well.—*P. D. Gurley.*

Now all men begin to see that the plain people, who at last came to love him and to lean upon his wisdom, and trust him absolutely, were altogether right, and that in deed and purpose he was earnestly devoted to the welfare of the whole country, and of all its inhabitants.—*R. B. Hayes.*

Abraham Lincoln mastered the problem committed to his hands. He felt that he was acting not merely for a single hour, but for all time. The question for decision was, "Whether this nation, or any other nation, conceived in liberty, and dedicated to the proposition that all are equal, can long endure."—*George W. Briggs.*

The grave that receives the remains of Lincoln receives the costly sacrifice to the Union; the monument which will rise over his body will bear witness to the Union; his enduring memory will assist during countless ages to bind the states together, and to incite to the love of our one undivided, indivisible country.—*George Bancroft.*

A man of great ability, pure patriotism, unselfish nature, full of forgiveness to his enemies, bearing malice toward none, he proved to be the man above all others for the struggle through which the nation had to pass to place itself among the greatest in the family of nations. His fame will grow brighter as time passes and his great work is better understood.—*U. S. Grant.*

Four years ago, oh, Illinois! we took him from your midst an untried man from among the people. Behold, we return him a mighty conqueror. Not thine, but the nation's; not ours, but the world's! Give him peace, ye prairies! In the midst of this great continent his dust shall rest, a sacred treasure to myriads who shall pilgrim to that shrine, to kindle anew their zeal and patriotism.—*Henry Ward Beecher.*

In his freedom from passion and bitterness; in his acute sense of justice; in his courageous faith in the right, and his inextinguishable hatred of wrong; in warm and heartfelt sympathy and mercy; in his coolness of judgment; in his unquestioned rectitude of intention—in a word, in his ability to lift himself for his country's sake above all mere partizanship, in all the marked traits of his character combined, he has had no parallel since Washington, and while our republic endures he will live with him in the grateful hearts of his grateful countrymen.—*Schuyler Colfax.*

To him belongs the credit of having worked his way up from the humblest position an American freeman can occupy to the highest and most powerful, without losing, in the least, the simplicity and sincerity of nature which endeared him alike to the plantation slave and the metropolitan millionaire. The most malignant party opposition has never been able to call in question the patriotism of his motives, or tarnish with the breath of suspicion the brightness of his spotless fidelity. Ambition did not warp, power corrupt, nor glory dazzle him.—*Warren H. Cudworth.*

Abraham Lincoln was born, and, until he became president, always lived in a part of the country which, at the period of the Declaration of Independence, was a savage wilderness. Strange but happy Providence that a voice from that savage wilderness, now fertile in men, was inspired to uphold the pledges and promises of the Declaration! The unity of the republic on the indestructible foundation of liberty and equality was vindicated by the citizens of a community which had no existence when the republic was formed. A cabin was built in primitive rudeness, and the future president split the rails for the fence to inclose the lot. These rails have become classical in our history, and the name of rail-splitter has been more than the degree of a college. Not that the splitter of rails is especially meritorious, but because the people are proud to trace aspiring talent to humble beginnings, and because they found in this tribute a new opportunity of vindicating the dignity of free labor.—*Charles Sumner.*

ANECDOTES.

ANECDOTES.

LINCOLN'S REPLY TO A MAN WHO KNEW HOW TO PUT DOWN THE REBELLION.

During the war a western farmer sought the president day after day, until he procured the much-desired audience. He had a plan for the successful prosecution of the war, to which Mr. Lincoln listened as patiently as he could. When he was through, he asked the opinion of the president upon his plan. "Well," said Mr. Lincoln, "I'll answer by telling you a story. You have heard of Mr. Blank, of Chicago? He was an immense loafer in his way; in fact, never did anything in his life. One day he got crazy over a great rise in the price of wheat, upon which many wheat speculators gained large fortunes. Blank started off one morning to one of the most successful of the wheat speculators, and with much enthusiasm, laid before him a 'plan' by which he, the said Blank, was certain of becoming independently rich. When he had finished, he asked the opinion of his hearer upon his plan of operations. The reply came as follows: 'My advice is that you *stick to your business.*' 'But,' asked Blank, 'what is my business?' 'I don't know, I'm sure, what it is,' says the merchant, 'but *whatever it is, I would advise you to stick to it!*' And now," said Mr. Lincoln, "I mean nothing offensive, for I know you mean well, but I think you had better stick to your business, and leave the war to those who have the responsibility of managing it!" Whether the farmer was satisfied or not is not known, but he did not tarry long in the presidential mansion.

HOW LINCOLN WAS LOVED.

"When I have had to address a fagged and listless audience, I have found that nothing was so certain to arouse them as to introduce the name of Abraham Lincoln." So remarked Dr. Newman Hall, of London, to me last year; and I have had a similar experience with American audiences. No other name has such electric power on every true heart from Maine to Mexico. If Washington is the most revered, Lincoln is the *best loved* man that ever trod this continent.— *Theodore L. Cuyler, D.D.*

HOW MR. LINCOLN TREATED AN OLD KENTUCKY FRIEND.

It was characteristic of Lincoln that while he did not often refer to his early life, he seemed ever mindful when occasion offered of those who were then his associates and friends. A case very aptly illustrating this point occurred at the time the ranks of the Union army were being repleted by the operations of the "draft" acts.

Through some technicality or other an injustice was done that section of Kentucky surrounding the county in which Lincoln was born, and several counties were not credited with the numbers of enlistments that had really been made from within their borders. Finally, Dr. Jesse Rodman, of Hodgensville, prominent as a citizen and politician, was sent to Washington for the purpose of interviewing President Lincoln and endeavoring to have the error corrected.

Lincoln received him with the greatest cordiality, and insisted that Dr. Rodman should remain several days as a presidential guest. During this time Lincoln made the fullest and most minute inquiry concerning persons whom he had known in his boyhood life among the Kentucky hills. The desired relief was also cheerfully given by the president.—*Mr. D. J. Thomas, now of The Voice, New York, late of The New Era, Springfield, Ohio.*

Nothing so moved Lincoln as injustice or oppression toward a fellow-man. During the campaign of 1864, when the president was a candidate for re-election, and was opposed by General George B. McClellan, a soldier was refused a pass through the lines to his New York home by some officious attache of the army because of the fact that he wore a McClellan badge. Friends brought the matter before the president, who investigated the charges, and found that the pass was refused on the grounds named, beyond doubt. The soldier was sent for by Lincoln, and presented with a pass in the president's own handwriting, accompanied by a hearty hand-shake and a "God bless you, my boy! *Show them that;* it'll take you home."—*D. J. Thomas.*

"TOO CUSSED DIRTY."

The following story is often told of Father Abraham about two contraband servants of General Kelly and Captain George Harrison: When the general and his staff were on their way up the mountains they stopped at a little village to get something to eat. They persuaded the occupant of the farm-house to cook them a meal, and in order to expedite matters, sent the two contrabands mentioned to assist in preparing the repast. After it was over the general told the negroes to help themselves. An hour or two afterward he observed them gnawing away at some hard crackers and flitch.

"Why didn't you eat your dinner at the village?" asked the general of one of them.

"Well, to tell the God's trufe, general, it was too cussed dirty!" was the reply.

"HIT OR MISS" INSTRUCTIONS.

Some simple remark that some of the party might make would remind Mr. Lincoln of an apropos story. Mr. Chase happened to remark, "Oh, I am so sorry that I had to write a letter to Mr. So-and-so before I left home!" Mr. Lincoln promptly responded· "Chase, never regret what you don't write ; it is what you do write that you are often called upon to feel sorry for."

Here is another: Mr. Stanton said that just before he left Washington he had received a telegram from General Mitchell, in Alabama, asking instructions in regard to a certain emergency that had occurred. The secretary said that he did not precisely understand the emergency as explained by General Mitchell, but he had answered back, "All right; go ahead."

"Now," he said, "Mr. President, if I have made an error in not understanding him correctly, I will have to get you to countermand the order."

"Well," exclaimed Lincoln, "that is very much like the occasion of a certain horse sale I remember that took place at the cross-roads down in Kentucky when I was a boy. A particularly fine horse was to be sold, and the people gathered together. They had a small boy to ride the horse up and down while the spectators examined the horse's points. At last one man whispered to the boy as he went by: 'Look here, boy, hain't that horse got the splints?' The boy replied: 'Mister, I don't know what the splints is, but if it is good for him, he has got it, if it ain't good for him, he ain't got it.' Now," said Mr. Lincoln, "if this was good for Mitchell, it was all right; but if it was not, I have got to countermand it."—*General Egbert L. Viele, in "Tributes from Lincoln's Associates."*

LINCOLN AS A LAWYER.

As a lawyer, according to Messrs. Nicolay and Hay, Mr. Lincoln, notwithstanding "all his stories and jests, his frank, companionable humor, his gift of easy accessibility and welcome, was, even while he traveled the Eighth circuit, a man of grave and serious temper, and of an unusual innate dignity and reserve. He had few or no special intimates, and there was a line beyond which no one ever thought of passing." They thus describe him in the court-room:

"He seemed absolutely at home in the court-room; his great stature did not encumber him there; it seemed like a natural symbol of superiority. His bearing and gesticulation had no awkwardness about them; they were simply striking and original. He assumed at the start a frank and friendly relation with the jury, which was extremely effective. He usually began, as the phrase ran, by 'giving away his case;' by allowing to the opposite side every possible advantage that they could honestly and justly claim. Then he would present his own side of the case, with a clearness, a candor, an adroitness of statement which at once flattered and convinced the jury, and made even the bystanders his partizans. Sometimes he disturbed the court with laughter by his humorous or apt illustrations; sometimes he excited the audience by that florid and exuberant rhetoric which he knew well enough how and when to indulge in; but his more usual and more successful manner was to rely upon a clear, strong, lucid statement, keeping details in proper subordination, and bringing forward, in a way which fastened the attention of court and jury alike, the essential point on which he claimed a decision. 'Indeed,' says one of his colleagues, 'his statement often rendered argument unnecessary, and often the court would stop him, and say: "If that is the case, we will hear the other side."'"

Judge David Davis said of him:

"The framework of his mental and moral being was honesty, and a wrong cause was poorly defended by him."

A WITTY REPLY.

On one occasion it is said that some of Mr. Lincoln's friends were talking about him and Stephen A. Douglas. The conversation led to the physical proportions of the respective men, and an argument arose as to the proper length of a man's leg. During the discussion on the subject Mr. Lincoln came in and quietly settled himself, and it was agreed that the question should be referred to him for settlement. They told him what they had been talking about, and asked him what, in his opinion, was the proper length of a man's leg. "Well," said he, reflectively, "I should think that they ought to be long enough to reach from his body to the ground."

A LINCOLN STORY ABOUT LITTLE DAN WEBSTER'S SOILED HANDS— HOW DAN ESCAPED A FLOGGING.

Mr. Lincoln on one occasion narrated to Hon. Mr. Odell and others, with much zest, the following story about young Daniel Webster:

When quite young, at school, Daniel was one day guilty of a gross violation of the rules. He was detected in the act, and called up by the teacher for punishment. This was to be the old-fashioned "feruling" of the hand. His hands happened to be very dirty. Knowing this, on the way to the teacher's desk, he spit upon the palm of his right hand, wiping it off upon the side of his pantaloons.

"Give me your hand, sir," said the teacher, very sternly.

Out went the right hand, partly cleansed. The teacher looked at it a moment, and said:

"Daniel, if you will find another hand in this school-room as filthy as that, I will let you off this time!"

Instantly from behind the back came the left hand. "Here it is, sir," was the ready reply.

"That will do," said the teacher, "for this time; you can take your seat, sir."

ADVICE TO A CLIENT.

To a man who once offered him a case, the merits of which he did not appreciate, he made, according to his partner, Mr. Herndon, the following response:

"Yes, there is no reasonable doubt but that I can gain your case for you. I can set a whole neighborhood at loggerheads; I can distress a widowed mother and her six fatherless children, and thereby get for you six hundred dollars, which rightfully belongs, it appears to me, as much to them as it does to you. I shall not take your case, but I will give a little advice for nothing. You seem a sprightly, energetic man. I would advise you to try your hand at making six hundred dollars in some other way."

DIFFICULT BRIDGE-BUILDING.

"I once knew a sound churchman by the name of Brown, who was a member of a very sober and pious committee, having in charge the erection of a bridge over a dangerous and rapid river. Several architects failed, and at last Brown said he had a friend named Jones who had built several bridges, and undoubtedly could build that one. So Mr. Jones was called in. 'Can you build this bridge?' inquired the committee. 'Yes,' replied Jones, 'or any other. I could build a bridge to the infernal regions, if necessary!' The committee were shocked, and Brown felt called upon to defend his friend. 'I know Jones so well,' said he, 'and he is so honest a man and so good an architect that if he states soberly and positively that he can build a bridge to — to —, why, I believe it; but I feel bound to say that I have my doubts about the abutment on the infernal side.' 'So,' said Mr. Lincoln, 'when politicians told me that the northern and southern wings of Democracy could be harmonized, why, I believed them, of course; but I always had my doubts about the 'abutment' on the *other* side."

THE PRESIDENT ADVISES SECRETARY STANTON TO PREPARE FOR DEATH.

Secretary Stanton, when secretary of war, took a fancy one day for a house in Washington that Lamon had just bargained for. Lamon not only did not vacate, but went to Stanton and said he would kill him if he interfered with the house. Stanton was furious at the threat, and made it known at once to Lincoln. The latter said to the astonished war secretary:

"Well, Stanton, if Ward has said he will kill you, he certainly will, and I'd advise you to prepare for death without further delay."

The president promised, however, to do what he could to appease the murderous marshal, and this was the end of Stanton's attempt on the house.

THEY SAW PRESIDENT LINCOLN.

The Chicago *Times-Herald* has printed some reminiscences of Lincoln, communicated by General John McConnell. He had been a close friend of Lincoln before the war. "He was to me a perfect being," General McConnell declares. "I do not know a flaw in his character."

Not long after Lincoln's election to the presidency, General McConnell was with him in his office in the old state-house in Springfield, when a tall, lank countryman, with his trousers tucked into his boots, put his head into the door, and asked to see Mr. Lincoln. He was from Kansas, he explained, and with his family was going back to Indiana. He had voted for Mr. Lincoln, and wanted to see him.

Mr. Lincoln, we are left to suppose, received his unconventional caller with politeness, and presently the man asked:

"What kind of a tree is that below there in the yard?"

It was a warm November day, and the window was open. Mr. Lincoln looked out, and said:

"It is a cypress. I suppose you would have known it if you had been on the ground?"

"No. I don't mean that," said the countryman. "I mean the other one nearer the house. You will have to lean farther out."

Mr. Lincoln leaned out, and then straightening up, he said:

"There is no other one."

"No?" said the man. "Well, do you see that woman and them three children over there in that wagon? That is my wife and children. I told them I would show them the president-elect of the United States, and I have. Good-by, Mr. Lincoln."

And so saying, he stalked down-stairs.

MR. LINCOLN'S KIND-HEARTEDNESS.

An incident connected with Mr. Shultz illustrates the kind-heartedness of Mr. Lincoln. On his return from his former imprisonment, on parole, young Shultz was sent to Camp Parole, at Alexander. Having had no furlough since the war, efforts were made without success to get him liberty to pay a brief visit to his friends; but having faith in the warm-heartedness of the president, the young soldier's widowed mother wrote to Mr. Lincoln, stating that he had been in nearly every battle fought by the Army of the Potomac, had never asked a furlough, was now a paroled prisoner, and in consequence unable to perform active duties; that two of his brothers had also served in the army, and asking that he be allowed to visit home, that she might see him once more. Her trust in the president was not unfounded. He immediately caused a furlough to be given to her son, who, shortly before he was exchanged, visited his family, to their great surprise and joy.

MR. LINCOLN'S KINDNESS OF HEART TO THE DISTRESSED.

Mr. Lincoln's kindness of heart was known to everybody. Vice-president Colfax says that his doorkeepers had "standing orders from him that, no matter how great might be the public throng, if either senators or representatives had to wait, or to be turned away without audience, he must see before the day closed every messenger who came to him with a petition for the saving of life." Accounts of many such cases are given. A woman, carrying a baby, waited three days at the White House to see Mr. Lincoln. Her husband, who had sent a substitute, had enlisted subsequently himself when intoxicated, and had deserted from the army, and had been caught and sentenced to be shot. On his way through the anteroom Mr. Lincoln heard the baby cry. "He instantly went back to his office and rang the bell. 'Daniel,' said he, 'is there a woman with a baby in the anteroom?' I said there was, and, if he would allow me to say it, I thought it was a case he ought to see; for it was a matter of life and death. Said he: 'Send her to me at once.' She went in, told her story, and the president pardoned her husband. As the woman came out from his presence, her eyes were lifted and her lips moving in prayer, the tears streaming down her cheeks." Said Daniel: "I went up to her, and, pulling her shawl, said: 'Madam, it was the baby that did it!'"

AN UNPATRIOTIC CONTRABAND.

One of the funniest stories of the war was related by Mr. Lincoln, as follows: "Upon the hurricane-deck of one of our gunboats, an elderly darky, with a very philosophical and retrospective cast of countenance, squatted upon his bundle, toasting his shins against the chimney, and apparently plunged into a state of profound meditation. Finding upon inquiry that he belonged to the Ninth Illinois, one of the most gallantly behaved and heavy losing regiments at the Fort Donelson battle, and part of which was aboard, I began to interrogate him upon the subject:

"'Were you in the fight?'

"'Had a little taste of it, sa.'

"'Stood your ground, did you?'

"'No, sa, I runs.'

"'Run at the first fire, did you?'

"'Yes, sa, and would hab run soona, had I knowd it war comin'.'

"'Why, that wasn't very creditable to your courage.'

"'Dat isn't my line, sa—cookin's my profeshun.'

"'Well, but have you no regard for your reputation?'

"'Reputation's nuffin to me by de side ob life.'

"'Do you consider your life worth more than other people's?'

"'It's worth more to me, sa.'

"'Then you must value it very highly?'

"'Yes, sa, I does, more dan all dis wuld, more dan a millian ob dollars, sa, for what would dat be wuth to a man wid de bref out ob him? Self-preserbation am de fust law wid me.'

"'But why should you act upon a different rule from other men?'

"'Because different men set different values upon their lives; mine is not in de market.'

"'But if you lost it, you would have the satisfaction of knowing that you died for your country.'

"'What satisfaction would dat be to me, when de power ob feelin' was gone?'

"'Then patriotism and honor are nothing to you?'

"'Nufin whatever, sa—I regard them as among the vanities.'

"'If our soldiers were like you, traitors might have broken up the government without resistance.'

"'Yes, sa, dar would hab been no help for it. I wouldn't put my life in de scale 'ginst any gobernment dat eber existed, for no gobernment could replace de loss to me.'

"'Do you think any of your company would have missed you if you had been killed?'

"'Maybe not, sa—a dead white man ain't much to dese sogers, let alone a dead nigga—but I'd a missed myself, and dat was de pint wid me."

LINCOLN AND COLONEL WELLER.

Weller was at Washington settling his accounts as minister to Mexico. After their adjustment he concluded to pay his respects to Mr. Lincoln, with whom he had served in Congress. He called at the presidential mansion, and was courteously received.

"Mr. President," said Colonel Weller, "I have called on you to say that I most heartily indorse the conservative position you have assumed, and will stand by you as long as you prosecute the war for the preservation of the Union and the Constitution."

"Colonel Weller," said the president, "I am heartily glad to hear you say this."

"Yes, Mr. President," said Weller, "I desire an appointment to aid in this work."

"What do you want, colonel?" asked Abraham.

"*I desire to be appointed commodore in the navy,*" said Weller.

The president replied:

"Colonel, I did not think you had any experience as a sailor."

"I never had, Mr. President," said Weller; "but judging from the brigadier-generals you have appointed in Ohio, the less experience a man has, the higher position he attains."

Lincoln turned off with a hearty laugh, and said: "I owe you one, colonel!"

JUDGE SHELLABARGER AND MR. LINCOLN.

Hon. Samuel Shellabarger (of Washington, D. C., and a native of Springfield, Ohio), whose congressional service covered President Lincoln's years in the White House, speaks of a visit to Mr. Lincoln, giving this incident:

"I, like many other members of Congress, did not see Mr. Lincoln often, because we felt that he was overwhelmed with the burdens of the hour, and people giving him no rest. But a young man in the army, Ben Tappan, wanted a transfer from the volunteer service to the regular service, retaining his rank of lieutenant, and with staff duty. There was some regulation against such transfer; but Tappan's stepfather, Frank Wright, of Ohio, thought it could be done. He had been to Secretary Stanton, who was an uncle of young Tappan by marriage, and on account of this so-called relationship the secretary declined to act in the matter. Wright and I therefore went up to the White House to see the president about it. After talking it over, Mr. Lincoln told a story, the application of which was that the army was getting to be all staff and no army, there was such a rush for staff duty by young officers. However, he looked over Lieutenant Tappan's paper, heard what Secretary Stanton had told us about his delicacy in transferring Lieutenant Tappan against the regulation because of the relationship by marriage. Then Mr. Lincoln wrote across the application something like the following indorsement:

"Lieutenant Tappan, of —— regiment, volunteers, desires a transfer to —— regiment, regular service, and assigned to staff duty with present rank. If the only objection to this transfer is Lieutenant Tappan's relationship to the secretary of war, that objection is overruled.

"A. LINCOLN.

"This, of course, threw the responsibility of breaking the regulation on Secretary Stanton. We never heard anything more about the transfer."

DWIGHT L. MOODY'S STORY OF LINCOLN'S COMPASSION.

"During the war," says Dwight L. Moody, the world's great evangelist, "I remember a young man, not twenty, who was court-martialed at the front and sentenced to be shot. The story was this:

"The young fellow had enlisted. He was not obliged to, but he went off with another young man. They were what we call 'chums.'

"One night his companion was ordered out on picket duty, and he asked the young man to go for him. The next night he was ordered out himself; and having been awake two nights, and not being used to it, fell asleep at his post, and for the offense he was tried and sentenced to death. It was right after the order issued by the president that no interference would be allowed in cases of this kind. This sort of thing had become too frequent, and it must be stopped.

"When the news reached the father and mother in Vermont, it nearly broke their hearts. The thought that their son should be shot was too great for them. They had no hope that he could be saved by anything that they could do.

"But they had a little daughter who had read the life of Abraham Lincoln, and knew how he loved his own children, and she said:

"'If Abraham Lincoln knew how my father and mother loved my brother, he wouldn't let him be shot.'

"The little girl thought this matter over, and made up her mind to see the president.

"She went to the White House, and the sentinel, when he saw her imploring looks, passed her in; and when she came to the door and told the private secretary that she wanted to see the president, he could not refuse her. She came into the chamber and found Abraham Lincoln surrounded by his generals and counselors; and when he saw the little country girl, he asked her what she wanted.

"The little maid told her plain, simple story—how her brother, whom her father and mother loved very dearly, had been sentenced to be shot; how they were mourning for him, and if he was to die in that way it would break their hearts.

"The president's heart was touched with compassion, and he immediately sent a dispatch canceling the sentence and giving the boy a parole so that he could come home and see his father and mother. I just tell you this to show you how Abraham Lincoln's heart was moved by compassion for the sorrow of that father and mother; and if he showed so much, do you think the Son of God will not have compassion upon you, sinner, if you only take that crushed, bruised heart to him?"

A CHARACTERISTIC LETTER.

EXECUTIVE MANSION, October 17, 1861.

MAJOR RAMSEY.

My Dear Sir:—The lady—bearer of this—says she has two sons who want to work. Set them at it, if possible. Wanting to work is so rare a merit that it should be encouraged.   A. LINCOLN.

LINCOLN'S PRIVATE SECRETARY IS WITTY.

The private secretary of the president was a wag. A young man decidedly inebriated walked into the executive mansion and asked for the president.

"What do you want with him?" inquired the secretary.

"Oh, I want an office with a good salary—a sinecure."

"Well," replied the secretary, "I can tell you something better for you than a sinecure—you had better try *water cure.*"

A new idea seemed to strike the young inebriate, and he vamoosed.

ANTICIPATIONS OF A HAPPY SECOND TERM.

The Hon. Henry Wilson, who was on the ticket with General Grant in his second campaign, as vice-president, says that on the day before his death the president said to his wife:

"We have had a hard time together since we came to Washington; but now the war is over, and with God's blessing upon us, we may hope for four years of happiness, and then we will go back to Illinois and pass the remainder of our lives in peace."

HOW A SENTENCE WAS IMPROVED.

On another occasion the public printer called the president's attention to a sentence in one of his messages which he thought awkwardly constructed. The president acknowledged the point of the criticism, and said: "Go home, Defrees, and see if you can better it." The next day Mr. Defrees took in to him his amendment. Mr. Lincoln met him by saying: "Seward found the same fault that you did, and he has been rewriting the paragraph also." Then, reading Mr. Defrees' version, he said: "I believe you have beat Seward; but, 'I jings' [a common expression with him], I think I can beat you both." Then, taking up his pen, he wrote the sentence as it was finally printed.

THE PRESIDENT SHAKING HANDS WITH WOUNDED REBELS.

A correspondent who was with the president on the occasion of a visit to Frederick, Maryland, tells the following incident:

"After leaving General Richardson, the party passed a house in which were a large number of Confederate wounded. By request of the president, the party alighted and entered the building. Mr. Lincoln, after looking, remarked to the wounded Confederates that if they had no objection he would be pleased to take them by the hand. He said the solemn obligations which we owe to our country and posterity compel the prosecution of this war, and it followed that many were our enemies through uncontrollable circumstances, and he bore them no malice, and could take them by the hand with sympathy and good feeling. After a short silence the Confederates came forward and each silently but fervently shook the hand of the president. Mr. Lincoln and General McClellan then walked forward by the side of those who were wounded too severely to be able to arise, and bid them to be of good cheer, assuring them that every possible care should be bestowed upon them to ameliorate their condition. It was a moving scene, and there was not a dry eye in the building, either among the Nationals or Confederates. Both the president and General McClellan were kind in their remarks and treatment of the rebel sufferers during this remarkable interview.

LINCOLN AND THE COLORED TROOPS.

General Grant intended that the army under Sherman, at Chattanooga, the Army of the Potomac, under Meade, and the Army of the James, under Butler, should move at the same time. General Burnside was at Annapolis, in Maryland, with the Ninth Corps, numbering nearly 30,000 men. He was directed to march to Washington, and from there to the Rapidan, to co-operate with the Army of the Potomac.

Down Pennsylvania avenue comes Burnside's troops, turning up Fourteenth street, where the president stands upon a balcony to review them. Some of the veterans have fought at Bull Run, Ball's Bluff, Roanoke, Newbern, in front of Richmond, Antietam, Gettysburg, Knoxville. The flags which they carry are in tatters, but they are the dearest things on earth to the men keeping step to the drum-beat. There is the steady tramping of the men, the deep, heavy jar of gun-carriages, clattering of horses' hoofs, clanking of sabers. General Burnside and the president, standing side by side, look down upon the serried ranks. The lines are deepening in the face of Abraham Lincoln. He is pale and care-worn. The soldiers behold him, swing their hats, and hurrah A division of veterans pass, and then, with full ranks, the platoons extending the entire width of the street, come brigades which have never been in battle—men who have come at the call of their country to lay down their lives on the battle-field. *Their country!* They never had a country till that pale man on the balcony gave them one. They never were men till he made them such. They were slaves; he made them freemen. They have been chattels—things; now they are owners of themselves—citizens—soldiers of the republic. Never before have they beheld their benefactor. "Hurrah for Uncle Abe! Hurrah for Mars Linkum!" No cheers like theirs. It is the spontaneous outburst from grateful hearts. Yes; in return for what he has done for them and for their race will they fight to the death!—*Coffin.*

TAD'S REBEL FLAG.

One of the prettiest incidents in the closing days of the civil war occurred when the troops, "marching home again," passed in grand form, if with well-worn uniforms and tattered bunting, before the White House, says *Harper's Young People.*

Naturally, an immense crowd had assembled on the streets, the lawns, porches, balconies and windows, even those of the executive mansion itself being crowded to excess. A central figure was that of the president, Abraham Lincoln, who, with bared head, unfurled and waved our nation's flag in the midst of lusty cheers.

But suddenly there was an unexpected sight.

A small boy leaned forward and sent streaming to the air the banner of the boys in gray. It was an old flag which had been captured from the Confederates, and which the urchin, the president's second son, Tad, had obtained possession of and considered an additional triumph to unfurl on this all-important day.

Vainly did the servant who had followed him to the window plead with him to desist. No, Master Tad, the pet of the White House, was not to be prevented from adding to the loyal demonstration of the hour..

To his surprise, however, the crowd viewed it differently. Had it floated from any other window in the Capitol that day, no doubt it would have been the target of contempt and abuse; but when the president, understanding what had happened, turned, with a smile on his grand, plain face, and showed his approval by a gesture and expression, cheer after cheer rent the air.

It was, surely enough, the expression of peace and good will which, of all our commanders, none was better pleased to promote than our commander-in-chief.

In response to a letter of inquiry by the author of this book to Hon. Robert T. Lincoln (formerly secretary of war, and minister to England) concerning " Tad," Mr. Lincoln replied as follows:

60 LAKE SHORE DRIVE, CHICAGO, 20th December, 1895.

MY DEAR SIR:—In reply to your inquiry, my brother Thomas died on July 15, 1871, from an illness resulting from a cold.

Very sincerely yours, ROBERT T. LINCOLN.

AN ENGLISH PORTRAIT OF MR. LINCOLN.

To say that he is ugly is nothing; to add that his figure is grotesque is to convey no adequate impression. Fancy a man six feet high, and then out of proportion; with long, bony arms and legs, which somehow seem to be always in the way; with great, rugged, furrowed hands, which grasp you like a vise when shaking yours; with a long, snaggy neck, and a chest too narrow for the great arms at its side. Add to this figure a head cocoanut-shaped and somewhat too small for such a stature, covered with rough, uncombed and uncombable hair, that stands out in every direction at once; a face furrowed, wrinkled and indented, as though it had been scarred by vitriol; a high, narrow forehead; and sunk deep beneath bushy eyebrows, two bright, dreamy eyes, that seem to gaze through you without looking at you; a few irregular blotches of black, bristly hair in the place where beard and whiskers ought to grow; a close-set, thin-lipped, stern mouth, with two rows of large white teeth, and a nose and ears which have been taken by mistake from a head of twice the size. Clothe this figure, then, in a long, tight, badly fitting suit of black, creased, soiled, and puckered up at every salient point of the figure (and every point of this figure is salient), put on large, ill-fitting boots, gloves too long for the long, bony fingers, and a fluffy hat, covered to the top with dusty, puffy crape; and then add to this an air of strength, physical as well as moral, and a strange look of dignity coupled with all this grotesqueness, and you will have the impression left upon me by Abraham Lincoln.

AN AMERICAN'S PORTRAIT.

In character and culture he is a fair representative of the average American. His awkward speech and yet more awkward silence, his uncouth manners, self-taught and partly forgotten, his style miscellaneous, concreted from the best authors, like a reading book, and yet oftentimes of Saxon force and classic purity; his argument, his logic a joke, both unseasonable at times and irresistible always; his questions answers, and his answers questions; his guesses prophecies, and fulfillment ever beyond his promise; honest yet shrewd; simple yet reticent; heavy yet energetic; never despairing, never sanguine; careless in forms, conscientious in essentials; never sacrificing a good servant once trusted; never deserting a good principle once adopted; not afraid of new ideas, nor despising old ones; improving opportunities to confess mistakes, ready to learn, getting at facts, doing nothing when he knows not what to do; hesitating at nothing when he sees the right; lacking the recognized qualifications of a party leader, and leading his party as no other man can; sustaining his political enemies in Missouri in their defeat, sustaining his political friends in Maryland in their victory; conservative in his sympathies and radical in his acts; Socratic in his style and Baconian in his method; his religion consisting in truthfulness, temperance; asking good people to pray for him, and publicly acknowledging in events the hand of God, yet he stands before you as the type of "Brother Jonathan," a not perfect man, and yet more precious than fine gold.

LINCOLN'S FIRST CONVICTIONS OF WAR—HIS GREAT SADNESS.

The Hon. Leonard Swett, in an address before the Union Veteran Club, at Chicago, gives the following interesting reminiscence:

I remember well the first time that the belief that war was inevitable took hold of Lincoln's mind. Some time after the election Lincoln asked me to write a letter to Thurlow Weed to come to Springfield and consult with him (Lincoln). Mr. Weed came, and he, the president-elect and myself had a meeting, in which Lincoln for the first time acknowledged that he was in possession of facts that showed that the South meant war.

These facts consisted of the steps which the disaffected states were taking to spirit away the arms belonging to the government, and, taking them into consideration, Lincoln was forced to the belief that his administration was to be one of blood.

As he made this admission, his countenance rather than his words demonstrated the sadness which it occasioned, and he wanted to know if there was not some way of avoiding the disaster. He felt as if he could not go forward to an era of war, and these days were to him a sort of forty days in the wilderness, passed under great stress of doubt, and, perhaps to him, of temptations of weakness. Finally, however, he seemed quietly to put on the armor and prepare himself for the great responsibility and struggle before him.

A MIDNIGHT PARDON.

A congressman who heard that a friend of his in the army had been court-martialed and sentenced to be shot, failing to move Secretary Stanton to grant a pardon, rushed to the White House late at night, after the president had retired, and forced his way to the president's bedroom, and earnestly besought his interference, exclaiming, earnestly:

"This man must not be shot, Mr. Lincoln. I cannot allow him to be shot!"

"Well," said the president in reply, "I do not believe shooting will do him any good. Give me that pen."

And so the pardon was granted.

LINCOLN ON BAYONETS.

"You can't do anything with them southern fellows," the old gentleman at the table was saying. "If they get whipped, they'll retreat to them southern swamps and bayous along with the fishes and crocodiles. You haven't got the fish-nets made that'll catch 'em."

"Look here, old gentleman!" screamed Old Abe, who was sitting alongside, "we've got just the nets for traitors, in the bayous or anywhere.'

"Hey? What nets?"

"*Bayou-nets!*" and Abraham pointed his joke with a fork, spearing a fish-ball savagely.

LINCOLN AGREEABLY DISAPPOINTED.

Mr. Lincoln, as the highest public officer of the nation, was necessarily very much bored by all sorts of people calling upon him.

An officer of the government called one day at the White House, and introduced a clerical friend.

"Mr. President," said he, "allow me to present to you my friend, the Rev. Mr. F., of——. Mr. F. has expressed a desire to see you and have some conversation with you, and I am happy to be the means of introducing him."

The president shook hands with Mr. F., and desiring him to be seated, took a seat himself. Then, his countenance having assumed an air of patient waiting, he said:

"I am now ready to hear what you have to say.";

"Oh, bless you, sir," said Mr. F., "I have nothing especially to say; I merely called to pay my respects to you, and, as one of the millions, to assure you of my hearty sympathy and support."

"My dear sir," said the president, rising promptly, his face showing instant relief, and with both hands grasping that of his visitor, "I am very glad to see you, indeed. *I thought you had come to preach to me!*"

HOW LINCOLN ILLUSTRATED WHAT MIGHT BE DONE WITH JEFF. DAVIS.

One of Mr. Lincoln's stories was told to a party of gentlemen, who, among the tumbling ruins of the Confederacy, anxiously asked "what he would do with Jeff. Davis:"

"There was a boy in Springfield," replied Mr. Lincoln, "who saved up his money and bought a 'coon,' which, after the novelty wore off, became a great nuisance.

"He was one day leading him through the streets, and had his hands full to keep clear of the little vixen, who had torn his clothes half off of him. At length he sat down on the curbstone, completely fagged out. A man passing was stopped by the lad's disconsolate appearance, and asked the matter.

"'Oh,' was the only reply, 'this coon is such a trouble to me.'

"'Why don't you get rid of him, then?' said the gentleman.

"'Hush!' said the boy; 'don't you see he is gnawing his rope off? I am going to let him do it, and then I will go home and tell the folks that he got away from me!'"

LINCOLN UNDER FIRE.

Leaving the ditch, my pass carried me into the fort, where, to my surprise, I found the president, Secretary Stanton and other civilians. A young colonel of artillery, who appeared to be the officer of the day, was in great distress because the president would expose himself, and paid little attention to his warnings. He was satisfied the Confederates had recognized him, for they were firing at him very hotly, and a soldier near him had just fallen with a broken thigh. He asked my advice, for he said the president was in great danger.

" What would you do with me under like circumstances?" I asked.

" I would civilly ask you to take a position where you were not exposed."

"And if I refused to obey?"

" I would send a sergeant and a file of men, and make you obey."

" Then treat the president just as you would me or any civilian."

" I dare not. He is my superior officer; I have taken oath to obey his orders."

" He has given you no orders. Follow my advice, and you will not regret it."

"I will," he said. "I may as well die for one thing as another. If he were shot, I should hold myself responsible."

He walked to where the president was looking over the parapet. "Mr. President," he said, "you are standing within range of five hundred rebel rifles. Please come down to a safer place. If you do not, it will be my duty to call a file of men, and make you."

"And you would do quite right, my boy!" said the president, coming down at once. "You are in command of this fort. I should be the last man to set an example of disobedience!"—*L. E. Chittenden's "Recollections."*

"PRING UP DE SHACKASSES, FOR COT SAKE!"

President Lincoln often laughed over the following incident: One of General Fremont's batteries of eight Parrot guns, supported by a squadron of horses commanded by Major Richards, was in a sharp conflict with a battery of the enemy near at hand, and shells and shot were flying thick and fast, when the commander of the battery, a German, one of Fremont's staff, rode suddenly up to the cavalry, exclaiming, in loud and excited terms, "Pring up de shackasses, pring up de shackasses, for Cot sake, hurry up de shackasses im-me-di-ate-ly!" The necessity of this order, though not quite apparent, will be more obvious when it is remembered that the "shackasses" are mules, carrying mountain howitzers, which are fired from the backs of that much-abused but valuable animal; and the immediate occasion for the "shackasses" was that two regiments of rebel infantry were at that moment discovered descending a hill immediately behind our batteries. The "shackasses," with the howitzers loaded with grape and canister, were soon on the ground. The mules squared themselves, as they well knew how, for the shock. A terrific volley was poured into the advancing column, which immediately broke and retreated. Two hundred and seventy-eight dead bodies were found in the ravine next day, piled closely together as they fell, the effects of that volley from the backs of the "shackasses."

TWO OF LINCOLN'S LAW-CASES.

At Clinton there was so interesting a case that men and women from all the surrounding country crowded the court-room. Fifteen women were arraigned. A liquor-seller persisted in selling whisky to their husbands after the wives begged him not to do so. He cared nothing for their protestations, but laughed in their faces. The tears upon their cheeks did not move him. What should they do? There was no law to stop him. They marched to the groggery, smashed in the heads of the barrels with axes, and broke the demijohns and bottles. The fellow had them arrested. No lawyer volunteered to defend them. Abraham Lincoln, from Springfield, entered the room. There was something about him which emboldened them to speak to him.

"We have no one to defend us. Would it be asking too much to inquire if you can say a kind word in our behalf?" the request.

The lawyer from Springfield rises. All eyes are upon him. "May it please the court, I will say a few words in behalf of the women who are arraigned before your honor and the jury. I would suggest, first, that there be a change in the indictment, so as to have it read, 'The State against Mr. Whisky,' instead of 'The State against the Women.' It would be far more appropriate. Touching this question, there are three laws: First, the law of self-protection; second, the law of the statute; third, the law of God. The law of self-protection is the law of necessity, as shown when our fathers threw the tea into Boston harbor, and in asserting their right to life, liberty, and the pursuit of happiness. This is the defense of these women. The man who has persisted in selling whisky has had no regard for their well-being or the welfare of their husbands and sons. He has had no fear of God or regard for man; neither has he had any regard for the laws of the statute. No jury can fix any damages or punishment for any violation of the moral law. The course pursued by this liquor-dealer has been for the demoralization of society. His groggery has been a nuisance. These women, finding all moral suasion of no avail with this fellow, oblivious to all tender appeal, alike regardless of their prayers and tears, in order to protect their households and promote the welfare of the community, united to suppress the nuisance. The good of society demanded its suppression. They accomplished what otherwise could not have been done."

There was no need for him to say more. The whole case had been stated, and the jury understood it.

"Ladies," said the judge, "you need not remain any longer in court unless you desire to do so. I will require no bond of you; and if there should be any fine imposed, I will give you notice." The judge was so polite and smiling that everybody in the room understood that there was no probability of a fine.— *William H. Herndon.*

Mr. Cass had a case in court. He owned two yoke of oxen and a breaking-up plow which he wanted to sell, and which Mr. Snow's two sons bought, giving their note in payment. Neither of the boys had arrived at the age of manhood. Mr. Cass trusted that they would pay the note when it became due; but it was not paid. Abraham Lincoln questioned a witness:

"Can you tell me where the oxen are now?" he asked.

"They are on the farm where the boys have been plowing."

"Have you seen them lately?"

"I saw them last week."

"How old are the boys now?"

"One is a little over twenty-one, and the other is nearly twenty-three."

"They were both under age when the note was given?"

"Yes, sir."

"That is all."

"Gentlemen of the jury, I do not think that those boys would have tried to cheat Mr. Cass out of his oxen but for the advice of their counsel. It was bad advice in morals and in law. The law never sanctions cheating, and a lawyer must be very smart indeed to twist the law so that it will sanction fraud. The judge will tell you what your own sense of justice has already told you—that if those boys were mean enough to plead the baby act when they came to be men, they at least ought to have taken the oxen and plow back to Mr. Cass. They ought to know that they cannot go back on their contract and also keep what the note was given for."

So plain the case the jury, without leaving their seats, rendered a verdict, and the young men were obliged to pay for the oxen and plow, besides learning a wholesome lesson.—*C. C. Coffin.*

NO MERCY FOR THE MAN-STEALER.

Hon. John B. Alley, of Lynn, Massachusetts, was made the bearer to the president of a petition for pardon of a person confined in the Newburyport jail for being engaged in the slave trade. He had been sentenced to five years' imprisonment and the payment of a fine of one thousand dollars. The petition was accompanied by a letter to Mr. Alley, in which the prisoner acknowledged his guilt and the justice of his sentence. He was very penitent—at least on paper—and had received the full measure of his punishment, so far as it related to the term of his imprisonment; but he was still held because he could not pay his fine. Mr. Alley, who was much moved by the pathetic appeals of the letter, read it to the president, who, when he had himself read the petition, said:

"My friend, that is a very touching appeal to our feelings. You know my weakness is to be, if possible, too easily moved by appeals for mercy, and if this man were guilty of the foulest murder that the arm of man could perpetrate, I might forgive him on such an appeal; but the man who could go to Africa, and rob her of her children, and sell them into interminable bondage, with no other motive than that which is furnished by dollars and cents, is so much worse than the most depraved murderer that he can never receive pardon at my hands. No! He may rot in jail before he shall have liberty by any act of mine."

A sudden crime, committed under strong temptation, was venial in his eyes, on evidence of repentance; but the calculating, mercenary crime of man-stealing and man-selling, with all the cruelties that are essential accompaniments to the business, could win from him, as an officer of the people, no pardon.

LINCOLN'S CUTTING REPLY TO THE CONFEDERATE COMMISSION.

At a so-called "peace conference," procured by the voluntary and irresponsible agency of Mr. Francis P. Blair, which was held on the steamer River Queen, in Hampton Roads, on February 3, 1865, between President Lincoln and Mr. Seward, representing the government, and Messrs. Alexander H. Stephens, J. A. Campbell and Mr. Hunter, representing the rebel confederacy, Mr. Hunter replied that the recognition of Jeff Davis' power was the first and indispensable step to peace; and to illustrate his point, he referred to the correspondence between King Charles I. and his Parliament, as a reliable precedent of a constitutional ruler treating with rebels. Mr. Lincoln's face wore that indescribable expresssion which generally preceded his hardest hits; and he remarked:

"Upon questions of history I must refer you to Mr. Seward, for he is posted in such things, and I don't profess to be; but my only distinct recollection of the matter is that Charles lost his head!"

Mr. Hunter remarked, on the same occasion, that the slaves, always accustomed to work upon compulsion under an overseer, would, if suddenly freed, precipitate not only themselves, but the entire society of the South, into irremediable ruin. No work would be done, but black and white would starve together. The president waited for Mr. Seward to answer the argument, but as that gentleman hesitated, he said:

"Mr. Hunter, you ought to know a great deal better about the matter than I, for you have always lived under the slave system. I can only say, in reply to your statement of the case, that it reminds me of a man out in Illinois, by the name of Case, who undertook, a few years ago, to raise a very large herd of hogs. It was a great trouble to feed them, and how to get around this was a puzzle to him. At length he hit upon the plan of planting an immense field of potatoes, and, when they were sufficiently grown, he turned the whole herd into the field and let them have full swing, thus saving not only the labor of feeding the hogs, but also of digging the potatoes! Charmed with his sagacity, he stood one day leaning against the fence, counting his hogs, when a neighbor came along:

"'Well; well,' said he, 'Mr. Case, this is very fine. Your hogs are doing very well just now; but you know out here in Illinois the frost comes early, and the ground freezes a foot deep. Then what are they going to do?'

"This was a view of the matter which Mr. Case had not taken into account. Butchering-time for hogs was away on in December or January. He scratched his head, and at length stammered:

"'Well, it may come pretty hard on their snouts, but I don't see but it will be root hog or die!'"

_____

ONE OF LINCOLN'S LAST STORIES.

One of the last stories heard from Mr. Lincoln was concerning John Tyler, for whom it was to be expected he would entertain no great respect.

"A year or two after Tyler's accession to the presidency," said he, "contemplating an excursion in some direction, his son went to order a special train of cars. It so happened that the railroad superintendent was a very strong Whig. On Bob's making known his errand, that official bluntly informed him that his road did not run any special trains for the president.

"'What!' said Bob, 'did you not furnish a special train for the funeral of General Harrison?'

"'Yes,' said the superintendent, stroking his whiskers; 'and if you will only bring your father here in that shape you shall have the best train on the road!'"
—McClure's "Stories and Speeches."

_____

SUFFICIENT CAUSE FOR A FURLOUGH.

President Lincoln received the following pertinent letter from an indignant private, which speaks for itself: "Dear President:—I have been in the service eighteen months, and I have never received a cent. I desire a furlough for fifteen days, in order to return home and remove my family to the poorhouse." The president granted the furlough. It's a good story, and true.

RECOLLECTIONS OF THE WAR PRESIDENT BY JUDGE WILLIAM JOHNSTON, OF CINCINNATI.

"I rendered," said Judge Johnston, "Mr. Lincoln some service in my time. When I went to Washington I observed that among congressmen and others in high places Mr. Lincoln had very few friends. Montgomery Blair was the only one I heard speak of him for a second term.

"This was about the middle of his first administration. I went to Washington by way of Columbus, and Governor Tod asked me to carry a verbal message to Mr. Lincoln, and that was to tell him that there were certain elements indispensable to the success of the war that would be seriously affected by any interference with McClellan. I suppose that the liberal translation of Tod's language would be thus:

"'I am keeping the Democratic soldiers in the field, and if McClellan is interfered with, I shall not be able to do it.' We all felt some trouble about it. McClellan had been relieved, and one bright moonlight night I saw a regiment, I suppose Pennsylvanians mostly, marching from the Capitol down Pennsylvania avenue, yelling at the top of their lungs, 'Hurrah for Little Mac!' and making a pause before the White House, they kept up that bawling and hurrahing for McClellan.

"I went to see Mr. Lincoln early next morning, and asked him if he had witnessed the performance on the previous night. He said he had. I asked him what he thought of it. He said it was very perplexing. I told him I had come to make a suggestion. I told him I would introduce him to a young man of fine talents and liberal education, who had lost an arm in the service, and I wanted him to tell one of his Cabinet ministers to give that young man a good place in the civil service, and to avail himself of the occasion to declare that the policy of the administration was, whenever the qualifications were equal, to give those who had been wounded or disabled in the service of the country the preference in the civil department.

"He said it was an idea he would like to think of, and asked me how soon I would wait upon him in the morning. I said any hour; and I went at seven o'clock, and found him in the hands of a barber.

"Says he, 'I have been thinking about your proposition, and I have a question to ask you. Did you ever know Colonel Smith, of Rockford, Illinois?'

"I said I had an introduction to him when attending to the defense of Governor Bebb.

"'You know,' said he, 'that he was killed at Vicksburg; that his head was carried off by a shell. He was postmaster, and his wife wants the place,' and he inquired if that would come up to my idea; and thereupon he and I concocted a letter—I have the correspondence in my possession—to Postmaster-general Blair, directing him to appoint the widow of Colonel Smith postmistress. in the room of her deceased husband, who had fallen in battle, and stating that in consideration of what was due to the men who were fighting our battles, he had made up his mind that the families of those who had fallen and those disabled in the service, their qualifications being equal, should always have a preference in the civil services.

"I told him that I was not personally acquainted with Mr. Blair, and he gave me a note of introduction to him, with the letter. I told Blair that I proposed to take a copy of Mr. Lincoln's letter, which he then had made out by the clerk. I took the letter to the *Chronicle* office in Washington, in which paper it was published, and the next morning I jumped into an ambulance and went to the convalescing camp, where there were about 7,000 convalescents, a great many of them Ohio men, and when I made my appearance, they called on me for a speech. I got upon a terrace and made them a few remarks, and coming around to the old saw, 'that republics are always ungrateful,' I told them I could not vouch for the republic, but I thought I could vouch for the chief man at the head of the administration, and he had already spoken on that subject; and when I read Lincoln's letter, the boys flung their hats into the air, and made the welkin ring for a long while.

"I hurried back to the city, and with a pair of shears cut out Lincoln's letter, and then attached some editorial remarks, and that letter went the rounds, and, I believe, was published in nearly every friendly newspaper in the United States.

"About that time Congress passed a resolution to the same effect, that those disabled in the military service of the country, wherever qualified, ought to have a preference over others. This may have been a small matter, but it made a marvelous impression on the army."

A "HEN-PECKED" HUSBAND.

When General Phelps took possession of Ship island, near New Orleans, early in the war, it will be remembered that he issued a proclamation, somewhat bombastic in tone, freeing the slaves. To the surprise of many people on both sides, the president took no official notice of this movement. Some time had elapsed, when one day a friend took him to task for his seeming indifference on so important a matter.

"Well," said Mr. Lincoln, "I feel about that a good deal as a man whom I will call Jones, whom I once knew, did about his wife. He was one of your meek men, and had the reputation of being badly hen-pecked. At last, one day his wife was seen switching him out of the house. A day or two afterward a friend met him in the street and said:

"'Jones, I have always stood up for you, as you know; but I am not going to do it any longer. Any man who will stand quietly and take a switching from his wife, deserves to be horse-whipped.'

"Jones looked up with a wink, patting his friend on the back.

"'Now, don't,' said he; 'why, it didn't hurt me any, and you've no idea what a power of good it did Sarah Ann.'"

SHE WAS SORRY SHE DID IT.

A secesh lady of Alexandria, who was ordered away into Dixie by the government, destroyed all her furniture and cut down her trees, so that the "cursed Yankees" should not enjoy them. Lincoln, hearing of this, the order was countermanded, and she returned to see in her broken penates the folly of her conduct.

LINCOLN AND GRANT—MARCH 9, 1864.

General Grant never had met the president, but was on his way to Washington in obedience to a summons. The Cabinet, Mr. Stanton and E. B. Washburne were in the White House when he entered.

"General Grant," said the president, "the nation's appreciation of what you have done, and its reliance upon you for what remains to be done in the existing struggle, are now presented with this commission, constituting you lieutenant-general in the army of the United States. With this high honor devolves upon you a corresponding responsibility. As the country trusts in you, so, under God, it will sustain you. I scarcely need add that with what I here speak for the nation goes my own hearty personal concurrence."

The words were spoken with trembling lips, so deep the feeling of Mr. Lincoln.

"Mr. President," General Grant replied, "I accept the commission for the high honor conferred. With the aid of the noble armies that have fought on so many fields of our common country, it will be my earnest endeavor not to disappoint your expectations. I feel the full responsibilities now devolving upon me; and I know that if they are met it will be due to those armies, and, above all, to the favor of that Providence which leads nations and men."

General Grant visited the Army of the Potomac at Culpeper, and made the acquaintance of General Meade, took a quiet look at the soldiers, and returned to Washington. Mrs. Lincoln had prepared a grand dinner expressly in his honor.

"Mrs. Lincoln must excuse me," he said. "I must be in Tennessee at the earliest possible moment."

"But we can't excuse you," said the president. "Were we to sit down without you it would be 'Hamlet' with Hamlet left out."

"I appreciate the honor, Mr. President, but time is very precious just now. I ought to be attending to affairs. The loss of a day means the loss of a million dollars to the country."

"Well, then, we shall be compelled to have the dinner without the honor of your presence," said Mr. Lincoln, as they parted.

Never before had a commander of any of the armies pleaded public necessity for declining a dinner at the White House; never a commander so absorbed as was General Grant in the business of the country. Possibly the declination gave the president more pleasure than he would have had from an acceptance of the invitation.—*Charles Carleton Coffin.*

A STORY WHICH LINCOLN TOLD THE PREACHERS.

A year or more before Mr. Lincoln's death, a delegation of clergymen waited upon him in reference to the appointment of the army chaplains. The delegation consisted of a Presbyterian, a Baptist and an Episcopal clergyman. They stated that the character of many of the chaplains was notoriously bad, and they had come to urge upon the president the necessity of more discretion in these appointments.

"But, gentlemen," said the president, "that is a matter with which the government has nothing to do; the chaplains are chosen by the regiments."

Not satisfied with this, the clergymen pressed, in turn, a change in the system. Mr. Lincoln heard them through without remark, and then said:

"Without any disrespect, gentlemen, I will tell you a 'little story.'

"Once, in Springfield, I was going off on a short journey, and reached the depot a little ahead of time. Leaning against the fence just outside the depot was a little darky boy, whom I knew, named Dick, busily digging with his toe in a mud-puddle. As I came up, I said:

"'Dick, what are you about?'

"'Making a church,' said he.

"'A church?' said I. 'What do you mean?'

"'Why, yes,' said Dick, pointing with his toe, 'don't you see there is the shape of it; there's the steps and front door, here the pews where the folks set, and there's the pulpit.'

"'Yes, I see,' said I; but why don't you make a minister?'

"'Laws,' answered Dick, with a grin, *I hain't got mud enough!*'"

TELLING A STORY AND PARDONING A SOLDIER.

General Fisk, attending the reception at the White House on one occasion, saw waiting in the anteroom a poor old man from Tennessee. Sitting down beside him, he inquired his errand; and learned that he had been waiting three or four days to get an audience, and that on his seeing Mr. Lincoln probably depended the life of his son, under sentence of death for some military offense.

General Fisk wrote his case in outline on a card, and sent it in, with a special request that the president would see the man. In a moment the order came; and past senators, governors and generals, waiting impatiently, the old man went into the president's presence.

He showed Mr. Lincoln his papers, and he, on taking them, said he would look into the case and give him the result on the following day.

The old man, in an agony of apprehension, looked up into the president's sympathetic face, and actually cried out:

"To-morrow may be too late! My son is under sentence of death! The decision ought to be made now!" and the streaming tears told how much he was moved.

· "Come," said Mr. Lincoln, "wait a bit, and I'll tell you a story;" and then he told the old man General Fisk's story about the swearing driver, as follows:

The general had begun his military life as a colonel, and when he raised his regiment in Missouri, he proposed to his men that he should do all the swearing · of the regiment. They assented; and for months no instance was known of the violation of the promise. The colonel had a teamster named John Todd, who, as roads were not always the best, had some difficulty in commanding his temper and his tongue. John happened to be driving a mule-team through a series of mud-holes a little worse than usual, when, unable to restrain himself any longer, he burst forth into a volley of energetic oaths. The colonel took notice of the offense, and brought John to an account.

"John," said he, "didn't you promise to let me do all the swearing of the regiment?"

"Yes, I did, colonel," he replied, "but the fact was the swearing had to be done then or not at all, and you weren't there to do it."

As he told the story, the old man forgot his boy, and both the president and his listener had a hearty laugh together at its conclusion. Then he wrote a few words which the old man read, and in which he found new occasion for tears; but the tears were tears of joy, for the words saved the life of his son.

LINCOLN AS A SHAKSPERIAN CRITIC.

A few days before General Grant received his commission, F. B. Carpenter, an artist, was installed in the White House to paint a picture commemorating the signing of the Emancipation Proclamation. He became a member of the household, and recorded scenes in the routine of the president's official life. Mr. Lincoln and the artist were together one evening, when the president turned from his paper as if weary.

"Tad," he said to his youngest son, "run to the library and get Shakspere." He read passages which had ever been a delight to him. "The opening of Richard III., it seems to me, is almost always misapprehended," he said. "You know the actor usually comes in with a flourish, and, like a college sophomore, says:

> "Now is the winter of our discontent
> Made glorious summer by this sun of York.

"Now, this is all wrong. Richard had been, and was then, plotting the destruc- tion of his brothers to make room for himself. Outwardly, he is most loyal to the newly crowned king; secretly, he could scarcely contain his impatience at the obstacles still in the way of his own elevation. He is burning with repressed hate and jealousy. The prologue is the utterance of the most intense bitterness and satire."

Mr. Lincoln assumed the character, and recited the passage with such force that it became a new creation to the artist.

LINCOLN NOT AN IMPROMPTU SPEAKER.

Mr. Lincoln was not a successful impromptu speaker. He required a little time for thought and arrangement of the thing to be said. I give an instance in point. After my election to the governorship of New York, just before I resigned my seat in Congress to enter upon my official duties as governor at Albany, New-Yorkers and others in Washington thought to honor me with a serenade. I was the guest of ex-Mayor Bowen. After the music and speaking usual upon such occasions, it was proposed to call on the president. I accompanied the committee in charge of the proceedings, followed by bands and a thousand people. It was full nine o'clock when we reached the mansion. The president was taken by surprise, and said he "didn't know just what he could say to satisfy the crowd and himself." Going from the library-room down the stairs to the portico front, he asked me to say a few words first, and give him, if I could, "a peg to hang on." It was just when General Sherman was en route from Atlanta to the sea, and we had no definite news as to his safety or whereabouts. After one or two sentences, rather commonplace, the president farther said he had no war news other than was known to all, and he supposed his ignorance in regard to General Sherman was the ignorance of all; that "we all knew where Sherman went in, but none of us knew where he would come out." This last remark was in the peculiarly quaint, happy manner of Mr. Lincoln, and created great applause. He immediately withdrew, saying he "had raised a good laugh, and it was a good time for him to quit." In all he did not speak more than two minutes, and, as he afterward told me, because he had no time to think of much to say.—*Governor* (*and Senator*) *Reuben E Fenton, of New York.*

ANOTHER LAW-CASE.

Another case was that of a poor woman, nearly eighty years old, who came with a pitiful story. Her husband had been a soldier in the Revolutionary war under Washington. He was dead, and she was entitled to a pension amounting to $400. A rascally fellow, pretending great friendship for her, had obtained the money, but had put half of it into his own pocket.

The poor woman was the only witness. The jury heard her story. Abraham Lincoln the while was making the following notes on a slip of paper:

· "No contract.
"Not professional services.
"Unreasonable charges.
"Money retained by defendant not given to plaintiff.
"Revolutionary war. .
"Describe Valley Forge.
"Ice. Soldiers' bleeding feet.
"Husband leaving home for the army. ¯
"Skin defendant."

He rises and turns to the judge. Of the lawyers sitting around the table perhaps not one of them can say just what there is about him which hushes the room in an instant. "May it please your honor," the words are spoken slowly, as if he were not quite ready to go on with what he had to say, "gentlemen of the jury, this is a very simple case, so simple that a child can understand it. You have heard that there has been no contract—no agreement by the parties. You will observe that there has been no professional service by contract." Slowly, clearly, one by one the points were taken up. Who was the man to whom the government of the United States owed the money? He had been with Washington at Valley Forge, barefooted in midwinter, marching with bleeding feet, with only rags to protect him from the cold, starving for his country. The speaker's lips were tremulous, and his eyes filled with tears as he told how the soldiers of the Revolution marched amid the snows, shivered in the wintry winds, starved, fought, died, that those who came after them might have a country. Judge, jurymen, lawyers and the people who listen, wipe the tears from their eyes as he tells the story of the soldier parting from friends, from the wife, then in the bloom and beauty of youth, but now friendless and alone, old and poor. The man who professed to be her friend had robbed her of what was her due. His spirit is greatly stirred. The jury right the wrong, and compel the fellow to hand over the money. And then the people see the lawyer who has won the case tenderly accompanying the grateful woman to the railroad station. He pays her bill at the hotel, her fare in the cars, and charges nothing for what he has done!

LINCOLN'S MOST CONSPICUOUS VIRTUE.

The character of Abraham Lincoln is not yet known to this generation as it will be to those who shall live in later centuries. They will see, as we cannot yet perceive, the full maturity of his wisdom in its actual effects upon the destinies of two great races of men. Probably he had an inadequate conception of his own work. Had he lived to full age, his guidance of the emancipation, that he decreed under military law, would have saved both races from many of the rough experiences that it has produced and will yet cause, by the effort to fuse the races into political harmony, against the mutual instinct that will keep them forever separated by race and social antagonisms.

The character of Mr. Lincoln was clearly displayed in his conduct of the war, but he was deprived of the opportunity for its full development in a period of peace and security. His most conspicuous virtue, as commander-in-chief of the army and navy, was the absence of a spirit of resentment, or oppression, toward the enemy, and the self-imposed restraint under which he exercised the really absolute powers within his grasp. For this all his countrymen revere his memory, rejoice in the excellence of his fame, and those who failed in the great struggle hold him in grateful esteem.—*Hon. John T. Morgan, Senator from Alabama and Confederate General.*

GARRISON IN BALTIMORE.

An account given in the *Independent* of a visit of William Lloyd Garrison and others to Baltimore, to find the jail where Garrison was imprisoned, states that when Mr. Garrison subsequently told Mr. Lincoln of it, the president said: "Well, Mr. Garrison, when you first went to Baltimore you could not get out of prison, but the second time you could not get in."

MR. LINCOLN ON THE "COMPROMISE."

When the conversation turned upon the discussions as to the Missouri Compromise, it elicited the following quaint remark from the president:

"It used to amuse me some to find that the slaveholders wanted more territory, because they had not room enough for their slaves, and yet they complained of not having the slave trade, because they wanted more slaves for their room."

STORY OF ANDY JOHNSON AND HIS DOUBTFUL INTEREST IN PRAYERS.

Colonel Granville Moody, "the fighting Methodist parson," as he was called in Tennessee, while attending a conference in Philadelphia, met the president, and related to him the following story, which we give as repeated by Mr. Lincoln to a friend.

"He told me," said Lincoln, "this story of Andy Johnson and General Buel, which interested me intensely:

"The colonel happened to be in Nashville the day it was reported that Buel had decided to evacuate the city. The rebels, strongly reinforced, were said to be within two days' march of the capital. Of course, the city was greatly excited. Moody said he went in search of Johnson at the edge of the evening, and found him at his office closeted with two gentlemen, who were walking the floor with him, one on each side. As he entered they retired, leaving him alone with Johnson, who came up to him, manifesting intense feeling, and said:

"'Moody, we are sold out. Buel is a traitor. He is going to evacuate the city, and in forty-eight hours we will all be in the hands of the rebels!'

"Then he commenced pacing the floor again, twisting his hands and chafing like a caged tiger, utterly insensible to his friend's entreaties to become calm. Suddenly he turned and said:

"'Moody, can you pray?'

"'That is my business, sir, as a minister of the gospel,' returned the colonel.

"'Well, Moody, I wish you would pray,' said Johnson, and instantly both went down upon their knees, at opposite sides of the room

"As the prayer waxed fervent, Johnson began to respond in true Methodist style. Presently he crawled over on his hands and knees to Moody's side and put his arms over him, manifesting the deepest emotion.   Closing the prayer with a hearty ' amen ' from each, they arose.

 "Johnson took a long breath, and said, with emphasis:

" 'Moody, I feel better.'

"Shortly afterward he asked:

" ' Will you stand by me?'

" ' Certainly I will,' was the answer.

" ' Well, Moody, I can depend upon you; you are one in a hundred thousand.'

" He then commenced pacing the floor again.   Suddenly he wheeled, the current of his thought having changed, and said:

" 'Oh, Moody, I don't want you to think I have become a religious man because I asked you to pray.   I am sorry to say it, I am not, and never pretended to be religious.   No one knows this better than you, but, Moody, there is one thing about it, I do believe in Almighty God! and I believe also in the Bible, and I say, d—n me if Nashville shall be surrendered!'

"And Nashville was not surrendered."

A LITTLE SOLDIER BOY.

" President Lincoln," says the Hon. W. D. Kelly, " was a large and many-sided man, and yet so simple that no one, not even a child, could approach him without feeling that he had found in him a sympathizing friend.   I remember that I apprised him of the fact that a lad, the son of one of my townsmen, had served a year on the gunboat Ottawa, and had been in two important engagements; in the first as powder-monkey, when he had conducted himself with such coolness that he had been chosen as captain's messenger in the second; and I suggested to the president that it was within his power to send to the naval school annually three boys who had served at least one year in the navy.

" He at once wrote on the back of a letter from the commander of the Ottawa, which I had handed him, to the secretary of the navy:

" ' If the appointments for this year have not been made, let this boy be appointed.'

" The appointment had not been made, and I brought it home with me.   It directed the lad to report for examination at the school in July.   Just as he was ready to start, his father, looking over the law, discovered that he could not report until he was fourteen years of age, which he would not be until September following.

" The poor child sat down and wept.   He feared that he was not to go to the naval school.   He was, however, soon consoled by being told that the ' president could make it right.'

" It was my fortune to meet him the next morning at the door of the executive chamber with his father."

10

LINCOLN AND JOHN HANKS.

"It was during the dark days of 1863," says Schuyler Colfax, "on the evening of a public reception given at the White House. The foreign legations were gathered about the president.

"A young English nobleman was just being presented to the president. Inside the door, evidently overawed by the splendid assemblage, was an honest-faced old farmer, who shrank from the passing crowd until he and the plain-faced old lady clinging to his arm were pressed back to the wall.

"The president, tall, and, in a measure, stately in his personal presence, looking over the heads of the assembly, said to the English nobleman, 'Excuse me, my Lord, there's an old friend of mine.'

"Passing backward to the door, Mr. Lincoln said, as he grasped the old farmer's hand:

"'Why, John, I'm glad to see you. I haven't seen you since you and I made rails for old Mrs. —— in Sangamon county, in 1837. How are you?'

"The old man turned to his wife with quivering lip, and without replying to the president's salutation, said:

"'Mother, he's just the same old Abe!'

"'Mr. Lincoln,' he said, finally, 'you know we had three boys; they all enlisted in the same company; John was killed in the "seven days' fight;" Sam was taken prisoner and starved to death, and Henry is in the hospital. We had a little money, an' I said, "Mother, we'll go to Washington an' see him." An' while we were here, I said we'll go up and see the president.'

"Mr. Lincoln's eyes grew dim, and across his rugged, homely, tender face swept the wave of sadness his friends had learned to know, and he said: 'John, we all hope this miserable war will soon be over. I must see all these folks here for an hour or so, and I want to talk with you.' The old lady and her husband were hustled into a private room in spite of their protests."

AN OFFICER'S SON SENT HOME.

In speaking of certain odd doings in the army, Old Abe said that reminded him of another story, as follows:

On one occasion when a certain general's purse was getting low, he remarked that he would be obliged to draw on his banker for some money.

"How much do you want, father?" said the boy.

"I think I shall send for a couple of hundred," replied the general.

"Why, father," said his son, very quietly, "I can let you have that amount."

"You can let me have it!" exclaimed the general, in surprise; "where did you get so much money?"

"I won it at playing draw-poker with your staff, sir!" replied the youth.

It is needless to say that the earliest morning train bore the "gay young gambolier" toward his home.

A "TIGHT SQUEEZE."

President Lincoln was very doubtful about his second election. He said that his poor prospect reminded him of old Jake Tullwater, who lived in Illinois. Old Jake got a fever once, and he became delirious, and while in this state he fancied that the last day had come, and he was called to judge the world. With all the vagaries of insanity he gave both questions and answers himself, and only called up his acquaintances, the millers, when something like this followed:

" Shon Schmidt, come up here! Vat bees you in dis lower worlds?"

" Well, Lort, I bees a miller."

" Well, Shon, did you ever take too much toll?"

" Oh, yes, Lort, when the water was low, and the stones were dull, I did take too much toll."

" Well, Shon," Old Jake would say, " you must go to the left among the goats."

So he called up all he knew, and put them through the same course, till finally he came to himself:

" Shake Tullwater, come up here! Well, Shake, what bees you in dis lower world?"

" Well, Lort, I bees a miller."

"And, Shake, didn't you ever take too much toll?"

"Ah, yes, Lort, when the water was low, and the stones were dull, I did take too much toll."

" Well, Shake—well, Shake (scratching his head)—well, Shake, what did you do mit dat toll?"

" Well, Lort, I gives him to de poor."

"Ah! Shake, give it to the poor, did you? Well, Shake, you can go to the right among the sheep, but it's a tam'd tight squeeze!"

SEWARD AND CHASE.

The antagonism between the conservatives in the Cabinet, represented by Seward, and the radicals, represented by Chase, was a source of much embarrassment to Mr. Lincoln. Finally, the radicals appointed a committee to demand the dismissal of Seward. Before the committee arrived, Mr. Seward, in order to relieve the president of embarrassment, tendered his resignation. In the course of the discussion with the committee, Mr. Chase found his position so embarrassing and equivocal that he thought it wise to tender his resignation the next day. Mr. Lincoln refused to accept either, stating that " the public interest does not admit of it." When it was all over, he said: "Now I can ride; I have got a pumpkin in each end of my bag." Later on he said: "I do not see how it could have been done better. I am sure it was right. If I had yielded to that storm, and dismissed Seward, the thing would have slumped over one way, and we should have been left with a scanty handful of supporters."

TRIBUTE TO MR. LINCOLN'S CLEMENCY, BY SENATOR DANIEL W. VOORHEES, A DISTINGUISHED DEMOCRAT.

Henry M. Luckett had been sentenced to be shot for disloyal conduct. Colonel Lane, Colonel William R. Morrison, Mr. and Mrs. Bullitt and Senator Hendricks had interceded in his behalf. Senator Voorhees says:

" We ascended the stairs and filed into the president's room. As we entered, I saw at a glance that Mr. Lincoln had that sad, preoccupied, far-away look I had so often seen him wear, and during which it was difficult to engage his attention to passing events. As we approached, he slowly turned to us, inclined his head, and spoke. Senator Lane at once, in his rapid, nervous style, explained the occasion of our call, and made known our reasons for asking executive clemency. While he was talking, Mr. Lincoln looked at him in a patient, tired sort of way, but not as if he was struck with the sensibilities of the subject as we were. When the senator ceased speaking there was no immediate response; on the contrary, rather an awkward pause. My heart beat fast, for in that pause was now my great hope, and I was not disappointed. Mrs. Bullitt had taken a seat, on coming in, not far from the president, and now, in quivering but distinct tones, she spoke, addressing him as 'Mr. Lincoln.' He turned to her with a grave, benignant expression, and as he listened his eyes lost that distant look, and his face grew animated with a keen and vivid interest. The little pale-faced woman at his side talked wonderfully well for her father's life, and her eyes pleaded even more eloquently than her tongue. Suddenly, and while she was talking, Mr. Lincoln, turning to Senator Lane, exclaimed:

"'Lane, what did you say this man's name was?'

"'Luckett,' answered the senator.

"'Not Henry M. Luckett?' quickly queried the president.

"'Yes,' interposed Mrs. Bullitt; 'my father's name is Henry M. Luckett.'

"'Why, he preached in Springfield years ago, didn't he?' said Mr. Lincoln, now all animation and interest.

"'Yes, my father used to preach in Springfield,' replied the daughter.

"'Well, this is wonderful!' Mr. Lincoln remarked; and turning to the party in front of him he continued: 'I knew this man well; I have heard him preach; he was a tall, angular man like I am, and I have been mistaken for him on the streets. Did you say he was to be shot day after to-morrow? No, no! There will be no shooting or hanging in this case. Henry M. Luckett! There must be something wrong with him, or he wouldn't be in such a scrape as this. I don't know what more I can do for him, but you can rest assured, my child,' turning to Mrs. Bullitt, 'that your father's life is safe.'

"He touched a bell on his table, and the telegraph operator appeared from an adjoining room. To him Mr. Lincoln dictated a dispatch to General Hurlbut, directing him to suspend the execution of Henry M. Luckett and await further orders in the case.

"As we thanked him and took our leave, he repeated, as if to himself:

"'Henry M. Luckett! No, no! There is no shooting or hanging in this case.'

"With what feelings we all left his presence; how the woman's heart bore its great flood of joy and its sudden revulsion from the depths of fear and despair; how she sobbed and laughed, and how tears and smiles were in her bright face together; how in broken words and choking voice she tried to pour out her unutterable gratitude to Abraham Lincoln; how some of the party returning in the same carriage with her and her husband were almost as deeply moved as she was; how all these things and others occurred in the swift transition from deep distress and overwhelming dread to happiness and security, cannot now be told. Perhaps they were recorded at the time somewhere else."

Mr. Voorhees gives this interesting sequel to his story:

"Two or three months later the object of all our solicitude and labors was released and sent North to his friends. I saw him but once. The first use he made of his liberty was to travel, poor as he was, to Washington to express his gratitude for his preservation from a violent and ignominious death. He called me from my seat in the House, and I met him exactly where I had met those who came to intercede for his life a little while before. He was a tall, spare old man, with an excited, startled, haunted expression of face. He wanted to call and thank the president in person for his great kindness, but the circumstances at the time were not favorable to such a call, and it was not made. He remained with me not more than fifteen minutes, and then in the hurried manner of one who has much to do and whose time is short, he moved away, and I saw him no more."—*North American Review.*

SPEAKING OF THE TIME.

When Mrs. Vallandigham left Dayton to join her husband, just before the election, she told her friends that she never expected to return until she did so as the wife of the governor of Ohio.

Mr. Lincoln is said to have got off the following:

"That reminds me of a pleasant little affair that occurred out in Illinois. A gentleman was nominated for supervisor. On leaving home on the morning of the election, he said:

"'Wife, to-night you shall sleep with the supervisor of this town.'

"The election passed, and the confident gentleman was defeated. The wife heard the news before her defeated spouse returned home. She immediately dressed for going out, and waited her husband's return, when she met him at the door.

"'Wife, where are you going at this time of night?' he exclaimed.

"'Going?' she replied, 'why, you told me this morning that I should to-night sleep with the supervisor of this town, and as Mr. L. is elected instead of yourself, I was going to his house.'

"She didn't go out, and he acknowledged that he was *sold*, but pleasantly redeemed himself with a new Brussels carpet."

CONSCRIPTING DEAD MEN.

Mr. Lincoln being found fault with for making another "call," said that if the country required it, he would continue to do so until the matter stood as described by a western provost marshal, who says:

"I listened a short time since to a butternut-clad individual, who succeeded in making good his escape, expatiate most eloquently on the rigidness with which the conscription was enforced south of the Tennessee river. His response to a question propounded by a citizen ran somewhat in this wise:

"'Do they conscript close over the river?'

"'Stranger, I should think they did! *They take every man who hasn't been dead more than two days!'*

"If this is correct, the Confederacy has at least a ghost of a chance left."

And of another, a Methodist minister in Kansas, living on a small salary, who was greatly troubled to get his quarterly instalment. He at last told the non-paying trustees that he must have his money, as he was suffering for the necessaries of life.

"Money!" replied the trustees, "you preach for money? We thought you preached for the good of souls!"

"Souls!" responded the reverend, "I can't eat souls; and if I could, it would take a thousand such as yours to make a meal!"

"That soul is the point, sir," said the president.

KNOWING TOO MUCH.

President Lincoln, while entertaining a few select friends, is said to have related the following anecdote of a man who knew too much:

During the administration of President Jackson, there was a singular young gentleman employed in the public post-office in Washington. His name was G. he was from Tennessee, the son of a widow, a neighbor of the president, on which account the old hero had a kind feeling for him, and always got him out of his difficulties with some of the higher officials, to whom his singular interference was distasteful.

Among other things, it is said of him that while he was employed in the general post-office, on one occasion he had to copy a letter to Major H., a high official, in answer to an application made by an old gentleman in Virginia or Pennsylvania, for the establishment of a new post-office. The writer of the letter said the application could not be granted, in consequence of the applicant's "proximity" to another office. When the letter came into G.'s hands to copy being a great stickler for plainness, he altered "proximity" to "nearness to." Major H. observed it, and asked G. why he altered his letter.

"Why," replied G., "because I don't think the man would understand what you meant by proximity."

"Well," said Major H., "try him; put in the 'proximity' again."

In a few days a letter was received from the applicant, in which he very indignantly said that "his father had fought for liberty in the second war for independence, and he should like to have the name of the scoundrel who brought the charge of proximity or anything else wrong against him.

"There," said G., "did I not say so?"

G. carried his improvements so far that Mr. Berry, the postmaster-general, said to him, "I don't want you any longer; you know too much."

Poor G. went out, but his old friend the general got him another place. This time G.'s ideas underwent a change. He was one day very busy writing, when a stranger called in, and asked him where the Patent Office was.

"I don't know," said G.

"Can you tell me where the Treasury Department is?" said the stranger.

"No," said G.

"Nor the president's house?"

"No."

The stranger finally asked him if he knew where the Capitol was.

"No," replied G.

"Do you live in Washington, sir?" said the stranger.

"Yes, sir," said G.

"Good Lord! and don't you know where the Patent Office, Treasury, president's house and Capitol are?"

"Stranger," said G., "I was turned out of the post-office for knowing too much. I don't mean to offend in that way again. I am paid for keeping this book. I believe I know that much; but if you find me knowing anything more, you may take my head."

"Good-morning," said the stranger.

LINCOLN AND THE CURIOSITY-SEEKER.

In answer to a curiosity-seeker who desired a permit to pass the lines to visit the field of Bull Run, after the first battle, Mr. Lincoln made the following reply as his answer:

"A man in Cortlandt county raised a porker of such unusual size that strangers went out of their way to see it. One of them the other day met the old gentleman, and inquired about the animal.

"'Wall, yes,' the old fellow said; 'Iv'e got such a critter, mi'ty big un; but I guess I'll have to charge you about a shillin' for lookin' at him.'

"The stranger looked at the old man for a minute or so, pulled out the desired coin, handed it to him, and started to go off.

"'Hold on,' said the other, 'don't you want to see the hog?'

"'No.' said the stranger; 'I have seen as big a hog as I want to see!'

"And you will find that fact the case with yourself, if you should happen to see a few *live* rebels there as well as dead ones."

LINCOLN'S IDEAS ABOUT SLAVERY.

The story will be remembered, perhaps, of Mr. Lincoln's reply to a Springfield (Illinois) clergyman, who asked him what was to be his policy on the slavery question.

"Well, your question is rather a cool one, but I will answer it by telling you a story. You know Father B., the old Methodist preacher? and you know Fox river and its freshets? Well, once in the presence of Father B., a young Methodist was worrying about Fox river, and expressing fears that he should be prevented from fulfilling some of his appointments by a freshet in the river. Father B. checked him in his gravest manner. Said he:

"'Young man, I have always made it a rule in my life not to cross Fox river till I get to it.'

"And," said the president, "I am not going to worry myself over the slavery question till I get to it."

A few days afterward a Methodist minister called on the president, and on being presented to him, said, simply:

"Mr. President, I have come to tell you that I think we have got to Fox river!"

Mr. Lincoln thanked the clergyman, and laughed heartily.

REV. DR. WAYLAND HOYT ON THE "SYMPATHY" OF LINCOLN.

Consider the sympathy of Abraham Lincoln. Do you know the story of William Scott, private? Mr. Chittenden gives the true version of it. He was a boy from a Vermont farm. There had been a long march, and the night succeeding it he had stood on picket. The next day there had been another long march, and that night William Scott had volunteered to stand guard in the place of a sick comrade who had been drawn for the duty. It was too much for William Scott. He was too tired. He had been found sleeping on his beat. The army was at Chain Bridge. It was in a dangerous neighborhood. Discipline must be kept. William Scott is apprehended, tried by court-martial, sentenced to be shot. News of the case is carried to Mr. Lincoln. William Scott is prisoner in his tent, expecting to be shot next day. But the flaps of his tent are parted, and Mr. Lincoln stands before him. Scott said:

"The president was the kindest man I had ever seen; I knew him at once by a Lincoln medal I had long worn. I was scared at first, for I had never before talked with a great man; but Mr. Lincoln was so easy with me, so gentle, that I soon forgot my fright. He asked me all about the people at home, the neighbors, the farm, and where I went to school, and who my schoolmates were. Then he asked me about mother and how she looked; and I was glad I could take her photograph from my bosom and show it to him. He said how thankful I ought to be that my mother still lived, and how, if he were in my place, he would try to make her a proud mother, and never cause her a sorrow or a tear. I cannot remember it all, but every word was so kind.

"He had said nothing yet about that dreadful next morning; I thought it must be that he was so kind-hearted that he didn't like to speak of it. But why did he say so much about my mother, and my not causing her a sorrow or a tear, when I knew that I must die the next morning? But I supposed that was something that would have to go unexplained; and so I determined to brace up and tell him that I did not feel a bit guilty, and ask him wouldn't he fix it so that the firing party would not be from our regiment. That was going to be the hardest of all—to die by the hands of my comrades. Just as I was going to ask him this favor, he stood up, and he says to me:

"'My boy, stand up here and look me in the face.'

"I did as he bade me.

"'My boy,' he said, 'you are not going to be shot to-morrow. I believe you when you tell me that you could not keep awake. I am going to trust you, and send you back to your regiment. But I have been put to a good deal of trouble on your account. I have had to come up here from Washington when I have got a great deal to do; and what I want to know is, how are you going to pay my bill?'

"There was a big lump in my throat; I could scarcely speak. I had expected to die, you see, and had kind of got used to thinking that way. To have it all changed in a minute! But I got it crowded down, and managed to say:

"'I am grateful, Mr. Lincoln! I hope I am as grateful as ever a man can be to you for saving my life. But it comes upon me sudden and unexpected like. I didn't lay out for it at all; but there is some way to pay you, and I will find it after a little. There is the bounty in the savings bank; I guess we could borrow some money on the mortgage of the farm.' There was my pay was something, and if he would wait until pay-day I was sure the boys would help; so I thought we could make it up if it wasn't more than five or six hundred dollars.

"'But it is a great deal more than that,' he said.

"Then I said I didn't just see how, but I was sure I would find some way —if I lived. Then Mr. Lincoln put his hands on my shoulders, and looked into my face as if he was sorry, and said:

"'My boy, my bill is a very large one. Your friends cannot pay it, nor your bounty, nor the farm, nor all your comrades! There is only one man in all the world who can pay it, and his name is William Scott! If from this day William Scott does his duty, so that, if I was there when he comes to die, he can look me in the face as he does now, and say, I have kept my promise, and I have done my duty as a soldier, then my debt will be paid. Will you make that promise and try to keep it?'"

The promise was given. It is too long a story to tell of the effect of this sympathizing kindness on private William Scott. Thenceforward there never was such a soldier as William Scott. This is the record of the end. It was after one of the awful battles of the Peninsula. He was shot all to pieces. He said:

"Boys, I shall never see another battle. I supposed this would be my last. I haven't much to say. You all know what you can tell them at home about me.

I have *tried* to do the right thing! If any of you ever have the chance. I wish you would tell President Lincoln that I have never forgotten the kind words he said to me at the Chain Bridge; that I have tried to be a good soldier and true to the flag; that I should have paid my whole debt to him if I had lived; and that now, when I know that I am dying, I think of his kind face, and thank him again, because he gave me the chance to fall like a soldier in battle, and not like a coward, by the hands of my comrades."

Was there ever a more exquisite story? Space forbids the half telling it. But the heart of Abraham Lincoln—how wide it was, how beautiful and particular in its sympathies! Who can doubt a gracious Providence, when at such a crisis such a wise, strong, tender hand was set to grasp the helm of things? What wonder that Secretary Stanton said of him, as he gazed upon the tall form and kindly face as he lay there, smitten down by the assassin's bullet, "There lies the most perfect ruler of men who ever lived."

THE QUAKER AND THE "COPPERHEAD."

Mr. Lincoln especially enjoyed this incident, occurring at Salem, Indiana, during John Morgan's raid: Some of his men proceeded out west of the town to burn the bridges and water-tanks on the railroad. On the way out they captured a couple of persons living in the country, one of whom was a Quaker. The Quaker strongly objected to being made a prisoner. Secesh wanted to know if he was not strongly opposed to the South.

"Thee is right," said the Quaker, "I am."

"Well, did you vote for Lincoln?"

"Thee is right; I did vote for Abraham."

"Well, what are you?"

"Thee may naturally suppose that I am a Union man. Cannot thee let me go to my home?"

"Yes, yes; go and take care of the old woman," said Secesh.

The other prisoner was taken along with them, but not relishing the summary manner in which the Quaker was disposed of, said:

"What did you let him go for? He is a black abolitionist. Now, look here, I voted for Breckinridge, and have always been opposed to this war. I am opposed to fighting the South, decidedly."

"You are," said Secesh; "you are what they call around here a copperhead, ain't you."

"Yes, yes," said the butternut, insinuatingly; "that's what all my neighbors call me, and they know I ain't with them."

"Come here, Dave!" hallooed Secesh. "There's a butternut. Just come and look at him. Look here, old man, where do you live? We want that horse you have got to spare, and if you have got any greenbacks, you shell 'em out." And they took all he had.

PASSES TO RICHMOND.

A gentleman called upon the president and solicited a pass for Richmond. "Well," said the president, "I would be very happy to oblige, if my passes were respected; but the fact is, sir, I have, within the past two years, given passes to two hundred and fifty thousand men to go to Richmond, and not one has got there yet."

The applicant quietly and respectfully withdrew on his tiptoes.

CHARLES A. DANA'S NIGHT RIDE.

In the beginning of May, Grant moved the Army of the Potomac across the Rappahannock and fought the battle of the Wilderness. For two days we had no authentic news in Washington, and both Mr. Lincoln and the secretary of war were very much troubled about it. One night at about ten o'clock I was sent for to the War Department, and on reaching the office I found the president and the secretary together.

"We are greatly disturbed in mind," said Mr. Lincoln, "because Grant has been fighting two days and we are not getting any authentic account of what has happened since he moved. We have concluded to send you down there. How soon will you be ready to start?"

"I will be ready," I said, "in half an hour, and will get off just as soon as a train and an escort can be got ready at Alexandria."

"Very good," said the president; "go, then, and God bless you."

I at once made the necessary preparations, and gave orders for a train from Alexandria to the Rappahannock. At the appointed time, just before midnight, I was on board the cars in Maryland avenue, which were to take me and my horse to Alexandria, when an orderly rode up in haste to say that the president wanted to see me at the War Department. Riding there as fast as I could, I found the president still there.

"Since you went away," said he, "I have been feeling very unhappy about it. I don't like to send you down there. We hear that Jeb Stewart's cavalry is riding all over the region between the Rappahannock and the Rapidan, and I don't want to expose you to the danger you will have to meet before you can reach Grant."

"Mr. Lincoln," I said, "I have got a first-rate horse, and twenty cavalrymen are in readiness at Alexandria. If we meet a small force of Stewart's people, we can fight, and if they are too many, they will have to have mighty good horses to catch us."

"But are you not concerned about it at all?" said he.

"No, sir," said I, "I don't feel any hesitation on my account. Besides, it is getting late, and I want to get down to the Rappahannock by daylight."

"All right," said he; "if you feel that way, I won't keep you any longer. Good-night, and good-by."—*Charles A. Dana, in North American Review.*

UNCLE ABE AND THE JUDGE.

Where men bred in courts, accustomed to the world, or versed in diplomacy would use some subterfuge, or would make a polite speech, or give a shrug of the shoulders, as the means of getting out of an embarrassing position, Mr. Lincoln raises a laugh by some bold west-country anecdote, and moves off in the cloud of merriment produced by the joke. Thus, when Mr. Bates was remonstrating apparently against the appointment of some indifferent lawyer to a place of judicial importance, the president interposed with:

"Come now, Bates, he's not half as bad as you think. Besides that, I must tell you, he did me a good turn long ago. When I took to the law, I was going to court one morning, with some ten or twelve miles of bad road before me, and I had no horse. The judge overtook me in his wagon:

"'Hallo, Lincoln! are you not going to the court-house? Come in and I will give you a seat.'

"Well, I got in, and the judge went on reading his papers. Presently the wagon struck a stump on one side of the road, then it hopped off to the other. I looked out, and I saw the driver was jerking from side to side in his seat, so I says:

"'Judge, I think your coachman has been taking a little too much this morning.'

"'Well, I declare, Lincoln,' said he, 'I should not much wonder if you are right, for he has nearly upset me half a dozen times since starting.' So, putting his head out of the window he shouted, 'Why, you infernal scoundrel, you are drunk.' Upon which, pulling up his horses, and turing round with great gravity, the coachman said:

"'By gorra! that's the first rightful decision that you have given for the last twelve month.'"

While the company were laughing, the president beat a quiet retreat from the neighborhood.

OLD ABE "GLAD OF IT."

A characteristic story of the president is narrated in a letter from Washington. When the telegram from Cumberland Gap reached Mr. Lincoln, that "firing was heard in the direction of Knoxville," he remarked that he was "glad of it." Some person present, who had the peril of Burnside's position uppermost in his mind, could not see *why* Mr. Lincoln should be *glad* of it, and so expressed himself.

"Why, you see," responded the president, "it reminds me of Mrs. Sallie Ward, a neighbor of mine, who had a very large family. Occasionally one of her numerous progeny would be heard crying in some out-of-the-way place, upon which Mrs. Sallie would exclaim, 'There's one of my children that isn't dead yet.'"

MR. LINCOLN'S GENEROSITY.

While President Lincoln was confined to his house with the varioloid, some friends called to sympathize with him, especially on the character of his disease. "Yes," he said, "it is a bad disease, but it has its advantages. For the first time since I have been in office I have something now to give to every person that calls."

LINCOLN AND STANTON FIXING UP PEACE BETWEEN THE TWO CONTENDING ARMIES.

On the night of March 3d, the secretary of war, with others of the Cabinet, was in the company of the president, at the Capitol, awaiting the passage of the final bills of Congress. In the intervals of reading and signing these documents, the military situation was considered—the lively conversation, tinged by the confident and glowing account of General Grant, of his mastery of the position, and of his belief that a few days more would see Richmond in our possession, and the army of Lee either dispersed utterly or captured bodily— when the telegram from Grant was received saying that Lee had asked an interview with reference to peace. Mr. Lincoln was elated, and the kindness of his heart was manifest in intimations of favorable terms to be granted to the conquered rebels.

Stanton listened in silence, restraining his emotion, but at length the tide burst forth:

"Mr. President," said he, "to-morrow is inauguration day. If you are not to be the president of an obedient and united people, you had better not be inaugurated. Your work is already done, if any other authority than yours is for one moment to be recognized, or any terms made that do not signify that you are the supreme head of the nation. If generals in the field are to negotiate peace, or any other chief magistrate is to be acknowledged on this continent, then you are not needed, and you had better not take the oath of office."

"Stanton, you are right," said the president, his whole tone changing. "Let me have a pen.'

Mr. Lincoln sat down to the table, and wrote as follows:

"The president directs me to say to you that he wishes you to have no conference with General Lee, unless. it be for the capitulation of Lee's army, or on some minor or purely military matter. He instructs me to say that. you are not to decide, discuss or confer upon any political question. Such questions the president holds in his own hands, and will submit them to no military conferences or conventions. In the meantime you are to press to the utmost your military advantages."

The president read over what he had written, and then said:

"Now, Stanton, date and sign this paper, and send it to Grant. We'll see about this peace business."

The duty was discharged only too gladly by the energetic secretary.

STORIES ILLUSTRATING LINCOLN'S MEMORY.

Mr. Lincoln's memory was very remarkable. At one of the afternoon receptions at the White House, a stranger shook hands with him, and as he did so remarked, casually, that he was elected to Congress about the time Mr. Lincoln's term as representative expired, which happened many years before.

"Yes," said the president, "you are from ——," mentioning the state. "I remember reading of your election in a newspaper one morning on a steamboat going down to Mount Vernon."

At another time a gentleman addressed him, saying:

"I presume, Mr. President, you have forgotten me?"

"No," was the prompt reply; "your name is Flood. I saw you last twelve years ago, at ——," naming the place and the occasion. "I am glad to see," he continued, "that the Flood flows on."

Subsequent to his re-election a deputation of bankers from various sections were introduced one day by the secretary of the treasury. After a few moments of general conversation, Mr. Lincoln turned to one of them and said:

"Your district did not give me so strong a vote at the last election as it did in 1860."

"I think, sir, that you must be mistaken," replied the banker. "I have the impression that your majority was considerably increased at the last election."

"No," rejoined the president, "you fell off about six hundred votes."

Then taking down from the bookcase the official canvass of 1860 and 1864, he referred to the vote of the district named, and proved to be quite right in his assertion.

BIG BRINDLE AND THE HIGHFALUTIN COLONEL.

President Lincoln tells the following story of Colonel W., who had been elected to the legislature, and had also been judge of the county court. His elevation, however, had made him somewhat pompous, and he became very fond of using big words. On his farm he had a very large and mischievous ox, called "Big Brindle," which very frequently broke down his neighbors' fences, and committed other depredations, much to the colonel's annoyance.

One morning after breakfast, in the presence of Mr. Lincoln, who had stayed with him over night, and who was on his way to town, he called his overseer and said to him:

"Mr. Allen, I desire you to impound Big Brindle, in order that I may hear no animadversions on his eternal depredations."

Allen bowed and walked off, sorely puzzled to know what the colonel meant. So after Colonel W. left for town, he went to his wife and asked her what Colonel W. meant by telling him to impound the ox.

"Why, he meant to tell you to put him in a pen," said she.

Allen left to perform the feat, for it was no inconsiderable one, as the animal was wild and vicious, and, after a great deal of trouble and vexation, succeeded.

" Well,"·said he, wiping the perspiration from his brow and soliloquizing, "this is impounding, is it? Now, I am dead sure that the colonel will ask me if I impounded Big Brindle, and I'll bet I puzzle him as he did me."

The next day the colonel gave a dinner party, and as he was not aristocratic, Mr. Allen, the overseer, sat down with the company. After the second or third glass was discussed, the colonel turned to the overseer and said:

" Eh, Mr. Allen, did you impound Big Brindle, sir?"

Allen straightened himself, and looking around at the company, replied:

" Yes, I did, sir; but old Brindle transcended the impannel of the impound, and scatterlophisticated all over the equanimity of the forest."

The company burst into an immoderate fit of laughter, while the colonel's face reddened with discomfiture.

" What do you mean by that, sir?" said the colonel.

" Why, I mean, colonel," said Allen; " that old Brindle, being prognosticated with an idea of the cholera, ripped and teared, snorted and pawed dirt, jumped the fence, tuck to the woods, and would not be impounded nohow."

This was too much; the company roared again, in which the colonel was forced to join, and in the midst of the laughter Allen left the table, saying to himself as he went, " I reckon the colonel won't ask me to impound any more oxen."

HE HAD ONLY LOST A LEG.

A gentleman visiting a hospital at Washington, heard an occupant of one of the beds laughing and talking about the president. He seemed to be in such good spirits that the gentleman remarked:

" You must be very slightly wounded?"

" Yes," said the brave fellow, "very slightly—I have only lost one leg."

AN APT ILLUSTRATION.

At the White House one day some gentlemen were present from the West, excited and troubled about the commissions or omissions of the administration. The president heard them patiently, and then replied:

" Gentlemen, suppose all the property you have were in gold, and you had put it in the hands of Blondin to carry across the Niagara river on a rope, would you shake the cable, or keep shouting out to him, 'Blondin, stand up a little straighter—Blondin, stoop a little more—go a little faster—lean a little more to the north—lean a little more to the south?' No! you would hold your breath as well as your tongue, and keep your hands off until he was safe over. The government is carrying an immense weight. Untold treasures are in her hands. They are doing the very best they can. Don't badger them. Keep silence, and we'll get you safe across."

DR. EDWARDS BUMPING THE PRESIDENT.

The popular editor of the *Northwestern Christian Advocate*, Dr. Arthur Edwards, is responsible for the following, which we take from the editorials of his excellent paper:

"Early in the war it became this writer's duty, for a brief period, to carry certain reports to the War Department, in Washington, at about nine in the morning. Being late one morning, we were in a desperate hurry to deliver the papers, in order to be able to catch the train returning to camp.

"On the winding, dark staircase of the old War Department, which many will remember, it was our misfortune, while taking about three stairs at a time, to run a certain head like a catapult into the body of the president, striking him in the region of the right lower vest pocket.

"The usual surprised and relaxed grunt of a man thus assailed came promptly. We quickly sent an apology in the direction of the dimly seen form, feeling that the ungracious shock was expensive, even to the humblest clerk in the department.

"A second glance revealed to us the president as the victim of the collision. Then followed a special tender of 'ten thousand pardons,' and the president's reply: "'One's enough; I wish the whole army would charge like that.'"

ONE OF MR. LINCOLN'S WITTIEST UTTERANCES.

Dr. Hovey, of Dansville, New York, thought he would call and see the president, and, on arriving at the White House, found him on horseback, ready for a start. Approaching him, he said:

"President Lincoln, I thought I would call and see you before leaving the city, and hear you tell a story."

The president greeted him pleasantly, and asked where he was from.

The reply was, "From western New York."

"Well, that's a good enough country without stories," replid the president, and off he rode. That was the story.

MR. LINCOLN AND THE GEORGETOWN PROPHETESS.

The president, like Old King Saul, when his term was about to expire, seems in a quandary concerning a further lease of office. He consulted again the "prophetess" of Georgetown, immortalized by his patronage. She retired to an inner chamber, and, after raising and consulting more than a dozen of distinguished spirits from Hades, she returned to the reception-parlor where the chief magistrate awaited her, and declared that General Grant would capture Richmond, and that Honest Old Abe would be next president. She, however, as the report goes, told him to beware of Chase.

AN INAUGURATION INCIDENT.

Noah Brooks, in his "Reminiscences," relates the following incident:
"While the ceremonies of the second inauguration were in progress, just as Lincoln stepped forward to take the oath of office, the sun, which had been obscured by rain-clouds, burst forth in splendor. In conversation the next day, the president asked:
"'Did you notice that sun-burst? It made my heart jump.'
"Later in the month, Miss Anna Dickinson, in a lecture delivered in the hall of the House of Representatives, eloquently alluded to the sun-burst as a happy omen. The president sat directly in front of the speaker, and, from the reporter's gallery behind her, I had caught his eye, soon after he sat down. When Miss Dickinson referred to the sunbeam, he looked up at me, involuntarily, and I thought his eyes were suffused with moisture. Perhaps they were; but the next day he said:
"'I wonder if Miss Dickinson saw me wink at you?'"

THE NATURALNESS OF LINCOLN.

The Rev. Robert McIntyre, in a Lincoln eulogy at the Auditorium, Chicago, among other good things, said:
"One day at the cabin in which Mr. Lincoln spent his early years I was told this story: Sometime before he was elected president, Mr. Lincoln visited some of his people there, and he stood in the doorway watching a summer shower hunted by a pack of sunbeams, which laid the rain in puddles gleaming in the yard.
"They say that Mr. Lincoln, taking up a little girl who was kin to him, carried her out into the yard and dipped her baby feet in the mud-puddle. Then, carrying her into the cabin, he lifted her and marked the ceiling with her feet, leaving marks that remained there for many years. We are told that something of that kind happened to him, by a power greater than himself that lifted him up among the heights and leaving those footprints that will shine forever in the annals of human endeavor. I do not like this theory because it takes away hope from our youth.
"Lincoln was like other men. He was not a miraculous man in any sense of the word. He had, indeed, less of the supernatural about him than any man in history, and more of the natural, and it was this that made him so great and lovable in the eyes of the people.
"Washington has been idealized until we have forgotten his real character. I confess he is a nebulous character to me.
"Now they are going to refine and sandpaper and veneer Lincoln until nothing of the simple, loving, commonplace soul is left to us. We don't want this. We want him just as he is."

AN AMUSING STORY CONCERNING THOMPSON CAMPBELL.

Among the numerous visitors on one of the president's reception-days were a party of congressmen, among whom was the Hon. Thomas Shannon, of California. Soon after the customary greeting, Mr. Shannon said:

"Mr. President, I met an old friend of yours in California last summer, Thompson Campbell, who had a good deal to say of your Springfield life."

"Ah!" returned Mr. Lincoln, "I am glad to hear of him. Campbell used to be a dry fellow," he continued. "For a time he was secretary of state. One day, during the legislative vacation, a meek, cadaverous-looking man, with a white neck-cloth, introduced himself to him at his office, and stating that he had been informed that Mr. C. had the letting of the assembly chamber, said that he wished to secure it, if possible, for a course of lectures he desired to deliver in Springfield.

"'May I ask,' said the secretary, 'what is to be the subject of your lectures?'

"'Certainly,' was the reply, with a very solemn expression of countenance. 'The course I wish to deliver is on the second coming of our Lord.'

"'It is no use,' said Mr. C. 'If you will take my advice, you will not waste your time in this city. It is my private opinion that if the Lord has been in Springfield once, he will not come the second time!'"

REMINISCENCES—THE TURNING-POINT.

It was while young Lincoln was engaged in the duties of Offutt's store that the turning-point of his life occurred. Here he commenced the study of English grammar. There was not a text-book to be obtained in the neighborhood, but. hearing that there was a copy of Kirkham's grammar in the possession of a person seven or eight miles distant, he walked to his house, and succeeded in borrowing it.

L. M. Green, a lawyer in Petersburg, Menard county, says that every time he visited New Salem, at this period, Lincoln took him out upon a hill and *asked him to explain some point* in Kirkham that had given him trouble. After having mastered the book, he remarked to a friend that if that was what was called a science, he thought he could "*subdue another.*"

Mr. Green says that Mr. Lincoln's talk at this time showed that he was beginning to think of a great life and a great destiny. Lincoln said to him, on one occasion, that all his family seemed to have good sense, but somehow none had ever become distinguished. He thought that perhaps he might become so. He had talked, he said, with men who had the reputation of being great men, but he could not see that they *differed much from others.*

During this year he was also much engaged with debating-clubs, often walking six or seven miles to attend them. One of these clubs held its meetings at an old storehouse in New Salem, and the first speech young Lincoln ever made was made there.

He used to call the exercise "practising polemics." As these clubs were composed principally of men of no education whatever, some of their "polemics" are remembered as the most laughable farces.

One gentleman who met him during this period says the first time he saw him he was lying on a trundle-bed covered with books and papers and *rocking a cradle with his foot.*

The whole scene, however, was entirely characteristic—Lincoln reading and studying, and at the same time helping his landlady by quieting her child.

A gentleman who knew Mr. Lincoln well in early manhood says:. "Lincoln at this period had nothing but *plenty of friends.*

Says J. G. Holland: "No man ever lived, probably, who was more of a self-made man than Abraham Lincoln. Not a circumstance of life favored the development which he had reached."

. After the customary hand-shaking on one occasion at Washington, several gentlemen came forward and asked the president for his autograph. One of them gave his name as "Cruikshank." "That reminds me," said Mr. Lincoln, "of what I used to be called when a young man—'*Long-shanks!*'"

Mr. Holland says: "Lincoln was a religious man. The fact may be stated without any reservation—with only an explanation. He believed in God, and in his personal supervision of the affairs of men. He believed himself to be under his control and guidance. He believed in the power and ultimate triumph of the right, through his belief in God."

A prominent writer says: "Lincoln was a childlike man. No public man of modern days has been fortunate enough to carry into his manhood so much or the directness, truthfulness and simplicity of childhood as distinguished him. He was exactly what he seemed."

Mr. Lincoln and Douglas met for the first time when the latter was only twenty-three years of age. Lincoln, in speaking of the fact, subsequently said that Douglas was then "the least man he ever saw." He was not only very short, but very slender.

OLD ABE NEVER HEARD OF IT BEFORE.

Some moral philosopher was telling the president one day about the under-current of public opinion. He went on to explain at length, and drew an illustration from the Mediterranean sea. The current seemed very curiously to flow in both from the Black sea and the Atlantic ocean, but a shrewd Yankee, by means of a contrivance of floats, had discovered that at the outlet into the Atlantic only about thirty feet of the surface water flowed inward, while there was a tremendous current under that flowing out.

"Well," said.Mr. Lincoln, much bored, "that don't remind me of any story I ever heard."

The philosopher despaired of making a serious impression by his argument, and left.

HOW LINCOLN AND JUDGE B. SWAPPED HORSES.

When Abraham Lincoln was a lawyer in Illinois, he and a certain judge once got to bantering one another about trading horses; and it was agreed that the next morning at nine o'clock they should make a trade, the horses to be unseen up to that hour, and no backing out, under a forfeiture of twenty-five dollars. At the hour appointed, the judge came up, leading the sorriest-looking specimen of a horse ever seen in those parts. In a few minutes Mr. Lincoln was seen approaching with a wooden sawhorse upon his shoulders. Great were the shouts and the laughter of the crowd, and both were greatly increased when Mr. Lincoln, on surveying the judge's animal, set down his sawhorse, and exclaimed: "Well, judge, this is the first time I ever got the worst of it in a horse-trade."

SENATOR CULLUM'S INTERESTING REMINISCENCES OF LINCOLN.

At the third annual banquet of the Lincoln Association of Philadelphia, given February 12, 1894, Senator Cullum, of Illinois, among other good things, gave the following reminiscences:

"It was my fortune to know Mr. Lincoln well. My knowledge of him dates back in my own life to the time I was ten or twelve years old; and even before this time I can remember that men would come twenty or thirty miles to see my father in those pioneer days to learn whom to employ as a lawyer, when they were likely to have cases in court. He would say to them, 'If Judge Stephen T. Logan is there, employ him; if he is not, there is a young man by the name of Lincoln who will do just about as well.'

"In my boyhood days I was permitted to attend the sessions of the circuit court one week twice a year. The first time I enjoyed the privilege I saw Mr Lincoln and the gallant Colonel E. D. Baker engaged in defense of a man charged with the crime of murder. That great trial, especially the defense by those great lawyers, made an impression on my mind which will never be effaced.

"Late in 1846, when Mr. Lincoln became a Whig candidate for Congress, I heard him deliver a political speech. The county in which my father and family resided was a part of his congressional district. When Mr. Lincoln came to the county, my father met him with his carriage, and took him to all of his appointments. I went to the meeting nearest my home; it was an open-air meeting in a grove. On being introduced, Mr. Lincoln began his speech as follows:

"'Fellow-citizens, ever since I have been in Tazewell county my old friend Major Cullum has taken me around. He has heard all my speeches, and the only way I can fool the old major and make him believe I am making a new speech is by turning it end for end once in awhile.'

"I knew him at the bar, both when I was a boy, and afterward when I came to the practise of the law in the capital of Illinois, his home then, mine now. I knew him in the private walks of life, in the law-office, in the court-room, in the political campaigns of the time, and to the close of his great career. I knew him as the leader of the great Republican party, when, as now, it was full of enthusiasm for liberty and equal rights; when the platform was, in substance, the Declaration of Independence, and he was its champion.

" He believed in 'preserving the jewel of liberty in the family of freedom ' Aye, he believed in making the American people one great family of freedom.

" I heard much of the great debate between him and Douglas, the greatest political debate that ever took place in America. I heard him utter the memorable words in the Republican convention of my state in 1858:

" ' A house divided against itself cannot stand. I believe this government cannot permanently endure half slave and half free. I do not expect the Union to be dissolved, I do not expect the house to fall, but I do expect it will cease to be divided. It will become all one thing or all the other.'

" What words of wisdom! He could look through the veil between him and the future and see the end. It is said that before this great speech was delivered he read it to friends, and all of them but one advised against its delivery. With a self-reliance born of earnest conviction, he said the time had come when these sentiments should be uttered, and that if he should go down because of their utterances by him, then he would go down linked with the truth.

" It lifts up and ennobles mankind to hear and study brave words of truth uttered by great men. ' Let me die in the advocacy of what is just and right,' he said again.

" In these days of apparent shallow convictions on many subjects, days of greed for wealth, of rushing for the mighty dollar, is it not well to pause and think over the lives of great men of our own country and the world? We are now [1894] in the very shadow of the death of a great and good man, George W. Childs, just passed away. A man who lived to do good; to make the pathway of his fellows smoother and easier; a great-hearted philanthropist whose fame is world-wide, and will endure as long as sympathy and generosity are found in the human heart.

" Mr. Lincoln was a great debater, as was Douglas. They often met in debate. On one occasion Douglas charged that there was an alliance between Lincoln and the Federal office-holders, and that he would deal with them as the Russians did with the allies in the Crimean war, not stopping to inquire whether an Englishman, Frenchman or Turk was hit. Lincoln replied, denying the alliance, but mildly suggested to Douglas that the allies took Sebastopol.

" Lincoln was a man of faith in the right when the great contest between him and Douglas ended, and the election was over. Lincoln had carried the popular vote of that state, but Douglas secured a majority of the Legislature.

When it was settled that Douglas had triumphed in securing a majority of the Legislature, I happened to meet Mr. Lincoln in the street, and said to him, ' Is it true that Douglas has a majority of the Legislature? '

" He said ' yes.'

" I felt greatly disappointed, and so expressed myself, when he said:

" ' Never mind, my boy, it will come all right,' and in two years from that day the country was ablaze with bonfires all over the land celebrating its first national Republican victory in his election as president of the United States.

" It has been said that Mr. Lincoln never went to school. He never did very much, but in the broad sense he was an educated man. He was a student—a thinker—he educated himself, and mastered any question that claimed his attention.

" In my belief there has been no man in this country possessing greater power of analyzation than he did. Webster and Lincoln, while unlike in intellect, were two of the greatest men intellectually this country has produced.

" Mr. Lincoln was said to be slow and timid when as president he walked along the danger-path before him. He learned the truth of an observation by Cicero, 'that whoever enters upon public life should take care that the question how far the measure is virtuous be not the sole consideration, but also how far he may have the means of carrying it into execution.' So in the great struggle for national life, he sought to go on no faster than he could induce the loyal people to go with him.

" As we look back over the period of agitation of slavery and of the great civil war, we see Lincoln towering above all as the savior of his country, and as the liberator of three millions of slaves. Lincoln was a shrewd and crafty man. After, as you remember, Vallandigham, of Ohio, was sent South, through the rebel lines, he got round on the Canada border, and finally returned home without leave. People thought his return would cause trouble.

" It is said that Fernando Wood called on the president, and cautiously inquired if he had been informed that Vallandigham had got home. Lincoln knew that by sending him South he had broken his power for evil, and in reply to Mr. Wood he said:

" ' No, sir; I have received no official information of that act, and what is more, sir, don't intend to.'

" Another illustration of his great good nature and shrewdness is told. As the war approached its close, Mr. Lincoln and General Sherman were in consultation at City Point. One of the questions considered was what should be done with Jeff. Davis when captured. General Sherman inquired if he should let him escape. Mr. Lincoln told him the story of the temperance lecturer who was plentifully supplied with lemonade. The host in a modest way inquired if the least bit of something stronger to brace him up would be agreeable. The lecturer answered he could not think of it, he was opposed to it on principle; but, glancing at the black bottle near by, he added:

" ' If you could manage to put in a little drop unbeknown to me, it wouldn't hurt me much.'

" ' Now, general,' said Mr. Lincoln, ' I am bound to oppose the escape of Jeff. Davis, but if you can manage to let him slip out unbeknownst-like, I guess it won't hurt me much.'

" Mr. Lincoln was never disturbed by little things. Mr. Chase was President · Lincoln's secretary of the treasury. As the time approached for the presidential nomination, Mr. Lincoln was understood to be a candidate, and Mr. Chase was a candidate, retaining his place in the Cabinet. Being in Washington for a time, I had a conversation with Mr. Lincoln about Mr. Chase's candidacy, and I advised Mr. Lincoln to turn him out. He replied:

" ' No, let him alone; he can do me no more harm in office than out.'

" When the president was considering Mr. Chase in connection with the high office of chief justice of the United States, a deputation of great men from Ohio (Ohio always had and has yet many) came to Washington to protest against Mr. Chase's appointment, and presented some letters at some time written by Mr. Chase, criticizing Mr. Lincoln. He read them, and, with his usual good nature, remarked:

" ' If Mr. Chase has said some hard things about me, I in turn have said some hard things about him, which, I guess, squares the account.'

" Mr. Chase was appointed.

" He was an American in the highest sense. He stood for America, for liberty, for the Declaration of Independence, for equality of rights, and he journeyed from his home to the national Capitol to obey the call of the people, and guide the ship of state through the portending storm; he came to his own historic city, and in old Independence Hall he declared ' that if the government could not be saved without giving up the Declaration of Independence, he would rather be assassinated on the spot than surrender it.'

" He was a Republican, as we are; he not only believed in union, liberty and equality, but under his guidance the policy of the government was established which has been maintained for more than thirty years, and never seriously interfered with until now, and which has given the people unexampled prosperity.

" Mr. president and gentlemen, his life and public utterances speak to us now in this period of peril to business and commerce. Yes, to sustain the honor of our nation as a republic, to stand fast by our colors, save the people from poverty and distress, the nation from financial wreck, and its flag in this and other lands from dishonor."

THE PRESIDENT WAS REMINDED.

A gentleman was telling at the White House how a friend of his had been driven away from New Orleans, as a unionist, and how, on his expulsion, when he asked to see the writ by which he was expelled, the deputation which called on him told him that the government had made up their minds to do nothing illegal, and so they had issued no illegal writs, and simply meant to make him go of his own free will.

" Well," said Mr. Lincoln, " that reminds me of a hotel-keeper down in St. Louis, who boasted that he never had a death in his hotel, for whenever a guest was dying in his house, he carried him out to die in the street."

LINCOLN'S VIEWS OF GRANT.

After he had satisfied himself with questions regarding the army, Mr. Lincoln turned to me and said:

"General, you have a man down there by the name of Grant, have you not?"

I replied: "Yes, sir; we have."

Fixing on me an earnest and somewhat quizzical look, Mr. Lincoln asked:

"Well, what kind of a fellow is he?"

I replied: "General Grant is a man of whom one can best judge by considering the results he has brought to pass. Belmont, Donelson, Shiloh and Vicksburg make a pretty strong record. He certainly has developed the elements of a successful commander. He is very popular with the army, which has full confidence in his military ability. When he makes his plans, he concentrates all his energies and all his resources upon their execution, and I don't think he ever entered upon a campaign or into a battle without a fixed determination, under all circumstances, to win, and with a consciousness that he would win. He fills the full measure of a great commander."

Mr. Lincoln listened closely to all I said, and then fixing upon me a most earnest and serious look, he put to me the blunt and startling question:

"Does Grant ever get drunk?"

I replied in most emphatic language: "No, Mr. President, Grant does not get drunk."

"Is he in the habit of using liquor?" asked the president, quickly.

My answer was: "My observation, depending on having excellent opportunities for judging, enables me to assert with a good degree of positiveness that he does not use liquor. Those opportunities have extended over a period of more than two years, during which time I have seen him often, sometimes daily, and I have never noticed the slightest indication of his having used any kind of liquor. On the contrary, I have, time and again, seen him refuse to touch it."

There was too much of whisky hospitality during the late war for the good of the service of the country. More than once did it happen that a movement miscarried because the officer charged with its execution had imbibed too freely of old Kentucky Bourbon.

"In all my intercourse with General Grant," I continued, in speaking to Mr. Lincoln, "I never saw him taste intoxicating drink. It has been charged in northern newspapers that Grant was under the influence of liquor on the fields of Donelson and Shiloh. This charge is an atrocious calumny, wickedly false. I saw him repeatedly during the battles of Donelson and Shiloh on the field, and if there were any sober men on the field, Grant was one of them. My brigade and myself gave him a Fourth of July dinner in Memphis in 1862. He, of course, as guest, sat upon my right, and as wine and something stronger were passed around, he turned his glass upside down, saying, 'None for me.' I am glad to bring this testimony to you in justice to a much-maligned man."

"It is a relief to me to hear this statement from you," said the president, "for though I have not lost confidence in Grant, I have been a good deal annoyed by reports which have reached me of his intemperance. I have been pestered with appeals to remove him from the command of that army. But somehow I have felt like trusting him, because, as you say, he has accomplished something. I knew you had been down there with him, and thought you would give me reliable evidence, for I have desired to get the testimony of a living witness. Your direct and positive declarations have given me much satisfaction. Delegation after delegation has called upon me with the same request, 'Recall Grant from the command of the Army of the Tennessee,' as the members of the delegations were not willing that their sons and brothers should be under the control of an intemperate leader. I could not think of relieving him, and these demands became very vexatious. I therefore hit upon this plan to stop them:

" One day a delegation, headed by a distinguished doctor of divinity from New York, who was spokesman for the party, called on me and made the familiar complaint and protest against Grant's being retained in his command. After the clergyman had concluded his remarks, I asked if any others desired to add anything to what had already been said. They replied that they did not. Then, looking as serious as I could, I said:

"'Doctor, can you tell me where General Grant gets his liquor?'

" The doctor seemed quite nonplussed, but replied that he could not. I then said to him:

"'I am very sorry, for if you could tell me, I would direct the chief quartermaster of the army to lay in a large stock of the same kind of liquor, and would also direct him to furnish a supply to some of my other generals, who have never yet won a victory.'"

Then, giving me a punch, as one will sometimes do when he thinks he has said something good, Mr. Lincoln lay back in his chair and laughed most heartily. He then added:

" What I want and what the people want is generals who will fight battles and win victories. Grant has done this, and I propose to stand by him. I permitted this incident to get into print, and I have been troubled no more with delegations protesting against the retention of Grant in command of that army." Continuing, Lincoln said:

" Somehow or other, I have always felt a leaning toward Grant, and have been inclined to place confidence in him. Ever since he sent that memorable message to Buckner at Donelson, when the latter asked for terms of surrender—'No terms but unconditional surrender. I propose to move immediately upon your works'—I have had great confidence in Grant, and have felt that he was a man I could tie to, though I have never seen him. It is a source of much satisfaction that my confidence in him has not been misplaced."

The conversation then turned upon other subjects, the condition of the country, politics, the rebellion, and the prospects of being able to suppress it. What seemed to cause Mr. Lincoln his greatest trouble was the state of feeling in certain of the northern states.

ent times of some move or thing, said "it had petered out;" that some other one's plan "wouldn't gibe;" and being asked if the war and the cause of the Union were not a great care to him, replied:

"Yes, it is a heavy hog to hold."

The first two phrases are so familiar here in the West that they need no explanation. Of the last and more pioneer one it may be said that it had a special force, and was peculiarly Lincoln-like in the way above applied.

In the olden time, everyone having hogs, assisted by neighbors, did their own killing. Stripped of its hair, one held the carcass nearly perpendicular in the air, head down, while others put one point of the gambrel-bar through a slit in its hock, then over the string-pole, and the other point through the other hock, and so swung the animal clear of the ground. While all this was being done, it took a good man to "hold the hog," greasy, warmly moist, and weighing some two hundred pounds. And often those with the gambrel prolonged the strain, being provokingly slow, in hopes to make the holder drop his burden. This latter thought is again expressed where Mr. Lincoln, writing of the peace which he hoped would "come soon, to stay; and so come as to be worth the keeping in all future time," added that while there would "be some black men who can remember that with silent tongue and clenched teeth and steady eye, and well-poised bayonet, they have helped mankind on to this great consummation," he feared there would "be some white ones unable to forget that, with malignant heart and deceitful tongue, they had striven to hinder it."

He had two seemingly opposite elements little understood by strangers, and which those in more intimate relations with him find difficult to explain. An open, boyish tongue when in a happy mood, and with this a reserve of power, a force of thought that impressed itself without words on observers in his presence. He was naturally a keen observer of men and events. And always a student, he grew in range and grasp with the increased demands upon him. With the cares of the nation on his mind, he became more meditative, and lost much of his lively ways remembered here in Illinois.

A biographer, already referred to, tells the following incident:

After the war was well on, a patriot woman of the West urged Mr. Lincoln to make hospitals at the North where the sick from the Army of the Mississippi could revive in a more bracing air. Among other reasons, she said if he "granted her petition he would be glad as long as he lived." With a look of sadness impossible to describe, he said:

"I shall never be glad any more."

A chill, raw day in February, 1861, found his friends at Danville again, waiting about the depot for the train that was to bear him on to Washington. Rumors of the rebellious acts of the slaveholding states, with threats of the dire war to come, filled the air. From the rear platform he spoke some kind words, the last he ever said publicly in Illinois. In a few moments he was beyond the limits of the state, from home and his well-known friends; not to return, and never to be glad any more.

LINCOLN ON THE MONROE DOCTRINE.

It will be remembered that at this time (the summer of 1863) Louis Napoleon was attempting to force a monarchy upon our sister republic of Mexico by the musket, the bayonet and the cannon. He had flitted the bauble of an empire across the sea before the easily impressible mind of the Austrian archduke, Maximilian, and his ambitious consort, the beautiful Carlotta, formerly Duchess of Brabant, and sister of the king of the Belgians. They caught at the bait, and Napoleon sent a French army to seat them upon the throne. This action of his and that of Maximilian was exceedingly offensive to the officers and soldiers of our armies in the field. It occurred to me to learn Lincoln's views on the subject. So I said to him:

"Mr. President, how about the French army in Mexico?"

Shrugging up his shoulders and wrinkling his eyebrows, he said:

"I'm not exactly 'skeered,' but don't like the looks of the thing. Napoleon has taken advantage of our weakness in our time of trouble, and has attempted to found a monarchy on the soil of Mexico in utter disregard of the Monroe doctrine. My policy is, attend to only one trouble at a time. If we get well out of our present difficulties and restore the Union, I propose to notify Louis Napoleon that it is about time to take his army out of Mexico. When that army is gone, the Mexicans will take care of Maximilian. I can best illustrate my position touching this subject by relating an anecdote told by Daniel D. Dickinson, senator from New York, in a speech delivered by him a few evenings since in New York City. He said that in a certain Connecticut town there had lived two men as neighbors and friends for more than sixty years. They were pillars in the village church, one of them being a deacon named White. The other was named Jones. After this long lapse of time a serious difficulty unfortunately sprang between these two brethren of the church.

"The feeling waxed so warm between them that it grew into a bitter feud. Mutual friends attempted a reconciliation, but the men would not be reconciled. Finally, Deacon White became dangerously ill, and drew nigh unto death. Mutual friends again interposed their kind offices to effect a reconciliation. They said to Brother Jones that it would be a sin to permit the sick brother to die with the quarrel standing. Jones was persuaded, and called on Deacon White. The two men talked over their mutual grievances, and agreeing to let them be buried, shook hands and exchanged mutual forgiveness in the presence of death. The deacon then lay back upon his pillow, awaiting his final summons, and Jones arose to leave. But as the visitor reached the door, Deacon White, with a great effort, raised himself on his elbow and called out, in a weak, fainting voice:

"'Brother Jones—Brother Jones! I want it distinctly understood that if I get well the old grudge stands.'"

Lincoln laughed at the conclusion of the story, saying that was about the way he felt toward the French emperor. He manifested strong feeling on this subject, and said the creation of an empire, especially by force, at our very doors was exceedingly offensive, and could not be overlooked by the United States. It had caused him great annoyance, as he was not in a condition to interfere so as to prevent it. He expressed himself strongly in favor of the position taken by President Monroe in his celebrated message to Congress, in which he declared against the acquisition of any territory on this continent by any foreign power.

Speaking of the French army and Maximilian's being in Mexico, led Lincoln to refer to Benito Juarez, then president of Mexico, for whom he cherished a deep sympathy and strong regard. He alluded to the similarity, in some respects, between his own case and that of Juarez. Both were presidents of republics; both were engaged in deadly struggles for the very existence of their respective nations, and both were beset by treason at home. Juarez was compelled, moreover, to meet a foreign invader and to be the defender of the very principle in the maintenance of which Lincoln felt so deep an interest—the inviolability of the American continent against foreign powers. Both came from the vales of humility, and both became great leaders. They were great lawyers and they were great statesmen and great patriots. Juarez had the nerve and the courage to cause to be shot to death, as he deserved, the scion of the royal house of Austria, and every throne in Europe was jarred, since the plain republican president of Mexico was a greater power than the kings and emperors who sought to save the fallen emperor.

Besides successfully defending his country against most unprincipled and most unscrupulous invaders, Juarez, in putting Maximilian to death, was the vindicator of the Monroe doctrine—he was the exemplar of what should be its real meaning, that any search after a throne or monarchical foothold on this Western Hemisphere is undertaken at the searcher's peril. It is full time the nations of Europe were made to understand that the Monroe declaration is not a string of mere glittering words, but is a living reality. Lincoln was in full sympathy with this view, and I am fully convinced from his own expressions to me that if we had not been engaged in a gigantic civil war, he would have enforced this view, and neither Napoleon's army nor Maximilian would have ever invaded Mexico.

My interview with Mr. Lincoln lasted over an hour, and it was one of the most important hours of my life. No one could have listened to the conversation with that great and pure man without having the conviction forced upon the mind that he was a sincere believer in an overruling Providence and had "full faith," as his own words declared, "that God was leading this nation through its firey trial to a triumphant issue."—*General John M. Thayer, in the New York Sun.*

CUTTING RED TAPE.

"Upon entering the president's office one afternoon," says a Washington correspondent, "I found the president busy counting greenbacks.

"'This, sir,' said he, 'is something out of my usual line; but a president of the United States has a multiplicity of duties not specified in the Constitution or acts of Congress. This is one of them. This money belongs to a poor negro who is a porter in the Treasury Department, at present very bad with the small-pox. He is now in the hospital, and could not draw his pay because he could not sign his name.

"'I have been at considerable difficulty and get it for him, and have at length ~~~~~~~~~~~~ you newspaper men say. I am now dividing the money and putting by a portion, labeled, in an envelop, with my own hands, according to his wish,' and he proceeded to indorse the package very carefully.

"No one witnessing the transaction could fail to appreciate the goodness of heart which prompted the president of the United States to turn aside for a time from his weighty cares to succor one of the humblest of his fellow-creatures in sickness and sorrow."

LINCOLN'S SPEECH TO THE UNION LEAGUE.

The day following the adjournment at Baltimore, various political organiza-tions called to pay their respects to the president. First came the convention committee, embracing one from each state represented—appointed to announce to him, formally, his nomination. Next came the Ohio delegation, with Mentor's band, of Cincinnati. Following these were the representatives of the National Union League, to whom he said, in concluding his brief response:

"I do not allow myself to suppose that either the convention or the league have decided to conclude that I am either the greatest or the best man in America; but, rather, they have concluded that it is not best to swap horses while crossing the river, and have further concluded that I am not so poor a horse but that they might make a botch of it trying to swap!"

LINCOLN'S ESTIMATE OF THE "HONORS."

As a further elucidation of Mr. Lincoln's estimate of presidential honors, a story is told of how a supplicant for office, of more than ordinary pretensions, called upon him, and presuming on the activity he had shown in behalf of the Republican ticket, asserted, as a reason why the office should be given to him, that he had made Mr. Lincoln president.

"You made me president, did you?" said Mr. Lincoln, with a twinkle of his eye.

"I think I did," said the applicant.

"Then a pretty mess you've got me into, that's all," replied the president, and closed the discussion.

www.ingramcontent.com/pod-product-compliance
Lightning Source LLC
Chambersburg PA
CBHW060536030726
47498CB00004B/1215